CRIMSON ANGEL

CRIMSON ANGEL

A Benjamin January Novel

Barbara Hambly

This first world edition published 2014
in Great Britain and in the USA by
SEVERN HOUSE PUBLISHERS LTD of
19 Cedar Road, Sutton, Surrey, England, SM2 5DA.
Trade paperback edition first published
in Great Britain and the USA 2015 by
SEVERN HOUSE PUBLISHERS LTD.

Hambly, Barbara author.
  Crimson Angel. – (A Benjamin January novel)
  1. January, Benjamin (Fictitious character)–Fiction.
  2. Free African Americans–Fiction. 3. Private
  investigators–Fiction. 4. Treasure troves–Haiti–
  Fiction. 5. New Orleans (La.)–Social conditions–19th
  century–Fiction. 6. Haiti–Social conditions–19th
  century–Fiction. 7. Detective and mystery stories.
  I. Title II. Series
  813.6-dc23

ISBN-13: 978-0-7278-8427-5 (cased)
ISBN-13: 978-1-84751-535-3 (trade paper)
ISBN-13: 978-1-78010-579-6 (e-book)

All Severn House titles are printed on acid-free paper.

Severn House Publishers support the Forest Stewardship Council™ [FSC™],
the leading international forest certification organisation. All our titles that
are printed on FSC certified paper carry the FSC logo.

MIX
Paper from
responsible sources
FSC
www.fsc.org FSC® C013056

Typeset by Palimpsest Book Production Ltd.,
Falkirk, Stirlingshire, Scotland.
Printed and bound in Great Britain by
TJ International, Padstow, Cornwall.

For Glen and Laurel

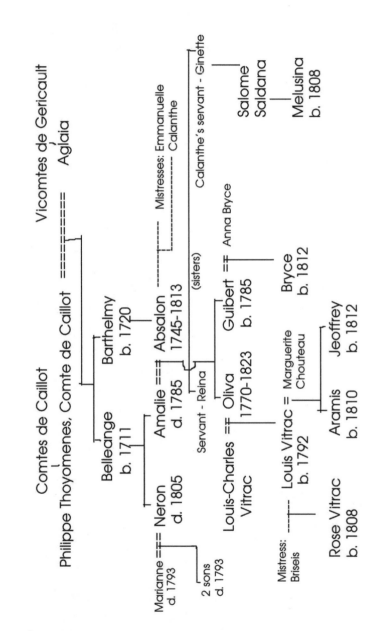

Comtes de Caillot
|
Philippe Thoyomenes, Comte de Caillot ========= Aglaia

Vicomtes de Gericault

Belleange
b. 1711

Barthelmy
b. 1720

Amalie ===‡‡ Absalon -------- Mistresses: Emmanuelle
d. 1785   1745-1813   Calanthe

Marianne ==‡‡ Neron
d. 1793   d. 1805

2 sons
d. 1793

(sisters)

Servant - Reina

Louis-Charles ==‡‡ Oliva   Guibert ==‡‡ Anna Bryce
Vitrac   1770-1823   b. 1785

Calanthe's servant - Ginette

Salome
Saldana

Mistress: -------- Louis Vitrac = Marguerite
Briseis   b. 1792   Chouteau

Bryce
b. 1812

Melusina
b. 1808

Rose Vitrac
b. 1808

Aramis
b. 1810

Jeoffrey
b. 1812

LOUISIANA

ONE

'Rosie!' The young man sprang from the cab in Rue Esplanade, took two strides toward the steps of Benjamin January's high-built old Spanish house, then turned back to pay the driver – which gave January the chance to put his head through the French door into the candlelit parlor and signal Tommy, one of the runaway slaves currently taking refuge beneath January's roof, to get the hell back under the house.

If one had to run a school without scholars in this poverty-stalked year of 1838, January reasoned, the least one could do was take advantage of the fact and give shelter to those fleeing through New Orleans, heading North.

In this poverty-stalked year of 1838, anything you could do to give God a better opinion of you and your family would be a help.

He stepped back on to the gallery as his wife rose from her bent-willow chair, her face alight with pleasure, and the young man bounded up the stairs: 'Look at you!' As their visitor caught Rose's hands and spread them out to suit his own action to his words, January wondered where he'd seen him before: tallish and a little awkward, with just enough blond in his walnut-brown curls to catch glints from the mosquito-smudges that ranged along the gallery rail in the humid summer dusk. His French was purest Creole, but his dark silk waistcoat and the cut of his frock-coat screamed *American.*

Only when Rose cried, 'Jeoff!' did January guess who this had to be, and who the young man's face reminded him of.

He looked like Rose's white brother, a planter down on Grand Isle named Aramis Vitrac.

And a little like Rose.

Rose and 'Jeoff' turned to him, and Jeoff caught his hand. 'You must be Ben.' Like Rose, this younger brother (*surely younger, since Aramis – younger than Rose – has the plantation*) had a lovely smile, though unlike Rose he displayed it freely. Like Rose he was tall, but he still had to look up at January's massive height. 'I have to start by thanking you, sir: I've never seen my sister look so happy.'

January returned the smile. 'I try, sir.'

'Jefferson.' The young man produced a card. 'Jefferson Vitrack.'
He pronounced it American-fashion, rhyming it with hat rack, instead
of putting stress on the final syllable and giving it a glottal French
'a'. Even before he held the card close to the nearest mosquito-
smudge to read it, January knew the address would be north of
Mason's and Dixon's Line.

He was half-right. One address was in Philadelphia, the other in
Washington City.

Both places where the younger son of an impoverished French
planter could find more opportunity to afford well-cut coats and
sober silk waistcoats than he'd have in the bayous of Louisiana.

Rose's hazel-green eyes sparkled with delight behind her spectacles.
'*Jefferson* now, is it? Jeoffrey is no longer good enough?'

Jeoff laughed, and Zizi-Marie – January's niece, who like the
runaways was sheltering under the big old house's ramshackle
roof, though in her case this was due to the fact that her father
hadn't worked since the bank crash eighteen months previously
– brought out a branch of candles from the parlor to set on the
little wicker table. But when she bent to gather up Baby John
from under his tent of mosquito-bar to take him inside, Jeoff
cried, 'Whoa, who's this?' and for a time they grouped around
the infant: talk, laughter, introductions all around. Gabriel, Zizi-
Marie's fifteen-year-old brother, came out with new-made coffee
and the last of the pralines from dinner – Gabriel had a genius
for small feasts on the spur of any given moment – and it was
full-dark before Jefferson Vitrack was able to get to the matter
which had brought him to New Orleans and to Benjamin January's
front gallery.

'Do you remember this?' He fished in his waistcoat pocket and
brought out something that he handed Rose. Something red and gold,
which glittered.

In the cobalt night, far down Rue Esplanade, the clang of bells
from the few steamboats on the wharves sounded as small as a night
bird's cry. A few streets closer, the dim commotion of gambling
hells floated like lingering smoke: it would take Armageddon to
shut down the gaming parlors of New Orleans, and even then January
was pretty certain the Four Horsemen would be able to find someplace to play a few hands before rolling up the heavens and the
earth like a scroll. Summer was the dead season in town, at the end

of a second disastrous year, with most of the city's banks still closed and one shopfront in three locked up for lack of business. Andrew Jackson, hero of the war with England, had proved a less than astute commander of a nation that depended on banking and credit for its prosperity, and though he was out of office now, everyone in the country was still paying the price of his prejudice against centralized banks.

So now, more than ever, the sparkle of gold was like a little twinkle of music in the candle glow.

'Good heavens!' said Rose. 'It's L'Ange Rouge!'

January took it: a Crimson Angel indeed, stiff and small and very old. On its ivory face, scarcely bigger than a child's fingernail, only traces of paintwork lingered in the lips and eyes. The robe of cloisonné enamel was bright as blood, as were the feathers of the half-unfurled wings. Altogether she was less tall than January's little finger, and a loop rising from the gold of her hair told him she'd once been a pendant on a necklace, or had hung, perhaps, on the corner of a candle-branch or lamp.

'She's supposedly the guardian of the de Gericault family. At least that's what our Granmère Vitrac, and her maid Mammy Pé, always said. Granmère had a ring with her on it as well.' Rose turned back to Jeoff. 'Where did you get this?'

'A pawnshop on Girod Street.'

'A *pawnshop*?'

He held up a finger mysteriously and turned to January. 'My brother Aramis writes me that you solve puzzles, Ben. Catch murderers and thieves, and find buried treasure.'

'I found *one* buried treasure, sir,' pointed out January with a sigh. 'And only because the crooks who were looking for it practically shoved it under my nose.'

Rose laughed – bright and flickering like her smile, and as quickly tucked away. 'Don't tell me the de Gericault treasure has finally surfaced?'

January's eyebrows went up. 'Is there a family treasure?'

'Supposedly. Nothing to do with us.' She turned back to her younger brother. 'But this particular Crimson Angel belonged to Mammy Ginette. If it's the same one,' she added doubtfully. 'There could have been several, for all we know.'

'I think it's the same.' With the air of a conjuror producing marvels, Jefferson Vitrack drew a thick yellow envelope from his breast pocket, and from it extracted two columns clipped from a newspaper. 'They're from the *Washington Intelligencer.*' He passed them to January. 'The last week of May.'

When I was still on the high seas, remembered January, *coming back from Washington myself . . .* With a bullet-hole in his side that still hurt like the very devil whenever he turned his shoulders, and a hundred and fifty dollars from a planter whose missing friend he'd located: funds upon which the January family would be able to live until Christmas.

ESCAPE FROM MURDER
Michael Donnelley

A small party of intrepid Americans – the Malcolm Loveridges of New York and their beautiful daughter Desdemona, Mr James Blakeney, also of New York, Mr and Mrs Thomas Powderleigh of Washington and Mr Loveridge's valet Hans Gruber, and the writer of this article – barely escaped from the vengeful machetes of rebelling slaves in the isolated Pinar del Río province of Cuba, by a combination of daring and miraculous luck . . .

'This was originally printed in the *Herald*,' said Vitrack as January's eye skimmed the columns. 'The writer, Donnelley, is a reporter for that paper.' He opened the yellow envelope again and thumbed quickly through the contents: newspaper clippings with dates and provenance written at the tops, neatly-ordered notes in a precise hand, letters carefully folded and arranged by date.

'It was reprinted in the *True American* as well.' Rose peered around January's shoulder. 'I remember thinking that it sounded like the Crimson Angel.'

. . . but Providence took a hand in the shape of an old slave-woman whom Miss Loveridge had earlier befriended. In the face of the smuggler-captain's adamant refusal to transport us to safety 'on credit,' as the saying goes, this woman produced from somewhere in the recesses of her rags a tiny golden angel, an exquisite miracle of crimson enamel, gold, and ivory. 'She be all dat left ob hidden treasure,' the old woman assured us. 'My mama's ole marse, he hide his gold – hide diamonds an' jools, 'nuff to buy de whole of Cuba! – hide it so none

*but de fambly can find it. But he gib dis to my mama, an' she
to me . . .'*

'I didn't know anything of theirs had survived.'
   'Neither did I,' said her brother. 'Until I read this.' He turned to
January, his handsome features – long and narrow, like Rose's, as
were his slender hands – filled with a grave brightness. 'I think it
ironic,' he said, 'and yet in a way fitting that this has come into my
hands. *None but the family*, she said . . . And only I – and Rose
and our brother Aramis – know the significance of this –' he held
up the little golden thing, ruby and flame in the candlelight – 'and
how it can lead to inestimable good for thousands of poor souls.
Yourselves included, I hope and trust.'

TWO

'In 1732,' said Jefferson Vitrack, taking a sip of Gabriel's excellent coffee, 'our great-great grandfather, Barthélmy de Gericault,
came to the colony of Saint-Domingue. The western third of
the Spanish island of Hispaniola had been ceded to France by the
Treaty of Ryswick thirty-five years previously, and a great many
Frenchmen – both of the nobility and of the bourgeoise – had
invested in sugar plantations there and were making substantial
fortunes.'
   'And were importing a hundred thousand slaves a year from
Africa, towards the end,' remarked January softly. Generally, the
old gentlemen who spent their days drinking coffee at the Café des
Refugies on the Rue de la Levée didn't care to be reminded of the
blacks who'd comprised seventeen out of eighteen inhabitants of
'the fairest jewel in the crown of France', as the colony had been
called. But if Vitrack was going to bring up why his forebears had
left that tropical paradise he couldn't very well pretend the slaves
hadn't been there. 'Most didn't last three years in the sugar fields.'
He watched his brother-in-law's face as he said it and saw, to his
surprise, not annoyance but sadness darken the hazel-green eyes
and tighten his mouth.
   'It was . . . barbaric,' agreed Vitrack. 'Inexcusable.'

And as it turned out, reflected January, *stupid as well. What did those planters on Saint-Domingue THINK was going to happen?*

But he knew better than to say that even to the most sympathetic of white abolitionists.

After a moment of silence, the young man went on. 'Barthélmy was the younger son of the Comte de Caillot; his mother was the only daughter of the Vicomte de Gericault. It was understood that the de Gericault estate was to come to him upon the death of her father. For whatever reason, the Comte thought it best that his younger son go to make his fortune in the Americas, and when the old Comte died, and then Vicomte de Gericault a year later, Barthélmy's older brother, Belleange, took BOTH his father's title of the Comte de Caillot AND the de Gericault title and lands for himself. Barthélmy sued to get the de Gericault title, but Belleange had married into one of the judiciary families that ruled the Parlement of Paris, and it was impossible to get a judgement against him.'

He paused, as if expecting the usual American exclamation of, '*What the hell—?*' and ready to explain the appalling mess of the French legal system before Napoleon had come along and straightened it out at gunpoint.

But January had spent sixteen years in Paris under the restored Bourbons, studying and practicing the arts of surgery and later – when it became obvious that even in the land of Liberté, Egalité, etc. nobody was going to hire a surgeon who looked like a cotton-hand – playing the piano, and he'd heard all about the Parlement of Paris.

'Well.' Their visitor broke a praline into precise quarters and arranged them symmetrically on his plate. 'The court case dragged on for decades. The best Barthélmy could manage was to arrange a marriage between his son, Absalon, and Belleange's daughter. But on Belleange's death, Belleange's son Neron claimed both titles, and the matter still hadn't been resolved when the Revolution came and made the entire point moot.'

'Our granmère,' put in Rose, 'was the product of Absalon's marriage to his cousin.'

The cheerfulness with which she spoke the words gave January, for an instant, a sense of seeing his wife across a vast chasm, as if she – and her white half-brother – were the inhabitants of a different world. *And MY granmère*, he thought, *was kidnapped from her home, loaded on to a ship, and raped by a sailor – possibly by the entire crew – on her way across before being sold to work as a field-slave for what little remained of her life. And she saw her half-white daughter grow up with no hope of ever being anything but a slave or a whore.*

And he didn't wonder at it, that the *librés* – the free colored – of New Orleans dealt with the blacks – slave or freed – as a different race, a different culture, a different species.

Rose – intelligent, educated, and kind, with a deep, cool kindness that had taken years to flower – was the daughter of the free people of color, descended from the mixed blood of black women and white men who had granted to their offspring many, but not all, the privileges of whiteness, the chief of them being assurance that they wouldn't be sold away from everyone they knew at a moment's notice. They were able to make their livings more or less as they wished, the boys from educations their white fathers paid for, the girls – if they were pretty – as the *plaçées* – the 'placed women' – of other white men who could afford such mistresses. That Rose was his wife and not a *plaçée* was due to a combination of temperament and circumstance, but she was, he saw now without anger or resentment, a *libré* to the ends of her ink-stained fingers.

She saw herself as primarily the descendant of white people.

She saw them – or some of them – as being her family, in a way January's mother, for all her pretense of being like the other free colored *plaçées* of New Orleans, never could.

His reluctant amusement at his mother's pretensions took away some of the sting of that chasm: she was what she was. And Rose, dearly as he loved her, was what *she* was. So he turned his eyes from the hell pit of that past, as he had taught himself to do, and only asked, 'And I take it Granmère married a man from Louisiana?'

'From Bordeaux, actually,' said Vitrack. 'Oliva de Gericault married Louis-Charles Vitrac –' he pronounced it in the French fashion this time – 'in 1786, when she was sixteen. He'd come to Cap Francais – the capital of Saint-Domingue – as clerk for a shipping company. I think they met at church. The de Gericault plantation, La Châtaigneraie, lay only five or six miles from the town. Their son – our father –' he nodded at Rose, with the friendly acknowledgement common in French Creole families of relatives 'on the shady side of the street' – 'was born in Cap Francais a year later, and they fled with Absalon de Gericault and his family to Cuba in 1791.'

In 1791. January turned the phrase over in his mind. For all Jefferson Vitrack's opinion that the importation of millions of men and women like his grandmother, to die in the cane fields of Saint-Domingue and Louisiana, was inexcusable, there was a little bit of this young white man that flinched from saying, '*When the slaves finally revolted.*'

When the slaves, who outnumbered the whites seventeen to one, had finally had enough of being beaten, being raped, being killed in any number of atrocious fashions at the merest hint of insubordination, being treated like animals, and had turned upon their captors, their rapists, their murderers in bloodthirsty and totally justifiable fury.

Maybe *when the slaves revolted* sounded a little too much, to white ears, like *we asked for it.*

In 1791 sidestepped the question of whose innocent wives and children had died, by whose hand and under what circumstances, and maybe that was for the best if this discussion were to proceed.

'Great-Granpère named his new plantation on Cuba "Hispaniola",' said Vitrack, 'after the island that he never ceased to consider his home.'

'Hispaniola is also the name of one of your brother's plantations in Grand Isle, isn't it?'

Both nodded. A cockroach the size of a small hummingbird threw itself, wings rattling, at the candelabra; it was definitely time to go indoors. January gathered up the candles and carried them into his room – officially a bedroom, but in practice a sort of study – and thence through to the parlor, Rose and her brother bearing the coffee things behind, like the mystical servants bearing the Grail to the Fisher King. When she'd attained her freedom as a white man's mistress, and acquired a house in New Orleans, January's mother had soundly beaten it into her son that only animals – or Americans, which amounted to the same thing – came straight into the parlor from the street, in spite of the fact that all openings in the walls of the house doubled as both windows and doors. You came in through the room of the master of the house, or its mistress, depending on who had invited you. Their slave cabin on Bellefleur Plantation having boasted only a single door and no windows at all, seven-year-old Benjamin had marveled at both the ridiculousness of this French Creole custom and at his mother's sudden conversion to the *libré* way of doing things, but had dared not disobey, and the habit had remained.

A completely different set of rules applied, of course, if the owner of the house happened to be white and if you happened to be black – or free colored – or if the owner was white and American . . .

They reassembled in the parlor, stuffy with the dense lingering heat of the day, but bug-free. Zizi-Marie brought more coffee.

'Granpère and Granmère Vitrac came to Grand Isle in 1803, as soon as Spain gave Louisiana back to France,' explained Rose. 'And Granpère never forgave Napoleon for selling the whole concern to the Americans – three weeks later! – not 'til the day he died. I can't say that I blame him.' She cast a glance at the windows, beyond which, even at this dead season of the year, freight wagons still hauled corn and salt pork, iron bars and silk hankies, along Rue Esplanade from the wharves to the bayou where it would be transshipped to plantations east of the city.

1803, January recalled, was the year he and his mother – and his younger sister Olympe – had first come to New Orleans. Where the wide 'neutral ground' along Rue Esplanade lay now had been the crumbling city wall, the drainage ditch in its center a sort of moat. Where the wooden houses of the suburb of Marigny stood had been sugar-fields.

Only a few streets over, as a child he'd sit in the evenings on the gallery above his mother's kitchen and hear the slaves singing as they were marched back to the quarters after work.

'I remember when we were children we were always talking about the treasure that Great-Granpère left behind,' Rose went on, 'either in Cuba or in Saint-Domingue. But I don't remember whether it was something we heard the grown-ups talk about, or something we made up. Do you remember Great-Granpère Absalon ever speaking of it, Jeoffrey?'

He shook his head. 'I was only a year old when he died. He came to Hispaniola – the Louisiana Hispaniola, not the Cuban plantation – in 1809, when the Spanish authorities on Cuba expelled all the French refugees. Granpère Vitrac was dead by then, and Papa ran the plantation. Aramis says Granmère Oliva was terrified of old Absalon, he doesn't know why. Our brother Aramis was only three,' he added, with a glance at January. 'He says he liked Great-Granpère, though he doesn't remember him very well either. And Rose was still here in New Orleans then. Granmère Oliva always pooh-poohed the treasure when we children would talk of it. Did Mammy Ginette –' Vitrack turned to his sister – 'ever say anything to you about the treasure?'

Rose was silent for a time, gazing with half-closed eyes at the little cluster of candles – like the village storyteller, January recalled, back in the quarters at Bellefleur Plantation when he was tiny. Calling out of the clear dark lake of his memories the tales of Compair Lapin and Bouki the Hyena, of High John the Conqueror and of the witches that waited for the careless at the crossroads on moonless nights.

Rose would be calling to *her* mind now herself as a gawky, short-sighted child who begged to be taught all those things that would be of no use to her, like mathematics and the wherefore of storms. Calling to mind the three-room 'big house' of her white father's plantation to which she'd been taken upon her mother's death, and the dreamy peacefulness of Grand Isle.

'No,' she said at length. 'She showed me the Crimson Angel, which she wore on a string around her neck, under her clothes. She said Great-Granmère Amalie – Great-Granpère Absalon's wife – had given it to her, and that it had been a symbol of the de Gericault family back in France – which I knew already, from Granmère Oliva's ring. She said it was the only valuable thing she had. But the treasure was real. I'm certain of that.'

'Why do you say that?'

Rose was silent for a moment, calling old memories back to mind. 'Mammy Ginette was . . . I think she'd been a servant in Great-Granpère's house in Saint-Domingue. Mammy Ginette came to Papa's plantation – the family was living at Chouteau Plantation then, which had come to Papa when he'd married Aramis' and Jeoffrey's maman – when I was ten. I'd just come there myself, after Mother's death. I was lonely and grieving, and Mammy Ginette was very good to me, telling me stories about Great-Granpère's plantation back on Saint-Domingue. We'd play games behind the barn, and she'd build the plantation for me out of bits of brick and lumber – I was always building things like that. I remember when I was twelve I reconstructed the entire city of Paris out of old shingles, and I was furious when Aramis stole them to make a bonfire.

'I think she took to me because she'd come to Louisiana looking for her granddaughter,' she went on after a moment. 'Mélusina was my age, she said, and had been kidnapped by slave-traders back in

Cuba. Mammy Ginette came to America to look for her – she only stayed with us on the plantation for a week – and she planned to use the Crimson Angel to buy her back—'

'Did she ever find her?' The candle-glow flickered in her spectacles as she looked across at her brother. 'Do you know?'

'I don't think she can have,' he replied, with a trace of sadness, 'if an "old slave-woman" traded it to a smuggler to get that bunch of Americans away from a slave-revolt to safety. But the treasure—?'

'Mammy Ginette told me that the year the Spanish drove the French planters out of Cuba – 1809, it would have been, nine years before she came to Louisiana looking for her granddaughter – an "old blind man" forced her to lead him back to Saint-Domingue – Haiti, it was called by that time – to find a treasure.'

'Great-Granpère's treasure?'

'I think it has to have been. Else why her? Why not someone else? But the slaves, once they'd won their freedom, were fighting among themselves by then. The Republic they founded had already split into *two* republics of Haiti, and Christophe made himself king of one of them a few years later . . .'

'If Mammy Ginette's daughter was a slave in Cuba back in May –' January turned the tiny gold-and-crimson figure in his powerful fingers – 'it doesn't sound like they did find the treasure.'

'She said they didn't make it far,' said Rose. 'She wouldn't talk about Haiti; said it was horrible, like a nightmare. She said she barely got back to Cuba, and I think the blacks there must have killed this "old blind man". But she said to me, more than once, that she was telling me this because I was "family".'

'Like the newspaper,' said Jefferson Vitrack quietly. *'None but the family can find it.'*

'So I think it has to have been the family treasure.'

'I do, too.' He fell silent for a time, long slender hands – duplicates of Rose's hands – folded on the table before him, while from the narrow dining-room behind the parlor a chair scraped softly and Zizi-Marie said, ''night, Gabe.' Her footsteps creaked. There was a little cabinet behind the pantry, from which a ladder ascended to the loft where the girls had slept, back when Rose's school had had pupils. In the ensuing stillness – for it was now late in the night – January heard also the faint scrape and rumble of someone moving in the little secret chamber that he'd walled off from the main storage area at street-level beneath the house, when he'd started taking in fugitives. There were three of them down there: Tommy, Boston, and Boston's wife Nell, scheduled to meet tomorrow with others of the organization that guided runaways north. Nell was with child, they said. Owners knew that once a woman bore a baby, she probably wouldn't run.

'It's not for myself that I want to find that treasure,' Vitrack said at last. 'Though of course, if you help me, I promise you'll have your share. Please hear me out,' he added as January drew breath to say that there was no way in Hell he was going anywhere near Haiti.

'My father-in-law – Congressman Ulysses Rauch – is President of the Philadelphia branch of the American Colonization Society.' From his yellow envelope he produced a folded paper, presumably credentials, and laid it on the table, as if he expected January to request documentation of his claim. 'He believes – as do I – that the only way in which the disgrace of slavery can be eradicated from our nation is for the slaves to be returned to Africa, the continent which God intended for their habitation. Only in this way can the white race secure itself against the inevitable retaliation by its former bondsmen.'

And make damn sure those former bondsmen aren't going to take jobs that white men want?

'Inevitable?'

'Of course.' Vitrack spoke as if the matter were self-evident. 'The events of 1791 have pretty much proved that if given their liberty, slaves will – with quite justifiable anger and outrage – turn on their former masters and seek revenge. Men from Thomas Jefferson himself on down have long recognized that the black race and the white are basically incompatible and cannot live side by side. Yet the expense of transportation to our colony in Africa,' he went on, again cutting off any objection that January might have made to either his reasoning or his evidence, 'and, in some cases, a very stubborn prejudice against the idea of repatriation, have often mitigated against this solution.'

January said nothing, which, he assumed, he was meant to do. He'd never encountered a single freed slave – himself, his mother, and the elder of his two younger sisters included – who had ever expressed the slightest interest in being sent to a primitive, tropical country where very few spoke his language and where, even within the 'American' black colony, the comforts of civilization were rudimentary. Nor had any of the runaways he'd ever hidden beneath his house ever exclaimed, '*I gotta find my way to Africa!*' And what, he wondered, did the American Colonization Society intend to do with the *librés*: half-white, three-quarters white, seven-eighths white or more?

He himself, with three African grandparents, had been born in Louisiana and considered himself an American.

'In 1824 an alternative destination was proposed, in the Republic of Haiti, on the island of Hispaniola. President Boyer was desirous of colonists to his nation, but of the six thousand or so free blacks who went there, many returned to the United States within a year, owing largely to the fact that there simply wasn't enough money to help them settle.'

The fact that the Haitians themselves had been engaged in bloody factional warfare for over half of the black republic's existence, January was careful not to say, might have had something to do with that as well.

'But that doesn't mean that the scheme is unworkable.' Vitrack leaned forward, as if with little encouragement he would have seized January by the lapels of his jacket and shaken him to make him see the wisdom of the plan. 'When I read in the *Intelligencer* about the Crimson Angel – when I encountered proof that the childhood tales we heard on the plantation about the de Gericault treasure were true – I came south at once. I spoke to Mr and Mrs Powderleigh in Washington, who said that the "old slave-woman" wasn't one of the slaves on the plantation where they were staying.'

From his yellow envelope he withdrew several sheets of notes and unerringly selected the page he sought. 'Mrs Powderleigh says she thought she'd seen the woman selling fruit in the streets of Guane, but wasn't certain. Her name might have been Sally, but the Powderleighs don't speak any sort of Spanish at all, much less the Creole Spanish of Cuba.'

And they were probably terrified, thought January. Whatever they were doing on an isolated coffee-plantation in Cuba – Mrs Powderleigh and Violet Loveridge had known Doña Clemencita, the plantation's mistress, in school, according to the *Intelligencer* – they could not have reckoned on the murderous confusion of a slave uprising. And having everyone around them in the jagged torchlight and blackness of the night attack shouting in an unfamiliar tongue would only have added to their shock and confusion. No wonder they didn't catch the name of the woman to whom they owed their lives. He wondered if 'Michael Donnelley', the writer of the article, had actually been as brave and intrepid as he described, or if he'd spent the whole night cowering under a bed until the time came to make a break for the beach.

'They did confirm that the old woman seemed to know the smuggler captain – Loup de la Mer, he's called – and that he put them ashore in New Orleans. I guessed that the first thing he'd do would be to pawn the Angel. From the owner of the pawnshop I learned where he stays when he's in town.' Vitrack sipped his coffee and made a face – it was now stone cold, or as cold as anything ever got in New Orleans in the summer, even at one in the morning. Through the wavy glass of the French doors out to the gallery, January could see that even the lights in the house of the Metoyer sisters on the other side of the Rue Esplanade neutral ground had been put out, the whole of the town (*except for the gambling parlors* . . .) asleep in the indigo velvet smother of the night.

'For it is, surely,' said the young man, 'the Hand of Providence that has manifested itself here. That the very fortune that was made from the blood and sweat of African bondsmen will be turned to good – sanctified – by this use. *Diamonds and jewels*, she said, *enough to buy the whole of Cuba*. The fortunes made by the sugar-planters of Saint-Domingue were legendary. This old blind man must have been connected with the family somehow—'

'Who was he?' asked January curiously. 'Not Great-Granpère Absalon himself, I assume?'

Brother and sister looked at one another. 'Mammy Ginette just said he was an old blind man. She only spoke of him the once, the first night of her brief stay at our plantation.'

'I never heard anyone say Great-Granpère was blind.' Vitrack shrugged. 'But the blind man, whoever he was, knew the treasure was there. And that it was worth risking his life for. Even as I do.'

He looked from January to Rose. 'Will you come with me?' he asked, his eyes almost shining. 'First to Cuba, to find this Sally, or whatever her name really is – Mammy Ginette's daughter – who can tell us exactly where the treasure lies. And then – Benjamin, this would of course be you only . . . to Haiti.'

THREE

Brother-in-law or not – advocate of 'eradicating' the 'disgrace of slavery' or not – Jefferson Vitrack was a white man, and so January refrained from saying, '*That's the stupidest idea I've ever heard.*'

Instead he simply said, 'No.'

'Your journey would not go unremunerated,' Vitrack hastened to assure him. 'Whatever we find, you will be entitled to half of it for your trouble. I understand it's a dangerous undertaking, particularly as you would be going into Haiti alone. As a white man, it would be impossible for me—'

'And as a black man,' finished January gently, 'the moment I set foot in Cuba, I would be at *extreme* risk of being kidnapped and shipped as a slave either back to the United States – where I promise you, nobody is going to ask if I've been enslaved illegally or not – or more likely to Brazil. The danger would be ten times worse for Rose. I don't generally play the Roman husband and patriarch,' he added, and he put a hand over his wife's wrist. 'But this time I will. I will not go; and I forbid Rose to even think about going.'

And Rose – who under other circumstances might have felt discomfort at saying nay to a younger brother whom she clearly cared for – cast down her eyes in wifely meekness, jaw-dropping to those who knew her, and said nothing.

'We have a son, sir,' said January. 'And we have enough money to last us for most of the rest of the year. It simply isn't worth the risk.'

Though Rose's brother wore an expression of profoundest chagrin (*he actually thought that any free black person in his right mind would consider for one moment going anywhere NEAR Cuba?*), he didn't argue. He would remain in New Orleans, he said, until Captain Loup de la Mer arrived, and he scribbled the name of his hotel – the Strangers, one of the best in the French Town – on the back of his card. 'In case you change your mind,' he said, with his dazzling smile. 'Or should you think of a man whose complexion is suffi-ciently dark that he won't be murdered out of hand as a spy the minute he sets foot on Haiti, who has not the responsibilities that keep you – as I know they must – from lending a hand to his brothers suffering in slavery.'

Though the corner of his mouth hardened a little at the imputation – intended or not – of cowardice and irresponsibility, January saw again the warmth in Rose's eyes as she looked at her brother and said cheerfully, 'Nonsense, sir. I hope we're going to see you Sunday for dinner. The cook at the Strangers is good . . . for a hotel cook. But my nephew can cook a duck in a way that makes even an atheist understand why God created ducks.'

Vitrack laughed and said, 'You have a guest for Sunday, then, Ben.'

It was one of the peculiarities, January had found, of the whole complicated system of what white people and black people could and could not be seen to be doing in relationship to each other, that while no white – French or American – would invite even the most fair-complected *libré* to eat at the same table with them (or even consume food closer to the interior of their house than the back gallery), it was perfectly acceptable for a white to eat in the home of *gens de couleur librés*, or even, in extreme circumstances, blacks (*if they'd just saved your life, for instance, and you were starving to death* . . .) as long as the whites 'didn't make a habit of it' and the blacks were sufficiently grateful for the honor.

Moreover, though Americans considered association with the free colored to be as socially damning as association with blacks, among the French Creoles no stigma whatever attached to whites having Sunday dinner at the home of *libré* cousins or aunts or brothers – the descendants of Granpère's (and sometimes Papa's) free colored mistress. This was probably, January guessed, because so many French Creoles *did* have free colored cousins and aunts and half-brothers . . . though of course no French Creole wife would admit to even knowing what her husband's *plaçée* looked like (with the exception of the extremely wealthy young wife of the lover of January's youngest sister Dominique . . . but that was another story. And even she didn't go to Sunday dinner).

'You think that treasure is still there, after all these years?' January came back into the candlelit parlor after escorting Vitrack as far as the corner of Rue Burgundy to hail a cab.

'Mammy Ginette spoke of treasure being hidden *inside a wall*.'

Rose had changed into her dressing gown and brushed out her hair, wavy and silken like a white woman's when taken down from beneath the tignon that had once been commanded by law as the only headdress permitted – and in fact mandated – to women of color in Louisiana. She carried the candle behind him as he passed from room to room, closing shutters and latching them, making the house safe for the night. 'I expect the house was burned to the ground, so it must have been a stone foundation wall if this "old blind man" who forced her to go back thought it would still be there. Maybe in the sugar mill?'

January nodded thoughtfully. The sugar mill was generally the only building on any plantation constructed of stone or brick, and it was frequently used as a hideout during hurricanes.

'I'll have to sit down tomorrow and write down everything I can remember of what she said to me; draw a copy of that little model of the plantation, too, if I can remember it, to give to Jeoff when he comes Sunday. I hope he won't be fool enough to try to go to Haiti himself, like the old man did.'

'When you're talking about *diamonds and jewels*,' replied January, 'you're talking about enough money to change your life if you're an "old blind man" – whoever he was – and doubly so now.' He followed the dim firefly of Rose's candle back across the parlor to the bedroom: with the shutters closed against night-walkers and mosquitoes, the house was like a cave.

'My family must have thought the slave uprising in their area was just a – a temporary problem,' said Rose. 'Gold is heavy. They must have shoved everything valuable in the safest place they could think of, meaning to come back.' She bent over Baby John's crib, the candle-gleam picking out momentarily those shut eyes, the little domed brow – like bronze silk – smoothed in sleep of the slight pucker of worry that characterized their son's waking hours. Often and often, at the balls where he played the piano, in the winter carnival season when New Orleans came alive, January had heard family stories recounted by men and women whose mothers and fathers had somehow thought the flower-filled paradise of Saint-Domingue would go on forever: how they'd waked in the night to the sound of the shutters cracking under furious blows, to the screams of the house servants as black shadows darted across the moonlight around the house. Since he was only at those balls to make music, and was thus to all intents and purposes invisible, he had been free to think, *They had it coming.*

His own master, Michie Fourchet, favored hanging a man who was insubordinate, or slack in his work, upside-down by his ankles naked from two corners of the sugar-house door and working him over with a cane, the tip of which had been wrapped in brass wire. A pregnant woman would be tied spreadeagled on the ground, with a hole dug for her belly so the future slave wouldn't be harmed. He'd heard that in Saint-Domingue it had been worse.

They had it coming.

Looking down at Baby John's face, he hoped that those whites who'd had infants this small – this precious, though they were the offspring of monsters – had made it out the back windows and into the jungle, and to the safety of boats. *They should have suffered* . . . He put out his hand, touched the incredible silken softness of that round cheek. *And what suffering would be worse than to lose a child, as thousands upon thousands of slave men had lost their children when they were sold away because of Michie's gambling debts or needing money to send Mamzelle to school in France?*

But still he hoped those people, unknown to him, dead now for years and lost in the shadows of what had been, had gotten their infants away safe.

Rose shed her dressing gown, slim sides, slim dust-brown flanks nude in the heat, and slithered under the mosquito-bar that tented the bed. January came to the bedside, blew out the candle, shed his own clothing in the black stifling velvet dark and thought about the old times and Saint-Domingue no more.

Even in fatter years than 1838, summer was a starving season for musicians. The previous February, January had had the misfortune to thoroughly offend one of the few American planters in New Orleans still wealthy enough for most of the *other* American planters to be leery of crossing him. After that, January had been out of the city for much of the spring and had thus returned to find what little work there was – mostly out in the resort villages of Milneburg and Mandeville by the lake – already contracted to others. It was a situation which he knew would shake itself straight eventually. He was one of the best piano players in town and pretty much everybody, French and American, knew it, and there was enough money hidden under floor-boards and behind attic joists in the old Spanish house to buy beans and rice for several months yet. Ironically, his unemployment put him in the position of playing 'man of the house' to the wives of several of the musicians who *had* gotten work out in Mandeville, if they needed someone to help move a trunk or fix a jammed window or give a talking-to to an erring son.

So it was a day or two before he visited the Café des Refugies.

Like most 'cafés' in the old French Town, it occupied what had originally been one of the hundreds of small stucco cottages built straight on to the brick banquettes of Rue de la Levée and consisted of the usual four rooms with a half-storey overhead. Even in the stifling heat of mid-morning, when January came to the French doors that opened on to the street, he could hear the subdued murmur of voices and the click of dice in the gambling rooms in the rear. The two front rooms – knocked into one years ago – were quieter, men at the small tables reading the latest newspapers and sipping *p'tit goaves* or coffee. In a corner, a dilapidated fiddler lilted his way through an air from *Così Fan Tutte*. The smoke of cigars or Spanish cigarettes blurred the dense brown shade.

When January had left New Orleans for Paris, twenty-one years ago in the spring of 1817, the tables of the Café des Refugies had always been filled, summer or winter, with graying men whose bitter eyes looked back from these smelly American streets across the gap of years to Saint-Domingue – the place that the world now called Haiti, which would always in their hearts be Saint-Domingue. They'd smoked, played dominoes, and read the newspapers, talking with a kind of eager spite about the internecine fighting between Pétion and his mulattos, and Christophe and the rebel slaves; jeering at Christophe for making himself king of half of their much-vaunted 'republic' and predicting conquest by the Spanish, by the British, by Bolívar – anything rather than admit that men who had been slaves were capable of forming or supporting a working government.

Americans, January had noted even then, didn't speak of the black republic at all.

When January had returned to New Orleans, and to the Café des Refugies, sixteen years later, though Haiti had still been torn apart by factional warfare, it was also still free. And though the Café had been moved from Rue St. Philippe to this location across from the market, these same few men, familiar faces crowned with white instead of gray, were still sitting here, playing dominoes and drinking guava cocktails and talking about their Saint-Domingue

plantations as if some miracle were going to occur and they were
going to get a letter any day now from a conquering general saying,
'And we're restoring your plantation to you with a full complement
of slaves . . .'

As if they could walk along the dusty streets of Cap Francais
again, to the little stucco cottages of their *plaçée* mistresses, and
find those same lovely quadroon and octoroon girls reclining on the
galleries under the shade of pomegranate and coco palms, smiling
a welcome while some obliging little servant rubbed their dainty
feet.

Where he stood in the French door, January could hear old M'sieu
Thierry – whose hair had been black when first he'd seen him in
exactly that same chair – declaiming loudly to M'sieu d'Evreux
(they were both stone deaf) that it was all the fault of the mulattos.
If the mulattos of the island hadn't started the whole trouble by
demanding of the General Assembly that they be recognized as
having the same rights as white Frenchmen when the Revolution
came (he meant the French, not the Haitian, Revolution) – if they
hadn't tried to get the blacks on their side against the whites – none
of it would ever have happened . . .

That was FORTY-SEVEN YEARS AGO, old man . . .

Have you done nothing since?

'Benjamin!' Jean Thiot, proprietor, crossed the room to the door
where he stood, white-haired now, like his customers, but his dark,
thin-featured face still smiling. 'I'd heard you were back in town.'

'I knew it would be summer here,' replied January gravely. 'How
could I stay away?'

Thiot laughed. 'And how is the beautiful Madame Janvier? And
le petit professeur?'

'Madame Janvier grows more beautiful every day. And I think
the first words out of John's mouth are going to be a speech in
Latin about phenomenological metaphysics.'

'Better that than a demand for some money so he could go
gambling,' said Thiot, grinning. 'Which was the first thing *my* son
said when he learned to talk. What may I help you with this fine
sunny day?'

Despite the brassy light crushing the street outside, thunder grumbled distantly, as if offended by the jest.

'I wondered if you knew anything about a planter named Absalon
de Gericault. Turns out Madame Janvier is related to the family.'

'Lord, yes! I can't tell you more than I told the other fellow who came asking yesterday—'

'Madame Janvier's half-brother?'

'Didn't say, but now you speak of it, yes, he had the look of her. Same nose, same chin . . . De Gericault was only in here once, back in 'ten or 'eleven, but everybody knew him, of course. His place was only a few hours' ride from the Cap, and he was a good man, his home and his hands open to all.'

'Was he wealthy, as planters went?'

'Heavens, yes! In those days it was impossible *not* to be wealthy, if one raised sugar. The world could not get enough of it. And even among the *grands blancs*, de Gericault was rich. Madame his wife coruscated with diamonds: she was famous for them. A colorless woman, always ailing, and thin as thread-paper. Her jewels wore *her*. And La Châtaigneraie plantation was like a town house. Furnishings of mahogany and ormolu, mantels of real marble, not wood painted to deceive. I suppose the other plantation he had in the south was like the plantations here, a business office, furnished only for the making of money. But La Châtaigneraie was his Trianon. Always the brokers and the merchants from town were on the road there.'

'You sound like you were one of them.' January studied the lined face, trying to guess how young Thiot would have been, forty-seven years ago.

'Once only, when I was eight. My father owned a theater in le Cap, so of course we saw everyone. He remembered me, too, when he came here, though Papa and I went to Havana in 'ninety-one and he to the far end of Cuba near Santiago. He recognized everybody. A very great gentleman.'

The blotched sunlight in the Rue de la Levée faded behind him. Thunder rolled again, stronger, and the smell of the storm swept the streets like cherubim announcing the coming of the Lord. Two men came out of the gaming rooms and moved in the direction of the bar, and Thiot went to greet them – white men, after all, and more worthy of the proprietor's attentions than a man who could only come through the doors on an errand from his betters. January noted that though they were French Creole, they weren't the fallen aristocrats of the Caribbean. New men, clerks or brokers – *petits blancs*, they would have been called then – who hadn't even been alive during those wild and rumor-filled days. Probably Napoleonistes or Orleannistes or some other flavor of politics utterly anathema to those last few refugees from the vanished world, the lazy tropical paradise that reeked of sugar and blood.

Looking up, January saw for the first time that the sign on the front of the building had been changed as well. It no longer said CAFÉ DES REFUGIES, but instead THE PIG AND WHISTLE.

'Thiot had it changed last week,' said Hannibal Sefton, when he'd packed up his fiddle and joined January on the street. 'He's been talking about it since Mardi Gras, but I think he was waiting for some of his oldest customers to die.'

They crossed the street to the market as the rain began, to buy coffee in tin cups from La Violette's stand among the brick pillars; both waved a greeting to Laurent Lamartine, playing the clarionet among the half-empty tables. It was summer, and if one could make a few pennies playing in the market rather than rolling cigars down on Tchapitoulas Street, that was all to the good.

'He thinks an English name will bring in Americans – or at least not turn them away.' The fiddler dug in the pocket of his long-tailed coat for the few cents that coffee would cost. La Violette – who had a soft spot in her heart for Hannibal – added a couple of pralines on a square of newspaper as *lagniappe*, and Hannibal bowed low and kissed her hand.

'Is it working?' asked January.

'Doesn't seem to be. *Omnia mutantur nos et mutamur in illis*, but Kaintucks seem naturally to shy away from any building which includes French doors and old men playing dominoes.' He settled in one of the rickety cane-bottomed chairs and slid a praline across the table to January. Hannibal was one of the few whites in New Orleans who didn't care who he was seen to associate with, with the result that he was regarded as rather degenerate by his fellow *blankittes*. 'But it's the first dandelion of what I assume will be an infestation of weeds within a year. And how fares the beautiful Rose?'

'As well as anyone can who's translating St Ignatius for the Ursuline nuns for two cents a page.' This was the means by which Rose was extending the slender funds hidden in the attic joists. 'Come to dinner and see for yourself.'

'I shall, thank you. *Oh, how much more doth beauty beauteous seem, by that sweet ornament that truth doth give! The rose looks fair, but fairer we it deem* . . . I should like to write a poem on your wife's perfections for her birthday, but my facility in that department seems to be returning only slowly – who started that rumor that one had to be a drunkard to produce great poetry? In my drinking days I never managed so much as a line.'

He coughed, turning aside and pressing a hand to his ribs, face chalky with sudden agony. In putting aside alcohol, January knew, his friend had perforce given up laudanum as well, and with its swoony oblivion went its undoubted powers to soothe. He waited in silence, and in time Hannibal collected himself and embarked on a cheerful account of a crooked poker-game in the back room of the Blackleg Saloon the previous night, which lasted them through the remainder of the brief downpour and the length of the walk back to January's house. By the time they turned on to Rue Esplanade, the sun had grown strong enough to burn away the brief freshness that the rain had brought. Steam rose from the wet bricks of the banquette, as if like Virgil and Dante they trod the murky floors of Hell.

'—at which point the Reverend produces from beneath his coat – God knows how he kept it concealed during the game – the shortest, biggest blunderbuss it has ever been my privilege to look down the barrel of . . . It made me wonder what sort of birds they had in Scotland. So taking as my motto, *Vir prudens non contra ventum mingit* . . .'

'Will you do me a favor?' asked January suddenly.

'Anything,' said Hannibal simply. 'Of course.'

'When we reach my house,' said January, 'I'm going to shake hands with you and go inside. You keep walking and turn on to Rue Burgundy. Do you see the man in the plug-hat, there by the tree?'

Hannibal looked. When the old city wall had been torn down thirty years previously, the area across the Esplanade had been developed, its neat wooden cottages housing either the mistresses of the French and Spanish Creoles who didn't own property in the old French town, or Europeans who didn't care for the idea of living among the Americans upriver of Canal Street. But Rue Esplanade remained wide enough to accommodate the wagon traffic to the bayou, and its drainage ditch was now lined with trees, beneath which stevedores and drovers would slouch for lunch or a smoke.

The man in the plug-hat was obviously doing just that. His shirt was coarse red calico, and beneath the brim of the hat January could observe that his hair was black and straight, his face dusky. Quadroon or octoroon, perhaps, though January was more inclined to think he was an Indian, descended from the Creek or Houmas tribes that had once hunted in the Louisiana forests before the French came and made their sugar-plantations . . .

'Don't stare. Don't let him see you've noticed him.'

'He someone you know?' They'd reached the steps that ascended from the banquette to January's gallery. The house was the oldest in the street and built high in the Spanish style, to preserve its inhabitants against the floods which had periodically inundated the town in earlier days, and set slightly crookedly, to catch the river breeze.

'Never saw him before yesterday.' January turned and clasped Hannibal's hand in the sort of friendly dismissal one reserves for casual encounters. The fiddler bowed in instant response, as offhand-edly as if January hadn't saved his life on several occasions. A gentleman's upbringing and several years at Oxford had given him an exquisite sense of how to look condescending. 'But he *was* there yesterday – well, he's changed trees, actually – and again this morning. Loitering like that. And, I think, watching the house.'

FOUR

'There's at least one other,' Hannibal reported, when he returned an hour after the swift-falling tropical nightfall had doused the city in ink. 'A white man, fleshy rather than muscled, fair, curly hair and a yellow sack-coat. Plug-Hat's staying at the Verrandah, which means that no matter how he's dressed he has money, or the man who hired him has—'

'You never followed him all the way to St. Charles Avenue?' Rose passed him the bowl of Gabriel's gumbo and the dish of rice. Despite the sticky heat, at this hour it was a better strategy to eat in the dining room, with smudges burning in each of the open windows, than to brave the wildlife of the open night on the back gallery where the family dinner had been conducted at twilight.

'He was so obliging – and so well-heeled – as to take a cab once he reached Rue Bourbon.' Hannibal accepted the glass of lemonade

Zizi-Marie brought him, cool from the buried jars in the yard. His long fingers shook so much that he had to use both hands to steady the glass. 'Which made it a relatively simple matter to climb on the back for most of the distance. I wasn't able to do so when he returned a few hours later to relieve Curly, but I knew where he was going and could take my time in pursuit. Sure enough, when I got here he was stationed across the street in the alley beside the Metoyer house, like Iago and Roderigo observing the dwelling of Brabantio. I don't think I was seen. I take it you have no – er – guests at present?'

January shook his head, Tommy, Boston and Nell having departed the evening after Vitrack's visit. But the fact that his house was being watched made him wonder how safe any of his fellow 'conductors' of escapees were.

As if she read his thoughts, Rose said, 'Surely if the police suspected us of harboring runaways they'd have taken out a warrant to search the house, rather than pay two men to watch us? And pay them enough to stay at the Verrandah and ride cabs down Rue Bourbon, at that.'

'Sheer wastefulness on the part of City Hall,' complained the fiddler, and coughed again. 'I shall write my Congressman . . .'

'It doesn't sound like the police.' January frowned through the dark parlor door to the line of shuttered front windows that closed off the view of the street. 'Even the secret police in France would mostly use neighborhood informers, not hire men specially. Not for anything less than politics.'

'But isn't sheltering runaways politics, Uncle Ben?' asked his niece quietly. She took the chair beside Hannibal, a slim, pretty girl of seventeen, with her hair bound up in a woman's elaborate tignon. 'Isn't that the whole point behind arresting people for doing it? Because Congress won't do anything about slavery?'

'And just because they haven't come up with something like the secret police so far,' added Rose, 'doesn't mean they haven't *just* started to use them.'

'If that's what's happening,' said January, 'it's an awfully expensive way to go about it.'

'Slaves cost upwards of a thousand dollars apiece,' pointed out Hannibal. 'There's a lot at stake.'

When the fiddler left – he was occupying the house of January's mother for the summer months while that lady stayed in much more bearable quarters by the Lake – January put on his darkest shirt and ghosted through the narrower of the two gates that led from the yard on either side of the house itself. This one – on the south-eastern or riverward side of the house – entered a damp little passway that January could have spanned with one arm and his back to the house wall, always supposing he wanted to put his back against whatever might be crawling on that wall on a sweltering night in July. The thin-waxing moon had vanished early behind murky over-cast, and the night was like pitch. January waited for his eyes to accustom themselves to the blackness, but when he reached the street he could see little besides dimly-flickering rectangles on the far side of the trees where Virginie Metoyer still had her parlor shutters open. The elfin sound of her piano floated above the metallic throb of cicadas, the multifarious chorus of the frogs. The trees themselves were barely suggestions in darkness. Whether a man stood in their shadow was impossible to tell.

As a child on Bellefleur Plantation, January had grown up watchful. You never knew when some white person would mention something you were doing – something that might have been perfectly permissible two days previously – to Michie Fourchet, which would set off his alcoholic temper and earn you a beating, or worse. In Paris, years later, the constant presence of the Secret Police had served to keep a familiar set of reactions sharp. The members of the revolutionary reading-group down at the Chatte Blanche had used to send January out to sniff around the alleyways before they went down to their meetings in the cellar.

January knew the smell of watchers. Felt their presence through his skin.

These weren't police.

He had no idea who they were, or why they were watching his house. But they weren't the police.

Would the slaveholders who dominated Louisiana's government – and the governments of every state south of Mason's and Dixon's Line – form a shadow organization devoted to tracking down the people who helped their slaves get away to the north? Had it become that important to them?

He knew it was going to, one day.

He glided along the walls of the buildings towards the river, then stepped out across the street, recalling uneasily that he'd sighted a four-foot alligator making its leisurely way along the drainage ditch last week. Groping blind, listening all the while for the sound of an approaching wagon – drivers often didn't bother to light up their lanterns, especially if they'd been drinking – he knew he could pass Michie Plug-Hat or Michie Curly within feet and not see them.

The fact that he saw no one didn't mean there was no one there.

In time he returned to the house, but slept little for what remained of the night.

As soon as it was light he ascended to the half-story attic that ran the length of the house and, from its two long, narrow dormers, scanned the wide waste-space of the Esplanade with Rose's good Swiss spyglass, not that he had much hope of seeing anyone in particular there. Even at this early hour, wagons and foot-traffic moved along beside the drainage ditch toward the Lake. January picked out the forms of two or three men who could have been Michie Plug-Hat or Michie Curly, but it was too far off to be sure.

'You want me to go out and watch, Uncle Ben?' Gabriel came into the hallway-like dormer behind him. 'I can get out of the yard over M'am Gardette's stable roof.' Like nearly every property in the French town, the old Spanish house had no back way in or out. Slaves, who in a more affluent regime would have lived above the laundry and kitchen in the rooms Rose used as a laboratory, would have had to pass beneath the eyes of their owners to get to the street. 'Or stay up here with the glass?'

'I want you to go to work.' January folded up the glass. 'You're late as it is. And not a word to anybody, mind you.'

The boy clattered away down the stairs – he was dressed already, the white linen coat he wore as an apprentice in the kitchens of the Hotel Iberville folded neatly over his arm. January followed and, after a little thought, sent a note via Zizi-Marie to her mother, Olympe, the older of his two younger sisters. He then dressed in the dark, formal coat he wore for his professional engagements, donned his tall beaver hat, and proceeded to their mother's house on Rue Dauphine where Hannibal made him coffee: 'Anyone following you?'

'I don't think so.' January unwrapped a couple of chunks of brown muscovado from a scrap of newspaper – naturally, his mother had left not a morsel in the house when she'd gone to the Lake – and looked down into the yard. The stucco cottage itself, given to Livia Levesque by the lover who had bought her and her children free of slavery, was shuttered tight, and the fiddler occupied January's old room in the garçonnière above the locked-up kitchen. 'But if it does have something to do with the runaways, I can't take chances.'

The previous day, immediately after sending off Gabriel with a warning to the other shelterers of runaways – the Underground Railway, people were beginning to call them – January had dismantled and hidden the false wall that partitioned off a section of the storage space beneath the house, in case someone *did* come in with a search-warrant.

'*Si vis pacem, para bellum*,' agreed Hannibal, whom death itself would not have found without an apt quotation. 'It must be difficult to shake off pursuit, at your height.'

'Watch and see.' January gave his hat, which sat beside him on the rail of the narrow gallery where they sat, an affectionate pat. 'In the Bible it says one can't add a cubit to one's stature by taking thought, but behold how with a little thought one can take at least a few inches away.'

Ten minutes later Olympe came into the yard, a slim tallish woman whose red-and-orange headscarf was tied in the style of the voodoos, its five points proclaiming her a priestess. She walked arm in arm with her husband, Paul Corbier the upholsterer, whose face and hands – January was pleased to note – had been blacked with charcoal and brick dust so that, at a distance, his skin had January's inky African darkness rather than his own natural cocoa hue. Since Paul was only a few inches shorter than January's massive six-foot-three, and not a great deal thicker through the chest and shoulders, it was the work of moments to swap coats and trade January's high-crowned hat for his brother-in-law's soft cap.

'We didn't see anyone like you described on the street.' Olympe folded her arms and leaned one shoulder in the doorway of the small garçonnière room – crammed now with Hannibal's books – to which they'd retreated to effect the transformation. 'But men of that stamp are a dime a dozen in this town.' As January had suspected, the request for such a subterfuge first thing in the morning hadn't discomposed his sister in the slightest. 'Any idea who they are?'

'Not a guess.' January settled Paul's coarse blue linen jacket over his shoulders. 'That's what I'm going to ask around about, once I'm sure I won't be leading my friend to anyone I'd rather he didn't know of.'

'You owe me,' said Paul Corbier, with a grin and a glance at his black-dyed face in Hannibal's broken shaving-mirror. 'I'm gonna be days scrubbin' this off, and my mama won't let me in her house tomorrow for Sunday dinner.' Like many former *plaçées*, Mère Corbier looked down her nose at those darker than herself ('*Slaves are black. I* am *colored . . .*') and had raised considerable objections to her son marrying Olympe, who shared January's *beau noir lustre*, as the slave-dealers described it. Their own mother had been known, in company, to deny any relationship to her two older children who had so obviously been fathered by one of the Bellefleur field-hands, and to claim that her only surviving offspring was Dominique, the lovely quadroon daughter she had borne St-Denis Janvier.

'Try butter.'

'You know what butter costs in the market?'

January left the house on Olympe's arm, and after escorting her home he made his way to the wharves. The man he sought out there was nearly of his height, and nearly of his complexion, but slender as a whip. Officially, Ti-Jon belonged to a man named Wachespaag, but Wachespaag – part-owner of a steamboat, a cotton-press, and the Louisiana Hotel on Rue Chartres – generally only saw his human possession on Friday afternoons, when Ti-Jon would go to his office and hand him five dollars. The rest of the money Ti-Jon earned was nobody's business, and January calculated that the arrangement – not an uncommon one, though city politicians, and Americans especially, tended to go into hysterics at the thought of it – had paid Ti-Jon's purchase-price two or three times over in the course of the years.

Ti-Jon, however – who bossed a stevedore gang on the deep-water wharves downriver of Rue Esplanade – knew everything that went on along the New Orleans waterfront: who was in trouble, which gangs worked at thieving which wharves, who was conning rubes and what their lays were, which hells (or churches) were simply skinning-houses, and whose games were crooked, and who was humping whose wife. He listened to January's account of the past twenty-four hours, and the descriptions – so far as January could give them – of Michie Plug-Hat and Michie Curly, presumably domiciled at the Verrandah Hotel, and shook his head.

'Don't sound like a police lay to me,' he opined. 'And I sure ain't heard of anyone shakin' around after runaways, beyond the usual cracker boneheads paying off the law to cherry-pick the jails. I take it your sister's heard nothing.'

'Not a word.' What gossip Ti-Jon didn't pick up on the wharves, Olympe heard through the multifarious whispers that came to the voodoos through their customers: *this man done me wrong; here's money to lay a curse on this man's crooked lottery game* . . . 'If they're after runaways, why not come up to the house with a warrant? And if they're not, what *are* they after?'

'How much of that silver you got left in the house? Not a lot have heard of it,' the slave added, when January hesitated. 'But you was gone all spring with your sister Dominique and that white planter of hers – *and* his wife – and when you came back, you paid down your bill at the grocery—'

January tried not to look annoyed. He'd deliberately let a portion of the tab stand, precisely so the desperate and the nosy *wouldn't* come to the conclusion that there was money in the house.

'*And* you gave Lala du Coudreau a dollar last week when her little boy was sick,' concluded Ti-Jon. 'People know things like that, Ben. And there's people who just figure, *I'm hungry an' he's not.* You got enough to make it worth somebody's while?'

'Not somebody who's staying at the Verrandah and riding in cabs up an' down Rue Bourbon, I don't.'

It was still early, and knowing that his house might still be watched – Paul was going to go there, dressed as Benjamin January in the black coat and the high hat that did in fact, at a distance, add nearly a cubit to his allotted span – January made his way to Rue St-Pierre where his friend Mohammed LePas had a blacksmith's shop. He'd known the old man from childhood, and LePas was another one who knew everyone in town . . . and who had been known to conceal runaways in the attic of his shop.

He worked the old man's bellows for him and spun once again the tale of Michie Plug-Hat and Michie Curly, who might or might not still be watching his house, who might or might not have followed him that morning . . . who might or might not have anything to do with anything, looked at in the brass light of mid-morning.

'They remind you of anyone you once knew?' asked the blacksmith, and he drew the square rod from the coals of the forge, locked it in the grip of his vise and bent it, with a single sure move, into the precise shape of the other four already-bent iron rods that stood ranged along the wall. 'Men take trouble like this for money, or for vengeance, or to protect themselves or those they love from harm.'

'Or because someone is paying them,' said January. 'And if that's the case, it could mean anyone or anything.'

With the noon sun grilling hot overhead, he left the blacksmith's and began a systematic round of the gambling parlors and taverns of the waterfront, knowing this to be the time and the route of Lieutenant Abishag Shaw of the New Orleans City Guards. Ti-Jon, or Olympe – or any of his old cronies at the Chatte Blanche back in Paris – would have smacked him upside the head at the mere suggestion of asking a policeman what the hell might be going on, and in his darker moments January had doubts about the matter himself. *Am I crazy, to let the police know that I'm aware of it, if the watchers are the police themselves?*

But something about the cab and the Verrandah Hotel caught like a burr on his reasoning: Hannibal was perfectly correct. The New Orleans City Council was simply too stingy to authorize observation like that, even if someone had suggested that Ben January was harboring runaways under his house.

LePas certainly hadn't observed anyone – with or without a plug-hat – watching his shop, and as a runaway himself the old blacksmith had an even keener nose for danger than January did.

It's something else.

He simply couldn't imagine what.

Shaw wasn't in any of the taverns along Gallatin Street behind the market, or along Rue de la Levée. For about three streets back from the wharves, every thoroughfare in New Orleans was thick with cafés, taverns, and grog shops large and small. Even at this slack period, during a bad year, these were crowded with sailors from the deep-water ships which docked below Rue Dumaine or the steamboats tied up all the way along the river to the Second Municipality. It would be the work of all afternoon to track the policeman down as he loafed from tavern to tavern, picking up gossip and listening to what people said.

Thus January cut short his search and, with the afternoon rain-storm gathering sullenly overhead, crossed the Place des Armes to the Cabildo. The grayish stucco block that stood next to the Cathedral housed the headquarters of the City Guard and up until recently had served as the Parish Prison as well. In the stone-floored watch-room he left a note for Shaw with the sergeant at the desk, then went next door to the Cathedral, to confess his sins and to pray for some desperately-needed guidance.

He prayed, too, as he had all summer, for the soul of the man he'd killed in Washington in the spring – a thoroughly despicable kidnapper of free blacks who sold them into slavery – and when that was done, he made his way back to Rue Esplanade, aware as he walked of an uneasy prickling sensation on the back of his neck, a tightening behind his sternum.

Neither LePas nor Ti-Jon nor Olympe had heard anything of surveillance on those who harbored runaway slaves.

Yet the house was being watched. Of that he was certain.

What Shaw might be able to tell him he had not the slightest idea, but he trusted the policeman's experience and judgement. Officially, the City Guards were supposed to watch over the possessions of the *librés* as tenderly as those of their white neighbors, though in fact most of the Guards probably wouldn't have lifted a finger to keep a black man's house from being broken into (those who were sober enough to ascertain that a crime was being committed . . . or weren't in the pay of the robbers themselves).

But if anything so organized as surveillance were afoot, Shaw would have heard of it.

Like January himself, Abishag Shaw could feel danger through his skin, even without knowing where it was coming from, or why.

And of course, reflected January dourly, at this hour of the day – nearly two o'clock, now – there was sufficient traffic on Rue Esplanade, drays and wagons and owl-hoot river-rats on their way to the taverns of the Swamp at the back of town, to conceal any specific watcher. He only hoped Gabriel, who had a venturesome streak and the confidence of a young man born in freedom, wouldn't do anything silly . . .

January was almost to the foot of the gallery steps of his house when Rose emerged on to the gallery, speaking to someone in the house behind her. She turned, saw him—

—and as January put his foot on the first step, Abishag Shaw stepped out of the French door of January's own room.

He must have got my note . . .

He could not possibly have gotten here before me.

Cold in his belly as if he'd been struck, January nearly ran up the stairs.

When he came on to the gallery he saw Rose's face was ashen. She held her spectacles in her hand; she had been weeping. She came quickly to him, her hands outstretched—

'What is it?'

'Jeoffrey.' She caught him round the waist as he folded her into his arms, pressed her forehead to his shoulder.

'Dead.' Shaw held out a piece of folded paper. 'Stabbed.'

January opened it. It said, in French:

> *Monsieur Vitrack,*
>
> *I reconsidered what we said Tuesday night and want to talk to your further about it. Please meet me in the morning at seven, in Trouard's brickyard next to the hotel.*
>
> *Benj. January fpc*

FIVE

'That's ridiculous.' January spoke, not angrily, but with a sensation as if he had just been punched hard in the solar plexus. 'Sir,' he remembered to add, Shaw being, after all, a white man, even if no free colored housewife would have permitted him through her front door.

Shaw spat tobacco over the gallery rail and scratched his greasy, dirt-colored hair. 'T'ain't your hand, that's for sure,' he observed. Shaw couldn't spell – as he had himself frequently observed – for sour owl-shit, but he had an eye for the minute differences in handwriting even as he had for such things as patterns of nail-settings when looking at the tracks left by horseshoes, or whether scratches in wood were weathered or not. 'Nor the paper ain't like any in your house, nor the ink neither. But the feller *was* here Tuesday evenin', accordin' to Mrs Janvier –' his nod indicated Rose – 'an' he *was* her brother . . .'

Thunder crashed suddenly, almost directly overhead. One or two hard spits of rain rattled on the gallery roof, followed – without transition – by silvery torrents that nearly hid the trees of the neutral ground beyond the street.

'Did she tell you about the house being watched?'

'She did. Looks like whoever was watchin' saw her brother come in an' knew who it was he wanted to talk to.'

Still feeling a little as if he'd fallen down a flight of stairs, January led the way back through into the parlor. 'I will have that coffee you offered earlier, m'am,' said Shaw, 'if'fn the offer's still open.'

Rose said, 'Of course.' She sounded stunned, disoriented.

January handed Shaw back the paper, guided Rose to a chair at the dining-room table, and went to the pantry for the coffee himself. 'Did Madame Janvier tell you what M'sieu Vitrack wanted?' he asked Shaw when he returned.

'She did,' agreed Shaw. 'An' it sounds damn hare-brained to me. I never met a black man yet that was on fire to move back to Africa, though I will say that if every slave in America was to be given his freedom this afternoon there'd be hell to pay for years, an' no mistake, seein' that three-fourths of 'em or more can't read nor write nor have never done nuthin' but pick crops. Thank you, M'am,' he added softly to Rose as he and January took chairs at the other end of the table. 'So I can see the colonizers' point, even if I do think it's a plumb fool way of dealin' with the problem. An' Mr Vitrack didn't say nuthin' about what he planned to do next, when you turned him down?'

'He said he was going to wait until Captain Loup de la Mer came back – the smuggler who brought the Loveridge party out of Cuba in exchange for this "old slave-woman's" pendant of the Crimson Angel . . . Was the Angel on him when he was found?'

The lieutenant shook his head. 'They cleaned his wallet out too.'

January's mouth tightened. '*Waste not, want not*,' he said, quoting one of America's Founding Fathers. 'I think Jeoffrey hoped to find out from Loup de la Mer where this "old slave woman" could be found in Cuba, and to track her down for more information. He did ask me if I knew a man who would serve as a guide or courier to go to Haiti, either with him or in his stead.'

'An' did you?'

'Haiti isn't a place you want to go,' January said quietly. 'They've been fighting amongst themselves ever since they killed off the whites. First the slaves against the whites, with the mulattos switching sides back and forth, trying to keep their plantations and their wealth. Then Christophe's ex-slaves against Pétion's mulattos about who was going to rule; then Christophe's soldiers against the ex-slaves, when Christophe tried to start up the sugar plantations again so that his government would have something to tax, and everybody taking time off to fight the French . . .'

'An' where'd the ex-slaves think they was gonna get an army an' weapons from, without taxes? It wasn't like the Spanish weren't sittin' there on the other side of the island waitin' to take over. Nor like there was a gunpowder factory anyplace on the island—'

'They weren't thinking like that, sir. All the former slaves knew was that they were free and that nobody was going to make them work sugar again. Even with an owner who takes care of his hands, they figure a man'll last only a few years in the cane fields, if the plantation's going to turn a profit.'

Shaw said nothing, but chewed like a ruminative beast.

'It was cheaper to work men to death and buy new ones from Africa when they needed them. The hate there runs deep. And killing whoever disobeyed was certainly cheaper than having a revolt on their hands. Later, Boyer took over the whole place and invaded the Spanish side of the island, and for all I know they're still fighting the Spanish. It's not anywhere I'd go, and a white man like Vitrack wouldn't last three hours.'

'You think there's treasure there?'

'I think so, yes.' January shrugged and glanced down the table at Rose, silent, with her untouched coffee-cup between her hands. 'Looks like someone else thinks so, too. Someone who knows that the Crimson Angel may have been part of that horde and who didn't want Vitrack getting there first. I trust you'll point out to the Coroner's jury,' he added, 'that the handwriting on the note isn't mine, and that "*I've reconsidered what we said*" works both ways to lure Vitrack out of his hotel: if I'd said no, he'd want to talk me into it; if I'd agreed and might be getting cold feet, he'd come out to keep me committed. Have you looked through his luggage?'

'Not yet. I wanted to get you – an' Mrs Janvier, if she's feeling able for it –' his eyes followed January's to Rose – 'first.'

Rose took a sip of her coffee and put her spectacles back on. 'Yes,' she said quietly. 'I'll come.'

The Planters & Strangers Hotel on Rue Chartres was one of the oldest in the French Town. It was barely larger than a good-sized town house, built in the Spanish style around a high-walled court-yard, and – like most town houses of the city – had only one way in or out after the gate of the arched carriageway was locked up for the night.

'Yes, M'sieu Vitrac –' Paul Hiboux, who worked the lobby desk and whom January knew from the Faubourg Tremé Free Colored Militia and Burial Society, pronounced the French form of the name that Rose's brother had abandoned – 'came through the lobby at about five minutes to seven. The dining room had not yet opened.' He nodded toward the door to the right of the long mahogany counter. 'And no other guests had yet come down. He bade me a civil good morning, but spoke no other words.'

'Do you remember who brought the note for him?' January asked.

Hiboux shook his head. 'One of the *p'tit drigailles* that hang about the wharves, I think, who'll run errands for a penny. I didn't know him.' A trim gentleman of middle age, he had himself, January knew, been born on Saint-Domingue, like so many of the *gens de couleur librés* of New Orleans; his parents mulattos who had thrown in their lot with their white kinsmen. It was not only the whites at the Café des Refugies who felt themselves to be exiles from their vanished paradise.

'He brought the note in midway through the afternoon, when M'sieu Vitrac was out. Had I known . . .'

'Not your fault.' January answered the note of genuine distress in the clerk's voice. 'How *could* you have known? May we see his room?'

January didn't expect to find much in his brother-in-law's hotel room, and in this he wasn't disappointed. Rose turned her face aside from the set of brushes laid out on the dressing table and stood for a moment looking out into the rain-drenched courtyard two floors below. January felt a pang of sadness as he looked at the coats and waistcoats in the armoire, the fine linen shirts in the drawer. The creaselessly folded cravats and regimented little oblongs of drawers, socks, handkerchiefs were an echo of the man's name, a memory of his light, breezy voice . . .

'Not a thing, far's I can tell.' Shaw closed the drawer of the little desk, reopened it to tuck in a rumpled corner of paper. 'For a man who keeps his cuff buttons all in one dish an' his tiepins stuck through their own little bits of cloth, he sure made a mess—'

He broke off, pale glance touching the neat drawer January still had open, the tidily-sorted garments grouped color by color in the armoire, and without a word went to the window. January, in his turn, stepped to look at the desk drawer.

It was chaos. Papers shuffled about – bills interleaved with

banknotes and visiting cards, a seal and a couple of pen nibs shoved
into the back of the drawer . . .

'The room's been searched.'

'An' by somebody who wasn't after money,' added Shaw, who
had opened the French door on to the gallery and was studying the
edge beneath its latch. 'This's been scratched recently, an' you'd
need a damn thin blade to slide in here to force the latch.' He turned
back into the room, his gargoyle mouth set. 'What he was after, we
got no way of knowin' . . .'

January knelt, pulled Vitrack's dressing case from beneath the
bed and opened it. Empty, without any kind of secret compartment
that he could detect. The small leather suitcase was the same. 'He
had a yellow envelope full of notes and clippings.' He glanced at
Rose for corroboration. She nodded. 'There might have been letters
from his father-in-law as well. Ulysses Rauch,' he added.
'Representative from Pennsylvania. It contained notes also about
his conversation with Mr and Mrs Powderleigh in Philadelphia—'

'Folks what escaped from Cuba?' Shaw had clearly read the
article as well.

'He have anything of the kind on him when he was found?'

'Consarn it.' Shaw opened the desk drawer again, searched more
carefully, unfolding and reading every scrap of paper. Bills for
laundry in Philadelphia and New Orleans, gambling vowels – none
for over forty dollars – on the stationery of the steam-packet
Montezuma, with a few on what looked like pages torn from different
memorandum-books, such as a man might accumulate in an evening
or two of gambling at the more genteel establishments in New
Orleans. A pack of visiting cards still wrapped in the printer's tissue,
and credentials from the American Colonization Society, signed by
his father-in-law.

Scribbled receipts for oyster suppers at La Belle Creole on Rue
Bourbon, for a cravat and a pair of gloves from At the Sign of the
Cotton Blossom, and for a half-day's rental on a gig.

Inspection of Jeoffrey Vitrac's clothing and effects in a small
whitewashed room off the First Municipality's morgue told the
same tale. Rose, a handkerchief soaked in vinegar held beneath her
nose, viewed her brother's body in the long chamber at the rear of
the Cabildo. Her face was like stone, as if she were viewing the
subject of a dissection, and not someone she'd gone crabbing with
on warm magic evenings of a shared childhood.

When she, January, and Shaw passed into the smaller room beyond to look at his possessions, she only said in a quiet voice, 'I'll have to write his wife. I feel bad,' she added, 'for the wives of those other men –' there had been two, on the other tables, one of whom had very obviously been pulled from a bayou infested with crawfish – 'if no one identifies them. How horrible, to be waiting and never to know.'

Her brother had been wearing the same gray frock-coat, the same collarless indigo silk waistcoat that he'd had on the previous Tuesday. Rose reached down to touch the breast and shoulder of the coat, as if the young man's sturdy flesh had still been in them, then drew her fingers back. The holes in both were in the front, slightly to the left of the solar plexus, where they would be if his killer had stepped close, seized him by the shoulder and pulled him into the blow. Judging by the amount of blood on the waistcoat, Vitrack's heart had been pierced by that single blow and he'd bled out very quickly. There had really been no need to cut his throat afterward, as the killer had then done.

'He wrote me when I left Chouteau,' said Rose, 'and was teaching my first school here in town. He said how much he admired me, for getting out of Grand Isle. For coming to a place where I could better myself. He was nineteen . . . Then a year later he came through town, on his way to Washington. He spent every penny above his train fare on clothes. He bought them above Canal Street, in the American town. *I don't want to look like some Creole from the sticks*, he said . . . He stayed with me at the school until the tailors had finished. He'd practice his American accent . . . *I want them to see me for who I am*, he said. *Not for where I come from or who they think my father is*.'

'If he was bound for Washington lookin' for a new life,' returned Shaw, 'he was goin' about it the right way. Seems to have worked, if'fn he married some Congressman's daughter.'

Rose laughed softly. 'I'm sure when he talked about "*my father's plantation*" he made certain his in-laws thought it was one of those big white houses with the pillars on it, and not three post-and-daub rooms in the middle of nowhere. Poor Jeoffrey.'

Jeoffrey's pockets, when he'd been found in the brickyard next to the hotel an hour after his murder, had contained a Morocco-leather wallet (empty), a seal and some wax, an octavo-sized volume of *The Last of the Mohicans*, and an ivory miniature of (presumably) his wife.

'No yellow envelope,' said January. 'No Crimson Angel. No article snipped from the *Washington Intelligencer*. And no notes – if he had any – about where he might have hoped to encounter Captain Loup de la Mer, or when. Or, for that matter, where to find this "Sally" in Cuba. They're after the treasure, all right.'

'Then what I'll need from you, m'am,' said Shaw as he led January and Rose across the Cabildo's courtyard – the tall walls of which trapped the twilight's suffocating heat – 'is a list of whoever you can remember is related to your grandma's family, an' where they might be. You say her daddy was one of the richest planters on Saint-Domingue, what married his French cousin . . . They have any other children 'sides granny?'

'I think a son. I have no idea what became of him. My brother Aramis might know . . . or rather my sister-in-law Alice,' Rose added with her quick-flash grin. 'All Aramis really knows about is what birds are flying over Grand Isle on any given day so he can shoot them, and when the tides are best for fishing. I'll write to him this evening – he always reads my letters to Alice – and with luck, if I tell Alice it's important, she'll make him write back within two weeks . . .'

'Sounds like my pa,' sighed Shaw. ''Ceptin' he couldn't read. Find out what you can, m'am, if you'd be so kind.'

'Of course.' Rose touched his hand as they halted in the wide-open doors of the Cabildo, with the strange wild stirrings of the river wind brushing at her skirt hems like a pack of invisible mice. 'And I'll write Jeoffrey's wife as well and ask what he might have told her.'

'I 'preciate it, m'am.' Shaw spat in the general direction of the gutter that ran before the Cabildo – in the gathering dusk it was alive with frogs – and missed it by feet. 'Either way, the feller what done it'll be long gone out of town 'fore you get an answer, but we'll see what we'll see. You didn't see none of your own little friends this mornin', did you, Maestro?' He glanced at January, who shook his head.

'Doesn't mean they weren't there.'

'No. But if'fn they was watchin' your place for Vitrack, they likely won't be back. So I'd appreciate hearin' if they *is* still around.'

Zizi-Marie had seen nothing of the watchers during the day, though she'd spent much of it playing backgammon on the rear gallery with her father and Rose, once the chores were done. Gabriel, returning from his work at the Hotel Iberville, had likewise glimpsed no one suspicious. But then, January wondered, how could one tell? 'There are at least two of them,' he said, exasperated, when supper was done. 'Nothing guarantees there aren't more.'

'Well, Mama says, if you need Papa to switch places with you again, you can do it by coming over to her house instead of them both going to Granmère's.' Zizi-Marie brought the basin of hot washing-up water up the steps from the kitchen across the yard, laid it on the towel Gabriel spread on the end of the back gallery's table. 'There's a dance out at the bayou next Saturday, and she says everybody in town is coming to her asking for *gris-gris*.'

Dusk was falling. Rose had moved her chair to the gallery rail so that she could see to stitch the mourning dress Olympe had lent her, mosquito-smudges flickering on the rail like smoky jewels.

'Will you go out to the bayou with her?' January asked the question quietly, and his niece hesitated before replying. At seventeen and a half, Zizi-Marie was considered a woman, old enough to go to the voodoo dances held in the woods along Bayou St. John. Her mother Olympe, January recalled, had started running away from their mother's house at fourteen, and going not only to the great dance, but the smaller, more frequent assemblies held in brickyards and in the vacant spaces at the back of town: dances that generally ended with the couples sneaking away to fornicate in the bushes.

Completely aside from the issue of the girl's immortal soul – if anything could be considered 'aside' from idolatry (and January didn't care how many people assured him that Papa Legba was actually St Peter, he knew full well that this wasn't the case) – and the possibility of pregnancy, the danger of being caught by slave-stealers was many times greater now than it had been in 1812 when Olympe was doing it. He knew Paul Corbier struggled daily with the conundrum of how to urge his children to be good Catholics without repudiating the tough, wise voodooienne whom he loved to distraction.

It was one reason, January knew, besides the desperately hard times that lay on the nation, that Paul had been relieved when January had offered to house the older two of his four children.

At length the girl asked, 'Is it a sin to go . . . Just to go? If I don't dance or anything?'

'If you want to go,' reasoned Gabriel, 'you can go to confession after, can't you? Then Père Eugenius will give you a couple of rosaries—'

'You really think God will think it's all right,' asked January, 'if you go in thinking, *Oh, God's GOT to forgive me if I say a couple of rosaries, so I'll do it anyway?* What does your mother say about it?'

'She hasn't said anything,' replied Zizi-Marie in a subdued voice. 'I think if she saw me there she wouldn't send me home. Have you been to one of the dances, Uncle Ben? Do people really . . . Have you seen somebody get ridden by the loa?'

'I have. Their power is real, Zizi. There's something really there. Whether it's demons working for the Devil, or spirits working for God to speak to African men and women in the language they'll understand, I don't know.'

He looked at the two of them in the soft silver of the evening light. Olympe's children. He saw Zizi-Marie the way she'd been four years ago when first he'd come home from France: thin and gawky as a half-grown colt, chasing around with her friends, her mind divided between devising the biggest and most fantastically-tied tignon within her little group and the lessons her father was teaching her of the upholsterer's trade. He saw Gabriel at eleven, scheming to acquire more marbles, or better-looking lead soldiers . . .

And now here they were, a young woman budding into beauty, a young man figuring out what he wanted from life. And looking at him as if they thought he knew the answer to the most fundamental of questions: what is God? Who is God? Which of the versions of God we're told about is right?

'And because I don't know,' he went on quietly, 'I play it safe and do what Père Eugenius tells me. I stay away from the voodoos, the same way I'd stay away from deep water when I don't know what's down there.'

Hesitantly, Gabriel asked, 'Can you really lose your soul?' And in his tone January knew he was thinking of his mother, and the altar in their house to Damballah Wedo, with its decorations of cut paper and its little dishes of tobacco and candy and rum.

'I don't know that either.' He took the cup Zizi had just washed, dried it and set it on another towel. 'Your mother does great good. She heals the sick, as I do. More than that, she gives people hope. Maybe she does give people good luck as well, and there's not nearly enough of that in the world. I don't think healing and happiness come from anyone but God. I don't know what shape God takes, to speak to her or through her. But I know it's dangerous territory.'

However, whether Zizi-Marie followed her mother to Bayou St. John on the following Saturday or not, January didn't learn until years later.

Long before then, he had other things to think about.

The following morning he slipped from the house early and made his way to the wharves.

Americans professed horror that the markets of New Orleans remained open and in full swing on Sundays as on any other day; that, after Mass, you could go to a café or a perfume shop or a gambling parlor if you chose – or a bordello, for that matter, or you could purchase a slave – but January noticed that Americans were perfectly willing to unload their cargoes or dicker for bargains along the levee on the Sabbath. He found Ti-Jon and his gang offloading corn from a flatboat, and the slave reported that, as far as he and his gang could tell, January's house had been watched at least part of the time by two Indians who were registered at the Verrandah under the names Three-Jacks Killwoman and Blueford Conyngham. Michie Curly – likewise at the Verrandah – was a man named Seth Maddox. All three listed their home city as Mobile. Both Killwoman and Conyngham had been seen near the house yesterday.

January added this information to the diagram Rose had drawn last night of her father's family, as far as she knew it: old Great-Granpère Absalon de Gericault; his cousin-wife and her perfidious father, who had cheated Great-Granpère out of his birthright back in France; his daughter Oliva, who had married Louis-Charles Vitrac; and a possible son who might or might not have escaped from Saint-Domingue with Absalon himself . . . Other sons? Other daughters?

Along with these notes, he had in his pocket Rose's letter to her sister-in-law Alice, asking further details. When the bells tolled for early Mass he walked across the Place des Armes, to take the Host and, with a clean soul, and in the grace of God, to pray for the soul of Jeoffrey Vitrac and for guidance in the murky and perilous darkness in which he now felt himself to be moving. He then left his notes with the desk sergeant at the Cabildo, for delivery to Shaw on the morrow, and, since the Post Office on Exchange Alley was just about the only place in the French Town that *did* close on Sunday, he directed his steps to the market.

There he found Hannibal at a table near the coffee stand, having what amounted to supper (it was eight in the morning) after a night playing in a gambling room somewhere. Two crème-café *filles de joie* shared one of the rickety little tables with him among the brick pillars, dipping bread in their coffee and blushing and blooming under his borrowed snippets of Catullus and Byron. As January approached, the girls took their departure, to greet with simulated ecstasy a gaggle of sailors. '*Bright as the sun, her eyes the gazers strike,*' Hannibal quoted thoughtfully as January took one of the vacated chairs. '*And, like the sun, they shine on all alike.* Those brave mariners just got in this morning, so they've still got most of their pay.'

'And have *you* still got most of *your* pay?'

'It depends on one's definition of *most.* I weep for the decline of the arts in this country – one would think the clientele of Davis's would show greater appreciation for Mr Mozart's genius. In the end I had to take Elbows Marrouguin's place dealing faro to make enough for groceries. Are you still playing host to Indian braves?'

Over another cup of La Violette's coffee, January related the most recent developments, and the fiddler's dark eyes grew grave. '*None but the family*, the old woman said,' January finished. 'I need to find someone to take Rose's letter –' he patted his pocket – 'to her brother's wife in Grand Isle: her older brother, the one who stayed on the plantation.'

'Try Jeannot Chigazola.' Hannibal got to his feet and drew a string shopping-bag from one pocket and, violin case under his arm, led the way among the market stalls. 'He's heading back there tonight.'

'Good. I'd rather not lose a day on this, though God knows how long it'll take her to answer.' He paused to let a couple of *march-andes* pass before him, with yokes of fresh milk on their shoulders and baskets of flowers balanced on their enormous and elaborate tignons. 'Ti-Jon tells me the watchers are still there, though I haven't seen them. I'd have thought they'd be on their way to Haiti by this time.'

'One can hope they will be soon,' murmured Hannibal. 'I understand that a white man's chances of survival on the island haven't improved in the slightest since August of 1791 . . . Good heavens, is that what eels look like when they're dead and I'm sober? *Thou deboshed fish, thou* . . . Beautiful Madame –' he took the hand of the stout Cajun lady among the baskets – 'like unto a mermaid among the dwellers of the sea, how much for a cooked specimen?'

On the other side of the aisle, January caught a glimpse of Rose, her own shopping basket on her arm, bending over a barrow of Natchitoches tomatoes. In the indigo gloom beneath the market's huge tiled roof, her black dress made her half-invisible among the gaudy calicos of the *marchandes* and the bright cotton gowns of good Creole housewives. With these workaday ladies, too, strolled gentlemen in evening dress, like Hannibal, just wrapping up an evening in the gambling parlors, now in quest of coffee and pralines for themselves and their mistresses before going to Sunday dinner with families and wives.

'Did you find Ti-Jon?' Rose turned to edge her way through the crowd around the tomato barrow. 'I forgot to ask—'

A cloaked man stumbled against her, and such was Rose's uneasiness over the events of the past several days that she sprang back from his touch with a cry.

Instead of regaining his feet, the cloaked man seemed to trip again and plunged at her, and at the last second January saw he had a knife in his hand.

'*ROSE*—!!!'

She cried out, twisted aside. January yelled, 'Stop him!' and as the housewives and market women stared in shock, the cloaked gentleman sprang to his feet and sprinted away through the crowd. January had a confused vision of Rose sitting on the brick pavement, staring at the blood that dyed her hand, Hannibal bending over her—

'After him!' yelled Hannibal, catching Rose as she slumped back, and January turned and plunged in pursuit.

SIX

Shopkeepers, market women, fishermen sprang out of the way. The gentleman shoved among the stalls, caught a farm woman with a yoke of milk pails on her shoulders and heaved her at January, sprang past a barrow of lettuces and cucumbers and overturned it. January yelled, 'Stop him! Murderer!' but no slave was going to tangle with a white man and precious few free colored would either. January tripped over the milk pails, scrambled around the trace poles of the barrow, slipping in lettuce leaves. He stumbled, blinking, out of the market's shadow on to the levee, among barrels of corn and crates of chickens off the flatboats that clustered the wharves. A pistol cracked from somewhere close, taking a chip out of the brick pillar just beside him.

January ducked back, panting. Knowing that in losing sight of the man, he'd lost him.

Rose.

He turned, strode back through the milling crowd of *marchandes, bonnes femmes, nymphes du pavé* amid trampled eggplants and spilled milk.

'She's at the Refugies.' The dark-eyed Cajun fishmonger caught his arm as he halted, staring at the blood-spattered bricks in front of the tomato stand. 'She crossed the street on her own two feet—'

January ran. And was enough a child of New Orleans (*if the wound went into her stomach or her gut she'll bleed out in hours . . .*) to stride around to the café's yard-gate, so as to enter the place through the back, shaking all over now as if he, and not Rose, had been knifed.

Rose had been carried upstairs to one of the family's bedrooms above the café. A sturdy little woman whom January recognized as Madame Thiot was shoving men out of the chamber and toward the outside stairway even as he ascended. 'Away with you! She's fine, I tell you—'

He looked around for Hannibal and didn't see him, thrust past old M'sieu Thierry, the deaf old Marquis d'Evreux, Thiot himself. 'I'm her husband,' he panted when Madame Thiot planted herself in the doorway, arms akimbo, to ward off the curious. 'And a surgeon.'

She squinted up at him as if it would have pleased her to deny him entrance, but stepped aside. Straw pallets had been laid down on the bed and the quilts of pink-and-white country-work stripped away and bundled in a corner. Rose lay propped on pillows, her eyebrows standing out black against a face gone ashen. Olympe's black mourning jacket, a dark blouse, and Rose's corset lay on the floor beside her, daubed – but not soaked – in blood. She'd taken her arms out of her chemise and pushed it down around her waist, and a bandage had been applied only moments ago, it appeared, from the bundle of lint and torn sheeting that lay on a corner of the naked mattress.

She turned her head as January came into the room, held out one hand. 'I'm all right.'

He crossed the room to her in two strides, checked the bandage – which had been competently applied and tied – and, because the knots that held it were tight, took the scissors that lay nearby and cut it, to have a look at the wound itself.

'Did you wash this, M'am?' He turned his head toward the innkeeper's wife.

'What kind of a question is that?' Madame Thiot puffed up like a pigeon. 'Of course I wiped the blood away. How else was I going to see what I was doing?'

'She didn't use soap or spirits of wine or anything,' said Rose, her voice tight with pain.

'Do you have any hot water in the kitchen, m'am?' January threw his most diffident respect into his tone. 'My masters in Paris always insisted on washing a wound in either hot water or spirits of wine before dressing it.'

'Your masters in Paris are imbeciles. My father had a precious French doctor look after his scratched arm and he bled him to death—'

'Flavia –' Thiot appeared in the doorway from the outside stair – 'do as the man says and fetch up the rest of the tea water.'

'I have raised five children,' retorted Flavia Thiot, up in arms at once, 'and they managed to cut themselves, mangle their fingers, slice one another . . .' Her husband took her firmly by the elbow and dragged her out the door. January heard her voice retreating down the stair and across the yard to the kitchen. 'What about the time Marie-Jeanne cut her foot on the glass, eh? No foolishness about hot water or spirits of wine *then*, and she was dancing at the St Genevieve's Ball the following night . . .'

'Truly,' whispered Rose through her teeth, 'I'm all right. I don't think it's very deep.'

January took a clean shred of the torn sheet, poured a little water from the bedside ewer on to it, and gently sponged the blood from his wife's side. Rose shut her teeth hard but shifted her shoulders a little so that she could watch what was going on; Olympe had told January not long ago that when she'd birthed Baby John, Rose had insisted on having a mirror set up so that she could observe.

'I think the blade snagged on my corset.'

The wound, as Rose had surmised, was a shallow gash about two inches long, which ended against the slight red pressure-mark where a corset bone had compressed the skin. Very gently, January ascertained that the blade had caught on her seventh rib as well.

She added thoughtfully, 'I never thought I'd give thanks for wearing the thing.'

He couldn't speak, but bent his head and pressed his lips to the side of her breast, just above the wound. A moment later he felt her hand stroke his hair.

When he looked down, he saw the wound repeated in the clothing that lay on the floor. Jacket, blouse, and the brown linen of the corset, though bloodied, weren't ensanguinated. Years of tending sailors and stevedores at the Hôtel Dieu in Paris, when they'd been carried in after fights in the river-front bars – of binding the wounds that drunkards and their wives inflicted on one another – had taught January that a blow that punctured the stomach or gut wouldn't necessarily look horrible. The bleeding would all be inside, unstoppably filling the body's cavities while the patient slid into darkness.

He took a deep breath. *Virgin Mary, Mother of God, thank you* . . . 'Did you get a look at him?'

'Only that he was white. I take it you didn't catch him?'

He shook his head. 'White, or Indian?'

'It sounds idiotic, but I don't remember. I think if he'd been an Indian—'

The door opened. Thiot entered with a brass can of steaming water and a small bottle of the potent, colorless medicinal alcohol. 'Is there anything else you need, my friend? You must excuse my wife – she talks like a parrot for the sheer joy of making noise. Is Madame Janvier all right?'

January held up Rose's corset, showed the short rent in it that ended against the stout bone. 'She thrust him away the minute he crowded up against her,' he said. 'When any woman in the world would have steadied a stranger—'

'Any woman in the world who hadn't just had her brother stabbed.' Rose drew up her bloodied chemise over her breasts. 'I think if I hadn't been thinking about the men outside our house – if I hadn't been thinking about Jeoff's death – I wouldn't have leaped like that. People fall against one in the market all the time.'

Her breath checked in what could have been a little gasp as January moved the chemise sufficiently aside to daub the cut flesh with first the water, then the alcohol. But her voice remained matter-of-fact. 'The minute I knew I'd been stabbed I told Hannibal to go to the house. Baby John is there,' she added, to January's blank look. 'And Zizi wouldn't know to keep someone out who came to the door.'

'Baby John—' He spoke his son's name stupidly, as if he'd been struck over the head.

Rose could have died . . .

Baby John . . .

'We don't know who these people are,' said Rose softly as Thiot departed – the opening of the door let through a dissipating mutter of voices from the yard. By the sound of it, the nine days' wonder of a white man stabbing a woman of color in the market had very little staying power. 'Or what their connection is with Great-Granpère's treasure. But they clearly think Jeoff told us something about the treasure – or that *we* told *him* something. If they're not already on their way to Cuba with whatever information Jeoff had in that yellow envelope of his – if they want to make sure of me, or of you – I think the next move would be to get hold of Baby John and use him as bait to lure us into a trap, don't you?'

'*Damn* them—' The words – not even in their true meaning of the vengeful fires of Hell – seemed to him like the ineffectual peeping of a cricket against the suffocating rage that swept through him.

His eyes met those of his wife, gray-green – true *libré* eyes – and very calm. She hadn't even taken off her spectacles, or the black tignon that closely wrapped her hair, so swift had been the attack, the remedy, the aftermath of thought . . .

In those eyes he saw his own thought reflected.

They're still watching the house. They're going to try again.

Olympe came to the house that forenoon, after January – and Paul Corbier, done up again in theatrical blackface in case need arose later to switch roles once more – carried Rose home. The voodooi-enne bore a large wicker basket of bandages and medicaments, and when she left the basket held Baby John, sleeping after a drop or two of valerian and invisible in a bundle of towels. January had suggested that she take away her own two children as well, but both Zizi-Marie and Gabriel had refused to go.

'I'm not leaving you two alone here in the house come nightfall,' stated Gabriel, and his sister had nodded firmly.

'Somebody's gotta stay awake tonight, while the two of you get some sleep.'

'I can't let you,' said January. 'These people aren't fooling around.'

'Well, neither are we.'

The afternoon rain started up just as Olympe was leaving. Gabriel, who'd been sent to Shaw's rooms on Basin Street with a note about the attempted murder, returned at the same time, with the information that the policeman had been gone when he'd arrived and wasn't at the Cabildo either. 'God knows if anyone will bother to tell him that a white man attempted to murder a woman of color in the market—'

He frowned as a thought snagged at his mind, but Hannibal – who'd been posted to the attic with a spyglass – came down at that point and asked, 'Rose didn't happen to make a copy of the family tree you sent along to him, did she?' They were sitting on the gallery, outside the open French doors of Rose's room – every French door in the house stood open, to let the rain-scented breeze blow through from the river – where Rose lay sleeping, a dim shape barely visible through mosquito-netting and the afternoon's silver gloom.

'I think I could draw it again,' provided Zizi. She was of an age and disposition to be fascinated by the histories of families and had looked over Rose's shoulder last night as she'd worked. This wasn't unusual – every woman January knew among the *libré* and *plaçée* ladies could spout volumes of who was whose cousin and which families were related to whom – but Zizi-Marie made a serious study of it and would make notes and draw up charts from these reminiscences. She darted indoors and fetched a piece of paper and a kitchen pencil and settled at the bent-willow table where January, Hannibal, and Gabriel sat with a pot of coffee between them. 'She said it wasn't very complete,' the girl added as she worked. 'She'd need to hear from her sister-in-law before she had all the details.'

'I don't think we can wait to hear from Madame Vitrac.' January looked aside from the sheets of rain that were rapidly turning the middle of Rue Esplanade into a yellow-gray river. Returning from the market, he'd seen an indistinct form loitering beneath the trees in the rain, but the man was gone by the time January drew near.

'You think they're gonna try again?' Gabriel's voice was somber and a little scared, but his dark eyes gleamed at the thought of adventure.

'I can't see any reason why they won't.'

At that point Abishag Shaw climbed the wooden steps from the banquette, sheltered by an umbrella so old that it had probably been first used by one of Noah's neighbors in the Great Flood. 'I been to the market.' He shook the umbrella – and himself – like a wet dog before approaching the table. 'Half the vendors is gone already, an' of the rest couldn't nobody give a description of the feller – naturally – 'ceptin' he was white. He was wearin' one of them broad-brim slouch hats, wasn't he? Some thinks he was dark-haired, others say he's blond. Mostly they say he wore a beard, but I'm bettin' that's the first thing that'll go. Mrs January gonna be all right?'

January nodded. 'But we've got to get out of this house unseen . . . Rose's brother Aramis, down on Grand Isle, might be able to tell us who else was in the family – who else would know enough about the Crimson Angel to be hunting the treasure.' He turned Zizi-Marie's diagram around for Shaw to see, and the policeman took from his pocket the much-smudged original that Rose had drawn up last night. 'All Rose could remember of family stories was that Absalon de Gericault had at least one son – name unknown – but there might have been others born in Cuba, after Granmère Oliva left for Louisiana, that we don't know about. And we don't know what cousins or nephews might have lived under his roof also, and how much they knew; or whether this "blind old man" that Mammy Ginette was forced to guide to the ruins of the plantation in Haiti told anyone – before or afterwards – of the treasure.'

'Or if the blind old man was the only one she guided,' put in Hannibal. 'A warning to Rose's brother Aramis might not be out of place too, if these people are out to silence members of the family. *Quid non mortalia pectora cogis, auri sacra fames . . .* And they probably won't be convinced,' he added plaintively, 'by your just taking out an advertisement in the *Bee* saying you haven't the slightest interest in looking for it. In these under-financed times, everyone in the United States can be presumed to have an interest in looking for it.'

'Mrs January gonna be up to the journey to Grand Isle?'

'In a day or two she will be. The wound was little more than a gash – which is not how I'm going to portray it to anyone who asks.' He looked from face to face around the little table. 'All of you – if anyone asks, Rose was badly hurt. By tomorrow she'll be in a raging fever –' *and please, God, don't make my words come true!* – 'and the fever will climb, which will be a good reason for me not to leave the house, either. Meanwhile, she and I can slip out and journey down to Grand Isle. Can you keep an eye on the place for a night or two?' He turned his glance to Shaw. 'Gabriel and Zizi, after the first few nights you're to go back to your mother's. Lock up the house – I'm not going to risk you getting hurt,' he added, when his nephew opened his mouth to protest. 'Check on the place in the daytime, but *don't* come here alone, and don't *ever* let yourself get into a position where someone can come on you unawares.'

'But you know who they are!' protested Gabriel. 'You said yourself, Uncle Ben, they're staying over at the Verrandah—'

'Which is where I'm goin' when I leave here.' Shaw folded his long arms and spat over the gallery rail without checking to see if there were pedestrians beneath. 'But I'm bettin' they's outta there an' gone, now they tipped their hands. Killwoman an' Conyngham is names you find among the Muskogee Creeks, an' there's whole counties of 'em in Alabama that you couldn't hardly tell from white men: they owns plantations an' slaves, wears shoes an' goes to church. I'll get a letter out tomorrow to the sheriff of Escambia County, askin' if the names Maddox, de Gericault, Killwoman or Conyngham mean anythin' to him, for all the good that's like to do. We'll be lucky if'fn he can read.

'Problem about bein' hunted, Gabe,' the Lieutenant went on, turning to the boy, 'is the hunter has all the advantage. Even knowin' your hunter's name – even knowin' his face – in heavy brush, or in a town the size of New Orleans, you don't know which way he's comin' at you 'til he's on your back. An' the only way to make sure he don't come at you again is to turn an' fight him when he comes, or lead him into a trap, both of which can be pretty risky propositions if he keeps his head.'

He held out his hand and clasped January's in a strong grip. 'I'll watch over these two for you whilst you're gone, Maestro. But you got to watch out for yourself.'

SEVEN

When the rain ceased and the banquettes smoked and the light turned molten with coming evening, Olympe returned. With her was Cora Chouteau, Rose's girlhood friend, with dishes of dirty rice, as if to a house in trouble. January made sure to emerge from Rose's room on to the front gallery with the dragging steps of a man stunned. He crumpled into one of the wicker chairs and buried his head in his hands; when Olympe came through the same door and approached him, he turned in his chair and clutched her like a drowning man.

It was not a difficult role to play-act. All he had to do was call to mind Ayasha dead, Ayasha his beautiful first wife, who had died in Paris of the cholera – *was it only six years ago?*

For a moment, the tears he shed on his sister's bony shoulder were real.

When January looked across to the neutral ground, he could see a familiar shadow slip behind a tree.

On the threshold of evening, other women came. Virginie Metoyer, the only one of the sisters across Rue Esplanade not being entertained by a gentleman friend out at the Lake (unkind gossip added, *This isn't her week . . .*). Marie Laveau, red-and-orange tignon tied into the seven points that in all New Orleans only she was permitted to wear, like a crown of fire, marking her as voodoo queen of the city, her tall daughter padding silent behind her with her basket of herbs. Liselle Ramilles, whose late husband had played at the same white folks' balls and parties as January did; Célie Jumon, whose marble-carver husband January worked with on the board of the Faubourg Tremé Free Colored Militia and Burial Society; La Violette, the coffee-seller from the market. January came out periodically on to the gallery, to pace, or to sit like a man numb with shock, while in the bedroom behind him – the jalousies had been closed, so that only needles of candlelight shone through the louvers – he heard the reassuring murmur of voices, Rose's among them.

'For Heaven's sake, Cora, I've done worse to myself in the kitchen trying to make dinner!'

Rose – though capable of estimating the ingredients for fireworks or intricate chemical compounds to within a few grains – was a truly dire cook.

It was well after dark when the women left, the tarry darkness of overcast clouds that gave no coolness. Cicadas roared in the trees. Mosquitoes whined above the many-voiced chorus of frogs. The women came down the stair from the gallery all together in a group, talking softly among themselves. A corner of the crookedly-set house utterly blocked the feeble rays shed by the lantern that swung above Rue Burgundy on its iron chain, and from the black pocket of that shadow, Olympe called, 'You sure you be all right, Ben?'

'I'll be well.'

'We'll be back come morning.'

He lifted his hand, as if mute, unable to reply. The women moved off up the banquette. Nine women, when only eight had entered the house with their rice and their shrimp and their expressions of sympathy.

January slumped on to the chair again and sat there, the picture of grief and shock, for as long as he could stand being bitten by mosquitoes, before at last he rose and stumbled into the house.

'They're still there, all right.' Hannibal emerged from the cabinet where the ladder-like stair ran up to the attic. 'It would be a shame to put on a performance like that for no audience.'

'Shaw was right.' January went into the room considered 'his' – the traditional bedroom of the master of the house, though he seldom slept there – and fetched, from its hiding place beneath the floorboards, his fowling gun and the bag into which, through the course of the day, he had collected all the money in the house from its dozen hiding places, a hundred dollars in silver and gold. 'The hunter has all the advantage in this case. He can say where and when. All *we* can do is wait for him to strike.'

'You think they'll try breaking in tonight?' Zizi came out of Rose's room, where she'd left a candle burning beneath the china *veilleuse*.

'I have no idea.'

'At least we have enough food,' said Gabriel cheerfully, and he waved toward the dishes on the dining-room table. 'Mamzelle Marie even brought strawberries for breakfast tomorrow.'

January slept and dreamed uneasily. Even knowing that Baby John was safe at Olympe's cottage, even knowing that Rose was safe, asleep in Hannibal's garçonnière behind his mother's house with her friend Cora sitting guard beside her, still his dreams were troubled. Again and again he saw Rose turn from the barrow of tomatoes in the deep shadows of the market, saw the cloaked man fall against her and, when she leaped back, fall again in a savage, grasping lunge.

Saw Rose sitting on the pavement bricks, taking her hand from her side, her palm red.

And I went after the man?!?

Rose sitting there with blood on her hand and *I CHASED THE MAN INSTEAD OF GOING TO HER SIDE???*

Even if he'd caught him, January knew that, as a white man, he had only to drop the knife and say, 'I don't know what this nigger is talking about.'

He saw her as he'd earlier seen her that afternoon, when in her first exhaustion she slept, veiled in the mosquito-netting, while the rain pounded down outside . . .

Pain, fear, grief for her brother sponged from her face by sleep. Like the young girl she'd been all those years ago, when her mother's death had sent her to her white father's little plantation on Grand Isle. Chouteau, where the slave woman Ginette had come, looking for her lost granddaughter.

Showing the child-Rose the Crimson Angel. Making a little model of the plantation, telling her about what Saint-Domingue had been and about guiding an old blind man there.

In his dream he saw Mammy Ginette in the market hall, trying to push her way through the crowd toward the barrow of tomatoes, holding the Crimson Angel up in her hand. Calling, '*Rose! Watch out, Rose . . .!*' as a cloaked man stepped up beside Rose, tripped against her, fell with a knife in his hand . . .

'Benjamin?'

He woke with a gasp. The dark-lantern's thready glow showed him Hannibal's thin features.

'It's four thirty.'

January washed and shaved in the pantry, moved with infinite care through his dark house, as if the watchers in the absolute blackness of the night could hear his tread. Once he ghosted up the ladder to the attic, felt his way along the narrow slot of the dormer to look out over Rue Esplanade: on the main floor, and on street level below it, solid shutters were fastened over the French doors every night, making the house a little fortress.

Lanterns bobbed and swung on the road out to the bayou, the first wagons on the road in the relative coolness of pre-dawn.

He glanced at his watch. *Five.*

The night before, he'd put together a bundle of what he'd need: clean linen, shaving things, a change of clothes. Copies of his freedom papers, the documents that supposedly – unless some white man decided to tear them up while he held him at gunpoint – would prove him a free man and not eligible to be taken up to the Territories and sold for twelve hundred dollars. He hated to leave the bird gun behind – it packed a hideous wallop and nobody in his right mind would go up against such a weapon's wide-flung pattern – but he could be jailed for carrying it. Could be jailed for carrying his knife, too, which stayed in his boot and never left him. Since 1791, slaveholders all over America had flinched at the sight of any black man with a weapon in his hands, and had told themselves they did so from righteous indignation, not fear.

Last of all, as he and Hannibal descended the stairs from the back gallery and from there entered the ground story of the house, he took his guitar. He knew he'd miss his piano – and a ridiculous corner of him felt, guiltily, that his piano would miss him, too – but at least he'd have music of a sort during the day or two they'd be in hiding at his mother's house, and on the three-day voyage via Natchez Jim's wood-boat down to Grand Isle . . .

Five after five.

Yesterday afternoon, he and Abishag Shaw had compared their watches. Though his was a silver Breguet that he'd bought in Paris and the American's looked like the product of some Yankee factory, they'd seemed to keep sufficiently close time. And, indeed, at precisely nine minutes after five he heard, through the heavy wooden shutter that opened into Rue Esplanade, the creak of wheels and the slow pat of hooves. There was a little Judas-window in the shutter. Through it, January glimpsed the lantern on the front of a wagon, the glint of harness brass, passing within feet of the door.

Hannibal whispered, 'Ο θεός να σας προστατεύσει,' and January opened the door, stepped out into the darkness, seized the ropes that secured the canvas-covered load and swung himself aboard. Hannibal had the door shut again before anyone in the dark of Rue Esplanade – *always supposing they're not home in bed like sane people* – could have seen the front of the house again.

The god protect us, indeed . . .

Rose and January remained in hiding at his mother's house for two days, before setting forth for Grand Isle.

Jeoffrey Vitrac was buried on Tuesday, Shaw and Hannibal his only mourners. In her bed in the *garçonnière* that January had occupied first as a child, and then again after he'd returned from his years in Paris, Rose wept for the brother who'd turned his back on his Creole French heritage and had sought the promise of money and power and a chance to do good for his children and the world at large under the American name of Jefferson Vitrack.

According to Gabriel, the house on Rue Esplanade was still being watched.

By Wednesday afternoon, Rose was on her feet again, in visible discomfort but no distress. The wound in her side was healing neatly, without complications and without (*thank you, dear God!*) infection. The worst of her suffering – as was the worst of January's own – was separation from Baby John and the fear that without her he suffered, too. Yet she was adamant, on the one occasion on which January tried to evolve some scheme by which Olympe might bring the baby to them undetected, that their son be kept hidden where he was. 'Olympe can take care of him,' she said quietly. 'I'd rather shed twenty times this many tears –' for he had come up from the kitchen to find her weeping – 'over whether he's lonely without me, than have even the slightest, even the *tiniest* chance that those people figure out where he is.' Her voice flawed, like a hairline crack in glass, but her gaze was unwavering into his. 'My fears are only in my mind.' She put her spectacles back on. 'I'll see him when we come back and it's safe to do so.'

Olympe was blunter, when she came to them that evening. 'Don't be a damn fool, Ben. Your boy's fine. And so long as he stays hid, he's gonna stay fine.'

Shaw came also, bringing the news that Killwoman, Conyngham, and Maddox had all now checked out of the Hotel Verrandah, along with two other Alabamans who'd been staying there also, Clint Cranch and Scenanki Goback: 'So now we knows their names, anyways.'

'They may just be hired troops.' Rose made a move to rise from the table – in the kitchen behind them, which January had crowbarred open the previous morning, the kettle on the hearth bubbled – and Olympe put a hand on her shoulder and pressed her back into her chair. 'But I'll ask Aramis – or more likely Alice – if any of those names is familiar.'

Like most cottages at the back of the French town, the one that St-Denis Janvier had long ago given to January's mother consisted of several buildings, and the height of the front house served to conceal any glimpse of the rear kitchen, which included the *garçon-nière*, the small laundry, and the room which had housed the workshop of a briefly-tenured husband whom the beautiful Livia had married after Janvier's death. Upon January's return from Paris, Livia Levesque had permitted her son to rent from her (at five dollars a month) the room he'd grown up in, a chamber she generally rented out (at seven dollars a month) to various young clerks at banks or law firms or cotton presses, (board not included). Only when these gentlemen fled the stifling heat, during the fever season of summer, did she allow Hannibal Sefton to stay there and watch the property while she herself retreated to a comfortable residential hotel by the Lake.

This being the first of August, however, most of their forty-eight hours of residence were spent in the little brick-floored loggia outside the kitchen's three wide doors. Hannibal had moved his few effects down to the old workshop – now used as a sort of lumber room – and it was understood that nobody was going to mention to the Widow Levesque that her son and his wife had had two days of free residence on the premises, much less that they'd permitted an American animal like Shaw into the yard and offered him coffee.

'If this de Gericault cousin of yours –' Shaw flourished at Rose's chart – 'or any of his brothers or sisters – has gone to the trouble of hirin' five people to kill your brother an' try to kill yourself, that says money to me. Not just the money that's hid in Haiti, but money on hand. Your great-grandpa bring any across from Cuba with him?'

'That I don't know,' said Rose. 'I'll have to ask Aramis. But if he had to take refuge in 1809 with his daughter and her husband on Grand Isle, and died there four years later, it doesn't sound like he brought much money with him. When the Spanish authorities in Cuba evicted the French planters, they gave them very little time to sell up their plantations.'

Shaw spat – aiming for the packed dirt beyond the edge of the bricks of the loggia, but as usual failing in the attempt. 'Money would make de Gericault easier to track, anyways,' he said. 'I tried yesterday to catch our Injun friends out there on the neutral ground, but couldn't get close: an' I got three men down with fever now an' the whole of the French Town to cover. So you watch your backs on your way south.'

Natchez Jim was a medium-sized man who could have been thirty-five or seventy, his graying hair and beard braided into ribbons like a pickaninny's, his eyes like the river at night. He ran his wood-boat, the *Black Goose*, from New Orleans down to La Balize, the half-ruined French fort on the East Pass where the river ran into the Gulf, trading not only in wood but also in calico, needles, salt and iron pans. Trading in information and gossip too, and, it was rumored, not above giving a man a ride who wanted to make the trip buried unseen under a stack of parcels and sticks. He went upriver as far as Baton Rouge sometimes, or down Bayou Segnette or Lake Salvador through the tortuous labyrinth of marshlands down to Barataria Bay, picking his way among the *cheniers* to pick up cargoes of game birds and oranges.

January and Rose had traveled with him before.

It was three days' journey down the bayous, a timeless world of water and sky where nothing was quite what it seemed. The trembling lands, the locals called them – green islands that turned out to be nothing more than vast masses of floating vegetation, and what looked like little hills were on closer inspection the shell dumps where Indian villages once had stood. Weathered gray houses of *bousillage* – mud mixed with Spanish moss – half hid among the trees, all roof, like mushrooms. In the warm evenings, after it rained, January glimpsed the black-haired children of Spanish and Indians swimming cattle across from the islets where they'd pastured to the islets where they'd be penned.

Despite daily rains the waters were low, treacherous with half-submerged logs and drowned trees, the branches of which scraped at the bottom of the boat. Basking turtles lay like mottled stones where the sun was warm; deer and wild pigs moved through stillness and fog in the early mornings. Brown flights of pelicans streamed low across the water, holding formation as if they'd rehearsed it like an opera chorus. Mosquitoes made the nights hideous despite the herbed grease Olympe had given them, and even Rose took to smoking cigars in the evenings, so that the tobacco fumes would drive the insects away.

Here and there they'd come across small sugar-plantations, the cane poor and the houses raised eight or ten feet high to avoid the floods. Small gangs of slaves worked waist-deep in water cutting wood to sell for the grinding season. 'Most of them don't have their own mills,' Rose remarked as the *Black Goose* skimmed past one such laboring crew along Bayou Dos Gris. 'My brother grinds cane for half his neighbors, and his equipment is so old, the wood costs him a fortune.' She put a hitch in the sheet she'd helped Jim adjust – they were teaching January to set the sails, but Rose had spent five years of her life in these waters and handled a boat like other women handled crochet hooks – and went back to the stern where January sat as the open water ended and the murky tangle of *flottants* and deadfalls closed in around them again.

'I hear Americans in town talk about "rich sugar planters" and I don't know whether to laugh or walk over and slap them. Just because my brother owns slaves doesn't mean he doesn't wake up every morning of his life wondering how he can keep from having his land foreclosed on.' She was dressed as a boy for the journey, her walnut-hued complexion darkened and freckled a little by the sun. Here, away from the city and its laws, she'd braided her hair and coiled it on her head; it was a few shades browner than her skin and curly, like a white woman's.

'I've often wondered why the smaller planters don't give up sugar altogether,' said January. 'Why they don't just support themselves and grow corn and vegetables for the town market.'

'Because they can't.' Rose turned her eyes toward a little huddle of cottages – barely huts – among the cypresses a few feet back from the bayou edge. A woman in a faded dress came down the path with a child on her hip and a bucket in her hand. 'Farming, you don't make a living. Unless you have something to sell, you slide into debt very quickly: for salt, for tools, for taxes. I've seen how the trappers live in the marsh, and even then the women have to tend the vegetables while Papa goes out and hunts muskrats for their skins. Here, if you don't raise sugar, you become a dirt-farmer until one of your neighbors buys your land out from under you.'

Her words returned to January on the following morning as the wood-boat – freed of the wet mazes of the trembling lands now and winging like her namesake across the shallow open waters – came in sight of the lift of land that marked Chouteau Plantation, the straggly tangle of laurel and oleander surrounding the house on its high stilts and the unkempt gardens beside it, and the wooded ridge behind it that hid the sea. January, who played the cornet in the Opera orchestras when he wasn't playing harpsichord, blew a couple of long blasts on Natchez Jim's old tin trumpet, and by the time they made the weathered wharf, Alice Vitrac and a swarm of shock-haired children came piling down the steps from the three-room 'big house' and dashed down the path.

'Rose, sweetheart, you should have said in your letter you were coming!' Madame Vitrac hugged her, a rabbity-looking little woman who was probably five years younger than Rose and looked ten years older, particularly in her home-dyed mourning.

'You didn't get my second note?' Rose had written on Monday, warning her brother that there might be an attempt on his life and that she and January were fleeing town.

Alice Vitrac shook her head. 'Aramis was going to write you, thanking you . . . Benjamin!' She clasped January's hands. '*Thank you* for seeing Jeoffrey laid to rest properly! We'll pay you back as soon as—'

'You will *not*.' January jabbed an admonishing finger at his sister-in-law's nose. 'Not *ever*, or Rose and I will take it personally amiss, Miss Alice. He was our brother, too.'

Alice flung her arms around him, pressed her face to his chest – the top of her head didn't reach his shoulder – and stepped back, half-laughing, as January bent to scoop up six-year-old Hilaire, who with his brothers and sisters was clamoring for their uncle's attention. 'And where is M'sieu Vitrac?' he asked, looking around him. 'We passed a wood gang this morning, but—'

Alice flung up her hands. 'Oh, everything is at sixes and sevens!' she exclaimed. 'Yes, he did go out with the wood gang this morning, but there was an accident. Some hunters—'

'It wasn't hunters,' protested Hilaire, turning from his perch on January's broad shoulder. 'It was pirates!'

'It was smugglers!' added four-year-old Pierrot, face ablaze with enthusiasm.

Alice rolled her eyes. 'It was nothing of the kind! There are no pirates hereabouts any more—'

And Marie-Rose, forgetting the dignity of her nine years, exclaimed, 'Papa was *shot!*'

EIGHT

'**O**f course I didn't see them.' Rose's brother made a move as if he would have propped himself more firmly on the moss-stuffed bolsters behind his shoulders, but turned suddenly very white under his tan and thought better of it. 'If they'd known there was anybody about they wouldn't have gone blazing away like they were at the Battle of Goddam Waterloo, or at least I hope they wouldn't. Likely it was that idiot DuPratz from L'Isle Dernier. There was no harm done. The bullet went right through—'

'May I have a look at it?'

'You turn your eyes away, Rose.' Aramis threw back the sheet draped over his lower body, to reveal a mass of bandages wrapped tightly around his right thigh.

'Like I've never seen your bottom,' she retorted, but obediently scootched her chair around so that she faced the wall. Aramis, though shorter than Jeoffrey and of stockier build, had the same long, rather rectangular face they both shared with Rose, the same straight nose and well-shaped lips. 'So you didn't send anyone to see—?'

'What good would that have done? Alice is as good a surgeon as a man could ask for,' he added proudly as January snipped away the wrappings. 'Last *roulaison*, when our sugar-boss Hercule got his hand caught in the mill gears . . .'

'Miss Alice,' said January diffidently, 'might you have one of your people fetch some boiling water from the kitchen? And if you have such a thing as spirits of wine in the house—'

'We do,' said Alice. 'Though myself, I didn't think it looked like it needed it.' But she got up good-naturedly and made for the door, Rose following, partly to reduce the impression that Alice – a white woman and the lady of the house – was fetching anything at the request of a black man, be he never so much her brother-in-law. Mostly, January suspected, Rose went to make sure that the rags they'd bring back for bandages would be clean. The ones wrapping the wound, while not precisely foul, had certainly been used to mop up a food spill and subsequently slept on by the household cats.

It was ten or fifteen minutes before they came back, with Lallie the maidservant in tow carrying the basket of medical impedimenta, and Rose bearing a tray of lemonade and cow-horn tumblers.

'The problem is,' said January as he examined the wound – which, as Aramis had said, was perfectly straightforward and had missed both the tibia and the femoral artery – and then washed the area carefully in hot water and spirits of wine, 'this almost certainly wasn't an accident. Were you alone when it happened?'

'I was riding out to the woods, but I was by myself, yes. Of course, Buck threw me – he's lucky he didn't take the bullet in his withers, poor old fellow! – but Hercule and the boys heard the shot and came running from the woods at once.'

'You were lucky,' said January quietly. 'A week ago the men who killed your brother attacked Rose, stabbed her in the market and fled. They're after your great-granpère Absalon's treasure, and when they killed Jeoffrey they got whatever notes he had about tracing it. They followed him to our house—'

'Tcha! That's grass-biting crazy!'

'Not if the treasure is large enough. These days, men will do just about anything to get money. They know enough about the family to have recognized the Crimson Angel from the newspaper description—'

'Newspaper?'

In a few sentences January described the role this last remnant of the de Gericault treasure had played in the spectacular salvation of a gang of white folks. 'So someone knows that Mammy Ginette's daughter is in Cuba,' he concluded. 'And that someone is either related to you, or connected with your great-granpère's plantation in Saint-Domingue. They think Rose knows something about it, and they may think *you* know something . . . or they may just think that when Rose was attacked I wrote to warn you, and they sent someone down here to put you out of the way as well. Did your great-granpère have any other children, besides your grandmother? Rose said she thought he had a son.'

'He did.' Aramis fixed his gaze on a corner of the ceiling and talked rather quickly as January packed the wound and bound it again with cleaner wrappings. 'When Great-Granpère Absalon came here in 1809 his son was with him, our Uncle Guibert. Our great-uncle, really, but he was only a few years older than our father, fourteen years younger than Granmère. I never saw him. He stayed on Hispaniola Plantation – Granpère Vitrac's original place over the other side of the island – less than a year, and when he left, just before I was born, Great-Granpère Absalon came back here to Chouteau – which was Mama's plantation, originally – and the Hispaniola house was allowed to fall to ruin. But the servants talked about him.'

'And he was the only other child besides your Granmère?'

Rose, who had resumed her contemplation of the wall, turned now in her chair, lemonade cup in hand. 'M'sieu Thiot at the Café des Refugies said Great-Granmère Amalie was fragile.'

'Well, she died only a few weeks after Guibert was born. I think she had two or three others before him who didn't survive,' said Aramis. 'That's what Mammy Zett told me.'

'Oh, good Lord, Mammy Zett! Of course, she'd know everything.'

'Mammy Zett's mama was one of the maids Great-Granpère brought from Cuba,' Alice explained to January. 'Old Mammy Pé.'

'I was *terrified* of Mammy Pé,' Rose affirmed.

'We was *all* terrified of Mammy Pé, Rosie.' With a trembling hand, Aramis steadied the cup January held to his lips: bitter willow-bark tea that Olympe swore strengthened the blood. 'She'd tell us tales about Uncle Gunnysack – Tonton Macoute – who came around at night snatching up children in the dark to eat for breakfast, or the Plat-Eye that hides in the woods near where blood has been spilled.'

'For Mammy Pé,' said Rose, '*everything* was some dark spell or other, or the work of demons or leopard men. I used to steal milk from the dairy and put it out in the woods, and then hide, to see if the spirits really would turn it into blood.'

'Did they ever?' asked January, who had been kept from wandering in the night woods himself, as a child, by tales of the Plat-Eye Devil. Only Rose, he reflected, would try to bait the thing in order to get a look at it.

'Usually, the wild pigs would knock it over trying to get at it.'

January laughed, recalling Mammy Zett's stories from his previous visit here with Rose in the summer of 1835. Those had mostly concerned the small incidents of life on the islands, or what had happened during this or that hurricane, or the secrets of animals. But clearly the old woman had inherited her skill as a raconteuse from her formidable mother, and he guessed that, if asked, she could produce plantation rumor and family gossip that went back well before her own birth.

Alice walked with January and Rose out to the weaving shed, where Mammy Zett and the older women of the plantation were to be found on summer days, while those able to do so knelt and stooped among the garden rows pulling weeds. Like the kitchens, the weaving shed had doors all along the side that faced the bay, and these stood open, so as they crossed through the gardens January heard the steady thump of the looms and the voices of the women, singing as they worked:

> *The winds roared, and the rains fell,*
> *The poor white man, faint and weary,*
> *Came and sat under our tree.*
> *He got no mother for to bring him milk,*
> *He got no wife for to grind him corn,*
> *No wife for to grind him corn, oh . . .*
>
> *The poor white man, faint and weary,*
> *Got no wife for to grind him corn . . .*

When Alice stopped to exchange words with the head woman of the gardening gang – Mammy Ti, January recalled her name was – he scanned the line of oaks and oleanders on the low ridge behind the house, looked out past the plantation buildings toward the head-high fields of dark-green cane, motionless in the yellow morning light.

Shaw was right. There's money behind this, money enough to split his forces, to send men after Aramis here while others waited outside the house in New Orleans . . .

Do they just want to put us down? Put us out of the race? Or is there something more? Something that's worth making sure of us: Aramis, Rose, and me?

The weaving shed stood on piers of brick, like the house, though not so high. Pigs rooted in the pen underneath. As he climbed the steps to the narrow gallery, January noted that the railing was in good repair and the plank floors had been swept. A sort of pen had been made from pieces of broken chairs in a corner of the weaving room, where two tiny girls and a boy – all three naked, and only one of the girls old enough to stagger – were being watched by a four-year-old girl, clothed in a sort of dress made from the faded scraps of a worn-out shirt. Two of the shed's three looms were being worked, one by a woman who looked to be in her sixties – though January guessed that in fact she was not much older than his own forty-three years – the other by a woman so bent and wasted that it was hard to tell her age. Flies roared around the shade of the peaked ceiling. Even from here, he could hear the slow beat of the surf on the other side of the island.

The singing stopped, and the two old women turned. The younger said, 'M'am . . .' And then, her lined face breaking into a smile, 'Miss Rose! And Ben, of all people! I hear it tell that you done made a fine baby boy—' Her French was the thick cane-patch pidgin of the slave quarters, French words grafted into African patterns, the first language January had learned.

Rose, he observed, had to listen more carefully, though she spoke it well enough to make herself understood.

'We have,' she said, and smiled in return. 'And who're these?' She knelt beside the makeshift pen and introductions were made. Time on Grand Isle wasn't like time anywhere else, but even in New Orleans, January would have made the time – despite the unexpected reminder that their enemies were close at hand – to re-establish the thousand homey connections with the people of Chouteau Plantation, the people who might unwittingly hold the key to the deadly puzzle of the de Gericault treasure.

'M'am Amalie.' When at last, in answer to January's eventual question, Mammy Zett spoke the name of Great-Granmère de Gericault, there was a note of sadness in her voice, as at the shadow of some old tale. 'My mama's brother was married to her maid – Reina, her name was – at La Châtaigneraie. She went with her, when Old Michie Absalon send her away to L'Ange Rouge by the mountains in the south.'

'L'Ange Rouge?' Rose frowned, as if at a name half-recalled.

'Michie Absalon's other plantation. Back in the forest, away from anywhere. My mama said her brother never saw his wife again.' And she shook her head at the tragedy that whites didn't even notice: even Alice, though she looked sympathetic, had, in her pale blue eyes, no true sorrow. Not the sorrow she'd show, or feel, at a white man losing the girl he loved.

'A little pretty lady, M'am Amalie, my mama said. Hair soft like a cloud, the color of dust, an' wavy like a waterfall.' The soft, regular thump of Old Mammy Dulcie's loom laid a warp of rhythm behind Zett's gravelly voice. 'She been born in France, and she longed all her days to go back there. An' she was a good lady, mama said, an' always try to help the field hands, an' keep 'em away from old Dr Maudit.'

'Dr Maudit?' January straightened up on the bench he'd brought in from the gallery.

The name meant *accursed*, and Mammy Zett's eyes narrowed dramatically. In the hunch of her shoulders, January detected the echo of her mama's scary tales. Not, he reflected, that it would take much imagination to make Saint-Domingue scary to the blacks who'd served there . . .

'He was an evil man, Dr Maudit. A *ouanga*-man that cast spells on Michie Absalon's mind, so he'd do his bidding like a *zombi*. Yes, and he'd make true *zombi*, mama said. Bring the dead back to life so they'd work for Michie Absalon, and steal little children and cut them up and eat them . . . yes, and sometimes their mamas and their daddies, too. I'm not make this up,' she added, seeing the startled glance January traded with Rose. 'You think this is like stories they tell about Tonton Macoute but it's not. Dr Maudit was an evil man, and he made Michie Absalon evil too, Michie Absalon that was as good a man as God made, in those parts, 'fore he met old Dr Maudit. Mama said he made Michie Absalon send poor M'am Amalie away to the south, 'cause she spoke out for the field hands against Dr Maudit when he'd steal their children.'

'White man can't make no *zombi*.' Old Dulcie spoke without pausing in her rhythmic passing of shuttle through warp. 'Nor is no white *bukra* alive gonna let nobody cut up an' eat pickaninnies that can grow up an' work for him. An' Mem say, that was valet to Michie Absalon on Cuba, that he heard Michie Absalon done send Miz Amalie away 'cause she need rest. She tire herself out, runnin' back an' forth to Cap Francais to go shoppin' an' take tea with her friends an' go to parties all wearin' her diamonds. She bear three babies that all break in two an' die, 'cause she runnin' around so much when she carry 'em, so he send her away clear to the south where she can rest an' bear him a healthy child.'

'Was your granmère not healthy?' January glanced curiously at Rose.

'She was fragile,' Rose replied, after a moment's thought. 'She seemed very old to me when I knew her, though I don't think she was even quite fifty when I came here in 1818. Her hair was mostly white, and she couldn't walk more than a few steps . . .'

'That's 'cause her mama was all gallivantin' around Cap Francais in her diamonds goin' to parties,' said Dulcie firmly. 'She'd been grow up in France in the King's palace, an' got used to it. An' for sure when Michie Absalon send her away to the south an' make her rest, she birth a big healthy boy.'

'You don't know what you talkin' about,' snapped Zett. 'Dr Maudit put a cross on Michie Absalon, got him to send M'am Amalie away where Michie Absalon couldn't keep an eye on her. An' as soon as Michie's back was turned, he poison her, on account of she tried to help the slaves 'gainst Maudit.'

Dulcie said, 'Huh.'

'*Huh* yourself, nigger . . .'

'Did Michie Absalon love his wife?' asked January, fascinated though not entirely certain any of this went any distance in explaining where the treasure might be or who would know of it.

'He did 'fore Dr Maudit come along,' put in Mammy Zett quickly.

'I heard he had two *plaçées* in town,' the older woman retorted.

'Hell, that don't mean nuthin'. Wasn't a man, white or colored, in Saint-Domingue didn't have women in town.' Mammy Zett turned back to January. 'You listen to me, Ben. Folks don't understand what it was like in Saint-Domingue. They was near twenty black slaves to every white man on that island, and the whites came up with ways of makin' their niggers too scared to even *think* about liftin' a finger 'gainst 'em. Slow beatin's that'd skin a man over the course of a day, then hangin' him up raw on a tree alive for the ants to swarm, or stuffin' their arse with gunpowder an' callin' every man, woman, an' child of the plantation to watch when he lit the fuse. M'am Amalie did what she could to stop Michie Absalon from doin' such things. But Dr Maudit, he was evil, evil an' crafty, like a stripe-eyed snake. My mama told me it tore Michie up inside, the things Maudit would do, but Maudit had a cross on him that he couldn't un-cross, even for M'am Amalie's sake—'

'Pah! Never in my life!' Old Dulcie snapped her fingers without breaking the beat of her loom. 'Michie Absalon married Amalie de Gericault 'cause her father done him out of his share of their gran-daddy's land in France, an' the title, an' when they got to Cuba I hear tell Michie Absalon went around callin' himself the Vicomte de Gericault. That's the only reason he wanted a strong son, was so's that son could get the title back from their uncle in France. An' he sent M'am Amalie away to where she couldn't get into any trouble, an' just went down there to get her with child, same as puttin' a stud horse to a mare, 'til she took, an' in the meantime had his ladies in town, Calanthe an' Emmanuelle, that was both so bright he'd take one or the other of 'em across to Martinique or Santiago, when there'd be balls there, an' introduce 'em as white.'

'Did he have children by them?' asked January. 'Children that might have lived in his household?'

'Huh.' Mammy Zett scowled at her rival. 'No man'd bring a child of his anywhere near Maudit.'

'No,' answered Dulcie flatly. 'Not as I ever heard.'

'Like you was there, nigger . . .'

'Like I ain't heard the tales your mama told about it, 'fore you was ever born . . .'

'What about Mammy Ginette?' asked Rose.

The two old women glared at each other. Mammy Dulcie sniffed. 'What 'bout her?'

Mammy Zett's eyes darkened with old sorrow. 'She was sister to M'am Amalie's maid Reina,' she said, 'the one that was married to my mama's brother. Michie Absalon, he gave Ginette to that plaçée Calanthe for a gift, same time he gave Reina to M'am Amalie.'

'High-yeller,' said Dulcie dismissively, 'an' proud as Lucifer.'

'When Ginette came here looking for her granddaughter, did she ever tell you anything about being forced to guide an old blind man back to Saint-Domingue, to the ruins of the plantation?' Rose looked from one to the other.

'Now, when'd we have had a chance to sit and pass the time of day with anyone?' returned Dulcie tartly. 'It was *roulaison* when she come here, an' everyone on the place was in the field haulin' cane.'

'She never did get on with my mama,' admitted Mammy Zett. 'Mama never did forgive her, for servin' that stuck-up bitch Calanthe, and then for bein' the one who ran away when her sister Reina died there on the island.'

'How did she die?'

'In a hurricane,' said Mammy Dulcie shortly, but Mammy Zett shook her head.

'It was old Dr Maudit that poisoned her,' she announced. 'Like he poison poor M'am Amalie, and her brother as well—'

'Her brother?' Rose's eyebrows shot up. 'I thought her brother was the Comte de Caillot, back in France.'

'He was,' declared Mammy Zett with morbid relish. 'But my mama told me that when there was the revolution in France and all them counts and dukes got their heads cut off, M'am Amalie's brother Neron come to Cuba, to shelter with his cousin Michie Absalon. An' Michie Absalon turned him out like a dog . . .'

Quick footsteps on the gallery stair vibrated the little shed, and a voice from outside called, 'M'am Alice?' It was a boy whom January recognized vaguely from his visit to Chouteau three years ago, Didi, grown now to a gangly adolescent. 'M'am Alice,' he said, 'Jacque told me to come tell you, this is twice now this afternoon he's seen men in the woods: men he don't know, men he says he got a bad feelin' about. He says their tracks look like those he found near where Michie Aramis was shot.'

NINE

Jacque was Aramis Vitrac's foreman, African-dark as January was, but – January was distressed to see – at least thirty pounds thinner than he'd been three years previously. There was a raspiness to his breath, even at rest, that spoke of overwork and poor food for too many years in a row. The first touch of pneumonia would take him, he thought, as it took so many.

Jacque told Hercule the sugar boss to keep the woodcutters at their work, and then took January up the ridge to show him the tracks. These meant little to January's unpracticed eye, save for the obvious fact that they'd been made by a man of above average height, with narrow feet, in slightly worn boots with square toes. A little distance away, Square-Toes had encountered a smaller man with wider feet, and – on the other side of the ridge – two horses had stood for a time and dunged. 'I found this same man's tracks near where Michie Aramis was shot, sir,' said Jacque, and he swatted – with wearied resignation – at the ever-present gnats that swarmed the stifling woodlands where the bay's breezes did not reach.

The fact that it rained every afternoon (and was, in fact, getting ready to do so again) provided a *terminus a quo* to the signs.

January took the shore path back to the house, though it was longer than the way through the woods along the ridge and got him soaked in the first of the storm. Even with a clear field of vision around him, he was deeply conscious of the island's isolation, and of the fact that there were a thousand places where a man might hide with a rifle.

'Much as I hate to say it, my nightingale,' he said, once he'd changed to dry clothes and was sitting with Rose on the back gallery with the gray downpour like a curtain before them, 'I think we're going to have to go to Cuba.'

She let her breath go in a sigh. The thought, he could see, had been in her mind from the time it had become clear that neither Aramis nor Mammy Zett – nor, probably, anyone on Chouteau Plantation – recalled sufficient information about the de Gericault family to show them in what direction danger would lie.

'There have to be people there who remember Absalon de Gericault, who remained in touch with the family, who can tell us where this Uncle Guibert is now, and who can give us some clue as to whether he's the one who's hunting this treasure – who's hunting us. They lived there for eighteen years; there might have been someone in the household, someone in the family, who can tell us who might be our enemy and who can give us some clue as to how to checkmate them. Otherwise all we can do is disappear and hope they'll pass us in quest of the treasure . . .'

'Which they may not do,' said Rose, 'if they think I know something they'd rather I didn't tell anyone else.' She turned her face a little away from him, her spectacles opaque ovals of silver in the shadow. 'And the plan has the virtue of leading them away from Aramis and his family – and from Baby John.'

He put his hand over hers, her long fingers cold in his grip.

Natchez Jim had promised to stop back at Chouteau the following morning, so as the afternoon darkened, January dug pen, ink, and paper from his slender luggage (none of these items being present in the house of Rose's brother) and wrote a letter to Hannibal. He folded it tightly together – the Vitrac household also lacked anything in the way of sealing wax or wafers (*thank God we didn't decide to wait til Aramis wrote back with information about the family!*) – and took two dollars from his slender hoard to make it worth Jim's while to deliver to the fiddler without waiting for a cargo. Heaven only knew what had become of Rose's second letter, warning Aramis of possible attack – given the way the post office operated on Grand Isle, it might arrive as late as Christmas. Around him, the house was deeply silent, save for the voices of the children on the back gallery and Aramis' deep, regular breathing in the bedroom. January was just rising to fetch a candle when Rose and Alice came in from the gallery themselves.

'Would you mind sleeping in the attic tonight?' Alice inquired. 'I'm thinking the cottage –' she nodded in the direction of the small guest house that had sheltered January and Rose on their previous visit – 'is a bit far from the house. I know Aramis would say I've been listening to too many of Mammy Zett's stories,' she added, with a self-conscious flush to her cheeks, 'but somebody *did* kill Jeoffrey . . . and *did* stab you, Rose. And in spite of what Aramis says, I believe Jacque when he says that wasn't just one of our neighbors he saw riding around in the woods.'

'Thank you.' The attic would be like a slow oven, January reflected, but at least he wouldn't lie awake wondering if each creak of the little cottage, on its tall brick piers, was a footfall, creeping up the steps.

For the next five days he made himself useful around the plantation, cutting kindling, going out with the shrimp boats, nursing Aramis and examining every one of the twenty slaves – men, women, children – for such ailments as could be rectified: hernias, sprains, inflamed tendons, female complaints. Old Dulcie doubled as midwife and herb doctor, and the condition of the children attested to her understanding of her craft. January found no signs of rickets or

worms among the dozen children (counting Alice's four) of the
plantation. But adults and children alike, he could see, still suffered
from the effects of last winter's overwork, and he knew that when
the time of summer vegetables and summer milk was over, they
would quickly slide back into the borderline malnutrition suffered
by all slaves, no matter how benevolent and well-intentioned their
owners. Plantations on the island grew their own corn, but as Rose
had said, there was always the drive to put more land into sugar
and let the slaves make up the difference in what they might
hunt and catch. With the price of sugar down, and expenses for salt
and tools and taxes up, that temptation would redouble. For the first
three days, Aramis himself was feverish, and January kept the wound
cleaned and dosed him with borage and willow-bark tea.

Several times a day he would take Rose's spyglass up to the attic
and sweep the horizon from each of its four windows, looking out
over the cane fields, the marshy shore, the oak-grown ridge behind
the house. All he saw were the thousand-and-one places where half
the British Army might lurk unseen: cane fields; palmetto thickets;
oak trees, all leaning weirdly in the direction of the bay, as if swept
by invisible, perpetual wind. He would walk up the ridge and through
the woods, looking for tracks, but he wasn't the tracker Lieutenant
Shaw was, and it made him deeply uneasy to get out of sight of
the house, even armed with Aramis' duck-gun. (*'Sure, go on, take
it . . .' So much for the laws against colored men laying hands on
weapons . . .*)

Two or three times he found the tracks of narrow square-toed
boots and those of wider, shorter feet. Once, he thought there was
a third set of tracks as well. *How many of them did our unknown
enemy hire?*

During those five days, both he and Rose tried to fit together the
half-remembered snippets of old rumor, old tales, hand-me-down
gossip from the children and grandchildren of the few slaves that
Absalon de Gericault had brought from Cuba, searching for names,
for clues, for anything of use. There wasn't a great deal. De Gericault
had had to sell most of his slaves before leaving Cuba, and Mammy
Pé had been the only one to live very long. De Gericault's valet,
Mem, had had two sons after coming to Louisiana, but both of these
had become field-hands, and both were already dead. Even with the
improvements that were beginning to lessen the hideous labor of
making sugar, cane was a brutal crop.

A whole cycle of tales revolved around the iniquities of old Belleange, Comte de Caillot's perfidy in stealing Absalon de Gericault's birthright – forged papers, swapped babies, murdered nurses, faithful shepherds, miraculous escapes, many blatantly reminiscent of the novels January's youngest sister Dominique read, and impossible to sort into fiction or fact. Another cycle centered on the insidious Dr Maudit. 'He can't really have cut up children and made stew of them,' protested Rose, on their way back from the quarters one evening. 'Aside from what the neighbors would have said, that would have gotten awfully expensive . . .'

'I'd say so,' agreed January. 'Except that you and I both know that Delphine Lalaurie made it a habit to imprison her slaves in the attic and torture them, and most of her neighbors still don't admit that she did it. A woman in her position "doesn't do things like that".'

He shivered at the memory of that stifling attic, of the agony in his shoulders and back, the terror of being helpless before those mad, self-justifying eyes. 'My old master on Bellefleur Plantation had a barrel with nails driven through its sides,' he went on slowly, 'that he'd nail people up in and roll them down from the top of the levee. If a man disobeyed an order, he'd have him hung up head-down in the chimney of the smokehouse for a couple of hours with the fires going. One of our neighbors killed more than one of his slaves with what he called the Water Treatment, and nobody in the district said a thing about it. He still got invited to parties because he had fifty arpents of land along the river and two marriageable sons. There's nothing to tell us that this Dr Maudit wasn't stark, staring crazy – and no guarantee that Absalon de Gericault simply refused to see what was going on under his nose.'

Rose looked unhappy, but made no reply. Her experience of servitude, January knew, had been at second-hand and relatively benign. On this, her father's plantation, she'd probably seen no more than a whipping or two.

Life on the island itself was incredibly primitive. There was no church closer than Crown Point – a priest was sent out from New Orleans once or twice a year to perform baptisms and marriages – and January missed the comfort of confession and the Mass. It was no wonder, he reflected, that townspeople looked upon the inhabitants of the Barataria as pagans.

Twice that week Rose took Aramis' skiff and sailed out beyond the rim of *flottants* into the Bay. Patiently, she taught January to trim sails and reef sheets, and to navigate by a hundred nearly-identical bumps and notches on the horizon: a bump here, an oak tree there, the gray blink of somebody's gable above a sea of grass and sedge that might or might not have roots on actual land. She seemed to know every shoal and creek and islet in the bay, the way he himself had learned the invisible geography of the woods around Bellefleur as a child: the shape of tree limbs, the taste of the damp air, the lie of the ground underfoot. It was good to be in the countryside again.

On Thursday she took them out through the Barataria Pass into the open Gulf, where dolphins swept along on both sides of the little craft and leaped from the water to regard January for a moment with wise, bright black eyes. Dressed in boys' clothing, her hair jammed under a fisherman's cap, Rose was in her element on the sea, handling the wheel with neat speed and reading the barely visible alterations of surface and color of the water like a Mississippi riverboat pilot.

'See how the waves get higher there? And their crests are closer together? That's shoal water . . . Now look where the color of the water changes, meaning there's a current . . .'

January blinked. It all looked perfectly identical to him.

'The Gulf is shallow for miles out. In close you'll find sheepshead and sandtrouts; you don't see things like bass unless you're very far from land. I used to sail out of sight of land, looking for different sorts of fish. Aramis would never go, but Jeoffrey would. Once we got caught by a current, and I didn't think we were ever going to make it back to shore . . .'

January cast a queasy glance back in the direction of where he'd last seen land. The quiet and scholarly Rose, he had found early in their relationship, had a blithe fearlessness when in pursuit of knowledge that frequently terrified him, and she would investigate nearly anything: gunpowder, incendiaries, lightning, storms. And, he reflected, they looked like they'd have the chance to witness the latter close up: black sky was building up to the south, and blue-white flickers of electricity sprang between water and clouds.

'If we were going to be here longer,' mused Rose as she regretfully put about, 'I'd like to try out the breathing tube I've been designing that would let a swimmer remain underwater. Even in a storm, I've heard, beneath the water it's calm.'

'Well, you're not going to swim out in the open ocean, with or without a breathing tube, until Baby John is grown up,' retorted January, only half in jest. 'He needs his mother. *I* need his mother,' he added, to Rose's wince of regretful agreement.

She hooked a bight of rope over the wheel, went to trim the sails. 'I wouldn't do it unless I'd made sure it was safe, first.' The wind snatched her cap away, tumbled her hair about her shoulders in a torrent.

January rolled his eyes. Rose considered making fireworks safe, also.

As they skimmed back toward shore, Rose pointed at the low silhouette of the island – barely a bump above the angry-looking sea. 'That's where Hispaniola was – Granpère Louis-Charles's plantation, where Great-Granpère settled when Papa married M'am Marguerite Chouteau. Aramis says Granmère Oliva was afraid of Great-Granpère—'

'I thought he was the kindest man in the world?' Only by narrowing his eyes could January make out the remains of the house, which – contrary to the custom of most of the small plantations of the island – faced the Gulf. 'Until the Evil Dr Maudit put a curse on him,' he added with a grin.

'It's what everyone says,' agreed Rose. 'And of course he was dead by the time I came to live at Chouteau, so I never met him. But I did know Granmère Oliva. And there was a note in her voice when she'd talk about him – which she almost never did – and she had a way of turning her head aside when Papa would speak of his kindness.'

She frowned, holding on to the sail lines as she studied the shore. 'I do remember her telling me, several times, that men thought girls were useless. And she was constantly apologizing to M'am Marguerite for being a trouble, and being a cripple, and not being able to do things, even though M'am Marguerite loved her very much and was sincerely happy about taking care of her. And now I wonder if her papa – Great-Granpère – scorned her because she was a girl and couldn't inherit back the title from his cousin, or because her bones were weak.'

January frowned as a thought snagged at the back of his mind – something he'd read? A name? Something he'd asked someone once, a long time ago, in France, maybe—?

But Rose was already scrambling to the wheel as wind blew up sharply from behind them and lightning sprang from the black mountain of cloud that now stretched over most of the sky. 'There! See the wharf? It's mostly in ruins, but we can still tie up at it – which is probably what we'd better do.'

January had at least acquired enough skill by that time to leap across from the gunwale to the few rickety beams that still united the pilings and haul the skiff inshore by the bowlines. Waves raced on to the shore, foam-fringed and angry, and spits of rain stung his face. Rose drew Aramis' fowling gun from beneath the seat, wrapped in its scraps of oilcloth, and tossed the weapon to January, though the likelihood of anyone attacking them in this desolate place was small. Hand in hand they dashed up the path to the half-rotted carcass of the old house among its tangles of hackberry and palmetto.

'The house is bigger than Chouteau, but the land wasn't as good, and they kept losing the roof when hurricanes would hit this side of the island,' Rose explained as they climbed the wrecked and splintery steps to the gallery. 'That may be why . . . Good Heavens!' she added as they ducked from the gallery into the house itself.

After a long moment January walked over to the remains of the mantelpiece – which Rose had been looking at when she'd exclaimed – and lit a match, for the storm was rapidly darkening such daylight as came through the holed roof and closed shutters. 'This is fresh,' he said. 'Within the last few days, I'd say.' The wooden mantle looked as if someone had taken an ax to it. The interior of the wood was unweathered and yellow-bright.

Rose moved quickly over to him. It was the gesture of a woman seeking protection, but in fact she bent and picked up a long shard of the oak (painted to look like marble) and held one end to January's sputtering match. Only by its light did he see in her eyes that, yes, she had moved to his side in fear.

The ruined house had been ransacked.

All furniture had gone decades ago, but in each of the six rooms, January and Rose saw as they moved from one to another, the ornamental fireplace mantles had been chopped open to search for hiding places and the protective bricks of their hearths crowbarred out. Boards had been torn up from the floor, and in the two tiny *cabinets* at the back of the house, where steps ran up to the attic, each step of the stair had been ripped up.

All the damage was fresh.

In four of the rooms, rain pounded through the open holes in the roof above. 'Only a few weeks of this would have weathered the wood,' said January, ducking back to the relative (but only relative) shelter of the front room where they'd entered.

'Looking for a treasure map?' Half-wondering disbelief tinged Rose's voice. The shutters had been unbolted on the French door through which they'd entered; they banged in the wind behind them. When January went to bolt them, he saw that the bolt had been chopped away as well.

'Or for information about the plantation in Saint-Domingue.' Though it was barely five in the afternoon, the storm was rapidly swallowing even the dim blue-gray light that came through the broken roof of the next room, and the old house creaked on its tall piers in the wind. This chamber, by its position, would have been Absalon de Gericault's bedroom, at the front of the house on the side nearer the far-off river. The bed was gone, and so was the desk at which he would have written whatever business he had: protests to Spanish authorities, demanding compensation for the Cuban plantation he'd been forced to sell? Notes to the old men in the Café des Refugies, lamenting the world they had lost? Letters to his Congressman? But nobody in Congress paid much attention to Frenchmen who'd had the misfortune to survive the destruction of their world. Schemes to recover his treasure?

Since 1789, as Jeoffrey Vitrac had pointed out, the issue of the de Gericault title had become moot.

'I think we'd better get out of here.'

Rain hammered down through the broken roof of the gallery. January pushed open the shutter, looked down the long path toward the wharf and the sea beyond it, trying to guess how long the storm would last and where they could shelter in the meantime . . . Surely the place had the ruins of a sugar mill . . .?

Two men were walking up the path to the house.

They carried what were clearly guns, wrapped in oilcloth but barrels protruding a little, to glint in the stormy light.

And Aramis' skiff was drifting free of the wharf, already fifty or sixty yards out to sea.

TEN

Rose turned at once to go to the back of the house. January caught her arm. 'There'll be one more coming in from the back.'

He'd kept the lock of Aramis' duck gun dry in its wrapping, but guessed that the powder in the cartridges in his pockets was damp.

'Boards in the dining room floor were pulled up,' she replied. 'We can drop through under the house.'

There'd be snakes down there – it was the reason they hadn't taken shelter in the thickets of palmetto that grew among the house piers in the first place – but now wasn't the time to hesitate. January ducked through the splattering rain in the dining room to the hole that had been chopped in the floor, where presumably someone had seen something that made him think a hiding place was there.

Only one board had been hacked completely free, but the opening gave January the leverage to wrench up the planks on either side. Rain rattled on the floor around him and thundered on the galleries, but he thought he heard, above the howling of the wind, steps cross the rear gallery as he caught Rose's wrists and lowered her through the hole to the sinister jungle below. He dropped the gun down after her, then slithered through himself.

The noise was less down there, and he could definitely hear the creak of weight on the floorboards above.

Rose took his hand, pushed her way through the thicket (*Virgin Mary, Mother of God, PLEASE send the snakes elsewhere . . .*) and, when they reached the edge of the house, dropped to her hands and knees to crawl through the scrubby growth beyond. January followed. He had a dim impression that the woods of laurel and hackberry that surrounded the house joined with the foliage higher on the ridge at some point, but between the stormy half-light and the violence of the rain, only Rose knew the direction for certain, and it was vital to put distance between themselves and the house immediately. It would take only moments for their hunters to see the enlarged hole in the floor.

The scrub ended. Twenty feet lay between them and the top of the ridge. Rose caught his hand again, gathered her feet under her to rise and make a dash; January withdrew his fingers, shook his head. Gestured: *You go that way, I'll go this way.*

Divide their fire.

Rose nodded and wiped futilely at the rain that blurred her spectacles.

They kissed, sprang to their feet, ran.

Fifteen feet to the ridge line. Ten.

A gun barked behind him, and he heard the soft *phut* of a bullet striking earth. Didn't dare look back for Rose, just kept his head down. Another gunshot . . .

On the other side of the ridge lay cane fields. Dark-green, elbow-high at this season and rank with undergrowth. (*More snakes. More rats . . .*)

The corner of his eye gave him a glimpse of Rose as she flashed down the short hillslope and straight into the cane, like a thin teen-aged boy in her pants and shirt. He darted in, instants later, fifty feet further along the field's edge. Leaves cut his arms like razor blades. Ants swarmed in outrage, up his legs and over his hands. He crawled across the rows in Rose's direction, splashing through the mud of the ditches between and wondering if the weight and size of his body were going to leave a visible trail. The men had to run down the gallery steps, climb the ridge . . .

He rolled himself longways against the cane on one of the hillocks on which it grew, in the middle of the unweeded mess of cane leaves, goat weed, Spanish grass.

A gun cracked, some distance to his left.

Shooting to flush us out?

The rain will wash our tracks . . .

He stayed where he was. The noise of the rain on the leaves drowned out other sounds, but he guessed they were looking . . .

How many of them? Two in the cane, one on the ridge, watching to see if we run? Have the Indians and Seth Maddox from New Orleans joined them yet?

At least he'd washed off the ants.

Rose . . .

He lay in the cane, hugging his useless bird gun, with the rain soaking his back and hair as it passed in audible waves over the lake of cane. It lightened to a drizzle, and the afternoon around him slowly brightened again and grew hot. The puddles steamed. January stayed where he was. Once he heard – or thought he heard – someone pass through the cane rows near him, crashing and rustling through the thick barricades of the leaves. It might only have been one of the island's wild pigs. The ant bites stung and throbbed. So did the wound he'd taken back in Washington, an aching pull deep in his side.

He'd seen his childhood playmates try to hide in the cane and knew that, with the plants at this height, if he moved the hunters could follow him by the threshing of the leaves.

Heat like steamed towels. Smoke rising eerily from the puddles in the ditches between the planted hillocks. Gnats like the wrath of a righteous God, and swallows like angels, gorging their fill.

Swift-falling tropical twilight.

Owls.

January crawled to the end of the row, looked up at the ridge above him. No silhouetted shape watched over the field. Still he crawled to the other end of the row before he dared stand, and then followed the road that divided the fields on the bay side of the island from the marshy, mosquito-haunted mudflats, going west toward Chouteau. On the bay, the shrimp boats were coming in, and in the distance the sonorous bray of the conch shells that in these parts still served as trumpets announced the end of the working day.

Enough light lingered in the sky for those who'd spent since cockcrow cutting wood or weeding Michie Aramis' corn to put in a few more hours of labor on their own gardens – *shell-blow grounds*, they'd been called on Bellefleur. Long before he came in sight of Chouteau's rooftops he smelled the smoke of the kitchen hearth and of the dozen open fire-pits that dotted the quarters. Then the cook fires came in sight in the warm dusk, and Chouteau's dim-lighted windows, and he heard the voices of the children as they played among the *flottants* in the dark.

Natchez Jim arrived the following noon, with Hannibal Sefton and – of all people – January's sister Olympe. January and Rose strode down the path to the landing, Rose with her face scratched from the cane leaves but otherwise none the worse for their adventure of yesterday: she'd been sitting on the dark gallery last night, watching for him, when he'd climbed its steps.

Olympe sprang over the gunwale and embraced January with fervor unlike her usual cool irony: 'I seen you in the cane,' she explained, looking up into his face. 'Just before sunset. You were crouched down in the cane rows. You had a gun with you, but you couldn't use it . . . You don't think I been lookin' in the ink for you, brother, since you went away?' she added, with her slight, crooked-toothed smile. 'You got bit by ants . . .'

She turned his hand over in hers and looked at the crusty dots of drying salt-and-soda paste on his skin.

'You don't think I been burnin' a white candle for you every night, and ask Ogun Badagris to watch your steps and see you safe?' she asked more softly. 'Every night I ask Mamzelle l'Araignée –' she named the private deity who lived in a black-painted bottle on a shelf in her house – 'for word of you.'

'*The effectual fervent prayer of the righteous availeth much,*' corroborated Hannibal, and he straightened up from kissing Rose's hand. 'And so, I am pleased to say, do some of the most ferocious mosquito-smudges I have encountered in my life. An enlivening journey. The bayous aren't as crowded or noisy as the gutters of Bourbon Street, but on the whole I think I've been wise in swearing off roofless nights for the time being.'

Olympe grinned and poked him with a sharp elbow. 'This worthless child came telling me he was off in the morning to keep you out of trouble in Cuba, and that night Mamzelle l'Araignée came and whispered in my ear, whispered to come with him here. *He gonna need brick dust on his shoes,* she say to me. *He gonna need iron in his pockets and the mark of Ogun on his brow, Ogun that watches over the strong.*' She spoke lightly, but her eyes, dark and somber as those of a prophetess, fixed on January's face, as if fearing he would turn away with some pious remark.

And as a good Christian, January knew he should do exactly that. *Get thee behind me, Satan* was universally recommended by the priests in New Orleans. Or at least, *Thanks but no thanks.*

Instead he asked, 'When did you see me?' as he gathered up Hannibal's two carpet bags (one of them was actually his sister Dominique's) and Olympe's satchel. 'Jim, I hope you're staying to dinner.'

'It's why I caught a couple of extra catfish.' The boatman lifted a string of them from the back of the *Black Goose.*

They travelled in a little procession up toward the house.

'I saw you night before last,' said Olympe quietly. 'Them ant bites look fresher than that.'

'You didn't happen to see the men after us?' inquired Rose, and Olympe shook her head.

'So far as I can tell the house isn't being watched any more,' added Hannibal. 'And the good lieutenant has heard nothing of the Mobilites. I have pursued enquiries of my own through the local dens of iniquity – an exhausting pursuit, considering how many of them there are in New Orleans – and have ascertained that though our friends were known by sight and by name, nobody recalled much about them. They certainly didn't go about the town asking after the Crimson Angel or the Vitrac family. *Belle Madame*—' He bowed deeply as Alice came smiling shyly down the gallery steps.

Rose made introductions.

'Please permit me to kiss your hands and feet in thanks for the shelter of your roof. *This castle hath a pleasant seat; the air nimbly and sweetly recommends itself* . . . I hope and trust your good husband's health has recovered enough to share this with you?' And he produced from the satchel at his side a bottle of very fine French wine which, January recognized, must have cost the fiddler a month's earnings and an advance against his best waistcoat at the pawnshop.

And he reflected briefly on his friend's commitment to sobriety. Three years ago the fiddler wouldn't have been capable of trans-porting a bottle of French wine two blocks, let alone sixty miles.

It served, needless to say, to elevate his welcome from 'the friend who's going to help Rose' to a valued guest in his own right and smoothed the social awkwardness occasioned by the presence of a quadroon half-sister's coal-black husband (who might eat with the family in private) and his equally coal-black sister (who couldn't, not without raising the stigma of, '*They eat with blacks* . . .'), to say nothing of Natchez Jim.

Rose and Olympe set a small table on the gallery of the 'cottage', fifty feet behind the 'big house' at the foot of the ridge. There they feasted on the excellent étouffée that Mammy Fanfan – Aramis' cook – made of catfish and shrimp, while across the yard, in the minuscule 'big house', Hannibal dined in state on the same viands with the family, at a table presided over – for the first time since his shooting – by Aramis.

Olympe, who – January was interested to note – appeared to be showing the beginnings of a pregnancy of her own, reassured Rose of Baby John's health and safety. 'I know you want to hear that he cries every night from missing you, but he's quiet. He look around for you, every time somebody comes into the room, but he loves for Chou-Chou to hold him –' she named her second son, Claud, aged eight – 'and Paul. When I went down to the wharf, to make Jim bring me down to you here, I got Zizi-Marie to come and take care of him at my house, and he was happy to see her. Have no fear for him, Rose. He born with the sign of thunder on him, and thunder's a strong sign.'

Rose smiled – probably at the thought of their solemn and methodical son bearing so impressive a badge – but leaned across and grasped her sister-in-law's hand. 'Tell me about seeing Benjamin in the ink,' she urged. 'What did that look like? How is it done?' She might be a scientist, January reflected, but her mind scouted out beyond the boundaries of the scientific, European education that both he and she had received. And he smiled at himself. *I say, 'That's nonsense, we know people don't see people in ink-bowls . . .'*

She says, 'What if it's not? What can I learn from it?'

And though Olympe had brusquely excluded his skepticism from her practice of voodoo when they were in their teens, now she explained, in the matter-of-fact tones of a woman explaining how to make bread, the lighting of candles, the drawing of vèves, the prayers to Papa Legba, the Old Man of the Crossroad, and to Fa of the Iron Cane. 'Most people ask a question, and for that I read the cards, or corn kernels on a tray. If I've prayed, I'll see the roads that run between the cards, or between the kernels, and like as not I see then that the question they're asking me isn't what they really want to know.'

'And I imagine,' January added gently, 'it helps that, as a voodoo, everyone in town tells you everything, so you know without your customer telling you that she's in love with her neighbor's husband or that her brother is soaking money off her . . .'

'For a Christian man, you got a limited view of God, brother,' returned Olympe with a smile, 'if you think God don't bring me all that information from one place and another for a reason. But sometimes –' she turned back to Rose, in the dim glow of the candles on the table, the smudges set all around them on the gallery

rail – 'I don't know enough. Then I'll pray to Papa Legba, and to
Fa of the Iron Cane, and look in a candle flame, or a bowl of ink,
and my hoodoo, my spirit, will come on me and ride me. Then I'll
remember the things she sees in the ink with my eyes. Not often.
I looked for sight of my brother's face every night for a week and
saw him only twice. Once, far off, I saw you on a little boat in the
ocean, turning before a storm. Your hair was all undone –' she
reached out to touch Rose's black tignon – 'and you were laughing
at him, for being an old hen about being on the sea.'

'That,' returned Rose with a grin, 'would be any time we've gone
sailing.'

But January was silent.

'The other time I saw him in the cane rows. It was just before
sunset, and the smoke was rising off the puddles between the rows.
Men were hunting him – hunting you both, I thought. I see these
things as if they're tiny as ants, but right up close to my eye; as if
they're reflected in the ink from someplace far off. These men that
hunt you, these men that tried to kill you in the market, that killed
your brother . . . I've tried to see them, too. Thought on them, went
to the place where they stayed – the Verrandah – and got the maid
to let me in their rooms, so's I could touch the walls they'd touched
and smell the pillows for the scent of their hair. When I looked in
the ink for them, Mamzelle l'Araignée wouldn't come. Wouldn't
show me anything. But for about a minute, the ink gave off the
smell of blood.'

The back doors of the main house opened then, and Hannibal
and the family emerged, Aramis leaning painfully on the arms of
his wife and guest. January and his party rose from their own little
table and, smudges in hand, crossed through the soft twilight of the
yard to join them on the back gallery, and Hannibal opened up his
fiddle case. The smudges were set around the gallery rail, and
Mammy Fanfan brought out coffee and pralines, white and pink
and gold.

Fiddle music of any kind was a rare treat on the island. January
fetched his guitar, and the men and women in the quarters, gathered
below the gallery, produced banjos, drums, whistles and spoons.
Even the four cane-hands whom Alice had placed as a perimeter
guard around the house – to the severe curtailment of the plantation's labor force – came in close to listen, grinning and tapping
their feet when the songs grew lively. Stories were told, not of

Saint-Domingue or murder or family treasure, but absurd tales of men and women of the parish, or of Alice's Uncle Dondon who claimed to have sailed with Lafitte.

It was long after midnight when all the company – there were now far too many to shelter in the attic, and Aramis appointed a couple of night guards – returned to the guest house. 'The *Triton*'s leaving New Orleans tomorrow, for Havana,' said Natchez Jim as he helped Rose unroll clean pallets – stuffed with new moss – on the floor. 'If we get ourselves out of here in the morning, we should catch them as they pass through La Balize.'

'Your Uncle Veryl contributed thirty dollars toward our passage,' added Hannibal, wrapping his violin in its usual cocoon of old silk scarves before stowing it in its case. He looked, January thought, better than he had in town, with his long hair braided into a tidy queue and some of the feverish exhaustion gone from his eyes. 'And, hoping it would be all right with you, I solicited another fifty dollars from Monsieur and Madame Viellard. *Nihil tam munitum quod non expugnari pecunia possit*: I have not the faintest notion what awaits us in Cuba, but if one is being hunted it's always better to have money in one's pockets. Or even,' he added wistfully, 'if one is not.'

'You are a scholar and a gentleman.' Rose embraced him. 'And if that wretched treasure isn't run off with somebody before we get to it – or wasn't looted years ago by the sinister Dr Maudit – you will surely be entitled to your share.'

'Dr Maudit?' Olympe frowned sharply.

'The evil "friend of the family", who might or might not have been the man Mammy Ginette was forced to guide back to Haiti in 1809,' Rose explained. 'Who might or might not have corrupted Great-Granpère into the ways of sin, according to Old Dulcie and Mammy Zett here. Though the old blind man Mammy Ginette guided could also have been the equally evil Comte de Caillot, Great-Granpère's cousin, or in fact—'

'He's a spirit.' Olympe sank back on to her pallet and unwrapped her tignon. Beneath it, her hair was ebony-dark and nappy as sheep's wool, and braided tight into a thick mass of narrow plaits like a pickaninny's, tied with kitchen string. It gave her face the wild aspect of a spirit herself. 'A *Guédé*, the get of Baron Samedei, the children of night and wickedness. Dr Maudit, that cuts up little children alive—'

'That's him,' agreed January.

Rose objected, 'Dulcie speaks of him as if he were a real person. Mammy Zett, too. He can't be both, surely.'

'Of course he can. Many of the *loa* were living men and women—' January glanced across at his sister for corroboration, and she nodded, dark eyes narrowed with thought. 'Great kings, some of them, or ancestors who watch over their children.'

'Yes, but this was only thirty years ago,' pointed out Hannibal.

'You ever see one of those silly pictures they paint back East,' asked January, 'of George Washington in a toga sitting amongst the Roman gods on a cloud, watching over Henry Clay or Daniel Webster or whoever? He's only been dead for forty years.' He turned again to Olympe. 'What do they say about him? Dr Maudit, I mean, not George Washington.'

'That he was an evil *blankitte*,' she replied softly. 'He walked the roads of Saint-Domingue in slavery times and would steal away children if they stayed out too late. Steal away women, too, and keep them locked in a stone house in the mountains guarded by *zombis* – by the walking dead. That he had a treasure in this house—'

January and Rose traded a glance.

'—and books, too, of evil magic that gave him his power.'

'Sounds like somebody's been reading *The Tempest*,' remarked Hannibal.

'Don't laugh, fiddler. Nor you, brother. And don't tell me there ain't power in the world greater than the bodies of the men it wells up through, the way water wells up through rock. I never thought to cross his path.'

'Who did you hear this from?' asked January after a time.

But Olympe had relapsed into thought and only shook her head. Her dark eyes seemed to gaze out past the barred shutters of the big, square chamber that constituted the whole of the guest house on its high piers. In time she gathered up her modest satchel and went outside.

Hannibal produced two decks of cards from a pocket and laid out a three-handed game of bezique around the single candle, for himself, Jim, and Rose. January lay for a time on the wide bed, listening to the murmurs of the card players and the slow pulse of the sea. Once it seemed to him that he was dreaming – only, it wasn't anything as definite as a dream – about the big, shadowy attic room he'd shared with two other medical students, when first he'd arrived in Paris: it had been like this, he thought. Nearly empty, save for a single table perennially littered with their pooled lecture notes, every corner of the room stacked with anatomy texts – Hunter, Browne, Vesalius – old medical journals, and assorted bones. In the darkness, around a single candle, they'd talk: Breyer from Nürnberg who lived across the hall, the thin bespectacled Indian Jogal, and January himself, the sounds of the Paris streets below whispering like the sea . . .

Then he woke from this half-dream and went outside. Wind had started up, but by the patchy light of a waning moon January could just make out the two guards Aramis had set still standing, one on either side of the guest house, halfway up the ridge.

And somewhere in the darkness an orange spot of fire burned, and when the wind shifted it brought him Olympe's voice, crooning to Mamzelle l'Araignée in her black-painted bottle, and with it, the whiff of blood.

CUBA

ELEVEN

They left Chouteau at first light, the *Black Goose* skimming through Caminada Pass and along the Gulf side of the islands, making for La Balize.

January had fallen asleep before Olympe returned to the guest house. When he woke in the stillness before first light, she gave him a circle of iron the size of a ten-dollar gold piece, strung on a leather thong. On it had been patiently scratched the diagonal checker-work and stars of Ogun, the blacksmith god. 'Wear it, brother,' said Olympe as they walked down to the wharf in the tepid dawn. 'For the sake of Rose, and of your son.'

Here, where there were no waves, the stillness seemed oceans deep, and the whisper of the surf on the other side of the island came like the breath of some sleeping thing. January turned the *gris-gris* over in his fingers. The Church was very clear on the wearing of such things, or of juju-balls tied into the armpit with string (all the way down to Grand Isle January had watched Natchez Jim, every night, take his off and dribble whiskey on it before saying his evening prayers).

Half the people he knew in New Orleans simply neglected to mention their *gris-gris* at confession (though they generally took them off before entering the church). A devout man and an educated one, January knew that to wear Ogun's mark with the prior intention of tossing it into the sea upon his return from Cuba and then going to confession and asking for absolution was exactly what he'd told Zizi-Marie and Gabriel not to do.

But he didn't cast the *gris-gris* away.

I don't understand Your ways, he prayed as the flat green line of the island dwindled to the north above the shallow waves. *And I know not if Ogun is one of Your names, or that of a spirit who does Your bidding – like St James, that loa's other name – or if this piece of iron is just a piece of iron. Protect us, if it is YOUR will, for nothing takes place but by Your command. If You tell me to throw this thing away, I will.*

Which meant, he supposed – turning to watch Rose as she hauled on one of the braces to bring the sail into the wind – that a part of him actually did believe in the power of amulets and spirits, and to hell with what he'd been taught in the St Louis Academy for Boys. Hannibal, in the prow, spread his arms to the wind and declaimed passages from the *Odyssey* in Greek. He was as thoroughgoing a pagan as Rose was: and one could make a fairly good argument that God (or Zeus) had looked after *him*.

'Any sign we're being followed?' asked Rose, and Hannibal broke off mid-metaphor, fished in the pocket of his old-fashioned swallowtail coat for Rose's spyglass, and with it swept the wine-dark sea.

'*Roll on, thou deep and dark blue ocean – roll! Ten thousand fleets* . . . Nary a thing.' He held out the glass to her. '*There is a pleasure in the pathless woods, there is a rapture on the lonely shore* . . .'

'They might be watching us from the trees,' pointed out Rose.

'Unromantic woman. I trust you'll display greater delicacy of soul once we reach Havana.'

It had been agreed that upon arrival in Havana, Rose would take on the character of Hannibal's concubine – a slave about whose disappearance any man would raise a great fuss with the Spanish authorities – and January, that of his valet. For this purpose the fiddler had brought with him from town a pink gown belonging to January's sister Dominique – now safely packed in their single trunk – and enough money over and above their passage, donated by Dominique's protector Henri Viellard, to purchase in Havana such additional raiment as would further this illusion. He'd also brought along January's second-best jacket and the knee-breeches that January wore to play at the Opera, a costume that was also the mark of a servant's livery.

Thus attired, on Monday, the thirteenth of August, Rose and January followed their new 'master' ashore at the low-lying cluster of post-and-*bousillage* huts of La Balize at the mouth of the Mississippi – 'ashore' being a relative term, since the buildings were constructed on wooden piers and the so-called ground between them was a squishy mush barely distinguishable from the *flottants* and cattail beds that surrounded it. Duckboards defined a path from the wharves to a tavern, where an unshaven proprietor in shirtsleeves – the day was suffocatingly hot and steaming from recent rain – assured Hannibal that, yes, the *Triton* was due today . . .

'Or maybe tomorrow,' reported the fiddler, re-emerging on to the gallery where Rose and January waited with their slender luggage. 'Or possibly the day after. Though he assures me that he can put us all up for a dollar a head, or fifty cents if you and Benjamin don't mind sleeping on the gallery.'

'Does he charge extra for mosquito smudges?' January fanned ineffectually at the gnats that swarmed around his face.

'I suspect he does. We can but pray for a southerly wind.'

Hannibal retreated into the tavern again, to join a poker game that appeared to have been in session for decades. La Balize, within rock-throwing distance of a crumbling French fort, was the head-quarters of the little colony of pilots that made their living bringing ocean-going vessels through the shifting mazes of the river's mouth. From the tavern's gallery, January could see half a dozen grounded hulks in various stages of decomposition, wrecked on the shoals and snags that stretched north and south of the cluster of oak trees and huts. South-east lay open water; north-east, sheets of what looked like clear sailing mixed treacherously with submerged trees and half-drowned islets. Some distance in that direction lay what appeared to be two long, parallel white sand-spits, with a chalky-looking yellow-brown aisle between: the currently most usable mouth of the Mississippi.

God knew where it would be in three years' time.

Snaggly-haired women and children moved about among the huts on the (marginally) higher ground, feeding chickens, tending vegeta-bles, hanging clothes out to dry. Gulls circled, crying, over kitchen garbage; along the wharves, fishing boats, pirogues, and snub-nosed pilot boats rocked. It could have been the seventeenth century rather than the nineteenth. The marshes that bordered the Styx would not have seemed as desolate.

'I wouldn't like to be here in a hurricane,' Rose remarked.

January grinned and shook his head, but the smile was forced. The desolation of the place was a reminder that their lifeline was now as slender as that of the runaway slaves he periodically housed in the cellar of the house on Rue Esplanade. It wasn't simply a matter of dodging danger for a time. If they didn't solve this riddle of murderous pursuit, they would lose first that house and all they had – if they didn't lose their lives – and then the community that made life possible, as the combined strength of the slave-villages made it possible for each man, each woman, to go on.

If we have to flee New Orleans, what have we to offer that will let us survive in some other place?

What have I to sell that a thousand others aren't offering as well?

He was an excellent musician, he knew – but he knew also that New Yorkers or Philadelphians were as unlikely to be lavishing money on balls and music lessons as New Orleanians were, in these hard times.

He was a competent surgeon. But without some extraordinary technique or specialty that others did not have, what chance had a black man (who looked like a cotton-hand) in a white market?

This has to work.

We have to find who these people are, what their weakness is, and either treat with them . . . or destroy them.

Across the waters of the open bay to the south, sails appeared. Russian flags flew at a merchantman's three masts; a pilot and a couple of boatmen emerged from the tavern and made their way briskly down to the tow boats. Not long after that, a schooner appeared, seeming to float over the marshlands to the north, and another pilot went down, and January understood that this horrible, shabby, bug-ridden place was in fact the center of a good deal of activity, a good deal of the time.

Just after noon the *Triton* came into view, a sloop-rigged brig laden with furs, sacks of corn, and bales of sacking from Kentucky mills. January shook hands with Natchez Jim, who'd helped carry the carpet bags down to the pilot's boat. By the size of the tip Hannibal gave Jim, January guessed he'd put in a profitable few hours unobtrusively fleecing the pilots in the tavern.

'We can but trust that our friends Maddox, Killwoman and Conyngham from New Orleans aren't on-board,' remarked Hannibal – in Latin – as the boatmen set the sail toward the brig.

'In a way, I hope they are,' returned January, in the same tongue. 'At least then I wouldn't worry about them being back on Grand Isle, murdering Aramis and his family.' The Jefferson Parish sheriff had been alerted to guard the little plantation and scour the island for the killers, but January had met the man and had his doubts.

Rose put up a hand, to hold her tignon in place, the ribbons fluttering on her sleeves. It vexed her that she couldn't observe the actions of the crew in the rigging, but Hannibal was adamant that lovely and valuable concubines did *not* wear their spectacles in public. 'I was keeping an eye out behind us and didn't see them,' she agreed softly. 'But if they're not already ahead of us, you know they're following fast.'

Still, it was a relief to spend three days at sea – if one had to do so on a ship where slaves dossed down among the crew – secure in the knowledge that one didn't have to be looking constantly over one's shoulder. Rose, at least, got to share Hannibal's minuscule cabin and bunk. ('I'd put a sword blade between us, *amicus meus*, only, believe me, there isn't room for such a thing . . .') January grew tired – and bored – of the sailors' talk in the fo'c's'le, which centered almost exclusively on women, drink, and the shortcomings of the ship's officers, but he'd long ago learned to let casual jests about niggers slide off his shoulders, and at least there was nobody in the crew who took it on himself to grudge him hammock room. It angered him to hear Rose discussed in lustful detail, but he reminded himself it was only to be expected. She was supposed to be Hannibal's concubine, and to spring to her defense would only have announced that there was something else going on. He certainly had not the smallest flicker of suspicion that the fiddler was anything but a perfect gentleman, lying side-by-side in an extremely narrow bunk with her, and that, he supposed, was the definition of both friendship and love.

He was nevertheless very glad when the *Triton* glided between the low headlands, and past the twin white fortresses that guarded the walled city, and came at last – just before sunset on Friday – to the long line of wharves beneath the walls of Havana's artillery barracks.

The flag of the Queen Isabella the Second fluttered above the ramparts.

They were on Spanish soil.

The day's heat had broken. Wind soughed across the bay and swayed the palm trees that grew between the stucco houses, reminiscent of New Orleans when January first had seen that low-lying pastel town as a child of eight: a smell of drains and fish and flowers and the sea. Rose put on her spectacles and looked around her, her hazel-green eyes very bright. 'It's beautiful.'

She loved their son, January knew. There was no greater happiness, for either of them, than to hold him, to steady his tottering steps, to meet that solemn, worried gaze.

But he knew she missed her freedom. Not every day, but many days.

The brother she loved had been killed. Her son – and January himself, and Rose as well – were in danger of their lives: her surviving brother and his family also, for all they knew, despite the assurances from the sheriff of Jefferson Parish.

But he saw how her cheeks colored in the salt-spanked air, and the way her gaze devoured the dark-skinned market women selling mangoes, the beggar boys lounging on the steps that led up toward the cathedral square, the bright flocks of parrots in the trees.

The captain of the *Triton* – who over the past three days had contributed substantially to the exchequer of the expedition, by way of Hannibal's adeptness at the card table – had recommended lodgings for them in the Calle San Ignacio: ground-floor chambers around the courtyard of a well-off planter's town house, an arrangement January was familiar with from his visit to Mexico two years before. Since their position as servants was their sole defense against the slave-stealers who abounded in the old town, Rose was given a tiny chamber adjacent to Hannibal's, and January a cubbyhole in the building's attic, three flights up, above the grand rooms of the householders themselves. The valets of two other gentlemen staying on the premises were up there as well. A third gentleman, a coffee-broker from Virginia, had his valet sleep on a pallet across the doorway of his own room, the arrangement many old-fashioned Americans still preferred.

After bringing Hannibal his breakfast the following morning, shaving him and helping him dress ('Honestly, Benjamin, you show a real genius for this sort of thing . . .'), when the fiddler went off to call on the American consul, January made the acquaintance of the other valets, and of the servants of the Orrente household. Señor Villaregal, the Orrentes' butler, was Peninsular Spanish and considered everybody but his master's Peninsular Spanish valet and the German butler of the house next door beneath him – including his own master, who was Cuban-born Spanish Creole and clearly not of the *limpieza de sangre* required, in Señor Villaregal's opinion, for Good Society. But the houseboys and the men who worked in the stables were native Cubans, of varying permutations of African and Spanish descent, and had heard all about the slave revolt in Pinar del Río last April.

'That was bad business, brother.' Ilario the head groom accepted the cigarette January offered him and set down the brush he'd been wielding to knock street mud from the wheels of the household *volanta*. 'Bad business. And stupid, you know, because if you just run away into the mountains, you hook up with the other *cimarrones* up there, and most of the time they don't catch you.' He took a long, considering drag of smoke, as if judging the quality of the Virginia tobacco and finding it wanting – but tobacco is tobacco, when all was said and done. 'Burning out the Big Folks' house and killing them – what does that get you, eh? The soldiers come in, and everybody suffers.'

'It's the sugar planting.' Bernardino – the boy who fetched water for the horses and mucked out the stalls – leaned on his pitchfork. 'On a *cafetele*, you work all day, but it's gentle, you know? It's not savage. The coffee trees need shade, so they plant them among fruit trees, and you go about picking the beans with everybody in the village – women, children, friends – and everybody helps between their chores. But sugar, there's a time you have to get the crop in or else, and you go out and chop canes and drag fuel to the *ingenio* –' it took January a moment to identify the word as meaning both a sugar plantation and the sugar mill itself – 'and the work is ten times harder, in the heat of the sun, with a machete in your hand and ants and cane rats around your feet, until after dark by torchlight. And men get angry.' He spread his hands. 'Then the *jefe* beats you because you got to get finished before the cane rots, and the *patrón* says, "*We got to get more cane because the price this year isn't so good as last.*" Anywhere you hear about slaves rising up, it's an *ingenio*, not a *cafetele.*'

'And did they kill the *patrón*?' January asked, though he knew from the *National Intelligencer* article that he and his family had escaped.

'No, but they got the *jefe* – the overseer. He was the real problem, everyone says.' The groom carefully crushed out the cigarette stub on the brick pavement of the *traspatio* – the rear courtyard – and returned to his wheel cleaning. 'The *patrón* got away, as did the Americans that were staying with him. Which is a good thing, because if Americans had been killed there would have been trouble with the American government.'

'Do you know the woman who got them away? Ginette, I think she was called . . .'

Ilario shook his head. 'Ginette's her mother,' he said simply. 'She only came into our barrio a couple of times, when I was little, selling knives and scissors and things: things we have to buy from Spain, and they're no good and cost a fortune, and the British ones and the Americans ones are better and cheaper, you understand. Salomé – the daughter, the one who got the Americans away – comes in every couple of months, you never know when.'

January raised his brows. 'That's how she knew this Captain Loup de la Mare, then?'

The head groom grinned. 'Ah, ask me no questions, dear heart, and you'll hear no lies. Sal knows all of them.' He wet a clean rag in his bucket, gave the little carriage's brass lantern a brisk rub. '*And* the *marones* in the mountains. Why else you think nobody sees her, unless she wants to be seen?'

January assisted man and boy in wheeling the *volanta* back into the passageway – the *zagún* was the local word for it – that lay like a vestibule behind the massive main doors of the house. Like the town houses of New Orleans – which were in fact far more Spanish than French – the stairway to the private quarters of the family ascended from the *zagún*, and there were houses in Havana – as there were in Mexico City – in which the family carriage occupied one side of the downstairs salon, an arrangement preferable to permitting even the slightest possibility that a well-born lady would ever be put into the position of stepping down out of the carriage into the actual street.

In Havana, due to the heat, most of the wealthy lived primarily in their courtyards, unless it was pouring down rain, which was pretty much every afternoon at this season. The not-quite-so-wealthy who rented out the lower rooms spent most of their time on the open arcades above the courtyard, and at least in the Orrente establishment the cook, Anazuela, provided for the roomers as well, to her own profit and probably, January guessed, at her employers' expense.

From Ilario the head-groom, January also inquired about entertainment in the town (approximately a thousand taverns within walking distance of the Calle San Ignacio all hosted balls, of greater or lesser formality, pretty much every night), when confession was heard in the cathedral (daily – there was no church of any kind in the Barataria, and January felt like he hadn't bathed), and the danger from *rancheradores*, or slave-stealers (extreme). It would not do to inquire too closely into the affairs and whereabouts of Salomé

Saldaña, purveyor of smuggled goods and associate of runaway slaves.

'Evidently, there are three mountain ranges on the island,' reported Hannibal, when he encountered January in the cathedral square that evening. January had donned his livery to go to confession, the knee-breeches and short jacket, in addition to proclaiming to slave-stealers that someone would make a fuss if he disappeared, serving to mark him as someone who probably wasn't carrying any money. Beggars swarmed the streets. 'The Sierra Rosario around Pinar del Río, to the west of here, the Sierra Maestra south-east around Santiago, and the Escambray in the middle to create a pleasing, artistic effect. The American consul's secretary – a helpful young gentleman named Butler – assures me that there are practically no slaves hiding out there and if there were they would never do anything so ill-natured as to attack or burn a plantation—'

'Did he somehow happen to gain the impression that you were thinking of investing in such a thing?'

'If he did I have no idea how he could have conceived such a notion.' Hannibal gravely scanned the cathedral square for one of the mule-drawn hackney cabs that infrequently plied the streets. Infrequently, January had already deduced, because in general those wealthy enough to afford the cab fare were wealthy enough to own their own two-wheeled *volanta* and at least a mule to pull it. Those who couldn't walked, and put up with the beggars, who were not, he had thankfully observed, either as numerous nor as aggressive as they were in Mexico City. 'He also informed me that not only were there no escaped slaves in the mountains, but there were also no persons so ill-intentioned as to seek representation for Cuba in Spain's government – if you can call what's going on in Spain these days by such a term – or, God forbid, independence from Spain altogether, and there never have been. So it would be perfectly safe for me to swear allegiance to Spain and acquire a plantation here, should I wish to do so . . . Ah.'

He stepped to the edge of the shallow platform on which the cathedral stood – the plaza had, January recalled, begun its life under the Spanish name for *swamp* – and signaled a dilapidated chaise emerging from the Calle Empedrado. The driver ignored him and drew rein beside one of the arcades that rimmed two sides of the square: 'He could be a private coachman,' January warned as Hannibal moved down the steps toward the man.

'I refuse to believe even the most poverty-stricken pettifogger in town would own an animal that sorry,' retorted the fiddler, with a gesture toward the dejected mule between the shafts. 'And unless you wish to act as a bully-boy keeping the mendicants at bay all the way back to our rooms, I suggest you help me in heading him off. At least there's no law here against you sharing the vehicle with me . . .'

Hannibal had reached the bottom of the steps and advanced about a yard toward the chaise when a man emerged from the arcade. January identified his clothing as a gentleman's – short Mexican-style jacket, black silk cravat – while the man himself had a native Cubaño's swarthy complexion, in the instant before three soldiers in the red-and-blue uniforms of the Spanish forces stepped from the shadows at each end of the colonnade and another two – with a crimson-breeched officer – turned from where they had been loitering among the passers-by around a coffee stand. A water carrier nearby shouted, 'Jucos, run!' and the well-dressed Cubaño made a dash for the cab.

It was only a matter of a few yards, but one of the soldiers brought up his rifle, and the driver, panicking, lashed his mule and fled – an act that did him little good, as the soldier fired after him and, amaz-ingly, hit him. The driver toppled from his high seat and screamed as the cab's iron-tyred wheel went over his leg, but nobody was paying attention. The Cubaño Jucos tried to dodge back into the colonnade, and the soldiers surrounded him, seized him by the arms and, though Jucos threw up his hands in surrender, knocked him to the pavement and began to systematically beat him with their rifle butts.

January was already down the steps and headed for the downed cab-driver, who was clutching his broken leg and sobbing. A market woman grabbed January's arm, pulled him back. 'You want to go to jail too, brother?'

Hannibal, who stood within a few feet of the driver, had been dragged back when he likewise made a move toward him.

January said, 'For what?' But a lifetime of instinct rose up in him, and there was no reason to think that slave-dealers didn't pay regular visits to the jails of Havana – as they did to those of New Orleans and of Washington City – in search of 'runaways' who could then be sold.

The square was clearing out, as if every building in it were about to burst into flames. Hannibal and January were hustled back with the crowd into the colonnade opposite: 'The man's a *mambí* – a seditionist,' said the market woman. 'A troublemaker, speaking against the King.'

The soldiers picked up their victim by his arms and legs, his head lolling, blood stringing from his pulped face, and carried him away in the direction of the Plaza de Armas. The driver lay where he'd fallen, and as soon as the soldiers were out of sight, market women, water sellers, servants, beggars hurried to him. January followed, digging in his pockets and wondering what he could use to get the bullet out. 'You're not going to help him?' The elderly market woman caught his arm again and jerked her head at the men clustering around the driver. 'One of them could be a police spy.'

A couple of boys had caught the mule – it had smashed the cab into the side of the cathedral's platform – and men were helping the driver inside. January said, 'I can help, I'm a surgeon,' but they looked at him doubtfully.

A man in a drover's rough jacket and boots stepped in front of him. 'Many thanks, señor, but he is best in the care of his family.'

'That's ridiculous. His leg is fractured, and he has a bullet in him . . .'

'It will be taken care of.'

Someone mounted what remained of the cab's box and took the reins. A man whose *guayabera* smelled of fish took January's arm, said, 'A man's friends and family are his best care, *surgeon*.' And there was a glint in his dark eyes that told January that his claim wasn't believed.

Gently, Hannibal murmured in Latin, 'I think they think *you're* a police spy, *amicus meus*.'

January stepped back. The cab was already gone.

Beggars followed them back to the Calle San Ignacio, but none importuned them for coin.

TWELVE

'**A**ccording to the helpful Mr Butler,' said Hannibal, when the account of these events had been related to Rose back in the quiet of their courtyard on the Calle San Ignacio, 'in addition to those who wish to establish Cuba as an independent nation, there is an even larger segment of the population – whom I don't imagine are the sort of people who get beaten up by soldiers in marketplaces – who have been trying to open negotiations with the United States to get the island annexed as the twenty-seventh state. These are mostly the owners of plantations, who naturally find they have a great deal in common with the owners of American plantations . . .'

'They will until it occurs to the plantation-owning Congressmen that their Cuban counterparts are all Catholics.' January set down the tray he'd fetched from the kitchen in the *traspatio*: chicken, fried plantains, and *Moros y Cristianos* – black beans, white rice. In addition to cooking for those who rented chambers, Madame Anazuela appeared ready to serve anyone who cared to come in off the street at dinner time, at rough trestles set up by her daughters in the courtyard.

'I don't expect he – or they – think anyone is any more serious about their faith than the Americans are,' remarked Rose. Hannibal's visit to the consulate having culminated in an invitation to attend a soirée that evening at the Marquesa de Lanabanilla's town palace, she had already put up her hair in an elegant chignon, and Dominique's borrowed garnets glinted in her ears. 'Americans turn Catholic all the time and become Mexican citizens in order to receive land grants without the slightest intention of even paying lip service—'

'It was a serious mistake to disband the Inquisition.' Hannibal shook his head sadly and took the pottery jug from the tray to pour coffee for all of them, followed by a dish of extremely dark muscovado sugar. 'I suspect that milk came out of a goat rather than a cow, but let us not be prejudiced. God made goats as well as cows – on an off-day, admittedly – and they're perfectly amiable creatures

'. . . I gather, however, that Cuban planters would prefer to deal with American planters rather than the Regent of Spain.'

The afternoon's rainfall had cleared the air. Though the courtyard's high walls sheltered it from the sea breezes, Havana's harbor – and the closeness of the Caribbean – prevented the city from turning into the Turkish bath that New Orleans did in the wake of the afternoon rain. On the second-floor gallery that circled the courtyard, maids and valets scurried back and forth with pots of pomade, fresh shirts, and polished shoes, and Ilario and Bernardino brought the team of black horses around to the *zagún* to harness them to the *volanta*.

January wondered whether his errant wife and her *soi-disant* protector were going to come face-to-face with their landlords at the Marquesa's soirée, and if anyone would care. He hoped not: he'd already bribed Ilario to return with the carriage after dropping off the Orrentes wherever they were going, to carry Hannibal and Rose to their destination. *A good thing Rose's mother spent all those years trying to educate her daughter in the graces of a plaçée after all . . .*

'And anything's better than total independence,' he said thoughtfully. 'Since the sugar-planters can't guarantee where the franchise line would be drawn. The people who actually fight for freedom from Spain would be small farmers and town artisans – people who have no stake in slavery . . . Like poor Señor Jucos, according to Ilario. They'd probably have to free and enlist slaves to help them, in order to have enough manpower to win.'

'Can't have that.' Rose spread her napkin across her pink silk lap.

'Be that as it may,' said Hannibal, 'according to Mr Butler, there exists, in the Santiago province, an *ingenio* called Hispaniola, owned by one Don Demetrio Gonzago. Since Mr Butler himself has only been in Havana a few years, he was unable to tell me if this Hispaniola had anything to do with the plantation of the same name in America, or with the de Gericault family . . . of whom I am a relative, by the way,' he added. 'Seeking information about the rumor that I was in fact related to the Comte de Caillot . . .'

'Considering what's happened to other relatives of the de Gericaults,' warned January, 'I'd be careful how many people you told that tale to.'

'*Id cum veritas dicere.*' Hannibal smoothed his graying mustache.

'But even the most bloodthirsty of American Democrats secretly nurses awe at the glitter that cloaked the *Ancien Régime,* particularly once revolutionists revealed themselves to be very common indeed. According to Butler, the Gonzago family has owned land in the Cauto Valley since 1742, and he has promised to introduce me to the appropriate people at the Palacio tomorrow to learn more about where and when Hispaniola came into Gonzago's possession, and who owned it before. More can be learned,' he added apologetically, 'at the soirée tonight . . . one reason for my acceptance of the invitation.'

'I'm perfectly resigned,' returned January, in his most martyred tones, 'to an evening playing solitaire. Or maybe going out to a *baile* at the local tavern with Anazuela—'

Rose slapped him with her napkin.

'It would serve you right,' remarked Hannibal. 'I have it from Ilario that she ate her last three husbands alive, like a mantis, leaving only their watch chains and shoes.'

In the event, January was forced to neither of these expedients for the evening. When Rose departed – resplendent in Dominique's second-best ball-gown ('Hannibal promises to buy me another tomorrow . . .' 'My seconds will be waiting when you get back from shopping, Mr Sefton.') – in the Orrentes' borrowed *volanta*, January and the valet of Mr Montrose of Virginia – William – walked down to the local tavern that Ilario had recommended and spent a quiet evening playing dominoes and listening to local gossip. The *mambí* Jucos – Damaso Juscobal, a journalist whose newspaper had been shut down by the government the previous year – was dead, though whether he had been shot while trying to escape, or had attacked his guards with such ferocity that they had been forced to kill him in self-defense, wasn't clear from official accounts. January told William about it, and some of the other men there – a few of whom knew a little English – came over to listen and to ask for the story in Spanish.

'What happened to the cab driver?' January asked one of them when he had done. 'He seemed badly hurt.'

The men glanced at one another, but one of them replied, 'He's been taken out of town, dear brother.' Like most Cubans he used the informal pronouns, and terms of affection, more than a Mexican and certainly more than a Frenchman would have, and the street-Spanish of Havana was markedly different from that of Mexico City or New Orleans. 'One cannot be too careful, you understand. Don't worry yourself. His mother is a *Santera*, an *Oliate*. She will cleanse his wounds and wash his head, and keep him safe in the forest.'

'Good,' said January. 'I'm glad.' And, when William protested about heathen practices: 'My sister is a *mambo*. She learned the ways of herbs and healing from the women who taught her, and to my mind they're better than some of the muck regular doctors come up with.'

They walked back to the Calle San Ignacio as the cathedral bells tolled midnight – early, for Havana, but William said that he wasn't supposed to be out and Marse Charles would 'take on' if he came home and his valet wasn't there. So January took a couple of candles out to the courtyard – the night was exquisitely warm – and sat at the little table where they'd eaten supper, reading the *Journal of the Royal Society of Medicine* until Hannibal and Rose returned.

'I met a woman in the tavern, fell in love, and married her,' reported January, closing the borrowed pages. Joaquin – valet to another of the courtyard's inhabitants, Dr Schlagmueller – had told him that his master, one of the most fashionable physicians in the town, was incapable of understanding a word of it. 'I hope you don't mind?'

Rose assumed an expression worthy of Sarah Siddons at her most tragic, put a hand to her forehead, and collapsed into January's arms.

'Now see what you've done,' said Hannibal mildly, and he felt the side of January's coffee pot to see if the contents were still drinkable. 'And me without smelling salts.' The cook's youngest daughter appeared momentarily in the archway that led to the *traspatio*, then darted off, to fetch two more cups.

Rose sat up on January's knee. 'I have a good mind not to tell you about Don Demetrio.'

'My new wife was tragically run over by a railway train.'

'That's better.' She fished her spectacles from her reticule. 'Hispaniola Plantation once belonged to Great-Granpère Absalon, all right. The Condessa de Agramonte remembered him, but the plantation itself lies so far from Havana – five days by sea at this season of the year, and well over a week by land – that he wasn't well known here.'

'He had a reputation as a philanthropist and a scholar,' added Hannibal, and he gave the returning girl – with her two gold-rimmed coffee-cups – a quarter of a silver reale. 'In Cuba, I'm not sure how they'd identify a scholar: someone who can make it through a newspaper unaided, I think.'

'He was one of the first sugar-planters in the east of the island,' said Rose, 'and went about it very scientifically. He had only one son, my informant said – of course, Granmère was already married and living on Hispaniola Grand Isle – Guibert, whom the Condessa recalls as exceedingly handsome. Both Absalon's name and Guibert's came up in discussions of possible matrimony, and the Condessa refused to consider either on the grounds that she didn't want to go to the other end of the island and never see her family and friends again, a position with which I can sympathize, even if Absalon weren't in his sixties at the time. Guibert was twenty-one. She remembers there was a huge party for his coming-of-age.'

'No other children in the household?'

'Not that anyone recalled. Upon the expulsion of the French, the plantation was sold to the Vizconde de Contramaestre, who owned – and still owns – most of the Cauto Valley. Don Demetrio Gonzago is the Vizconde's nephew.'

'I suspect,' said Hannibal, 'that we'll have more luck speaking to this Don Demetrio than we would trying to track down Salomé the Smugglers' Friend. Particularly since, as you pointed out, I have announced to all Havana that relatives of the de Gericaults are at large and asking questions. Nobody at the soirée seized me by the hand and cried out, "*But your long-lost cousins are here in this very room, asking about the de Gericaults and the Crimson Angel—!*"'

'I'd have given a lot to see your face if they had,' put in Rose.

'We'd have fought our way out,' retorted Hannibal, 'in the best tradition of Dumas . . . But like Time's Wingèd Chariot, I cannot help hearing their footfalls at our backs. 'T'were the better part of valor, as our friend Lieutenant Shaw would say, to absquatulate without loss of time. At least in the wilds of Santiago we'll have a better chance of seeing them coming.'

'If they're not there before us,' said January thoughtfully. 'The helpful Mr Butler made no mention of anyone asking after the de Gericaults before me.'

January grunted. Beautiful as Havana was – and much as he longed to explore those narrow streets with Rose – he heartily agreed with Hannibal. As the hunted, all they could do for the moment was to keep ahead of the hunters. Moreover, in the course of the evening, the valet William had told him of three separate occasions on which attempts had been made by *rancheradores* to corner him alone: 'I swear it, Ben, sometimes I think they're watching this house for me!' One reason William – who seldom left the courtyard even when his master wasn't expected back for hours – had been so glad to go to the Posada Caballero that evening was because the place had been vouched for by Ilario as relatively safe, and because he would be with another black man who spoke Spanish.

Walking back, even the hundred yards or so from the district along the canal, January had been deeply conscious of the narrow blackness of the streets around them, and had been careful to keep to those ways where lights still fell from the windows above.

THIRTEEN

After forcing Hannibal – with equal applications of black coffee and threats of violence – from bed shortly before noon the following day, January took Rose, and a portion of the fiddler's winnings of the previous evening, and went to the harbor to look for passage to Santiago while Hannibal paid a call on the colonial archives. Since giving up liquor and opium, Hannibal's card-playing had improved, considerably aided by the fact that since giving up liquor and opium, the fiddler was frequently the only sober person at any given gaming table. Every social occasion in Cuba or anywhere else included a card room, with the exception of the house parties of the Americans in New Orleans ('Why is it considered Christian not to have a good time?'), so Hannibal had spent the previous evening at the Marquesa's putting a lifetime of dissipation to good use.

At early Mass that morning, January had encountered a number of men he'd met at the Posada Caballero on the previous evening, and a number of them had recommended the small coastal trader *Santana*. Its captain, Serafin Castallanos, was honest, and plied these waters regularly, and when January booked passage 'for my master and myself' he was favorably impressed with the man. On the way back from the harbor, he and Rose stopped at a shop in the Calle San Pedro which dealt in second-hand clothing, and though most of the frocks there had been handed down from mistress to maidservants and worn to dilapidation, Rose found three that not only fit her, but that would also not contradict her claims to be the mistress of a reasonably well-off gentleman related (possibly) to the Comte de Caillot.

'But I'll continue to wear what I have until we set sail,' she decided as the shop-boy raced away to find a hack for them. 'The last thing I need is to be confronted in the street by that yellow silk shawl's former owner.'

Across the street, January mentally identified two men watching them, of the rough bully-boy type he guessed were *rancheradores*. At least, he reflected dourly, there was no law in Havana against black persons taking cabs.

Back at the Calle San Ignacio they found Hannibal in the court-yard. 'A brief entr'acte,' the fiddler explained, 'between making free among the colonial land records in the Palacio de Capitan-General, and paying for the privilege by having dinner with the Archivist, whom I understand to be one of the dullest men on the island. He was assistant to the head of the Spanish College of Heralds under King Charles back before the days of Napoleon, and the only way I could obtain assistance in tracking down the de Gericault family here in Cuba was to promise my fullest attention to him this evening, on the fascinating subject of the precise relationships between the Cordoba-Figueroa y Moncado family and the Perez de Barrada branch of the Condes de Empúries, and similar enthralling topics.' He dropped a lump of muscovado sugar in a cup of Anazuela's coffee. He was in shirtsleeves in the blistering heat, his long hair pinned up with a lady's comb, and around them the courtyard was somnolent: the hour of siesta was at hand.

January removed his hat and bowed low. 'Such self-immolation on the altar of duty renders me speechless.'

'*Dulce et decorum est pro patria mori* bore,' Hannibal punned. 'An hour and a half of listening to the Conde de Montevierdo – the Archivist insists upon the title, though I think he was stripped of it by the Bonapartes, and no wonder – would render you not only speechless, but numb and blind as well. I was irresistibly reminded of those Roman nobles who faked their own deaths in order to be carried out of the Emperor Nero's mandatory recitals upon the lyre. But no matter! To serve my friends is the whole of my aim in life, not counting the cost—'

'Benjamin's already said thank you,' pointed out Rose heartlessly, and Hannibal grinned. 'What did you learn for your trouble?'

'Not a great deal beyond what gossip unearthed last night. No record of children by either mistress – neither of whom seem to have made the voyage from Saint-Domingue with Grandpa. A *plaçée* in Santiago – at least a woman in Santiago to whom he gave a small house and a hundred and twenty dollars a month. Two sons and a daughter: one son died in 1820, and the other, Alejandro, would be thirty-two now and the daughter thirty – Felicia is her name. God knows where they are now. But obviously de Gericault made no effort to bring any of them to the mainland with him, and in 1811 Felicia and Alejandro's mama was given *another* house, also in Santiago, by a planter named Zapata, so she clearly wasn't spending all her nights weeping into her pillow. She died in 1834.'

He flipped a page in the much-battered shagreen notebook he'd pulled from his pocket. Torn-off fragments of notepaper and scented billets-doux fluttered like petals to the rough wooden table. 'As that idiot Madame de Agramonte informed Rose last night, de Gericault and his son came seldom into Havana, but nothing is known against them. They were expelled strictly on the grounds of an unfashionable nationality when Napoleon foisted his older brother on to the throne of Spain.'

January picked up one of the loose notes. Creased, as if it had been folded small, it contained only the words '*Tonight, 1. Aphrodite statue in garden*' in Spanish, in a woman's rather ill-formed hand. January rolled his eyes as he handed it back. 'I hope you'll remember that the tide turns at four and we need to be on the *Santana* by then?'

Hannibal glanced at the note. 'This was last night's.'

'What about the old blind man?' asked Rose, to forestall January's clearly-upcoming remark on his friend's love life. 'The evil Dr Maudit? Nobody I spoke to last night seemed to have heard of him.'

'Opinion is divided,' said Hannibal. 'And no official *dramatis personae* of the de Gericault household exists in the records. A report dated March of 1809 mentions the departure of Absalon de Gericault, planter and widower, and Guibert de Gericault, his son, along with a number of slaves. A planter named de Herredia at the gambling table last night seemed to recall his own mother telling him about the family, and he rather thought she'd said Grandpa Absalon's wicked cousin the Comte de Caillot lived with them for a time, corroborating Mammy Zett's story. She seemed to think

Grandpa Absalon murdered the Comte, but others contend the Evil Dr Maudit was in reality a harmless old man who had been Amalie de Gericault's personal physician.'

'A Frenchman?' January frowned, with a momentary sensation of having his sleeve snagged by a rose thorn. A recollection . . .

'Presumably, though his name might not actually have been Maudit. *Accursed* sounds a little melodramatic to have occurred naturally. I expect, if Madame's health was poor, de Gericault was wealthy enough to attach a man to keep her going, particularly if he hoped to get his hooks into one of the family titles for his son. Cap Francais was by all accounts a fairly sophisticated place before the rebellion, where one could obtain the latest Paris fashions and the latest Paris politics.'

'Except that, unlike the situation in Paris, one man in twenty literally held the power of life and death over the other nineteen.' January spoke softly, anger over the myth of the tropical paradise drawing his mind aside from that tugging sense of something important, like a half-remembered dream . . .

It had been in Paris, whatever it was.

Something he'd heard? Something he'd said?

To whom? Why?

'One man in twenty could, with very little trouble, rape a woman – or a child, boy or girl – whenever or however he wanted to do so. Could have a man, or a woman, or a child for that matter, killed, just by saying, "That man struck me," or, "That woman tried to put poison into my food . . ."' Mammy Zett's words came back to him, and the terrors of his own childhood. 'The *grands blancs* – the rich whites – didn't know what it was to open their own windows, to wash their own clothing or pick it up off the floor if they dropped it. Every slave in their households was desperate to be favored by them, pandered to them, tried to make himself or herself indispensable, to avoid being passed along to something worse.'

But as he spoke he wondered what had brought back the memory of that stifling loft he'd lived in, before he'd met his beautiful Ayasha in Paris. Before he'd turned his face from the care of the sick and the injured . . .

'And if you don't think men of wealth and social position in Paris couldn't do precisely the same thing to the perfectly white poor who live in the city – both before and after 1789 –' the lift of Hannibal's eyebrows carried a whole ladder of parallel wrinkles up his forehead – 'you clearly never spent much time visiting the law courts there, or talking to people who'd been in its prisons.'

Hannibal finished his coffee, and rose. The sun had past its zenith, but heat transformed the courtyard into a crucible of molten gold. Beyond the gate, the street was silent. 'And so to bed, to ready myself for the unbearable jollities of the night. My beautiful one . . .' He took Rose's hand. 'Can I by any means persuade you to accompany me to the *palacio* of the Conde de Montevierdo the Excruciating this evening, to keep me from running mad with boredom? He has assured me that his wife is a spritely young minx of sixty, given to washing the feet of the poor and investigating the morals of indigent women, and she would be most pleased to make the acquaintance of any companion I should choose to bring—'

'Not a *café-crème plaçée*, I'll wager,' returned Rose primly.

'I shall introduce you as an Italian widow whom I encountered at the consulate.'

'You shall have no opportunity to do anything of the kind. We were at sea for a week and in Havana for two days, and I haven't spent more than a few peaceful hours in the company of my husband since we left Louisiana . . . and part of *that* time we were hiding from assassins in a cane field.' She put her hand over January's, and her eyes met his with that quicksilver smile. 'I must and will spend an evening as a wife.'

'*πάθει μάθος*. It is by suffering that one learns.' Hannibal handed January his notebook and disappeared into the cobalt shadows of his doorway. January thumbed the scraps of notepaper and the jotted memoranda. There were three more love-notes, besides the one from the previous evening; Hannibal re-emerged from his room like a dilapidated squirrel from its hole, plucked them from January's fingers, sorted through them for the one that said '*North-east corner of the square, midnight – M*', and thrust it in his pocket.

'Just as well we're sailing before dawn,' sighed January as his friend disappeared once more into the gloom of his chamber. 'The last thing we need is an irate husband demanding satisfaction. And I,' he added as he led Rose to the servants' stair that ascended to his own stifling cubbyhole, 'will cease to be an irate husband once *I* have achieved satisfaction – and given it, I hope and trust.'

They anchored in the shelter of Guadiana Bay the first night, after a day of sailing which began with Hannibal scampering down the wharves in the pre-dawn darkness with his boots in his hand and smudges of rouge on his shirt, to spring aboard as the tide turned. The second evening, with the sun like spilled treasure on the waters and the green mountains rising above the palm-fringed shore, they put in at the Isle of Pines; the third they spent in the small bay at Trinidad, the hub of the sugar plantations along the lush San Luis Valley. The fourth day they skimmed to the west of the long archipelago called the Gardens of the Queen, tiny islets separated from Cuba's shore by twenty miles of shallow, sparkling water . . .

'And crawling with smugglers,' added Captain Castallanos, when Rose and January stood mid-afternoon by the rail of the little sloop to admire those low green benches scattered like floating carpets on the turquoise glitter of the waves. 'All these islands give the *rancheradores* a perfect hiding-place from the British navy – they're the ones who're really trying to stamp out the trade – and give smugglers hideouts from the Spanish authorities in Havana.'

Smoke from his brown cigarette trickled into the following wind.

'Most of the American dealers come into Manzanillo rather than Havana, to arrange cargoes into the Barataria. In Havana the liquor's better –' he grinned with his white teeth – 'but you never can tell whether the man you're dealing with is actually working for the government. In Manzanillo you can be sure . . . and the liquor's not that bad.'

'Remind me,' said January, 'not to go ashore in Manzanillo. You've been around these islands,' he added. 'Have you ever heard of a woman named Salomé Saldaña?'

'Salomé, sure.' The brown eyes flicked to Olympe's *gris-gris* that January wore around his neck. 'You a friend of hers, my brother?'

'I was a friend of her mother's,' said Rose. 'Her mother came to Louisiana many years ago, looking for – I think – Salomé's daughter—'

Sadness and anger darkened the man's eyes. 'Siney,' he said. 'Mélusina.'

'Did she ever find her?'

He shook his head, a small gesture. 'I had the privilege of slitting open the guts of the man who took her,' he said quietly, 'and leaving him to die in an alley in Trinidad . . . But no. Ginette never found her.'

At the helm, the pilot called out something to one of the men in the rigging; sunlight flashed on the sea. The water here was so clear that January could see the pale forms of the sharks that followed the ship, dozens of them, sinister triangular dorsal-fins cutting the waves.

'Would she be in these parts?'

'Like you, my beautiful sister,' Castallanos said, 'she don't go into Manzanillo. Only if she has business to transact with one of the smugglers, or . . .' He hesitated. 'Or with somebody else. Mostly she keeps to the mountains, and she keeps on the move.'

'And did she ever speak to you,' asked January, 'about her mother making a journey to Haiti with an old blind white man? This would be just before or just after the French were expelled.'

'Ah, I was just a gleam in my mama's eye then.' January could tell the man was lying, but he did it smoothly and well. '*Mambo* Ginette kept quiet in her home and didn't travel much – except that one time, to Louisiana, to seek for her granddaughter. But when she came home, she dropped out of sight again.'

'Hiding?' It passed through January's mind that whatever information Jeoffrey Vitrac had had in that yellow envelope about Salomé Saldana's whereabouts, their pursuers now knew.

The dark eyes cut sidelong to him. 'In this country,' returned Castallanos, 'if you're *Negro*, or close to it, you're always hiding from someone.'

Nevertheless, the *Santana* put in at Manzanillo on Thursday night, and January and Rose stayed on-board and out of sight, while Hannibal went ashore with the captain for a little discreet card-playing and hobnobbery with the Brotherhood of the Coasts. Castallanos traded goods he shouldn't have been selling for things that were loaded in the corners of the hold and covered with tarpaulins: tobacco, coffee, and rum free of Spanish trade regulations or American or British duties. Both men came back full of news about who was bringing in Africans from Dahomey and selling them to Americans – in defiance of US law – to be resold at the big smuggler-depots in the swamps outside New Orleans, and who was running in weapons and gunpowder and the writings of the exiled Padre Varela to the Cuban Suns of Liberty.

Running along the edge of the north-west winds, the *Santana* left the swampy coast and swung wide to avoid the treacherous shallows of the bay of Guacanayabo, the Sierra Maestra rising before them, straight out of the water like an emerald wall. 'Will we be safe in Santiago?' January asked, when they rounded the mountain tip of the island, set their course straight east into warm gray squalls and the smell of a hurricane somewhere at sea.

'Compared to the French Town in New Orleans? No.' The captain raised one mobile eyebrow at January's livery of knee-breeches and tailed jacket. 'Compared to Manzanillo or Havana?' He shrugged. 'You watch your back and you keep close to that "master" of yours . . . and you're safe as any black man on this island. There's no American consul in Santiago,' he added, turning to Hannibal. 'But you take rooms at the Fonda Velasquez on the Plaza des Armas, and you'll meet pretty much everyone in town in the gambling rooms. Most of the planters from the Cauto Valley have town houses in Santiago rather than Manzanillo – there's fewer mosquitoes, and the water's better. You'll be able to meet Don Demetrio there at this season of the year. Ask old Rosario the innkeeper to introduce you. It's perfectly respectable. But watch out you don't win too much off him at cards,' he added, shaking his finger at the fiddler. 'He's a bad loser.'

Hannibal raised his brows in shocked dismay. '*I*? I have no control over the fall of the cards.'

Castallanos sniffed. 'And if Don Demetrio invites you to his *ingenio*,' he added, 'which he doubtless will, since Santiago is about as interesting as stale bread without oil, stay away from his wife. Her parents married her to him to keep her out of trouble, and he's like an insane Turk if any man so much as looks at her. Other than that, he's a good host and he's got a good cook. But if you even get to see her, don't kiss her hand.'

Dressed in his best waistcoat (courtesy of the second-hand shop in Havana) and with his long hair tied back in an old-fashioned queue, Hannibal stepped ashore in the velvety torchlit blackness with the stylishly-gowned Rose clinging to his arm: she'd put off her spectacles again and couldn't see a thing. January arranged for the luggage to be transported to the Fonda Velasquez before following them up the hill – Santiago seemed to be all hills – to the Plaza des Armas. Entirely ringed in a wall of mountains, the long bay seemed to trap the heat of the day, but even so, the place was, as Castallanos had said, drier and more comfortable than Manzanillo.

This being Cuba, of course, even at eleven at night – which it was by the time January reached the Plaza – candlelight streamed from every door and window, guitars and fiddles wove their music to the clacking of heels on tiled floors, and market women in bright colors still strolled the steep ways with baskets of fruit, shrimp, or pralines on their heads. Both the cathedral and the Fonda were illuminated like ballrooms, as were, indeed, half a dozen other houses around the square. When January entered from the long colonnade, the downstairs salon was filled with the rattle of dominoes, the smoke of cigars, and the leisured music of voices, and Hannibal was already deep in conversation with the innkeeper.

Yes, of course there was room for the gracious señor and his servants, immediately, right away. 'Téo! Fetch in the luggage of the gracious señor! This is your manservant? Excellent! By the gracious señor's speech he is English?'

'My father was English,' said Hannibal. 'My mother was French – and it is in quest of my mother's family that I have come to Cuba, in fact. My mother's name was de Gericault – you know it?'

The man's whole face brightened with recognition. '*Naturalmente*, my dear brother! At one time my uncle was tailor to Don Absalon!'

'I know very little of the family,' explained the fiddler, with an extremely convincing air of diffidence, 'my mother having been a sort of poor relation in France who became estranged from the Comte de Caillot . . . But chance has brought me to this part of the world, and chance has provided me with word that this was in fact their home.'

'*Por supuesto*! Think of that! Don Demetrio—!' The innkeeper put an arm around Hannibal's shoulder and tugged him across to a table near the open French doors where a small group of men sat. Well-dressed men, January observed, following with quiet respect in their wake. Linen suits in the close-fitting Spanish style, short jackets, many of them as fair-haired as Frenchmen or Germans. *Criollos*, Spanish Creoles, like the Spanish Creoles still to be found in the French Town or in Mexico. Tributes to the Spanish tradition of *limpieza de sangre*, with the blood of the conquistadores still pure in their veins though their families hadn't lived in Spain for fifteen generations.

'Don Demetrio!' cried the innkeeper again, and a man looked up. Big-shouldered, sturdy and square-faced, the lines around his eyes proclaiming him to be a dozen years older than January, but his hair still the crisp brown of a younger man's. 'Here is Señor Sefton of England, that is related to old Don Absalon de Gericault!'

'Don Absalon?' Don Demetrio Gonzago leaped to his feet and caught Hannibal in a breathtaking embrace. 'In truth? But I knew Don Absalon well, señor! His son Guibert and I were raised together. Guibert was my dearest friend.'

FOURTEEN

hat is it that I remember?
January looked around him at the forest on both sides of the road, the shabby little *bohios* that surrounded the outskirts of Santiago, rough walls and roofs of thatch. Women in faded skirts cooked over open fires like the women in the quarters back home. The morning's heat was already brutal, trapped by the thick foliage. Ahead of him, Don Demetrio – who had remained in town last night, in order to conduct his guests personally back to the *ingenio* called Hispaniola – gestured as he spoke; January touched his borrowed horse's flank, moved closer to listen.

But that sense of recalling something – something he'd heard or said or thought in France – returned, stronger than before.

Something about Saint-Domingue.

Something about Haiti.

Something that had almost surfaced when Hannibal had spoken of Amalie de Gericault and her tame physician whom the slaves called Dr Maudit.

Something that at the time had turned him almost sick with rage and shock.

I'd never heard of these people then . . .

Had I?

'Amalie's brother, Neron de Gericault – yes, Neron was her brother – did indeed come to live with his cousin at Hispaniola, the year after old Absalon settled there,' the planter was saying, dividing his warm smile between Hannibal and Rose. 'He was half-mad by then and a complete nuisance. He insisted on being addressed as the Comte de Caillot, and in his final illness, indeed, he thought he was back in France, with servants to do his every wish and peasants to step out of the road and pull off their caps as he and his family rode by. Poor man, and no wonder: he was in England when the troubles started in France, and his wife and his young sons were arrested. He spent three years in London trying to get them out, and in the end word came to him that they were in the prison of La Force when the mob broke its doors and massacred the prisoners in the courtyard. He was destitute by then, and came to Cuba because he had nowhere else to go. I remember he would fly into rages and accuse Don Absalon of murdering his sister. It upset Guibert very much.'

'I understand Madame Amalie died in childbed?'

Don Demetrio sighed. 'She was always . . . brittle. This is what Guibert told me. That whole side of the family was. Such a contrast with a man like Don Absalon, a lion who never tired. Her megrims and crotchets drove him mad, his valet told my uncle's coachman . . .'

'Could her brother have meant that?' asked Rose diffidently. 'That Guibert's birth was too much for her frame to bear?'

'Perhaps. Guibert was a big boy, handsome and strong as a hero, even at six. Often when a woman dies in childbirth, the father will take against the child, but Guibert was absolutely the apple of his father's eye. But he had a loathing of the deformed and the weak, and had nothing but contempt for his daughter Oliva, who like her mother suffered from a weak back and a deformed pelvis and could not perform the duties of a plantation wife.'

Rose looked as if she would protest that her granmère had made a home for her husband – and borne him children – in Louisiana, weak back or not, but closed her mouth, as if remembering that she was no more than Hannibal's concubine. She shifted the angle of her pink-and-white parasol and tried to look bored.

'If Don Absalon hated weakness,' inquired Hannibal, 'what possessed him to marry a woman who spent all her time on a chaise longue with a personal physician in attendance?'

'Well, Don Absalon originally hired old Dr Maurir to cure her, you see.' Don Demetrio nudged his horse to the edge of the trail to let a line of charcoal-burners pass, leading laden donkeys and black with the soot of their trade. They raised cheerful hands in greeting to the planter, who bowed a little in his saddle and called out, asking after his uncle and cousins: 'My uncle's men, you understand,' he explained. 'The Vizconde. My family has planted coffee in the valley since 1720, though my uncle, like most of our neighbors nowadays, is turning to sugar-planting. When Don

Absalon first came there was a good deal of talk that sugar-planting was not the province of a gentleman, as a *cafetele* is, not to speak of requiring a far greater number of slaves. People were very nervous about blacks, in 1791 . . . as, indeed, still they are. Don Absalon made his fortune, and had the last laugh, on them and on Cousin Neron. But even with all his money, to the end of poor Neron's life, Don Absalon tried to force him to sign over to him the de Gericault title and the lands – lands that had been confiscated by the revolutionary government and a title that no longer existed! – in return for a roof over his head. He was absolutely mad on the subject of his "birthright".'

'And did he sign?' Rose leaned a little from her saddle as the horses continued up the pass. 'His sons, I believe you said, were dead? An infamous thing to have done to the poor old man!'

'He never lost hope that one of his boys survived.' The planter sighed, distressed at the tale of those two old men, squabbling viciously over words in the ruin of their world. 'He would not disinherit him, he said. Poor Guibert went to his father when Neron was dying – Guibert and I must have been eight or nine at the time – and said to him, "*I will have Hispaniola when I'm a man. Why do I need some land in France that I'm never going to see?*" It was the only time I ever saw Don Absalon strike his son; he must have lectured him for an hour after that, at the top of his lungs, about the honor of the family and the wrong that the Comtes de Caillot had done him. Poor soul, to be so obsessed.'

His brow furrowed for a moment at the memory, of the child he had been – a square-faced, sturdy little Spanish boy, January reflected, fair among the dark Cubaño and African faces all around him – and of his grief at these ugly corners of his friend's family. 'Poor Neron begged Don Absalon to send his body back to France for burial in Caillot, and for spite he laid him to rest instead at Hispaniola. I'll show you the stone. *Neron Thoyomènes*, it says – Thoyomènes was the family name of the Comtes de Caillot. Not even his title. A very sad business.'

'And Dr Maurir . . .?'

The planter turned in his saddle and stared January with much the same expression as if one of the horses had spoken.

January – remembering that he was Hannibal's valet – immediately ducked his head and said, a little shyly, 'Forgive me speaking out, señor. But back in Louisiana, I heard tell around the quarters bogey-tales about a Dr Maudit, from back in Saint-Domingue, that used to make zombies and eat little children.'

'Good Lord, yes,' said Hannibal promptly. 'A couple of the old mammies whose mothers used to belong to the de Gericault family went on about that old doctor in a way that would give you nightmares!'

'Which I'm sure was their intention.' Rose looked loftily down her nose.

Don Demetrio let out a crack of laughter. 'Lord, yes, I'd almost forgotten that! Fancy that poor old man's fame crossing to America.'

'I take it he was nothing of the kind?'

'Oh, heavens, no! He was a dust-dry old stick, cold-blooded as a fish. Don Absalon originally hired Maurir to cure Madame Amalie of her back problems. He couldn't stand to be around physical weakness. Lucien Maurir was some kind of specialist in diseases of the bones back in France, but he hadn't the money to pursue his researches properly, Guibert said. I know he delivered Guibert – and the two other babies before him who didn't survive – and nursed Amalie . . .'

'And then murdered her?' Hannibal's eyebrows quirked.

'I thought Don Absalon murdered Amalie,' put in Rose, and their host laughed again.

'Supposedly – though Neron's story changed from one day to the next. Don Absalon eventually sent poor Amalie to a distant plantation so she could rest – she was always running off to Cap Francais, and she may have been a bit of a flirt. So what is a man to do, eh? She must have been driven mad with boredom on Saint-Domingue, and I shouldn't wonder if her husband sent her to L'Ange Rouge Plantation to keep her out of trouble.'

'L'Ange Rouge?' asked Hannibal. 'The Crimson Angel?'

'Don Absalon's other plantation in what was called the "Cul de Sac", the plain beside Lake Azuei. The Crimson Angel was supposedly the guardian of the Comtes de Caillot. Guibert was born at L'Ange Rouge, and it was Dr Maurir who brought him back to La Châtaigneraie Plantation after his mother died. Cousin Neron may have blamed Don Absalon for keeping Amalie in that isolated place, though with a medical specialist there he can hardly have thought that contributed to her death. Guibert was very fond of old Dr Maurir, though I admit he was a formidable old man and the slaves absolutely hated him.'

'Why?' asked Rose. '*Did* he eat babies?'

'I never saw him do so,' returned the planter, with a chuckle. 'I suspect the Negroes who cleaned his quarters had a peek at his medical books. Guibert and I used to sneak looks at them, when we wanted to scare one another – you know how boys are. Some of the color plates in them were pretty horrifying, and what they must have looked like to the Negroes you can only imagine.' He grinned again, at the foolish superstitions of savages incapable of understanding.

'He was a small man, I recall, and thin as a monkey. But the biggest bucks from the cane field would walk all the way around the other side of the quarters to keep from crossing his path. Don Absalon was always whipping one or another of the maids for not keeping old Maurir's room as clean as she should have, for fear of being in the same four walls with him. Even after we were grown, Guibert used to go into Dr Maurir's rooms every morning and afternoon, to check that the maids had actually cleaned the place and hadn't just gone in and rattled the washbasin a little, and he would never fail to ask Dr Maurir if he needed anything done, after he began to go blind.'

'Dr Maurir was blind?' Hannibal's glance flickered back to January, but January barely saw it.

Looking out over the dark acres of sugar cane revealed by the turn of the trail as it began to descend, January already knew that it was Lucien Maurir – Dr Maudit – who had forced Mammy Ginette to take him back to Haiti.

Lucien Maurir. That was the name.

Dark acres of sugar cane: the riches of Saint-Domingue, rebuilt here . . . The neat French-style house surrounded by a moat, the *bohios* of the quarters fenced in by a stout wall of *mamposterìa* – rubble, stone, and mortar – and a spiked iron gate, legacy of the fear kindled by the fire that had swept over Haiti. A tall gray tower rose above the wall; another marked the sugar mill.

Yet the sight brought back to him not the sticky heat and constant fear of his childhood, but rather the drum of cold French rain on an attic roof in Paris, and the smell of dusty papers. The very weight and texture of the pages in his hand, and the taste in his mouth of the coffee he'd lived on in those days to stay awake.

The smell of tallow candles.

The eyes of the other two medical students who shared the attic with him all those years ago, staring at him in surprise as he had cursed, quietly and from the bottom of his soul, the name of that unknown physician Lucien Maurir.

FIFTEEN

'He practiced vivisection.'

Hannibal and Rose merely looked at him, momentarily too shocked to respond.

The little cavalcade of Don Demetrio's horses and servants had reached Hispaniola just before the hour of siesta, having taken a leisurely halt for bread, cheese, and wine at a small *cafetele* on the footslopes of the mountains, where the road from the pass went down into the valley of the Cauto. Upon their arrival Don Demetrio had ordered Claudio, his major-domo, to show them at once to their rooms, built in the French fashion in two long wings behind the main house, which funneled the evening breeze. January was given a tiny chamber beside Hannibal's – in much of Cuba, he knew, as in Mexico, many masters clung to the old habit of having their servant sleep in the same room with them, on a pallet on the floor, rather than in some other part of the house.

The day's heat was at its height. The gallery outside the room and the courtyard, under its vertical golden hammer of heat, were as still as Sleeping Beauty's Castle. No sound came from the fields outside save the occasional rattle of beetle wings against the side of the house, or the cry of a parrot in the trees.

As he'd laid his saddlebags on the narrow cot – Don Demetrio had sent a runner ahead to tell Claudio to have rooms made up – January had thought, *I'm under Absalon de Gericault's roof.*

I'm under the same roof where Lucien Maurir slept, for eighteen years.

The wave of anger that swept through him at the thought of the man made the hair rise up on his scalp.

When Rose and Hannibal had come in, and Rose had said cheerfully, 'Well, it sounds like Dr Maudit was the one Ginette went back to Haiti with,' January turned upon them, as if she had jested about the dead.

'He practiced vivisection,' he said.

After a startled moment, Hannibal said, 'Can you be sure? How do you—?'

'I read his articles. When I was a medical student in Paris. I didn't remember his name, but I knew there was something about a physician who I was certain had worked in Saint-Domingue . . .'

'Where no one would care,' said Rose softly, 'what a master did with his slaves?' She dropped the train of her riding dress and took her spectacles from her reticule and put them on.

Hannibal's eyebrows were halfway up his forehead. 'You were in Paris . . . When? Just after the war? And Maurir – or Maudit, and no wonder they called him *Accursed* – can't have written them after 'ninety-one . . .'

'The attic I lived in was crammed with them,' said January. He sat down on the bed; the ropes beneath the mattress creaked softly with his weight. 'With scientific journals, I mean – English, French, German, Swedish, going back fifty years, some of them. The house belonged to a physician named Des Essarts. His father had been a physician before him – before the revolution – and had been a member of just about every scientific society in Europe. He'd collected journals on everything: minerals, frogs, wedding customs of the Chinese. Two-thirds of them, the pages hadn't even been cut. Des Essarts *fils* had simply packed them away in the attic, and then rented out the space that was left to students.'

'A built-in library.' Rose's voice was filled with scholarly delight, and Hannibal – a student of human nature in all its forms – brightened with an enthusiasm that he had once reserved for cocktails of laudanum and sherry.

'We went after them like rats in a cheese room. Well, Jogal and I did – Jogal was from Pondicherry, and few enough Frenchmen would share a room with either of us. God knows what he finally ended up doing for his living – probably went back to the Coromandel Coast to practice among his own people. Boissière – our room-mate – spent all his days either in the taverns around the Jardins du Luxembourg or at his uncle's, trying to talk the old man into giving him more money. Jogal and I – and a German student who lived in the other attic – combed through every one of those journals, looking for material on the structure of the body, the operation of the heart and lungs, the progress and cure of disease . . .'

His face clouded. 'And we found Lucien Maurir's articles on

poisons, on the function of organs, and most especially on diseases of the bones.'

In his silence, Rose sat beside him. 'And you could tell, couldn't you,' she said quietly, 'if a drawing was done from a dissection.'

'I can tell.' He tried to keep his voice normal, but heard in it a deadly flatness as he tried to turn his thoughts aside. Even as it had come into his mind – *he could not have learned this except by observing a living body, its flesh opened before him on the table as the organs reacted* – he had been unable to stop reading the information gleaned. Had been unable not to take in and profit from what had been learned. 'I wondered at the time if Maurir were writing in America. In someplace where he could buy a human being, take him to some isolated plantation, drug him – or her, as the case occasionally was – and nobody would ask when he or she dropped out of sight.'

After a long time, Hannibal whispered, 'Nobody would—' and January only looked at him.

'We're talking about people who discouraged insubordination by packing the culprit's anus with gunpowder and lighting a fuse,' he said eventually.

The fiddler looked aside.

'Mammy Zett was right,' January added, after another long silence. 'None of us – including myself, who grew up under the complete domination of a drunkard with the power of life and death – have any idea of what it was like in Saint-Domingue, during the days of slavery. Can I prove it happened? No. Do I think it happened? I don't think he could have made some of those observations any other way.'

Rose sighed, pushed up her spectacles and brought up a corner of the sheet to wipe the sweat from her face. 'You think he was doing that at this second plantation of Don Absalon's? L'Ange Rouge, hidden away in the Cul de Sac?'

'Even in Saint-Domingue,' remarked Hannibal, 'surely the neighbors would have talked if it had been close to town. At least I hope they would have, for the sake of our common humanity. The question is, if Don Absalon were the kind and generous gentleman everyone recalls – other than his *idée fixe* about being the rightful Vicomte de Gericault – wouldn't he have had something to say about his wife's physician periodically chopping up the help? Even if cane hands were half the going price they are these days in New

Orleans, six or seven hundred dollars is still a lot to pay for a look at somebody's duodenum in action, not to speak of the effect this is going to have on morale in the quarters.'

'He probably didn't operate on cane hands,' replied January quietly. 'Planters – or traders – are always happy to get rid of weak or ageing or sick stock for a fraction of what they'd ask for someone who's fit. And I can only surmise that if de Gericault gave Dr Maurir license to perform experiments of this kind, it might pay us to ask if Dr Maurir – Dr Maudit – had something on his employer. Something for which he was trading de Gericault's silence and acquiescence.'

'Blackmailing him, in other words?'

'Unless the man was a total monster himself,' Hannibal ventured. 'Maybe he *did* murder his wife, or have Dr Maudit murder her, or whatever it was.'

'In any event,' January went on, 'it leads me to wonder if what we're looking for, what someone is trying to keep anyone in Rose's family from finding, is a treasure at all . . . or, instead, a secret.'

'What kind of secret?' demanded Hannibal. 'Given that the gentry of Saint-Domingue didn't blink at explosion or, apparently, vivisection, what sort of behavior *would* they take pains to conceal?'

'Satan worship?' Rose cocked her head. 'Black masses? It's been almost fifty years since the family fled Saint-Domingue.'

'And yet they still consider it a threat – if it is a secret we're pursuing, and not simply a whacking great pile of diamonds hidden someplace for the taking.' January leaned his back against the wall, the cot ropes creaking at his movement, and laid his hand over Rose's. 'If it's a treasure, hidden at La Châtaigneraie before they fled, all we have to do is get sight of our pursuers when they cross to get it, or when they come back. *If* they come back . . . Which they may not, if they're going to set foot on Haiti. Either ambush them, or notify the Haitian authorities of where they're headed, or simply stay out of their way. They may lose interest in us once they see they're going to win the race. But if it's a secret, it's one they think we already know. So we're going to *have* to learn what it is and use it against them if we can. Else you and I, my nightingale –' his hand tightened over hers – 'will never again know a moment's peace.'

'*Not poppy, nor mandragora, nor all the drowsy syrups of the world, shall ever medicine thee to that sweet sleep, which thou ow'dst yesterday.* Which causes me to reflect,' added Hannibal, pausing in the doorway into his own large chamber, 'upon the fact that Mamzelle Ginette – and her daughter, apparently – have stayed hiding in the mountains for all these years, long after Maudit has been gone.'

After that, January and Rose lay for what remained of the siesta in the shuttered gloom of the little servants' chamber, crowded together on the cot, their bodies curved together even in the stifling heat. When he finally slept, January dreamed of those yellowed journals, resurrected from the dust of the Paris attic: saw with the vividness of reality the neat, workmanlike drawings of hearts and lungs, of crooked pelvises and spinal columns split or splayed or butterflied open in grotesque horrors of nerve and bone.

Dreamed that these had somehow all been transported to the attic of his own house on Rue Esplanade, and that there was one article in particular that contained the answer. That contained the secret, like a toxin which remains deadly for centuries buried in a tomb. But he didn't know which it was, or where. He could only hunt through the familiar chambers – office, parlor, dining room, the bedroom where Baby John slept, the pantry that looked out on to the crooked little backyard, the attic where Rose's students had slept – peering under mattresses and behind chairs, until he woke with Don Demetrio's *casa de vivienda* still as death around him and burning slits of afternoon sunlight traced in the gloom.

Somewhere, in that unearthly silence, he heard far off the muffled sobs of a woman weeping in terror or grief.

The following morning, Don Demetrio rode out with Hannibal and Rose to show them the plantation of Hispaniola, an *ingenio* of some three hundred acres at the feet of the Sierra Maestra mountains. He treated Rose with the courtesy an American would only have extended to a legitimate white wife, though he had not, of course, introduced her to the women of his own family nor asked her to sup with them on the previous evening.

Before setting forth on the tour of inspection, the planter had Claudio bring down from the attic the four trunks of family papers left behind by the de Gericaults when the orders had come from Spain that all Frenchmen on the island must sell their goods and depart within the month.

'I recall no woman named Reina among Don Absalon's servants,' he said as the trunks were piled in January's tiny cubicle. (*God forbid he should inconvenience his white guest*, reflected January as he moved his own few effects under the bed to make room for these records). 'Nor Ginette . . . His wife's servant, you say, Señor Sefton? There must be a ledger of his slaves in there somewhere, as well as the plantation daybooks. I fear they're all in French – Don Absalon spoke Spanish perfectly, and Guibert of course was more Spanish than French, coming to the island as he did so young. Claudio speaks French and reads it a little—'

'—and has his own work to do,' finished Hannibal politely. 'Benjamin will be able to assist me, and Rose also . . .'

Don Demetrio bowed to Rose. 'Surely you would never ask so lovely a lady to perform so dismal a task?'

Rose widened her nearsighted hazel eyes at him. 'My mother instructed me in all matters concerning business and finance, sir,' she said, which January knew was no more than the truth. '*A lady must always remain a lady*, she would say, *but in this world a girl must look out for herself.*'

The planter laughed and flourished an arm toward the gallery which led to the main house, beyond the doors of which grooms would be waiting with the horses.

'A moment, by your leave,' said Hannibal, and he turned toward January as if about to give him detailed instructions, and with another bow Don Demetrio made his exit, footfalls dying away along the wooden planks.

'I'll bet his poor wife is tearing her own skin off with boredom in this place,' commented Rose. 'I haven't seen a book anywhere yet – have you? When the ladies retired to the back gallery after supper –' she nodded in the direction of the main house, the rear gallery of which, like those in New Orleans, was fitted up almost as an auxiliary room – 'I didn't hear the girl so much as open her mouth.'

'I doubt she could,' agreed Hannibal, 'with Don Demetrio's two sisters squawking like parrots.'

Young Doña Jacinta, January had observed last night, had retired early to her rooms, which were in the other wing of the house opposite those assigned Hannibal and Rose. Though he hadn't shared the excellent supper that Rose had been brought in her room, for fear of the servants talking, afterwards he'd sat on the gallery outside it with her, until Don Demetrio's mother and two sisters had likewise retired, and Rose had gone to help Hannibal regale the planter with the gossip of New Orleans and Havana. The *casa de vivienda* was furnished with both piano and harp, but he had yet to hear anyone play them. They were, Hannibal had reported, lamentably out of tune.

'We'll come back and help you with these as soon as we can,' said the fiddler, opening the first of the chests. 'Though I suspect we're going to be required to sing for our supper most of the time we're here. I can burn a good deal of midnight oil in a good cause. I'm not sure which was worse,' he added, offering Rose his arm. 'Old Madame Gonzago's minute account of her last twenty card-games with her daughters, or having Doña Jacinta looking through everyone at the table as if we were window glass. Dirty window-glass,' he added plaintively. '*Nature never framed a heart of prouder stuff . . . Disdain and scorn ride sparkling in her eyes . . .* A terrible waste of doe-like eyes and raven hair.'

'She's seventeen,' pointed out January. 'Girls are intolerant at that age, and someone probably told her that her husband's guest had brought his mistress with him. Depending on how high in the instep her family is – and I understand they're one of the oldest in Cuba – she may have taken it as an insult that he'd even have Rose in the house.'

Was that, he wondered, the meaning of the weeping he'd heard yesterday afternoon? It had been stifled, not loud, as women often wept from anger and pride. And he'd heard no shouted accusations to go along with it.

Or was it one of the sisters who'd wept? Stout, stolid women in their forties, without even the dowers to get them into a good convent, much less a suitable marriage. How did they like living as their brother's pensioners on an isolated sugar plantation?

'She can't be too intolerant, surely,' said Hannibal, 'if what Captain Castallanos said is true. I wonder what sort of trouble she got into back in Havana?'

'*That*,' said January, 'is not your business – and had better remain not your business for the rest of our stay here.'

The fiddler gave him a look of such startled surprise that January almost laughed. Though Hannibal did not, like many so-called 'ladies' men', regard every woman he saw as a challenge to his manhood, he did regard every woman he saw as a potential inamorata, not from lust but from a genuine friendliness and enjoyment

of mutual enjoyment. In most situations January could only shake
his head over his friend's philandering. But at the moment, he
reflected as Hannibal and Rose retreated along the gallery, the last
thing they needed was a blood feud with Don Demetrio Gonzago.

At least until he'd had a look at the contents of Absalon de
Gericault's trunks.

SIXTEEN

As January suspected, Don Demetrio was right. The four
trunks left in the attics of Hispaniola plantation, when the
government of Spain ordered the French to leave Cuba in
the spring of 1809, were filled mostly with plantation records, and
searching through them was like eating dust with a spoon.

The purchase of slaves ('I thought Don Demetrio said that Cubans
in 1791 wanted there to be *fewer* slaves, because of what had
happened in Haiti . . .?' 'You ever cut sugar cane, Hannibal? They
just couldn't get whites to do it.'). The installation of the newest
types of grinding and boiling equipment, including steam boilers
when they became available, which was very different (again
according to Don Demetrio's recollections) from the lackadaisical
business methods employed by the Spanish Cubans.

'In truth, Don Absalon – and all the French who came here from
Haiti, many thousands of them – went about making money like a
Frenchman.' Don Demetrio's brows knit in a little frown as he
surveyed the stacks of daybooks, ledgers, receipts, letters, and bills
of lading that covered the table which Hannibal had requested be
brought into his chamber, as if this fact about his friend's father
were to be infinitely regretted.

'My uncle the Vizconde, and my grandfather before him, were
good Spaniards. They farmed their coffee like gentlemen, they
visited their friends, they opened their hands and hearts and houses
to all . . . and the French made three times as much money on
half the land they did, and then bought their land out from under
them. This land that is now Hispaniola . . .' His gesture took in
the dark, flat cane-fields along the river, visible through the French
windows, beyond the trees. 'It used to be one of my grandfather's

cattle ranches. Don Absalon bought it for next to nothing, and my grandfather was horrified when he started building a sugar *ingenio* and bringing in slaves. For two hundred years the Gonzagos had ruled this land like the noblemen of olden times. Then, poof! Here are the businessmen, saying, "*It is the modern world, after all, and we must do this and this to make money*." He shook his head. 'All over Cuba it was the same tale.'

Then he smiled and offered Rose his arm: they were to sail downriver to Deliciana Plantation to visit Don Demetrio's cousin Silvestro, leaving the plantation yet again to the management of the overseer and Don Demetrio's mother.

Even two days at Hispaniola had served to show January that no improvements had been made on the place for thirty years. When, after another hour's sorting, he went walking for some air, he observed that the sugar mill still had the steam boilers installed in 1806, but had not converted over to the vacuum system now in use even in such isolated spots as Grand Isle. Coming back toward the house in the growing heat, he saw how many of the fields had gone back to weeds and maiden cane.

'It's a shame, good land gone to waste like that,' he observed, stopping at the corner of a woven-reed fence where a woman was weeding a garden, and the woman straightened up, glad as anyone would be for a few minutes' rest and someone to talk to.

'Ah, Don Demetrio like his father,' opined the woman, whose wrinkles and fallen lips proclaimed the age that her bright-colored headscarf hid. Her Spanish was extremely African, but no worse than Mammy Zett's French had been. 'Always here, there, and everywhere . . . You should hear the way the Vizconde scold him! And what would you have, with your good master come to visit him, eh? Of course, he'll want to meet others of the family.'

'Were you here when Don Absalon had the place?' asked January, in a tone of interested curiosity. 'My master says the French were very different . . .'

The French were indeed very different. Old Nyssa – who fetched January a hospitable gourd of sugar water and was pleased when he asked her to share it with him – had been only a little girl on the Vizconde's plantation when Don Absalon was here on Hispaniola. Her uncle was one of those the Vizconde sold to Don Absalon when he started growing sugar, though, so she'd heard all about how the Frenchman had run his *ingenio*, and another of her uncles had been

Don Demetrio's personal groom back then, when there was a great deal of coming and going between the Vizconde's plantation at Soledad and Hispaniola. She remembered those days well.

'Ginette?' The old woman frowned when January asked after the name. 'No one by that name lived here then, not that I ever heard. And my mama and my aunts, they knew everyone up and down the valley. Yana was the midwife on our place, the best between Santiago and Manzanillo; there wasn't a woman she hadn't helped in her time. She knew everybody's business.'

'Maybe a friend of Don Absalon's in town . . .?' The little red angel gleamed in his memory, crimson enamel feathers catching the stormy daylight back on Rue Esplanade, in Jeoffrey Vitrac's palm.

The old woman shook her head decisively. 'No, Dolores Moreno was his *plaçée*, and a haughty girl she was, my aunt told me . . . And well it served her, when the King threw the French out, and poor Don Absalon had to sell the land and the house and all his slaves for whatever he could get for them to get himself a new start in America. That should have taught her not to go looking down her nose at honest women, but of course it didn't. But that's not what your master's after learning about his family, after all, is it?'

'In a way it is, though.' January looked from the bench where they sat toward the gate of the walled village, with its steep African-style roofs and the chickens pecking in the dust in quest of bugs. Thunder rumbled softly, and the wind had a wildness to it that whispered of a storm to come. 'Michie Hannibal is trying to find his family – or find out something *about* his family, whether he can ever prove himself to be the Vicomte de Gericault back in France or not. So all those papers in the trunks, and anything anyone can remember, are indeed what he seeks to learn. Some names, some hints, somewhere to start.'

Some way to find out who they are, and where they are, before they find US . . .

'Don Demetrio says he was great friends with the boy Guibert, but he hasn't spoken of what happened to him when he went with his father to America.'

'It's because he doesn't know.' A younger woman came down the path between the shell-blow grounds, a basket of damp clothing on her hip. A quick smile passed between her and old Nyssa, then she nodded greeting to January: 'You're Señor Sefton's man? I'm

Fia . . . My mama did the laundry for the Vizconde, back in those days.'

'He doesn't know?' January's brows drew together. 'He said they were like brothers.'

'And so they were. And Don Demetrio – I will say that for him –' and there was a trace of something, like an obsidian glint, in her voice as she said his name – 'tried to get his uncle to get the governor to let Don Absalon stay. But, of course, there were too many people – and the Vizconde the first among them – who wanted to buy this land, after Don Absalon had made such a success of it. So they went to America, to stay with Don Absalon's daughter and her husband, poor girl.'

'I thought Don Absalon was so kind and thoughtful a man as to be welcome anywhere?' *Tell me differently . . .*

'Not if you were a cripple.' The brittleness in her voice was like dry wood splintering into a wound. 'The way he used to speak of that poor woman – when he'd speak of her at all – my mother says, it was no wonder she ran away and married the first man who'd have her. Don Demetrio's cousin Lucio had a club foot – and a kinder and brighter boy, and young man, you'd never meet in the whole eastern end of the island, Mama said – and Don Absalon couldn't bear the sight of him. Mama said she'd overhear him say at dinner that those born like that should just be put out on the mountain, like the people in old times used to do their babies, and let the wild dogs and buzzards eat them. She said Guibert picked this up from him, and when he'd be with other people – not Don Demetrio – he'd call Lucio things like Gimpy and Stump-Along, pretending it was in jest, but it wasn't.'

When her dark brows pulled together under the red-and-yellow line of her tignon, her square-faced resemblance to Don Demetrio was strong enough that January could guess at the closeness of her 'mama' to the family.

'But Don Demetrio never got over Guibert leaving.' Old Nyssa's dark eyes narrowed as she looked across to the house, among its groves of banana and orange trees. 'He wrote him there in America, but Don Guibert never wrote him back.'

'What happened to him?'

Both women shook their heads.

'Will you stay to eat with us?' asked the younger woman, Fia, giving the clothes basket a little hitch. 'It's only beans and rice, but that's all you'd get up at the *casa de vivienda*, with the master away. Old Madame and her daughters make a hearty meal, but they keep a sharp eye on what goes to the servants when Don Demetrio's gone, and of course poor little Madame stays to her rooms and eats hardly a thing.'

'I'd be delighted.'

When Fia went down the path to the drying ground by the river, and January extended a hand to help Nyssa to her feet, the old woman paused and glanced at Olympe's *gris-gris* around his neck. 'There's a man across the river,' she said quietly, 'who it might be can help you find what happened to Guibert Gericault. A *babaaláwo* who reads the shells. They not coming back tonight – the master, and your good master. The way Don Silvestro talks, they lucky if they get back by Sunday. You be inside the walls here –' she nodded toward the enclosed village – 'when the overseer locks the gate tonight. Lazaro Ximo can come down off the mountain and be here too.'

January glanced uneasily in the direction of the house. In the days he'd been there, he'd become very well aware of which servants carried tales to Old Madame. He'd taken care to flatter them, and given them small pickings of money, but even so he had no surety that they wouldn't take it on themselves to mention it to her, if Don Hannibal's valet went missing for an evening. Old Madame, though fat and indolent, had a reputation for petty sadism, and might consider herself justified in locking up a guest's errant servant in the plantation jail.

Or possibly getting the white overseer to administer a whipping 'for his own good'.

As he watched, young Doña Jacinta emerged on to the gallery, petite as a child in white gauze that flickered around her in the restless wind. Both sisters – Doña Terecita and Doña Griselda – bustled out of another French door almost immediately, tugging at her and coaxing; the girl stamped her foot, jerked her arm away from their touch. At that Old Madame appeared, pounded her cane on the gallery planks, and said something that made her daughter-in-law flinch and retreat into the dimness of the house.

'You want me to ask,' said Nyssa behind him, 'can he throw the shells for you tonight?'

Olympe's power, reflected January, fingering the iron *gris-gris* of Ogun around his neck, lay in information. In secrets.

All secrets came to the voodoos.

And it was secrets, he sensed, that would save them all. That would let them lead their enemies into destruction.

'Yes,' he said. 'I'll come.'

SEVENTEEN

*T**his is the legacy of the rebellion in Saint-Domingue.*

Through the door of Nyssa's *bohio*, January could see the little plot of open ground among the huts and the wall with its iron-barred gate.

This is how badly the whites were scared by Toussaint, and Dessalines, and Christophe.

In Louisiana, and elsewhere in the United States, slave-owners paid county sheriffs to mount nightly patrols of the roads, to pick up straying bondsmen. In Cuba, they dealt with the problem closer to home, locking the slaves in at night.

There was a tower on the wall, where one of the overseers – there were four, on Hispaniola Plantation – would watch: for slaves going over the wall, or for runaways from other plantations or from the nearby mountains sneaking in to 'make trouble' by whispering to those in bondage that there was another way to live.

Halfway between the village wall and the overseer's house stood the *barracones*, the stone building where the single men were locked up each night. Only the families dwelled in the village, which was slightly more than half of the slaves. Of the twenty *bohios*, with their huge African roofs thatched in palm leaves, four stood vacant and broken down. Even with the British government trying to close down the slave trade entirely, on a sugar *ingenio* it still made better economic sense to buy only young men from Africa, work them to death and replace them, rather than go to the expense of raising stock from babyhood as the Americans were supposed to be doing. ('Although they don't,' January had said earlier in the day, when sharing a light *merienda* with the major-domo Claudio in the loggia outside the kitchen. 'They buy them from smugglers when they can, or from dealers who get them from the old worked-out tobacco plantations in the East. There isn't a *blankitte* in the country who wants to feed black children till they're old enough to work.')

The women of the village were herded in just before sunset, along with the older children who'd been helping them at their vegetable patches outside the wall or with picking coffee in the few acres of high ground behind the house. The gates were locked, and Old Nyssa came in and set about making supper for her husband and children, and for January. 'You can go out and walk around now,' she said with her wry-mouthed smile. 'They don't have a guard up on the tower till the men come in.' The married men came in by torchlight, long past dark, dirty and wearied from cutting wood in the forest beyond the cane fields. Nyssa's husband Kimo greeted January a little shyly, but her children gathered around him right away.

'You not *ara-ni* like Claudio an' Cellie.' The youngest daughter, Losa, named Doña Jacinta's maid. 'It's like they think they're doin' you a favor, lettin' their shadow fall on you.'

On other nights, when the still heat pressed like black velvet on the cane fields, January had heard the far-off beat of drums in the mountains. But tonight, either there was none, or the changeable, humid winds carried the sound away. Rain splattered briefly on the thatch, and the banana plants among the huts rustled like a thousand ladies in silk dresses fleeing for their lives; lightning flared across the sky to the east. Between flashes, the overcast night was tar black, and after the cook fires had died down, outside the huts, men and women began to come into Nyssa's hut, sitting on the bed, the table, the bench.

And it wasn't, January observed, so very different from the voodoo gatherings in New Orleans. The presence of an overseer on the tower outside precluded dancing or drumming, but everyone brought food – fried plantains, *Moros y Cristianos*, *vianda* thick with *mojo*. Someone brought a jar of herbed rainwater, put into a corner of the hut. Someone else brought rum – enough to earn a whipping, if they were caught. The talk, he guessed, would go on for most of the night, as it did at parties at 'the back of town', after the whites had all gone to bed.

Lazaro Ximo himself was a slender young man of medium height, with a quiet air of modesty. He had an *ilé* in the mountains, Nyssa said, a couple of miles into the forest; January guessed that, like himself, the *santero* had slipped into the village sometime in the afternoon and lain hidden in one of the empty huts. Thick necklaces of beads gleamed on his chest; dark eyes sparkled under a long mass of curly black hair. He greeted January with a smile and clearly knew everyone in the village: he talked to everyone, asked after babies and husbands and crops.

Nyssa explained to him that January sought information about where Don Guibert had gone when he'd left Hispaniola, but after that, for a long time the *santero* occupied himself with everyone else. Five or six of the men and women present retreated one by one with the *santero* to the corner, for him to wash their heads with the rainwater, the same way that the *mambos* in Congo Square would bless celebrants with dripping branches of gladiolus flowers. He'd brought a carved *opun* – a tray with a shallow rim around it – and a little gourd of red dust, and others besides January crouched at the table with him near a couple of stubs of household candles, to have him scatter the dust into the tray and read the shells.

When Ximo finally came back to him through the crowd in the little hut, he recognized that the young man was about half drunk . . . and that he was being 'ridden' by whatever it was – *orisha*, spirit, African god or demon, as the priests would insist – that came upon the dancers in the voodoo ceremonies. Even his voice was different, deep and hoarse, and his dark eyes had a mocking glitter.

'So you come lookin' for Absalon's boy, that went off to America?'

January bent his head. 'I do, lord.'

The beautiful eyes, black with the dilation of the darkness, measured him. 'Nyssa say your *patwon* chasin' gold, but I see fear in you. Hidin' in the cane field, waitin' to see his face.'

January said, 'That's true.'

The *orisha* grinned, took January by the elbow and steered him back to the rainwater jar. January knelt and let Ximo wash his head, then followed him to the table. Olympe would cast dried beans; Ximo threw cowrie shells, scattering them a few at a time from his big hand. 'God damn, you run a long way, brother.'

'That I have.'

'He scared you good. He wrote a letter – Gilbert did. I see it there—' His long finger traced a line between the shells. 'From America, from New Orleans. Wrote a letter to his friend, sayin', *I'm not having it no more. Doors slam on us, people turnin' away their faces. Tell us, "Move on."'*

His eyes narrowed to slits, and he rocked a little on the corner of the bench, repeating words as if from rote. *'I'm goin' into the*

country, not be French no more, not be Spanish. I'm American now.
I'm a-turn my coat, I'm a-turn my name, I'm a-turn myself, 'cause
that's where there's money. With money come power can't nobody
take away. And I never write you no more 'cause you're what I
used to be. That's where he gone.' His eyes opened, but his gaze
remained unfocused. 'America.'

'You know his name?'

'Gericault.'

'His name now?'

'Gericault.'

January gave that one up. Even without the presence of an African
god in his brain, Ximo smelled like he'd been drinking steadily all
evening. 'You know why he's coming after us?'

'Hell.' The *santero* swept his shells into his hand again. 'Don't
need no reason for an American to go after a black man, a black
woman. If it ain't gold, it's blood; if it ain't blood, it's gold. Blood'll
bring you gold, doctor, but that gold'll bring you blood.'

'Why do you call me a doctor?'

'Ain't you?'

For a moment his gaze changed, went beyond January to focus
on the darkness, and his brows knit as if listening. Then he shook
his head. 'I see him—'

'Gericault?'

'The angel,' said Ximo. 'The angel behind you with blood on
his golden wings. He holdin' out his hands at you, and his hands
full of flame.' He stretched out his fingers, hesitantly, like a drugged
man grasping at fire because it's pretty.

Then he shook his head and turned back to January with a smile.
'He gone now. He come back maybe when it's quieter and speak
to you. Meantime you walk ahead careful, brother, till it's time to
close the trap. And you say hello for me, next time you see your
pretty sister. You tell her Lord Ogoun he say hey.'

'Did he never write to you from America?' Hannibal's light, rather
scratchy voice drifted from the rear gallery, and January paused in
his patient perusal of daybooks and accounts, of slaves' and
mistresses' names. The planter had returned with his guests just
before dinner time, and through his own discreet supper with Rose
behind the closed doors of the guest room, January had related what
had passed in the walled village the night before.

Now, on the gallery outside the guest room again with the plantation records around them, they pretended to be friendly acquaintances, listening to the after-dinner chat and smelling the drift of Don Demetrio's cigar. 'Guibert? You said he was a friend—'
'Never.' The planter's reply was like a dry stick quietly snapping. 'It was the worst of it, you know? Yes, I understand that he would be angry. They had less than thirty days, to sell up all they owned, and of course they got no kind of decent price for any of it. And, yes, he spoke with great anger of . . . of having thought that our neighbors would have held forth their hands to help. *We were driven out like dogs by blood-maddened savages*, he said. *It was only to be expected of Negroes. We did not expect such treatment from civilized men who claimed to be our friends.*'
'What could you have done?' asked Hannibal reasonably. 'You were, what, twenty-three? Just one of the young men living in your uncle's house.'
Servants brought coffee and sweets to the back gallery and lighted mosquito smudges as the twilight turned with tropical suddenness to night. The shorter of the two sisters, Terecita, bawled for the card table, and she and her sister Griselda began pestering stridently for Hannibal to join them. Little Doña Jacinta sat back in her wicker throne, watching them with contempt in her narrowed gaze, as still as a child who fears a beating.
After listening to the talk in the *bohio* last night, January now understood that her disdain was the only fortress her spirit had.
He want her to have child, the slave woman Fia had said. *She had two babies slip on her already – she take the malaria bark, like the women in the quarters. So Don Demetrio, he get his mama to watch her all day, and his sisters to sleep in her bed with her at night, to make sure she don't do it again.*
The laundry woman had spoken, too, of the welts that all the slaves had seen on the girl's arms, particularly after her husband had had guests in the house. *Last time that young cousin of his, Gracio, come here and talk a little too much with Young Madame, Don Demetrio kept her locked up for five–six weeks. When she gave him back answers about it, he took and burned her books. She loved them books.* The woman had shaken her head wonderingly. *He won't let her have any now. Says they're bad for women, they give them bad thoughts.*
In the cricket-creaking stillness, Don Demetrio might have shaken

his head. 'His father was very bitter. When I rode up to the house
– to this house, where now I live – the day after the news came,
Don Absalon sent word to his butler that I was to be turned away.
I lingered in the woods on the edges of the cane fields all day,
hoping Guibert would come out to me, but he didn't. I never saw
him, never heard from him again.'

''Metrio!' shouted Old Madame. ''Metrio, come take this bad
man's place! He's flirting with Terecita—'

Both sisters hooted with laughter.

'—so she can't play properly, and if I don't got my play, I can't
sleep!'

'What, that lazy girl I gave you to rub your feet is not doing her
job?'

'She's a fool, and she steals from me. And that lazy wife of yours
thinks she's too good to chat with me—'

Doña Jacinta turned her face aside, haughty and completely alone.

'All she wants to do is read those old newspapers she got,' jibed
Griselda. 'Nothing jolly or good—'

'T'cha!' scolded Old Madame. 'You know what Father Alonzo
says about books.'

'No wonder Don Demetrio spends most of his time with his
mistress in Santiago,' murmured Rose, setting down a stack of letters
from Don Absalon to his lawyers and drawing her yellow silk shawl
up over her shoulders again. 'And no wonder his poor wife—' She
turned back to look across the dark of the yard between the wings
of the house and said softly, 'Oh, damn.'

January followed her gaze.

The card game had subsided into the silence of absolute concen-
tration, the planter, his sisters, and his mother completely absorbed
in their play.

Doña Jacinta was gone.

So was Hannibal.

'We did nothing!' protested the fiddler, considerably later in the
evening, when he returned to his chamber. January, who'd sat up
in a card game of his own with Rose as the lights went out in the
main house and the wing across the yard, gave him a sidelong look.
It was true that first Hannibal, then Doña Jacinta, had returned to
the rear gallery fairly promptly, but January had been on pins and
needles, watching Don Demetrio, until they did.

He also knew that Hannibal could accomplish a great deal towards the winning of a woman's heart in an astonishingly short span of time.

'The question isn't what you did, but what you plan to do in the future.'

'The girl is lonely,' said Hannibal. 'And frightened – she told me how he uses her – and desperate. He—'

'I know all about what he does to her,' returned January quietly. 'I've talked to the servants. But first, I'd rather we didn't lose what seems to be the best chance we have to trace de Gericault and whatever his secret might be – and I'm less than halfway through the materials in those trunks. And second –' he hardened his voice as Hannibal opened his mouth to protest what January himself knew was a heartless view of the case – 'I'd rather you weren't the cause of that poor girl getting another beating for slipping away to whisper sweet nothings with one of her husband's guests.'

Hannibal looked aside, his mouth taut under the graying fringe of his mustache.

At least he didn't protest – as nine out of ten men would – *we won't be caught* . . .

Behind him, January could feel Rose's torn silence. 'There is very little that we can do,' he went on after a moment. 'Unless you're prepared to get her away not only from him, but also from Cuba entirely, the best thing that you can do for her is to leave her alone. According to the servants, her family are the ones who arranged her marriage to Don Demetrio, so it's unlikely they'll come to her rescue. More likely, they'll report to him any plea for help.'

Hannibal dropped his voice to a furious whisper. 'The man is a tyrant! The life that poor girl is leading—'

'*We are running for our lives*,' said January. 'We can't—' He turned his head sharply at the sound of soft scratching at the louvers of the French window. His eyebrows went up; Hannibal shook his head with an expression of innocence and surprise. *I knew nothing about this, honestly* . . .

But even before he reached the jalousie to open it, Doña Jacinta slipped through, a couple of dark silk shawls wrapped around her shoulders, her midnight hair braided down her back like a young girl's, and only the thinnest of batiste nightdresses sheathing her slim form. She saw January and Rose, and drew back. Even in the light of the few candles, January could see the flush that dyed her face. Hannibal put a hand on her wrist. 'It's all right,' he whispered, though January could see that the disconcerted expression on his face at her semi-clothed appearance was genuine. 'What on earth are you doing here, Jacinta?'

'It isn't what you think.' Her glance darted to Rose and January again, then to Hannibal. 'Can they be trusted?'

'Of course! But truly, you shouldn't—'

'I will take that risk.' She looked up into his face – she stood barely taller than a fourteen-year-old girl – clutching her shawls close around her shallow breasts. 'Hannibal – Señor Sefton –' she corrected herself self-consciously – 'I think I would take any risk, to get out of this place. You said you would help me.'

'Not at the risk of putting you further into your husband's bad graces.'

'I am not in his bad graces.' She turned those haughty dark eyes toward January and Rose again, and in the candlelight he saw the glimmer of tears. 'Satan isn't angry at the sinners in Hell, Señor Sefton. They are sinners. They're there for him to torment. It is as it should be, to him. That's the worst of it, I think: that my husband isn't even angry when he says I'm out chasing after men . . . Which I *do* not do! Which I *never* did!' Passion shook her voice, but it never grew louder than a whisper, and Hannibal drew her into the room and away from the windows as January pinched out two of the candles and carried the third one into the door of his own little chamber, leaving the room dark, as if all within were innocently asleep.

'It's just the way women are, he says . . . And they need to be locked up, like bitches in their season.' She faced January, trembling. 'When my husband has Claudio tie me to the bed, so that he can have his marital rights when I refuse him – when I try not to be gotten with child—'

She bit her lip, steadying herself, and added, 'Believe me, I would not have come to you so – naked like a *puta* – if Madame didn't take my clothes away from me, as she does every night, and lock them in a cupboard in her room. My sisters-in-law take turns sleeping in my room with me, in my bed with me, but Griselda had a few too many cups of wine and is snoring like a muleteer. Please listen to me.'

Hannibal put his hands around hers, wrapped as they were in the silk of the shawls. 'Of course—' He visibly bit off another word, probably *querida* or *corazón* . . .

'When you go to Havana,' she said, and her low voice shook, 'will you take a message for me? It isn't to my parents, but to my cousin Enrique. He's the only one of the family who won't write to my husband, telling him that I'm trying to get away from him. Enrique has been to Spain, and to America, and has studied and doesn't believe the whole good of a woman's life is to bear her husband children. Will you do that?'

'Of course.' He didn't even glance at January.

From beneath her shawls she produced a folded sheet of paper – when January saw it later, in daylight, he saw it was the sheet out of a ledger book.

In a whisper even softer, she went on, 'Don Demetrio lied to you. Guibert Gericault did write to him from America, from New Orleans—' She held up a second folded sheet. 'He keeps this in his desk, even still, even now, after all those years. You must give this back to me, and I'll put it back tomorrow. They were very dear to one another. What he says in the letter hurt my husband very much, although it is every word of it true.'

She put the paper into Hannibal's hand.

EIGHTEEN

Hispaniola Plantation
Grand Isle, Louisiana
October, 1810

Metrio,

 You remember that old nigger Pardo, that Papa got into such trouble for killing back in the year of the big hurricane? Never a more blockheaded disobedient buck ever stood up on his hind legs. He'd run off into the jungle, and when he was brought back Papa would whip him with the lead whip till the bones showed through the blood. He'd starve him, break his bones, pull out his teeth, cut off fingers and toes, put him in chains, and put him to every kind of rotten job on the place; nothing you could do to that nigger would make him obey, even when he KNEW what Papa would do. And I'd watch Papa doing this and think, Why doesn't that stubborn son of a bitch just knuckle under and be a good nigger?

Papa just got back from New Orleans. There's not a man in that city will give him credit, now that all the banks are in the hands of the Americans. He's spoke with about a dozen of the big planters – Marigny and Trepagier and Allard – and they all say the same. They'd surely like to help, but with the Americans moving in, times are tight. They can offer him work, they can offer us shelter, they're happy to extend charity, but we're just refugees. We're just people who got ourselves kicked out of two places, and there's only so much they can do.

We're all right (they say) here on with Aunt Oliva on Hispaniola. We have a place to live, acres to farm, even if they belong to that sanctimonious cripple Vitrac. What more do we want?

What indeed?

I'm writing to tell you, I've had enough. It's time for me to take my own advice, to knuckle under and be a good nigger.

Havana is crawling with men who I know, for God's own truth, their fathers were casta *– musterfino and yellow as cheese – who left their end of the island and come to Havana and pass themselves off as white. Back in Saint-Domingue, every other white man you saw had a grandma or great-grandma as black as pitch. (Hell, our butler was lighter than I am!) But move to another city, and take an Italian or maybe a Spanish name, and say, 'I'm white,' and they're asked to every house in the town.*

If they can pass for white men, then I can pass for an American.

I speak English without flaw now. I've been working for a year on my accent. If I go to someplace like Boston, all they'll think is that I'm from someplace like Virginia. In the territories, nobody asks if the name you go by is really your own: how can they check on you? A Spanish man won't do; a French man won't do. So to hell with them all. I'm American, from the soles of my shoes to the bear grease in my hair, and the devil take the man who refuses me help or money or a hearing then.

I will turn my coat and dress like an American in their tweeds and checks and flappy pantaloons. I will turn my name, so that no man can say to me, 'He is a foreigner – no money for him.' I will turn my life, so that no man will turn away from me.

It will be some time before I write to you, or to Papa, or to anyone from Cuba or Saint-Domingue. I have to be able to say, 'Ah, that's a man I met when I was traveling in the Caribbean . . .' It's a hard world, Metrio, and harder for those who have no money. It is as if I go to a far country, to make my fortune before I can return to my old friends.

I hope you understand. Papa doesn't. And so Papa will die in another man's house, eating the bread another man chooses to give him, because he's too proud to change. Because he's too proud of being a Frenchman, too proud of having been master back in Saint-Domingue, once upon a time.

But I will think of you often, and look forward to the day when we can again be friends.

Always your brother,
Gui

Only, the scrawling handwriting made the signature look like '*Gil*'.

I'm a-turn my coat, I'm a-turn my name, I'm a-turn myself, the *orisha* had said, through the lips of the priest he rode.

January had known both men and women, who had made the decision to become *passe-blanc*. To turn away from their families and friends. *In the territories, nobody asks if the name you go by is your own: how can they check on you?*

Rose had teased her brother: *Jeoffrey is no longer good enough?*

For a fair-complected man of African parentage, the stakes were far higher than money – to become a man who couldn't be whipped for disobedience until the bones showed through the blood. Still, January was familiar with the sting of sadness, and of anger, at those who chose to turn their backs, not only on what they were themselves, but also on what their friends and family were as well.

To trade everything you had, and were, for everything you could become.

To pretend that those you had loved – those who had loved you – were nothing, and never had been.

No wonder Demetrio Gonzago was angry.

If they can pass for white men, then I can pass for an American . . .

Jefferson Vitrack. Jeoffrey Vitrac.

Lazaro Ximo's long finger pointing at the shells, *He wrote a letter – Gilbert did . . .*

Not Guibert. Gilbert.

Not Gericault . . .

'Jericho,' he said, and handed the letter back to Doña Jacinta.

'I beg your pardon?'

'Let's check the port records,' he said, turning back to Hannibal, 'for a name that *sounds* like Gericault. He could be calling himself Andrew Jackson in an effort to sound more American, of course – but I think a trip back to Santiago is in order. And then probably to Havana. With luck our friend will be in town by then, and we can get a look at him and figure out where to go from there.'

After some discussion it was agreed that Rose would remain at Hispaniola Plantation and continue the work of sorting through the records the de Gericaults had left behind. 'Our second line of defense is to find out what old Dr Maudit had on de Gericault's father,' she said, when their young hostess had slipped away into darkness again. 'And the sooner we do that, the better. De Gericault – or whatever his name is now – knows we're coming here to Cuba. It's only a matter of time before he comes knocking on Don Demetrio's door.'

'You think Don Demetrio would let him in?'

'He kept Guibert's letter.'

Thus, on the following morning, January and Hannibal rode over the pass to Santiago and spent an extremely cautious day inquiring of Rosario at the Fonda Velasquez – and of Captain Castallanos, who was in port on his way back from Jamaica – if any Americans had come into the town asking after a couple of color, or after the de Gericault family, or Hispaniola Plantation. If any of those Americans were named Maddox, or had been accompanied by dark-faced men named Killwoman or Conyngham . . .

None.

Was Castallanos bound back to Havana soon?

A day, two days . . .

An agreement was reached. Having been Don Demetrio Gonzago's guest for a week, Hannibal still had most of the money he'd won in La Balize and at the Marquesa's in Havana. 'And it's a wonder I do,' he added as they rode out of the little town the following morning, 'considering how that old witch Doña Elena cheats.'

Rose and January spent most of the evening patiently plowing through correspondence regarding Absalon de Gericault's lawsuit with Cousin Neron, which had still been in the courts when the Bastille fell and rioting swept the streets of Paris, while Hannibal copied odes in Greek from a volume of Theocritus he'd stolen from Cousin Silvestro's library at Deliciana Plantation the previous week.

'I'm tempted to simply tear them out,' he explained, 'but one of Silvestro's penniless uncles is a scholar, so I do actually want to get the volume back to him intact. ψυχῆς ἰατρὸς τὰ γράμματα . . .'

'I must say, my heart aches for poor Amalie.' Rose lowered a sheet dated April of 1780. 'However much everyone's always saying what a charming, kindly gentleman Grandpa Absalon was, he seems to have been as much of a domestic tyrant as Don Demetrio. Here's a letter to his lawyer in Paris inquiring if it's possible to sue Cousin Neron for false pretenses and entrapment, because Amalie "is incapable of bearing a healthy child", without surrendering the legal right their still-unborn son has to the de Gericault title. He also accuses Cousin Neron of dosing Amalie with some "perfidious substance" before the marriage, to ensure that she would not bear "normal" babies.'

'Hence his employment of Maurir, as far as I can make out.' January looked up with distaste from the shuffle of letters, account books, and a kitchen slate that lay on the table before him. 'My recollection is that a number of his articles involved congenital malformations of the bones, so Don Demetrio is right about him being an expert in heredity. Possibly, Absalon was trying to find proof that Cousin Neron "knew" in some fashion that Amalie would give birth to fragile children . . . You haven't found any further letters from Maurir to Absalon, have you?'

'Not yet.' Rose rearranged the combs that held her hair up off her neck. 'We still have half of this trunk and all of the last one to go. But, as of that batch you're looking through now, he was certainly working for Absalon by 1781.'

'And well enough in his trust to be purchasing slaves for him.' January glanced at the slate before him, with its list of names. 'And not all of them show up on the daybooks of the plantation, either. He writes that he's sending them to the other plantation, L'Ange Rouge. But it sounds like he's spending a lot on them – four thousand livres for a "house servant", and almost that much for another "manservant of fair complexion".'

'Was a livre in 1781 the same as a franc now?'

'Almost. Four maidservants—'

'Sounds like he's getting the house ready for Amalie to be sent there. Maybe he did murder her.'

There was a faint scratching at the jalousie. With barely a creak of the floorboards, Hannibal slipped across to it, opened it a crack and slipped outside. He was in shirtsleeves in the heat of the night; January saw him dig something from his trouser pocket and hand it to the dim form that vanished almost immediately into the rainy darkness. 'I hope and trust,' he said, 'that you're not doing anything that's going to jeopardize Rose's position here, should certain female members of the Gonzago family start wagging their tongues when you and I are gone?'

'Upon the lyre of Apollo I swear it.' Hannibal lifted his hand. 'Whatever his sisters say, our host has enough regard for a man's property – with all due respect and apologies, Fair Athene –' he bowed to Rose, who gave him a sidelong glance over the rims of her spectacles – 'to at least wait for our return before he takes me to task about carrying letters for her.'

'And that packet contained . . .?'

'Opiates,' said Hannibal. 'At Jacinta's request I visited a *botica* in Santiago yesterday afternoon while you were chatting with old Rosario—'

'And you still think her cousin Enrique is going to defy their family, leap on his white horse and come here to rescue her? Did your adventures in Santiago also involve a visit to a blacksmith versed in the manufacture and cutting of keys?'

Hannibal managed to look shocked. 'Benjamin!'

'She got out of her room Wednesday night before you'd been to Santiago,' pointed out Rose, thumbing through the borrowed Theocritus. 'So she's either learned to pick that lock—'

'You slander an honest woman, and I shall be forced to call you out!'

'—or is counting on the opiate to permit her to get the key away from her sleeping guardian.'

'Benjamin, will you act as my second?'

'He can't,' retorted Rose. 'He's going to be *my* second, and as the challenged party I name home-made cannons, with home-made gunpowder, at two hundred paces.'

'Hmf,' said Hannibal. 'In that case I shall take the matter under advisement and shall send a second to you as soon as I find one suitable.'

'Which won't be until 1870,' finished January, a little wearily.

'Hannibal, I ask you to remember—'

'I'm not making love to her.' The fiddler's face grew suddenly grave. 'She's a young girl, she's alone, and she's frightened. She's doing everything she can to keep from conceiving by her husband, because she says – quite rightly – that if she's with child she won't be able to flee. Opiates wasn't the only thing I obtained for her in Santiago. But she's running out of strategies, and she's running out of time.'

'And do you think your meddling – and her cousin's meddling, if he'll even reply to her message – is going to do anything but make matters worse for her in the long run?'

'I can't not try.' Hannibal sat on the bed. Though there wasn't a clock in the house, January guessed it must be long past midnight, and owing to the hour of the outgoing tide, the stablemen had been alerted to have horses ready for them at the first whisper of light. 'Besides,' he added as January and Rose began to replace the plantation records in the trunk, 'you remember Guibert's letter to his friend Demetrio? How he compared himself to a slave that his father had tortured repeatedly for disobedience and eventually killed because he wouldn't knuckle under and be good?'

He regarded January steadily, and it was January who looked away.

There was long silence, broken only by the rattle of the wings of a huge brown moth, fluttering around the candle on the table.

Rose said, 'Even if Don Demetrio should learn of Jacinta's letter while you're away, Benjamin, I'll come up with some story. And I'll do what I can to protect her as well.'

NINETEEN

Ever the perfect host, Don Demetrio rose in the blackness of pre-dawn to bid his guests Godspeed, with the light of the candles in the hands of sleepy servants gleaming gold in the eyes of the horses. A very small stable-boy held a lantern that illuminated nothing, as January and Hannibal mounted, and followed them on a scrawny old nag into the dripping gloom of the morning, to lead the horses home from Santiago. For a long time they rode in silence, surrounded by the croaking of the frogs that filled Cuba's forests. As he'd done as a child, January made names for them: that tiny peep, like a silver bead dropped on to marble, was Monsieur L'Argent, the deeper, slow-paced glug was Old Madame Gonzago . . .

They pressed on over the mountain ridge and reached Santiago late in the afternoon. Just before the scattered *bohios* and gardens of the town's outskirts gave way to the more substantial houses of stucco and tile, January drew rein. 'I think here might be a good place to send the horses back,' he said. 'Hannibal, would you be able to walk from here to the harbor? It would be less conspicuous than riding – and just because Gericault and his minions hadn't arrived as of the day before yesterday, it doesn't mean they aren't waiting for us now. Particularly,' he added, 'if someone around the wharves mentions to him that the Americans have taken passage on the *Santana*.'

He was already starting to dismount when the stable lad said, 'No,' in a small and rather frightened voice.

January turned, startled – the boy had stayed well behind them for the whole of the day, and this was the first time he had heard his voice.

Her voice, January realized.

Jacinta Gonzago's voice.

The small, raggedy figure reined over to them and, yes, under the brim of the battered straw hat he recognized the oval face, the doe-like brown eyes.

He glanced immediately at Hannibal and saw the fiddler was as startled as he was himself.

'Don't send me back.'

She sat straight on her sorry old gelding; he'd mentally registered that their 'stable lad's' bare wrists and feet were nearly as fair as Hannibal's, but long acquaintance with the congress of masters and enslaved women had taught him that many slaves were in fact as light as their owners.

'He'll know by this time that I'm gone. He can only be a few hours behind us.' She swallowed hard, but kept her eyes and her voice steady. 'Please, please, señores, help me. Take me on the ship with you. If I can get to my cousin Enrique's . . .'

'You really think he won't just hand you back to your husband?' January exploded.

She answered his thoughts instead of his words. 'He won't harm Señorita Rose.' When January reached for her horse's bridle, she tried to retreat, but the old nag was tired and probably had a mouth like iron: it didn't budge. In a flash she was down from its back and out of the range of his grasp, looking quickly from his face to Hannibal's. 'He'll know you wouldn't have left her there if you were planning to run away with me.'

'Oh, will he?' demanded January.

'He'll at least wait till you return – you and Señor Sefton.' Her moth-fine eyebrows pinched a little, as if adding up the fact that it was the so-called slave who expressed angry concern, not the so-called master. The supposed slave who, the minute they were out of Don Demetrio's sight, was clearly in charge of the expedition.

'Please,' she said again. 'You can tell him when you return that you saw nothing of me. That you thought I was Pablo all the while, that I never spoke, and why would you look at a servant? Just the fact that you'll go back will tell him that I didn't flee with Señor Sefton—'

'You're making a lot of assumptions about what he'll think.'

She glanced again at Hannibal, standing now beside the head of his horse, still without having said a word.

'I swear I won't go back,' she said. 'If you send me back I'll go into the forest and try to reach Enrique's men that way. He isn't in Havana,' she added quietly. 'He's in the mountains, with the *mambises*, the rebels against the King. The ones who want Cuba to be free, as I do.'

'Is that why your parents forced you to marry?' inquired Hannibal gently. 'Because you're a *revolutionista*?'

She nodded.

'You'd never make it.' January spoke more quietly now. 'From what I heard in Havana, the rebels could be anywhere, and the hills are crawling with bandits, with *rancheradores* who'd see a girl of your complexion and sell you as a musterfino in Kingston or Rio or—'

'Do you think I'm anything but a slave now?' The dappled light showed tears in her eyes. 'Out here, away from everyone except that family of his, who want a son from him as much as he does, he can do anything to me. *Anything.* They believe whatever he tells them because he has told them I'm a liar. They're right outside the door when he comes into my room and takes me by force – even a whore has a pimp to turn to! Señores, I have no one. Even the priest tells me that I must submit with good grace – good grace! He wants me with child, and he wants a son, and he knows that the moment I'm with child I won't be able to flee.'

No, reflected January. Every slave-owner in Louisiana knew that, too. Most of the runaways he concealed for a night, or two, or three, in the secret room beneath his house were men, who had left their womenfolk – burdened with babies – behind. *I'll send for you later . . .*

Only, later, the woman had been given by her master to another man and was with child again.

'If we're going to catch the tide,' said Hannibal in his mild, scratchy whisper, 'we'd probably better get to the harbor.'

'I'll take the horses to the inn,' said January after a little time. 'With loud complaints about how the boy ran off in the forest, the first time we turned our backs.'

'Good man!' Hannibal slapped him on the shoulder. 'As for you, *Pablo*,' he added, snapping his fingers at Jacinta, 'you can demonstrate what a good stable boy you are by carrying our saddlebags down to the harbor.'

And Jacinta, for the first time that January had ever seen, smiled, a mischievous girl's smile, though a tear of relief leaked from the corner of her eye. 'Of course, señor,' she said, forcing her voice to a boy's roughness. She jammed her hat more tightly down over her piled-up hair. 'As you command.'

If Captain Castallanos had any suspicions about the gender of the 'boy' that Hannibal had added to his party, he didn't voice them, and he greeted her as 'Pablo' on those few occasions when Jacinta came up on deck. His crew – two nephews and a plump little Yoruba named Sammy with 'country marks' carved into his face – simply ignored her, and Jacinta took care to stay below for most of the five-day voyage. 'Seasick,' Hannibal explained.

This was a shame, partly because the cabins were penitential coffins, stinking of raw cow hides and bilge water, and partly because the waters among the tiny islets of the Gardens of the Queen were a turquoise paradise under the glare of the sun. They put in at Manzanillo the first night, at Trinidad the second, and towards sunset of the fifth afternoon glided gently past the bristling stone fortifications that guarded the harbor mouth and down the long canal into Havana harbor itself.

From the coachman Ilario, January had earlier learned where to find far less costly accommodations in Havana than the Casa Orrente on Calle San Ignacio, and that evening, leaving Hannibal and Jacinta in the modest little rooms they'd rented by the harbor, he made his way to the Posada Caballero. There he renewed acquaintance with Ilario and others he'd met there, and he asked to whom one would give a message for Enrique Jivara . . . and felt the glances that passed among them.

'We know nothing of the man,' said Ilario carefully, 'save that he is wanted by the police.'

'I know nothing of him either,' returned January. 'I only found a piece of paper lying in the highway, addressed to him from a member of his family, whose name I could not make out.'

The coachman smiled. 'Well, I'll ask around, dear brother. Maybe someone knows something.'

It was the last the matter was mentioned that evening. But the following afternoon, when January and Hannibal returned from the shipping offices of the harbor, they found Jacinta in the shabby yard behind their rooms, radiant, with a scruffy, bearded man whose peasant *guayabera* accorded ill with the upper-class perfection of his Spanish. 'I thank you both,' he said, shaking January's hand and then Hannibal's, 'for bringing my cousin here. For treating her with honor and kindness, as she assures me you have. Maybe I was a fool to believe my parents when they told me –' his dark brows drew down over piercing dark eyes – 'when I returned from my schooling last year, that she was content to marry this Gonzago. I am ashamed to say that there were other matters occupying my mind.'

'We all of us make errors of judgement,' said January. 'I certainly have. I am only glad that this was one that could be rectified. So many cannot.'

Under the shaggy beard, the man's mouth hardened, and the thoughts that fleeted across the back of his eyes made January realize suddenly that he was younger than he seemed, not even thirty.

'*No, let my father seek another heir,*' Hannibal quoted the absconding princesses of *As You Like It*, and took Jacinta's hand. '*Therefore devise with me how we may fly* . . . I take it you're planning to do something rash, like run away with the *mambises* . . .?'

Enrique put a protective arm around the girl's shoulders. 'Where would you have her run, señor? Back to the family who sold her like a whore to a man who abuses her, for five thousand pesetas and ten *caballerías* of land? To Jamaica, maybe, to seek work as a sewing woman or a governess? In the mountains I can protect her.'

'Until you're killed,' said Hannibal, and he looked, with quiet sadness, into Jacinta's eyes.

Another runaway, thought January. As Hannibal himself had bidden his own father seek another heir and fled from a world whose expectations he could neither tolerate nor fulfill.

'I'm an outcast already,' reasoned the girl. 'Maybe being shot by the King's soldiers will be better than dying in childbed with the son of a man I despise.'

'I don't want you to find out that, in fact, that isn't the case.'

She smiled, put her hands on his shoulders, and tiptoed to kiss him. 'Soldiers do it every day, dear brother,' she said.

'She won't be the only woman in our band,' said Enrique. 'Nor the only one in the mountains. We will protect her, to the best of our ability, that I promise.'

'*Vaya con Dios*, then,' said Hannibal, and kissed Jacinta again, on the forehead this time. '*Si finis bonus est, totum bonum erit.*'

'*Saepe ne utile quidem est scire quid futurum sit,*' returned the rebel. 'Nor should we seek to know what lies ahead . . . How can I thank you?'

Hannibal shook his head, and January was about to deny thanks also – they had, in fact, found what they were looking for, on the incoming passenger-list of the *Laurel Glen* from New Orleans on the fourteenth of September: Bryce Jericho, of Mobile, Alabama, and party.

Then he thought about it and said, 'Yes. In fact, there is something you can do for me.'

TWENTY

'The treasure of the Crimson Angel.' Salomé Saldaña glanced from the narrow circle of the pierced lantern's light toward the door of the hut. Like the walls, it was a patchwork of cane, scrap wood, and banana leaves, insufficient even to keep out the wind, let alone the incessant creaking of cicadas in the jungle night. The gold gleam of the candle showed the whites all around the dark of her pupils. She was straining to listen.

Bracing herself to flee.

January estimated her age at fifty. She looked closer to seventy, mouth fallen in over missing teeth, a battered face that had once been beautiful. *C'est d'umaine beaulté l'yssue!* Villon had mourned, in the words of the helmet-maker's wife. *So this is the end of beauty.*

Ainsi emprent à mains et maintes . . .

So it goes for all of us . . .

She closed her eyes, and for a long while the thatched shed to which Ilario had led January was silent, save for the quiet voices among the other huts in the clearing. But in the tension of the woman's body, January could almost hear the swift hammering of her heart.

Who the hut belonged to, January had not the least idea. It lay somewhere beyond the last of the handsome houses of Havana, where the trees began to get thick. The simple bed with its banana-leaf mattress, the bright skirts and scarves hung on pegs, the straw hat on the table, the cradle and the water jars – portraits of an absent family.

It had taken two days of nerve-racking waiting, for Enrique Jivara to send word to him that Salomé Saldaña would meet him, days during which it had taken all January's resolve not to go down to the harbor to look for a ship back to Santiago.

Whatever Don Demetrio is going to do when he finds out his wife has run off, he's already done . . .

*And Rose will brain me with a Greek lexicon if I walk away from
the chance to speak to this woman.*

Even at the cost of her own safety.

Two sleepless nights gave an air of unreality to the hot dimness
of the hut, to the night bird cries and the murmur of a woman's
voice asking Ilario something outside the rickety door. January
had gone to Mass daily since his arrival in Havana, sometimes
twice a day, seeking both comfort and distraction and finding
neither. He had lighted half a dozen candles, watched light and
smoke ascend with his prayers, and had tried to keep at bay the
superstition of a child – hammered into him when he *was* a child
– that God would punish him for his conversation with the *orisha*
by harming Rose.

She'll be all right . . .

*We now know who it is who pursues us. And tonight we will find
out why.*

'Yes,' Salomé Saldaña said at length. 'Maudit came to my mother's house. It was the year the French were expelled. She was to
go with him back to Saint-Domingue, to Michie Absalon's plantation, or else he'd go to the police and accuse her of poisoning white
men. After he left her house she came to me at midnight, not weeping
but trembling all over, for she had lived twenty-three years in fear
that he would find her.'

January counted back in his mind. 'They weren't on the island
twenty-three years.'

'She fled Saint-Domingue for fear of him, señor. My mother was
born in Saint-Domingue and sold together with her sister to Don
Absalon de Gericault when she was fifteen. He gave my mama to
his mistress, Mamzelle Calanthe; her sister Reina to his wife.
Calanthe was mean, Mama said, and spiteful. But Reina loved
M'aum Amalie. When Reina married Don Absalon's coachman, it
was M'aum Amalie that gave her a dress and shoes, and had the
wedding held in the Church at Cap Francais.'

'Did your mama go to the wedding?' January recalled a dozen
friends – boys who'd been like brothers to him – whom he'd
never seen again after he and his mother were sold away from
Bellefleur.

'Oh, yes, señor. The Cap wasn't but an hour's ride from the
plantation, and M'aum Amalie would go there often. She'd never
have spoke a word to Mamzelle Calanthe if she saw her in the street,

but my mother and her sister loved each other. They never let that love go cold.'

A sound outside made Salomé turn with a gasp, but it was only the rising wind, stirring in the banana leaves. January recalled again that this woman's name and whereabouts had been in the envelope in Jeoffrey Vitrac's pocket.

'I've heard that Reina died in Saint-Domingue,' he said quietly. 'That Dr Maudit poisoned her.'

'He'd buy people in the market,' whispered Salomé, 'just on purpose to cut them up alive. He had a house with a stone jail behind it, on stone foundation so nobody could dig their way out. Sometimes instead of cutting them up he'd turn them into *zombi* – he knew how to make the *coup de poudre*, the powder-strike that brings back the dead to be his slaves. Or he'd use other drugs to keep them alive while he cut them up, alive but not able to move . . .'

Like a corpse floating into momentary view in a river's sluggish tide, January's mind cast up a sentence from one of Lucien Maurir's articles: *effects were observed over the course of forty-eight hours . . .*

'Don Absalon offered Mamzelle Calanthe a lot of money, if she'd go stay at L'Ange Rouge, at the feet of the mountains in the Cul de Sac. My mama begged her not to go. But Don Absalon, he said she'd have her own house there, and many servants. He sent both his *plaçées*, both Calanthe and Emmanuelle with their servants. Later he sent M'aum Amalie there as well. So Mama and Reina were there together. Mama was shocked, that a man would send his wife to the place where both his mistresses were.'

'Did Madame Amalie object? Or try to flee?'

'Flee where, señor?' The woman regarded him with a matter-of-fact sadness in her hazel eyes. 'Her husband sent her to that place, and her family were all in France.'

Like Doña Jacinta. The best part of a day's journey, over rough country haunted by bandits and *rancheradores*, lay between her and the nearest people who weren't relatives of her husband.

'The Cul de Sac country was mostly cattle ranges, and she was not a strong woman, and with child besides.'

'But your mother fled.'

'On the night of the hurricane, señor. The rain hid her tracks and kept the men from following her.'

'She's lucky she wasn't killed.' January had been outside during hurricanes. It wasn't an experience he cared to repeat. 'Why did she flee?'

Salomé Saldaña shook her head. 'She made her way across the mountains and got some fishermen to bring her here to Cuba. She stayed in Havana for a time, where she met my father, and worked as a hairdresser, but she never felt herself safe. I asked her once what she was afraid of, when I was a little girl, and that was when she told me about Dr Maudit. Then, when so many French came to Cuba, she got my father to move to Pinar del Río, where his cousin had a farm. That was where he found her. Maudit.'

'How did—' January began, but some sound in the night – the bark of a dog, Ilario calling out, *'Who's that?'* – made the woman jerk around as if she'd been given an electric shock. She sat frozen, listening, her lips stretched back against her teeth with terror. January wondered how far Enrique's influence would go in holding her here, and if it would be long enough for him to discern the pattern that was beginning to form up in the darkness at the back of his mind.

The stableman Ilario had come to his rooms in the Calle San Pedro and arranged the meeting, even as, yesterday, it was Ilario who had led him to a café across the street from the American Hotel on Calle Obispo, where they'd idled for half an hour before a group of men had emerged from the hotel: *Is that he, dear brother?* Acceptance by Cousin Enrique, and by the shadowy confraternity called the Suns of Liberty, who whispered of Cuba as an independent country, had the effect with which January was already familiar from his dealings with the network of men and women in New Orleans who aided runaway slaves. Once someone in the group vouched for you, you found that there was always somebody who knew what you needed to know – or knew somebody else who would know it.

January hadn't needed to be told which man he meant.

The family resemblance wasn't striking, but it was there. A description of Jeoffrey Vitrac would easily fit Bryce Jericho. It could well have been he, not Jeoffrey, who had gone to the Café des Refugies in New Orleans, of whom Jean Thiot had said, *'He had the look of her . . . Same nose, same chin . . .'*

'The man in white?' he had asked, and Ilario had nodded.

'Bryce Jericho he is called in the registry of the hotel. Those others with him are his servants. Brown and Green, they are called—'

Less noticeable names than Killwoman and Conyngham, certainly, and possibly these were not the same men. Their dusky-dark faces looked far more African than Indian.

'There are others of his party at the hotel as well. I am told they are asking about these Americans who escaped from the rebellion in May and about the "old slave-woman" who helped them. This Jericho showed my friend the red-winged angel you spoke of.'

L'Ange Rouge, which last he'd seen in Vitrac's hand.

Bryce Jericho. Beyond doubt, the son of Guibert de Gericault. He looked in his mid-twenties, active and strong. His white linen suit was crisp, unstained, and fit him well, his gestures those of a man used to command.

The men who'd killed Jeoffrey Vitrac in a New Orleans alleyway.

The men who'd stabbed Rose in the market. Who'd shot Aramis on the edge of his own cane field.

The blood will bring you gold, the *orisha* Ogoun had said, Ogun whose talisman he wore around his neck. *And the gold will bring you blood* . . .

The men who would kill Salomé Saldaña to keep her quiet, unless she got out of Cuba within days.

Stillness returned outside. Salomé let her breath trickle from her lips, though she didn't stop trembling.

'And Maudit asked your mother to take him back to Saint-Domingue?'

'He was nearly blind.' The woman looked back at him, eyes gleaming in the tiny glow of the tin lantern. 'He had a slave who led him around, a *zombi*: you looked in his eyes, and there was nothing there. Maudit called him Caliban. He'd do whatever Maudit said. Guard him, fetch him food, kill for him like a trained dog. But there wasn't enough in his mind even to know to pull down his pants when he made water.

'Maudit told my mother, she had to take him back to L'Ange Rouge Plantation, in the Cul de Sac. My mother told me there was treasure hidden there. M'aum Amalie's diamonds, and gold besides. Don Absalon had let Maudit draw to his credit for whatever he needed. That's how he bought the slaves he cut up. That's why neither Don Absalon, nor his son Don Guibert, came with him to L'Ange Rouge. They didn't know what he was doing there—'

'Are you sure?' broke in January. 'Are you sure they didn't know?'

Her eyes widened at the thought. 'How could they know?' she

whispered. 'How could they know that he did such things? No, señor. He hired Maudit to make M'aum Amalie well enough to bear him a son, you see. My mother knew that, everybody knew it. He needed a strong son, one who could make the journey back to France and push and quarrel with the lawyers there, so he could get the lands and the title away from M'aum Amalie's brother. "You make her give me a strong son, a big boy," he say to Maudit – this my mother heard from Mamzelle Calanthe, who heard him say it to poor M'aum Amalie. "You take whatever it cost." But Maudit took the money and spent it on slaves to cut up, to sacrifice to the devil.'

To sacrifice to the devil of his pride, anyway, reflected January, remembering those precise drawings in *Les Procédées de la Société des Sciences Francaise.*

Or was it the devil who had whispered to Dr Faustus, who had sold his soul, not first for the charms of Helen of Troy, but for knowledge? Adam's original sin, the fruit of the tree of knowledge . . .

'So why did he send his mistresses there?' January asked. 'And what became of them?'

'Huh.' She sniffed her contempt – stronger, for a brief moment, than her watching and her fear. 'Nasty sluts, my mama said, and both pregnant by the houseboys before the first month was out.'

'Houseboys?' He'd read the lists of slaves for L'Ange Rouge Plantation, and there were no young men listed as working in the house.

But Salomé had already taken up her tale again. 'When the French were thrown out of Cuba, Maudit came and found my mother. My mother came to me that night and begged me to go with them. *I won't be alone with him*, she said, though he was a blind man, and old, near to eighty he was then, like a dried-up spider. *I won't be alone with him and his zombi.*'

She froze again, at the sudden flurry of urgent whispers outside the door.

'It's them,' she gasped. 'The men hunting me. My mother said—'

She scrambled to her feet, and had January not caught her by the wrist she would have been out the hut's single window, which looked out on to the jungle behind them.

Nails scratched the wooden door. 'Put out the light,' whispered Ilario, opening it. 'Men coming, *blancos*. This way.'

January flipped open the lantern door and blew out the candle, never releasing his hold on Salomé's wrist. A hand closed around

January's elbow in the dark. He felt his head scrape the lintel of the doorway as he passed through. After the velvet blackness within the hut, the ragged moonlight fleeting through clearing seemed bright. Three or four men, bearded like Enrique Jivara and, like him, in the ragged clothes of peasants, surrounded January and Salomé and led them into the jungle.

'Don't let anyone go back to that hut.' January kept his voice to the ghost breath that he'd used as a slave child, eluding the patrols along the back roads and bayous at night. 'They're killers—'

'No fear, brother.' Ilario's hand steadied his elbow as they descended to the gurgle of a stream. Starlight flickered on a tiny falls. Windy darkness swallowed them, smelling of the sea.

The thin wrist in his grip twisted, trying to pull away. 'They said these men were asking for me,' Salomé whispered frantically. 'My mother said they would come. All her life she said they would one day come after us.'

'Even after Maudit was dead?' With his free hand January dug in his pocket, pulled out all his coin and slapped it into her palm. He felt her grow still as she estimated the unmistakable weight of the silver.

'Take that and get off the island,' he said as the bearded revolutionaries hustled them deeper into the trees. 'Can you arrange that, Ilario? There's thirty-two American dollars there.'

Hannibal had better be winning tonight . . .

'I can arrange it.'

'Then tell me what happened in Saint-Domingue.' He spoke to the darkness, to the hard shape of bone that he held on to like a traveler in legend gripping the coat-tail of a demon. 'Did you go?'

'I went.' Her voice was barely audible above the rattle of the palm fronds overhead. 'I was twenty, and had just had my daughter, my child, Mélusina. I left her with my husband and went with my mother, with Maudit and his *zombi*. Fishermen took us across. Even now, fishermen and smugglers cross back and forth to the island, you know, though these days there is little enough to buy. In those days Christophe and Pétion were at war with one another, north against south, blacks against mulattoes. Maudit was killed within hours of coming ashore. Mother and I hid in the jungle – the partisans who killed Maudit would have killed us too, for being fair-skinned – and we finally found fishermen to take us back here. But Maudit had reported to the authorities, before we left, that my father and my husband had poisoned white men with our complicity. They had been arrested, and we, too, were being sought. I managed to get Mélusina from my husband's sister, and the three of us – Mother, Mélusina, and I – fled to the partisan bands in the mountains, to make our living as smugglers and healers and fugitives. Because of Maudit. Because of L'Ange Rouge.'

January stood silent, his hand still locked around her wrist. They'd come to the edge of the trees, where the land sloped down to the sea. Moonlight shimmered through the fleeting clouds, edged the waves in silver as they ran up on to the beach.

Baby John was back at home in New Orleans. Asleep in Olympe's cluttered little parlor, surrounded by *vévés* and *gris-gris* and the beaded gourds where the *loa* hid. Safe, January hoped . . .

As he prayed Rose was safe at Don Demetrio's plantation.

January tried to convince himself that Hannibal was right, that the chances were good that even if Don Demetrio didn't entirely believe January's outraged tale at the inn, of how 'Pablo the stable boy' had deserted them in the middle of the jungle, that the planter would wait to see if, in fact, Hannibal would come back. Rose was a hostage, collateral for Hannibal's return, and as time was reckoned in Cuba, it was early days yet. Hannibal – and Jacinta – had been gone for less than a week.

Virgin Mary, Mother of God, keep her safe. Let her be there when I get back . . .

When I get back with the news that I've seen the son of Guibert de Gericault.

And that he looks enough like Jeoffrey and Aramis to be their brother.

He shivered at the thought of what he knew he'd have to do now. *Hannibal will take care of Rose, anyway . . .*

'The Crimson Angel belonged to M'aum Amalie, didn't it?' he asked, and she nodded.

'But she was dead, Mama said, by the time she took it. Maudit had it with M'aum Amalie's diamonds, and the gold he'd got from Don Absalon to buy slaves, and jewelry from Mamzelle Calanthe and Mamzelle Emmanuelle. It was hid in his house, but Mama knew where, and we lived on that jewelry for years after we got back from Saint-Domingue and the police were hunting for us. The Crimson Angel was the last of it. Señorita Loveridge – the girl who was staying at Los Flores, the plantation where the slaves rebelled last spring – she showed me many kindnesses during her stay there. How could I let her be raped and killed by angry men? And I'm an old woman now, and the Suns of Liberty take good care of me. Of course I gave the Angel to Loup de la Mare, to carry them away to safety. I think the thing must have had a curse on it, the way all things did that Maudit touched.'

January was silent, thinking about Lucien Maurir's research. About those precise, medical engravings, and the blood on the golden angel's feathers.

About Jacinta Jivara, and an isolated plantation in the Cul de Sac.

He drew in his breath to speak, thought about it for a moment more, then asked, 'Was there ever a rumor that Guibert de Gericault wasn't his father's son?'

She almost laughed. 'Of course there was, señor! Every woman in Cuba – especially those of the rich! – face those rumors, every time they give birth. Particularly when a woman like M'aum Amalie, who was never brought to bed of anything but wizened little monsters that never breathed, poor things – save for the one sickly girl – suddenly brings forth a strapping lad like a young warhorse. Of course people will say she played her husband false. But Michie Absalon kept her strictly, and sent her to L'Ange Rouge at Candlemas, the moment she missed her courses, to be kept strictly to her room and watched over day and night by this Maudit.'

She shuddered. 'Such a nursemaid! It would be enough to make you birth a monster, seeing no face but his for eight months.'

'Then your mother fled,' said January after a moment's calculation, 'when the child Guibert was born?'

'That I don't know, señor.' She glanced again toward the darkness of the trees, where a trace dappling of moonlight caught on the barrel of a rifle held by one of the men. 'Let me go now, señor. I have told you what I know. Maudit died badly. The partisans on Saint-Domingue knew who he was, and he lasted many hours, staked out on the beach with his entrails pulled out for the seabirds to peck at. But his shadow has lain over my life, and over my mother's. Leave off searching for that treasure – for Madame's diamonds, and Don Absalon's gold. It is an accursed thing. Your life will be better without it.'

'I have no doubt that it's accursed,' January replied. 'But if I

don't want to spend the rest of my life as you've spent yours – if
I don't want to lose those I love, as you lost your husband – I need
to find what Maudit hid, and find it soon. And I'm afraid,' he added,
turning his eyes to the dark of the ocean, 'that means Haiti.'

TWENTY-ONE

'**W**ell, old Rosario at the Fonda Velasquez did say Amalie
de Gericault got herself sent away to the other side of
the island to keep her out of trouble,' pointed out
Hannibal, who returned to their room on Thursday morning about
forty-five minutes after January did so. He was ashy with fatigue
and his hands shook, but he carried a jug of coffee from their land-
lady, a couple of pottery cups and a plate of pandolce with the
casual ease of a waiter. Chickens were crowing, and the first hot
streak of sunlight gilded the thatch on the western side of the yard.
'Could that be what Maudit tucked away with his pickings and the
girls' jewels? Proof – *can* one have medical proof of something like
that? – that Guibert de Gericault wasn't actually the son of Great-
Granpère Absalon?'

'There's none that I've ever read of.' January took the breakfast
from his hands, and the fiddler sank, coughing, into a chair. 'And
for Great-Granpère's purposes, the proof would mean nothing to
anyone after 1789 anyway. Besides, Guibert's son Bryce has the
same nose as Jeoffrey, the same jaw . . .'

Hannibal dug in his pockets and dropped a couple of handfuls
of reales and francs. 'I'm sorry about the cash. The Marquesa cheats
like a Greek – a terrible slur on the Greeks, now that I think of it.
I would say "cheats like a Congressman", but that's a terrible slur
on the Marquesa. And proof that Guibert wasn't the son of Amalie
would likewise lose its killing power in the summer of 'eighty-nine,
unless, of course . . .' He paused trenchantly, brows raised.

'Unless, of course,' January finished for him, 'the proof was that
the alternate parent in either case was a man or a woman of color.'
He poured coffee in the cups, divided the pandolce in two. 'What
did Guibert say in his farewell letter to Don Demetrio? "*Every other
white man you saw*" had an African ancestor somewhere. "*Hell, our*

butler was lighter than I am!" And it would be reason enough for Absalon to exile Amalie to his more distant plantation . . .'

'Until he saw how light her child was.'

'Which would be proof of nothing if her lover were an octoroon or musterfino. And when presented with a strapping, healthy, and apparently perfect white boy, do you think Great-Granpère was going to turn him away? The reverse would be true as well. And it is a weapon that would still be sharp after forty years. Proof – if such proof existed – that would be worth killing over, if de Gericault has any sort of position in society anywhere south of Mason's and Dixon's Line.'

'Which means that he probably does.' Hannibal dunked his pandolce into his coffee and coughed again, a dry rasp that January did not like. 'If we're going to argue in a circle. But it also means that he's not going to give up. It's too vital to his survival. Nor is he going to risk you and Rose going after the treasure that's possibly hidden along with the proof – if there is proof – and finding what's hidden with it.'

'What it means,' said January with grim simplicity, 'is that I'm going to Haiti.'

Captain Castallanos had taken the *Santana* on to Jamaica, but the local friends of Enrique Jivara in Havana vouched for the honesty of Captain Oldcastle of the *Samothrace*. Before departing Havana, January wrote a letter to Abishag Shaw, asking for information about a Gil or Gilbert Jericho, who had a son named Bryce and probably lived in or near Escambia County, Alabama. Either Gil or Bryce Jericho were probably to be found to be implicated in the murder of Jeoffrey Vitrac and the attempted murders of Jeoffrey's brother and half-sister. Anything he could relate about the Jerichos, please send on to Hannibal care of the American ministry in Havana.

'I suppose it would be safer for you, upon your return,' mused Hannibal as the leaky and overladen *Samothrace* wallowed its way into harbor at the Isle of Pines, 'if Rose and I should wait for you in Santiago, but quite honestly I'd feel safer with the length of the island between myself and Don Demetrio. *Honi soit qui mal y pense* and all that, even if I do convince him that I had no idea that "Pablo" was anything more than he seemed when we rode out of the stable yard two weeks ago . . .'

'I'll manage.' January felt in his pocket for the jotted names Ilario had given him, of fishermen to contact in the vicinity of Santiago, who could be trusted to get him across to Haiti rather than dosing him with opium and selling him in São Paulo. Nevertheless, the sheer riskiness of the venture turned him queasy. Haiti was still too great a prize to European powers for its inhabitants to look upon outsiders as anything other than potential spies, and, conversely, its mountains and forests were overrun with *Trinitarios* from the other side of the island, which had been conquered by Haiti a decade and a half previously. Fighters for their own freedom, they were likely to kill anyone who looked like a Haitian.

Moreover, Hannibal's run of bad luck at the Marquesa's gaming tables meant that January had only a few reales wherewith to pay the fishermen who'd take him to the island and, presumably, who could be bribed to bring him back. Hannibal had little more, to get himself and Rose back to Havana to wait.

Hail Mary, Mother of God, the Lord is with thee— His fingers sought the comfort of the rosary in his pocket. The *gris-gris* of Ogun, swinging against his chest, seemed hot from the sun against his flesh.

Keep them safe . . . Keep Baby John safe, whatever the hell is going on in New Orleans . . .

Bring us together again.

But out of the dark at the back of his mind he heard the Santeria incarnation Ogoun whisper, '*Blood and gold . . . gold and blood.*'

Whatever help the Mother of God might be on hand to talk her Son into offering, he suspected the *loa* weren't done with him yet.

For a reale, Captain Oldcastle anchored at the Bahia de Cayuna, a shallow inlet hidden from Santiago by a point of land on the opposite side of the main bay. It was a walk of three miles along the bay into town – nearly five, if they didn't pay one of the shrimp fishers in the lower bay to come across and ferry them to the eastern side – and the path, January had been warned, was haunted after dark by *rancheradores* out to pick up whatever people of color they could catch walking alone.

Still, he was chary of going into town without reconnaissance about Don Demetrio's feelings.

On the night of their arrival, they left their slender luggage in one of the broken-down bohios of a deserted fishing camp among the palm trees on the bay's western shore and paid a discreet visit to the Fonda Velasquez. Téo the stableman there was willing, for a reale, to take a note to Rose with the understanding (for an additional reale) that it wouldn't be shown to Don Demetrio. January could ill spare the coins, but needed the man in good humor.

'T'cha!' said the young man good-naturedly, pocketing both the coins and the note. 'You just lost me ten *centavos* – I bet the cook that your master run off for good . . .'

'How is Mamzelle Rose?'

'Oh, she's well.' Téo grinned. 'Fia in the laundry says, you never heard such screaming and cursing, when Don Demetrio found out Doña Jacinta was gone. Mamzelle Rose, she called your master every kind of *cabron*, saying she didn't believe a word of that "Pablo disappeared in the woods" tale, and if Señor Sefton had run off with that *puta*, when he came back she'd kill him. Then she clung to Don Demetrio's neck and wept, and I think that's the only reason Don Demetrio didn't take and sell her off out of pure spite, because between you and me, brother, he's got a nasty streak in him. They're all waiting to see if your master comes back.'

He leaned closer – though there was no one else in the inn's stable yard at the moment – and whispered, 'Did La Doña run off with your master?'

'No!' January was rather proud of the combination of exasperation and horror he managed to throw into his voice. 'Good God, he knows as well as anybody else Mamzelle Rose would murder him! We only heard yesterday in Manzanillo that people were saying he did!'

Téo shook his head. 'You tell your master he better be careful when he go up to Don Demetrio's, then. I hear from Fia that all the servants at *la casa* are saying, when Don Hannibal show up again, Don Demetrio's going to poison him and blame old Nyssa, who's a witch.'

'Oh, excellent,' grumbled Hannibal, when January gave him this piece of news in a quiet alleyway near the plaza. 'Just what I always wanted. A lifetime of running off with other men's wives and debauching maidens in hedgerows, and the one time I *don't* seduce a woman, *that's* when her husband makes trouble.'

'The world is an unfair place.'

They'd planned to take supper at the Fonda and listen to a more complete version of the local gossip, but given the possibility that someone would see Hannibal and get word to Don Demetrio – or simply oblige a friend by assassinating him on the spot – the two men chose the better part of valor and wound their way through Santiago's waterfront alleys and thence to the wharves, where a fisherman waited to take them across to their campsite among the palms. The sun dipped behind the wooded hills; the salt-smelling air was tinged with woodsmoke.

'I just hope she's able to get out of there undetected,' said Hannibal quietly as the fisherman set his sail to the gentle wind that flowed down from the mountains behind the town. Tropical night was falling swiftly; January groaned at the thought of locating their camp in the darkness.

'And I just hope,' he returned grimly as he shed his jacket to lend a hand with the ropes, 'that she doesn't run into *rancheradores* between Don Demetrio's and our camp.'

January guessed that Téo wouldn't leave Santiago until morning, and it was a day's ride across the mountains to Hispaniola Plantation; longer yet for Rose to return. On Wednesday, therefore, he walked westward, to a little bay hollowed into the shoulder of the Sierra Maestra where the mountains crowded down on to the coast. A little colony of fishermen – recommended by Ilario, and all named Vargas – agreed, for three reales, to carry him across to Haiti.

'But it's a bad place, señor,' warned the gray-haired patriarch of the clan. 'If you don't get shot for a spy and the Trinitarios don't kill you, the mulatto planters will see in you a man who has no family, no one to search for you if you vanish. They pay the *bokors* – the sorcerers – to find them such men, to kill them and make them *zombis*, and work them until their bodies rot and fall to pieces.'

Nevertheless, for a consideration, they thought that Cousin Cristobal (who was a friend of smugglers) could be talked into carrying January across to a secluded beach on the Môle-Sant-Nicolas, the tip of the island's north-western peninsula. Cristobal would go back for him the following Sunday . . . 'He will be here tomorrow,' promised the patriarch. 'He comes by to see his wife, on his way through to Manzanillo. Return in the afternoon to make arrangements.'

January agreed, but, weary though he was when he returned to the deserted *bohío*, he collected the fiddler, and together they walked across the point of land to the main bay and got one of the shrimp fishers to take them up into Santiago again to make sure the Vargas clan could, in fact, be trusted.

'They can,' Rosario assured them. 'That's just old Abuelo Vargas' way. If you're worried that he's just luring you out to their cove to be picked up by *rancheradores*—'

'In fact,' said Hannibal frankly, 'we are. Although we were told –' he cocked an eye at the innkeeper, who had, rather surprisingly, figured along with Téo the stableman on Enrique Jivara's list of 'Those Who Can be Trusted' – 'that he was not given to double-dealing, still I would rather not find out that we were misinformed. The cove is a very isolated one, and the road there runs very handily close to the sea.'

January had, in fact, taken the road itself as little as possible and had a fine set of insect bites and scratches from scrambling along in the thickets of palmetto that flanked it. A few yards below him, for close to three miles, the waves had lapped lazily on the beaches, and he'd been vividly conscious of how easy it would be, for slave-stealers to bring a boat up and pick a lone man off the road.

'It's all right,' said the innkeeper decidedly. 'The Vargas family deals with smugglers, but not slave-stealers . . . Well, of course I don't know about the smugglers,' he added quickly and smoothed his long-handled mustache. Through the back door of the common room someone called out his name, and he bowed apologetically. 'I must go, señores.' The stable yard where they'd met him – still cautious about encountering Don Demetrio's friends – was lively with the horses and *caretelas* of men from the plantations round about, and the music of guitars started up inside.

More seriously, Rosario went on, 'But I do know about the *rancheradores*, my friends. The Vargas have lost more than one nephew to such scum, and I promise you, this isn't a trap.'

Nevertheless, on the following morning January armed himself with his pistol, a rifle that Rosario lent him, and a knife before setting off along the coast road once again. 'Will you be all right?' he asked Hannibal, before leaving the camp. The fiddler was stowing what remained of their food – they'd replenished supplies in town yesterday afternoon – preparatory to setting off himself to meet Rose on the road behind town.

'Perfectly.' Hannibal stifled a cough. 'I think I can talk old Rosario into lending me a horse, and as I recall the jungle is thick enough, going up over the ridge, to keep me concealed while I await the Beautiful Athene. If she slipped away from Hispaniola as soon as it got light this morning, we should actually reach the top of the pass at about the same time, and there's enough other traffic on the road that she shouldn't be in too much danger before that time. *Fortes fortuna adiuvat* – don't worry, *amicus meus*. We'll be all right.'

As he threaded the paths through the wooded country south-west of the bay, paths that he recognized as the secret trails used by the slaves of the *cafeteles* that dotted this rolling land, January tried to tell himself that Rosario was right, and all would in fact be well. At least with Hannibal and Rose, he added grimly, and he shivered at the thought of landing on the isolated northern peninsula of Haiti, of making his way down the barren coast to Port-au-Prince, and thence along the feet of the mountains to L'Ange Rouge. Salomé Saldaña had sketched a map of the plantation for him, which agreed with Rose's recollection of the place old Ginette had created for her in play. House, sugar mill, quarters, woodsheds . . . 'Of course, it's pretty much the plan of every plantation I've ever been on,' Rose had reminded him. 'It could be Aramis' plantation at Chouteau. Or La Châtaigneraie. I'm sure if we'd had time to grub around in the underbrush at Hispaniola-Grande-Isle we'd have found the remains of the mill and the quarters and the mule barns in pretty much the same place.'

Rose.

His heart seemed to squeeze tight in his chest: love, dread, fury at the men who'd stabbed her in the market. Panic at the thought of losing her.

And losing her to what? To some ancient plot, to some idiot panic by a man who feared that someone might call him 'nigger' . . .

A man who couldn't let well alone. Who couldn't let the past stay dead.

Which brought the next thought as January came clear of the woods and the clean salt silk of the Caribbean wind flowed over his face from the sea. *WHY can't he let the past stay dead?*

A man doesn't come to New Orleans with premeditated murder and the expense of tracking down all members of his family – solely on the news that someone has uncovered the location of the old family treasure – unless he's driven by something.

So what's really going on?

He scanned the sea: sails, big craft and small, coming and going from the harbor mouth where the old Castillo mounted guard, but nothing near the road along the rugged hill-feet. Scanned the road. *Fortune helps the bold*, Hannibal had said.

The face of Bryce Jericho – long and firm-jawed, with a nose like Jeoffrey's and Aramis' honey-colored hair – remained in his mind as he turned his steps along the road, seagulls crying overhead.

TWENTY-TWO

He returned to the *bohio* – after successful negotiations with Cristobal Vargas and his grandfather – at the hour of siesta. It would be the act of a husband and a friend to set forth at once to meet Rose and Hannibal on the road.

A husband and a friend who hasn't just walked ten miles.

He mixed himself some water with vinegar and ginger and lay down in one of the hammocks he and Hannibal had strung up in the little hut. By the time he'd signaled one of the shrimp fishers to carry him across to the Santiago side, his friends would in all probability be already walking along the eastern shore road in quest of shrimp fishers to carry them over to this side. Tired as he was, January couldn't shut his eyes, listening to the rustle of the sea breeze in the banana groves and wondering if each flurry of bird calls was prompted by the stealthy approach of *rancheradores* who would tear him from Rose, from his child, from his friends and his life and his freedom, forever . . .

He woke with a start, and the angle of light through the chinks in the wall and the flimsy door told him it was nearly sunset.

Softly, the waves continued to wash on the beach nearby.

Where the hell are Hannibal and Rose?

He rolled out of the hammock, took bread and cheese from the crock on the table, walked out of the *bohio* and, after a moment's hesitation, clear of the trees and up to the weed-grown track that led around the bay, the long way to town. From there he walked down to the waterside, a prickling uneasiness growing in him. After a little hesitation, he set off up the trail through the palmetto thickets that led across the point and looked out across the bay – half a mile wide here – to the road that led up its eastern side toward Santiago.

A couple of women were walking along it towards town, carrying baskets. A fisherman had drawn up his boat on the shingle, about half a mile up from where January stood.

His first, panicky thought was, *Rose never reached the rendezvous.*

Don Demetrio intercepted my note to her . . .

His stomach turned over.

Then, *Hannibal could have been taken ill.* The fiddler hadn't looked well. Though giving up drinking had seemed to rally his strength against the slow wasting of consumption, January had seen the toll that travel and exertion were taking on him. At any time the disease could return full force: fever, infections, lesions opening in his damaged lungs.

But if that happened on his way up the pass to meet Rose, she'd have found him . . .

He waved, whistled, and shouted, and eventually the shrimp fishers noticed him and in a leisurely fashion cleared up their nets and baskets, set their sails, crossed the bay.

They only took him across the bay, not up to town, and he couldn't spare the half-reale it would take to pay them for the extra distance.

The sun went down as he walked. Tropical night closed in.

'*Dios*, man!' Young Téo emerged from the harness shed, ran across the stable yard as January came through the gateway. 'I was praying you'd come—'

The cold that had been growing like a poisoned seed in his heart all the way up the lonely road along the bay clenched tight in his chest, almost stopping his breath. In the light of the cressets burning around the yard, the groom's face told its story.

'What happened?'

'*Rancheradores.* They got your master's woman; your master gone after her—'

'When?' And then, as his mind sorted the words, 'Where? How do you know this?'

'Santos told me, one of the fishermen in the bay. He was taking your master across this morning, when your master points to the road and says, "There she is! Saves me the cost of the horse!" She was wearing a yellow shawl, Santos said, and a pink dress. Santos said your master said his lady friend must have started out walking in the night instead of waiting for morning. That must have been soon after I gave her your note, maybe the minute everybody at *la casa* was in bed.

'Santos said she was walking fast, looking behind her, like she was afraid. And while Santos and your master was still about a half-mile off from her – the wind was offshore, so Santos wasn't making much headway – a rider comes from town, and a boat comes from the same direction, a skiff with a black hull. Your master's lady, she tries to run inland, but the rider overtakes her, grabs her by the waist and drags her to the boat. Your master's yelling and cursing, and the men in the black boat shoot at him, so Santos won't follow them—'

'Damn it!'

'Santos got a family.' Compassion filled the young man's eyes. 'Santos told me he took your master up to the harbor where your master hired Lobo – that's Santos' cousin – to follow them in his boat, and the last he saw them, Lobo and your master were heading down the bay after these slave-stealers in their skiff. Santos said they were dark-skinned men, mulattos, he thought, so they're probably El Chirlo's men from Manzanillo. El Chirlo's a mulatto. Lobo isn't back yet, and his wife's fit to kill somebody, 'cause he's always getting into trouble . . .'

Manzanillo. A long day's sail around the western arm of the island, *if* that was where they'd taken her . . .

The world seemed to collapse, burying him in darkness.

'You love her, don't you, brother?' asked Téo softly. 'For all she's your master's—'

'I love her.' His mind felt blank. There had to be something he could do, but nothing came to him. 'Where is Lobo's house?' he asked at last.

'They won't hear nothing till Saturday night at the earliest, depending on the wind. More like Sunday. Believe me, you'll be first to hear.'

January opened his mouth to protest, but asked himself, *What do you want to do? Sit on Mrs Lobo's doorstep?* He felt as if he'd been struck by lightning, or had taken a stunning blow to the head. Walking back to the *bohio* on the other side of the bay seemed unthinkable—

Walk there and do what? WAIT? All night tonight, all day tomorrow . . . 'More like Sunday . . .'

He pressed his fist to his lips, trembling as if smitten with deadly chills. *Holy Mary, Mother of God . . .*

The words circled on themselves, going nowhere.

Holy Mary, Mother of God . . .

Thank you. Thank you that Hannibal saw it. Thank you that he's in pursuit.

Dear God, where do I even start?

I brought her here.

Endless pacing, miles, like trying to outwalk the Devil. Back and forth across the rickety little hut. Back and forth across the point of land between the bay and the cove behind the point. Around and around the thickets of palmetto and banana plants, stealing out fifty times during the course of Friday to watch the road, or stare at the passers-by on the path along the bay. Cursing himself, cursing Don Demetrio, cursing the slave-stealer El Chirlo – if that was indeed the man who'd taken her – through the endless sweltering hours of Thursday night, Friday night, and all over again Saturday as he listened to the grasshoppers creak, the frogs peep and grunt and glak their never-ending hellish chorus.

I brought her here.

He knew well enough that if they'd remained in New Orleans they'd both have been killed: possibly Baby John as well.

He knew if they'd stayed on Grand Isle, Bryce Jericho's men would have overtaken them and killed them there.

It made no difference. The pain in his heart did not lessen by the weight of a single hair.

Rain on the thatch.

The slow surge of wavelets in the cove.

She can't be gone.

Old Ginette, who had voyaged from this island to Grand Isle when Rose was ten, must have said the same thing of her granddaughter, when *rancheradores* carried her away. Salomé Saldaña had never seen her child again.

It can't be true.

Follow her? Seek her? For how long?

Months? Years?

Or go back to New Orleans and be the best father I can be to Baby John?

Or will Jericho and his men still come after me there?

He wanted to weep and couldn't. It wasn't yet time for tears.

There was bread and cheese and oranges in the *bohio*, but he ate none of it. Had Rose simply vanished, had Hannibal not been there to set out in pursuit, he, Benjamin, would have already departed for Manzanillo – that hive of slave-traders – alone . . .

Though he told himself there was no certainty that this El Chirlo of whom Téo spoke was in fact the slave-stealer who'd taken her. It was only a guess.

Manzanillo was only a guess.

It could have been anyone. Going anywhere.

Sometimes he found himself cursing Hannibal, though the fiddler hadn't been aware that Doña Jacinta was with them when they'd left Hispaniola Plantation. Even had she not fled, would Don Demetrio have assisted in finding a stolen slave-woman?

He didn't know.

Other times he knew, with the clarity of a man on the scaffold, that the whole of his life, of his heart, lay in the shaky hands of a consumptive fiddler to whom he had been kind.

His faith told him that it was impossible that Rose had been taken because he, Benjamin, had gone seeking the *orishas*, had listened to Lazaro Ximo, though he had no doubt that any number of his acquaintances – both white and black – would tell him that this was so. In the deeps of the second night, he wondered if they were right.

Late on Sunday afternoon, on his tenth or eleventh aimless prowl to the shore, he saw one of the shrimp boats crossing the bay toward him with three men in it, one of whom wore a red shirt such as Téo wore. January had, through these endless days, taken care never to show himself on the beach when he walked there, keeping instead to the fringe of banana plants just above the tideline. Now he waited until they were halfway across, and, yes, that was Téo in the boat, with a smaller man, stout and gnarled like a wind-bitten tree-stump, in a faded *guayabera* and a raggedy straw hat.

He stepped clear of the trees.

The only other man in the boat was the shrimp fisher. No sign of Hannibal.

Heart pounding, he walked down to the pebbly shore with a sense of dreadful vertigo.

Téo sprang from the boat as the other two men beached it and called out to him before they even came close, 'She is in Haiti.'

January stopped in his tracks. '*What?*'

The short man finished helping to pull the boat up on to the beach, came to join them; Téo's gesture indicated him before he came near enough to speak himself. 'Lobo here followed them out to sea. He thought at first they were going to Jamaica – there are slave-dealers who operate there in spite of the British. When he started to turn, to come back here – for Mariana his wife would surely strike him with a stick of firewood, if he was away overnight – your master held the pistol on him and told him he would shoot him if he gave up the chase.'

'And I should have let him do it,' added Lobo with a single-toothed grin. 'We were right out in the ocean, and Don Hannibal had no more idea of how to steer a boat and set his sails than my baby daughter.'

'Thank you.' *HAITI?* He felt breathless with shock. 'I have no money, but I promise you, I will give you some, as much as you ask, when I get some . . . I swear to you . . .'

'Yes, yes.' The fisherman waved his hand. 'I'll tell my banker to get in touch with your banker, brother. He fell asleep, your master, in the deep of the night, lying on the bench with his pistol under his hand, and I had not the heart to waken him, seeing as it was clear then to me where this black-hulled skiff was headed. We had lost sight of them – they could spread more sail than we and keep on course to the south-east when the winds turned in the night. I did take his pistol away from him. It was clear to me that Haiti was the only place they could be going.'

Dear God. His mind felt blank.

Dear God.

Slave-stealers would have gone up the coast to Manzanillo, or crossed the Windward Channel to Jamaica.

Bryce Jericho was back in Havana, or had been when he and Hannibal had left there over a week ago. There was no way he could have reached Santiago before them.

He had to forcibly bring his mind back to the voices of Téo and Lobo: *not slave-stealers.*

Treasure-hunters.

Bryce's men . . .

But why not kill her, as they'd killed her brother?

They could have easily done so on the shore.

They would certainly do so when they'd found what they sought.

They're going to one of de Gericault's plantations: La Châtaigneraie, or L'Ange Rouge.

'. . . put him ashore at a cove right at the end of the Môle,' Lobo was saying. 'The wind was hard from the north-east; I don't think they'd have gone around that way to Le Cap. Not if they'd had to pass the fort of Saint-Nicolas. I tried to talk your master into coming back with me – he's a dead man the minute anyone sees him. But he wasn't having any of it.'

Téo's eyes slid sidelong to January. 'He must love her a good deal, this woman.'

'He was like a man distracted.' Lobo shrugged. 'You see so many men, they are jealous of their mistress if she look at another man, but if that other man offer them money for her? She'd be gone.' He made a motion, as if flicking muddy water from his hands. 'She is a free woman, your master's mistress?'

January nodded. 'And he is more like a brother to me than a master. I owe him my life – and more else than I could ever say. The men who took her think she knows where a treasure is hid, a treasure from the old days before the rebellion.'

'They were mulattos,' said Téo. 'There was a white man with them, Santos said, tall and plump and fair-haired . . .'

Seth Maddox. Michie Curly, who'd watched his house in New Orleans. 'I don't know the whole of the tale.'

Lobo sucked at his lip where he'd lost teeth. 'And you're about to ask me to sail you over there for nothing, eh? And lose me another three days' catch on top of the two that your master just cost me, making me go across to that devil-cursed island at pistol point with nothing to feed my family on but the two reales he had in his pocket. Ow,' he added as Téo punched him in the arm.

'Let me take your boat, then,' said Téo.

'Oh, yes, so I can feed my family fishing for shrimp with a hook and a line from the shore . . . and you know no more of sailing than this *zambo* here—' He nodded at January.

'For the love of God, man!'

'Why doesn't God ever tell us to help the rich who'll pay us money, eh?' Lobo shook one calloused finger at January. 'You tell me that. And you –' he turned in disgust back to Téo – '*you* go tell my Mariana that *you* talked me into taking this crazy *zambo* back across to the Môle, where he's gonna get shot for a spy, or worse, before he's even off the beach, and I have his death on my conscience the same way I have his crazy *patrón*'s. And it's only 'cause I been such a sinner I'm doing this, and God better forgive me one or two or three of the worst ones . . . Go get your things.' He glared at January. 'We got to wait for the evening tide.'

HAITI

TWENTY-THREE

They veered along on the edge of north-westerly winds that kept the deep passage between Cuba and Hispaniola perpetually choppy and rough. Twenty-one years previously, January recalled, he had clung to the rail of the French merchantman *Fleur-de-Lys*, outbound through this Windward Passage from New Orleans to Bordeaux, and had watched the turquoise waters of the Caribbean transform into the heavy gray-green swells of the Atlantic.

And his heart had sung to him: *Never going back. Never going back. In America the shadow of slavery will lie over me always. In France I will be truly free.*

It amazed him that he'd been young enough to believe that.

The winds backed hard to the north-east just before dawn, and rain swept them. Lobo and his nephew Tómas fought the tiller against the driving darkness, and when full light came Lobo curled up in his blankets and slept. January knew he should do the same, and couldn't. 'Your *indios* could have been running for Baie-de-Henne,' Lobo said when he woke up, and the westering sun showed them the pine-shrouded mountains of Hispaniola in the distance. 'Maybe Red Beach, or run clear into Gonaïves. Smugglers run in and out of Gonaïves all the time—'

And is that how YOU know so much about it, old man? January wondered.

'—so a couple of *indios* maybe won't be noticed. But the troops on the Môle-Sant-Nicolas, they watch for deep-water sail, and I knew if they caught me bringing a white man ashore, they sure weren't going to believe no story about a friend of his having his wife kidnapped by a bunch of *indios*. I put you ashore where I put him ashore. This whole coast got few real harbors, but there's a beach about ten miles from Baie-de-Henne.'

January said, 'I understand.'

'More than President Boyar's troops, you got to watch out for the Egbo, the Leopard Society. Every little village, there's men that belong to it, men that know there's nothing Spain or France or maybe even the United States would like better than to take Haiti back again and make them all slaves again, and make the country pour out money like it used to. To them, all strangers are spies – or else Spanish *Trinitarios* raiding from the east of the island, who hate the rule of Boyar. They eat the flesh of the men they catch and drink their blood.'

Through Rose's spyglass, January watched the land draw near. The northern peninsula seemed to be mostly scrubland, with patches of forest which grew thicker as it ascended the low mountains that protected the island's central gulf from the Atlantic winds. Trails of smoke rose from a village. What looked like fishing boats were putting out, and he wondered if the villagers had reported – either to the military or to the local Leopard Society – Lobo's earlier visit. He also wondered if this was anywhere near where Dr Maudit had come ashore some thirty years previously.

He thought of Hannibal alone ashore – he'd been here three days already – and shivered.

But scanning the beach as they approached – a long, shallow crescent of sand a couple of miles east of the village – he saw no column of vultures in the air that would mark a corpse on the beach.

Now let's make sure I don't end up a corpse on the beach myself.

'You got to wade in from here,' Lobo told him, when they were about a hundred feet from the sand. 'Any farther in, we couldn't get the wind to get ourselves out of here.'

January dropped overside and found himself breast deep in water, warmer and calmer than he'd seen all day. This was the Caribbean side of the island, and though the evening was drawing on, heat seemed to radiate from the land.

The boy Tómas handed him a straw gunnysack containing bread, cheese, oranges and two water-bottles. January balanced it on his head, like the women who carried baskets of tomatoes and strawberries around the streets of New Orleans.

'Good luck finding your lady and your master.' Lobo hooked the sheets free, sail canvas snapping as it filled with the wind. 'You surely going to need it.'

It was nearly fifty miles, Lobo had told him in the course of that afternoon, to the little port of Gonaïves, and almost twenty to the fishing village of Red Beach. Between those harbors the coast was mostly deserted, lacking anyplace where a vessel of any size might put in. The *lakou* – the family compounds – of the mountainous country behind were primitive and hostile to strangers. Only in the towns, he had said, would January find anyone who spoke French.

As January waded ashore, he reflected that Rose's captors would almost certainly be making for Cap Haïtien – Le Cap, Lobo had called it – the old capital at Cap Francais. La Châtaigneraie – Absalon de Gericault's primary plantation – lay only a few hours' walk from it, and to anyone who had not spoken with Salomé Saldaña it would make sense that old Maurir had hidden his treasure – and his secret – there.

From old Lobo's description, Jean Thiot at the Café des Refugies would probably barely recognize the place. It had been burned by Dessalines and his men, and close to 20,000 whites had been slaughtered there. Mulatto brokers and traders still ran the town, said Lobo, the way they ran all the towns in Haiti – it was their money that kept the government afloat. But the 'Paris of the Caribbean', with its three theaters, its newspapers and its dozens of graceful little houses where the planters' quadroon mistresses dwelled, was long gone.

And when they don't find what they're seeking at La Châtaigneraie, January thought, his feet pressing the underwater sand, *they'll head for L'Ange Rouge.*

And I need to reach it before them.

The thought of leaving Rose in their hands for that long made him nearly sick.

The thought of moving on at once, without looking for Hannibal – who had come to this place only to help him, who had set out alone for Haiti to rescue Rose with one bullet in his gun and barely the price of dinner in his pockets – tore his heart like broken glass. But the surgeon in him – the man who could, and had, look at a woman sobbing in a blocked labor and say, *'The baby must be killed for the mother to live'* – heard in his mind Abishag Shaw's light-timbred drawl: *'The hunter has all the advantage . . . The only way to make sure he don't come at you again, is to lead him into a trap . . .'*

The trap could only be set if he reached L'Ange Rouge first.

Where Guibert de Gericault had been born.

Whatever happened, happened there.

How can I leave Hannibal?

How can I hesitate, when hesitation will mean Rose's life?

A thousand lesser questions pricked his mind, as if he'd thrust his hand in a jar of pins – what had become of Calanthe and Emmanuelle? Why were they at L'Ange Rouge in the first place? What sent Ginette fleeing into the night in the wildness of a hurricane after Amalie de Gericault died giving birth to a healthy son? But, like a greater torment driving out a lesser, he saw a thousand memories as well: Rose with her long cloak fluttering in the storm winds, that first day he'd walked her from her school on Rue St-Claude to his mother's house where he'd been living then . . . Rose with her brown curls tumbled about her shoulders, smiling up at him with Baby John nestled against her shoulder. Rose rising from her chair on the gallery of their house, spectacles flashing in the lights from the parlor window.

Rose crouched beside him in the cellar of the old house at Hispaniola, listening to the creak of boots overhead.

I'd better be right about them needing her to find the treasure . . .

The thought that he might be wrong turned him sick with panic.

And whatever we find there, he reflected as Lobo's boat was swallowed by the sun glare, as if sailing into a gate of fire, *there'd better be at least SOME treasure left at L'Ange Rouge, if the three of us – Holy Mother, please let it be the three of us! – plan to get off the island alive.*

By the last of the fading daylight, he searched the mile-long curve of the beach for any sign of Hannibal. Last night's rain had destroyed whatever tracks there might have been, but he'd formed a good enough opinion of Lobo's seamanship to trust the old man's assertion that this was, in fact, the place he'd brought the fiddler ashore.

At least he wasn't murdered the minute he set foot on land.

January himself had food for two days if he was stingy with it, a rifle, a pistol, several knives and five reales in his pocket. Hannibal, he guessed, had been set ashore with nothing. Before he reached the headland that ended the beach, night had fallen, so he made a bed for himself in the landward edge of the thickets of palmetto, far enough into the scrub to be free (he hoped) from sandflies. He ate his bread and cheese by moonlight, drank sparingly of his water bottle, and lay listening to the whisper of waves on the beach, the liquid calls of the birds as they settled themselves, each in its own territory.

What country, friends, is this? Viola had asked, cast ashore at the beginning of *Twelfth Night.*

The only one in the Western Hemisphere where I'm NOT in danger of being kidnapped by white men as a slave.

And I'm still not safe.

From westward along the beach – from the fishing hamlet in its cove? – came the throbbing of drums. Yet he found the sound comforting, knowing – as most whites did not – that it only meant that the villagers were dancing in the hot moonlit night. Happy – forty years later – to be free.

With daybreak, he ate, sparingly, of his slender supplies and walked to the headland that bounded the beach to the east. He scrambled over the steep land, to another shallow curve of sand barely ten yards wide and still blue with the shadows of the mountains inland, and at the far end, where the mountains advanced to the water again, saw what he'd dreaded all along: a dark column of birds circling in the clear dawn light.

He broke into a run.

There'd been a camp there. Charred rocks and burned wood in a fire pit, makeshift shelters wrought of palmetto fans and banana leaves, the smell of a hastily-covered latrine pit. The body lay in the thickets of palmetto between the camp and the woods on the higher ground, three days dead by the smell of it, squirming with maggots.

The buzzards grunted and hissed at him as he came close. They'd left little of the face – which was invisible, in any case, under its living, wriggling shroud – and what skin remained visible was dusky with the lividity of decay. But the boots weren't Hannibal's. Neither was the hair long like the fiddler's, but straight and coarse. Indian hair.

A Muskogee Creek, presumably, from Escambia County, Alabama.

And by the behavior of the buzzards, the only corpse (or near-corpse) on the beach.

The thought of searching the body, for either money, papers, or evidence of how the man had died, was literally nauseating. January backed away and returned to the abandoned campsite. The palm tree that had formed the corner of one of the shelters bore marks where a rope had fretted and scratched.

They tied her here.

Rage swamped him like a hurricane surge, momentarily
blinding. Rage, terror, dread.

Fresh bullet scars pocked the palm trunk, and another one nearby,
but search as he might he found no blood in the sand near that tree.
There was a great splash of it some ten feet away, and a trail that
led into the fan-palm thickets behind the camp. It ended in the marks
of scraping and dragging.

The Leopard Society? Hannibal? One of Rose's kidnappers –
Maddox, Killwoman, Conyngham . . .?

*Have they somehow mislaid their own map to the treasure? Are
they trying to double-cross Jericho? Get to the treasure – the secret
– before him?*

Like a child's wail, his prayer went up, *Please, God, don't let
them have hurt her . . .*

*Please, God, don't let the world be as I know perfectly goddam
well the world is.*

He tried to breathe, tried to steady his mind. This had all happened
Saturday night, while he was pacing frantically back and forth in
the *bohio* on Santiago Bay.

There's nothing I could have done. No way I could have saved her.

He'd had whippings less terrible than the guilt and horror he felt.
Than the fear that there was worse to come.

*They came ashore Saturday – because of the wind and rain? Did
they anchor here the night, meaning to put out when the sea grew
calm again and risk running around the Môle of St-Nicolas under
the noses of Boyar's troops and along the north coast to Le Cap?*

*Or did they plan to take the easier route along the southern coast
of the peninsula to Gonaïves?*

In any case, the camp had been attacked, driving them back into
their boat.

Hannibal?

The Egbo?

Someone else?

Wherever they sailed, Hannibal remained behind, afoot. Alone.
Maybe wounded badly.

*In Gonaïves – maybe sooner – I can find or steal or beg a place
on a boat down the coast to Port-au-Prince. That's the way Hannibal
will have gone, if he's still alive.*

He turned his steps eastward along the beach, beside the innu-
merable laughter of the turquoise sea.

TWENTY-FOUR

The coast stretched east in a succession of shallow crescent beaches, thin strips of sand below mountains cloaked in light woodlands of ceiba and palms. Many times he had to scramble over steep slopes rising straight from the sea. No streams trickled from the thin tree-cover above him, and though the sea winds mitigated the hammering heat, still the sun oppressed him like a physical weight.

His only companions were his thoughts . . . and fear.

Educated in New Orleans and Paris, heir to the wisdom of Socrates and Shakespeare, Harvey and Newton, January knew himself to be as much a stranger in this land as if he'd been set ashore in Africa.

Here, deceased ancestors still took a lively interest in the doings of their descendants. Secret brotherhoods united men of families and tribes against outsiders. Old gods whispered to *mambos* and root doctors from out of bottles and gourds. Those whose hearts and minds sought dreams beyond eating, sleeping, farming and their families were obliged by ignorance to give them up.

He was a stranger, protected by no clan and no tribe.

Holy Mary, Mother of God, walk beside me . . .

He came around a long shoulder of scrubland and found a potholed, uneven trace presumably used by the inhabitants of whatever *lakou* eked out a living here, by charcoal burning and fishing and maybe growing a little coffee. He was weary, and thirsty, though he'd gone fairly slowly, searching as he went for any sign that Hannibal had passed this way, and as he rounded that shoulder of cliff, he could see a village on the shore where a river came down from the jungled mountains inland.

Baie-de-Henne, Lobo had called the place. A little harbor with fishing boats.

He wondered if he could find someone there to sell him food and transport him across the gulf. Or would they simply whisper to the Egbo that there was a stranger – possibly a spy – afoot?

The path widened, and by the animal droppings he found along it he guessed that there were *lakou* in the neighborhood, whose members led donkeys to the village to get supplies. Farmland spread along the river below the town, and January followed the edge of the woods inland, to remain unnoticed.

He remembered the drumbeats of last night.

At the woods' edge, however, he met two men and a woman, leading a donkey laden with provisions from the direction of the village. They hailed him in cane-patch French similar to that he'd grown up with – '*Mo kiri mo vini*,' his mother called it with scorn, as if she hadn't worked like a devil to learn proper French when she'd been freed and had moved to town.

Flight, he knew from childhood brushes with the pattyrollers, would call more attention to himself than foreign speech. So he called out, '*Bonjou*,' half-expecting his mother to magically appear and slap him for it, and the woman lifted her hand to him with a friendly smile. When she spoke it was with French words strung together on an African weft, like beads.

'You not from here, brother,' she said, and January shook his head with a rueful expression.

'I'm come from Cuba.' And, thankful that he didn't have to come up with a fabrication which could be checked, he went on, 'Three men, *indios*, kidnap my wife in a sailing boat. I thought they were slave-traders, but the fisherman who saw it – who followed them, may God reward him a hundred thousand times! – says they brought her here, to Haiti. Is that Baie-de-Henne down there ahead?' He pointed toward the village, and all three of the farmers nodded. 'Have you heard anything of this? Of Indian men, with a mulatto woman among them?'

He didn't expect that they had – he'd scanned the wharf with Rose's spyglass and had seen no sign of the black-hulled skiff that Lobo had described – but one of the men, with a nod at the *gris-gris* around January's neck, said, 'You go ask Papa Grillo in Red Beach. He got a *humfo* just past the town, and he know everything. He hear everything.'

'Would any in the town sell me food?' He gestured to his own nearly-empty gunnysack – *macoutes*, they were called here. 'Or any you know of, be willing to take me down to Gonaïves, or Port-au-Prince?'

'The fishermen there are all out.' The younger man nodded toward the jewel-blue waters of the gulf. 'They're not in till evening.' He was skinny, with the thinness they all shared, the thinness of malnutrition and overwork.

.

'And maybe better you not stay in the town that long,' added the woman, glancing at him with worried eyes. 'There's men in town that watch for strangers, that work for the *bokors*. A stranger that no one will miss—' She shook her head. Though her clothing was hand-woven, faded and shabby, still she wore a tignon bright and brave and fashioned of at least half a dozen kerchiefs, like the market women in New Orleans. The style of wrapping he dimly recognized as that signaling a married woman, but only the older market women these days kept closely to the old system of using a tignon to denote status. Except for the voodoos, women in New Orleans pretty much tied their headwraps as they pleased, the fancier the better.

He thanked them and went on, giving the village wide berth. It was in his mind that he might also ask at the church for some help on his journey, but he'd heard no sound of bells. Priests, he recalled, had fled with the other whites, or been killed, and the church in Haiti had broken from the church in Rome. Once past the village, he turned his spyglass back upon it and saw that the steeple of the little church there was in ruins.

There was a road, however, past the town – unpaved, and gashed with evidence of the summer's torrential rains – and this made the going easier. Towards noon January retreated to the shelter of the woods, ate the remainder of his food and drank as little of the water as he could stand. He'd come, he guessed, about a dozen miles from where Lobo had left him on the beach; when he lay down in a palmetto thicket to sleep, he took a certain amount of care to pick a place where he wouldn't be easily seen.

He slept and dreamed of the corpse on the beach.

A mile or so from Red Beach, with the evening beginning to come on, a man came down from the woods above the road and hailed him in a friendly fashion: was he a stranger here? Where was he bound?

'I'm Tullio, I got a little farm up in the hills . . .'

He spoke French, not the local language, and his hands weren't a farmer's hands. His clothes, though old, were of store-bought cloth, not homespun. When Tullio offered to buy him a *p'tit-goave* at a tavern he knew in the village ('My cousin's husband owns the place, best rum in the north-west . . .') January excused himself.

'My cousin, he said he'd meet me on the road past town.'

'Where's your cousin coming from? There's nothing past town, brother, not for twenty miles. It's not safe, walking when darkness falls.' Tullio shaded his eyes and looked suggestively westward, where the sun was sliding towards the sea beyond the tips of Hispaniola's two long peninsulas. 'Much better you spend the night in town. My sister, she can put you up.'

January couldn't shake the man off until they'd passed the village – which was so small that it barely boasted a wharf – and he turned up the twisty little path which led, according to the farmers that afternoon, up the wooded shoulder of the hills to the *humfo* – the sacred compound – of Papa Grillo.

Tullio put a hand on January's arm, brow drawn with concern. 'You want to watch out for old Grillo,' he warned, dropping his voice almost to a whisper. 'He works with both hands, you know? Poisons people and then sells them cures. Puts the cross on people and then they got to pay him to take it off. He's a *bokor* – a werewolf as well, some say. Men who go through his gate sometimes don't come out again.'

Not much to January's surprise, the first thing Papa Grillo told him – when one of the women pounding grain in the yard of the modest compound sent a child to fetch the white-bearded and thoroughly ugly *hougan* from the largest of the several houses – was that Tullio was the one who worked for the *bokor*, Efik, further up the valley. It was Efik who poisoned strangers, and then revived them as *zombi* and sold them to the mulatto planters on the south coast.

'The smuggler boats, they come in and put out from Red Beach,' grumbled the old man as he seated himself on one of the benches in the peristyle, the thatch-roofed marquee in the middle of the compound where the dances were held to honor the *loa*. 'The President, he don't care how *les grands* along the south coast get their workers. Mulattos.' He spit. 'Christophe should have killed them, along with the whites.'

Cut-paper banners hung from the rafters overhead, bright against the shadows of the thatch. The central post – the avenue of the gods, before which Grillo sat on his bench – was painted red with black stripes, the table of stones built up around it scrubbed spotless. 'President wants the *súceries* back, so he can get taxes from them. Free men, free women, they had enough of that kind of work in slavery times, they won't do it. They just want to work their farms and raise their children. This Boyar say – this mulatto who call himself President – they're strangers who got no business here anyway, why should he care?'

He shrugged and offered January a gourd of ginger water. Just behind the peristyle stood a small house, and through its door January could see the shadowy altars of the various families of gods, Guédé and Rada and Petwo, gay with cut paper, beaded bottles, little dishes of candy and tobacco and cups of rum.

'Since I'm a stranger here myself,' said January, shaking his head in thanks, 'and there's two others who'll die if I disappear, I'm going to say no. But thank you.' He'd set down his rifle against the bench where he sat, but it was in easy reach of his hand.

The *hougan* tilted his wall eye at him, then saluted him with the gourd.

'I heard of those men,' he said, when January had told him what he sought. 'The *indios* that bring that mulatto woman ashore. There was shooting. One of the *indios* was killed and a *blan'* shot, who got away into the trees bleeding—'

'A white man?' *Shit.* His heart turned cold at the recollection of the marks where the injured man had been dragged away.

A stranger . . . who got no business here . . .

'*Indios* shove the woman into their boat, climb in and row out a little. They set their sails when the tide turns and go east. The fishers say they seen them go by, in the dawn Sunday. They be going to Gonaïves, I bet.'

They'd go straight across the gulf if Port-au-Prince was their goal. *Heading definitely for Le Cap . . .* 'You didn't hear what became of the *blan'*?'

Grillo shrugged again, but his good eye rested probingly on January's face. 'The boys that seen all this, they were too scared to look for the *blan'* in the night. When the men from the village go back in the morning, that *blan'*, he gone. I heard nothing of Tullio having him – they say he was bad hurt – but Tullio's not the only one.'

DAMN it. Horror filled him, and the knowledge that unless he reached L'Ange Rouge ahead of the Creeks and found what they were looking for before they did, they would have no further reason to keep Rose alive. But, against that, the memory of Hannibal stepping jauntily off the *Black Goose* on to the wharf at Grand Isle.

He didn't have to come with us. Rose and I had to come to Cuba for our lives, but he came only for friendship.

Only because I asked him to.

Hannibal had said to him once, *I've never been anything but a waste of air and boot-leather.*

But not leave him like this. To have his brain killed by whatever drug the *bokors* used, and his body – with who knew what dazed shred of consciousness still aware – turned over into slavery . . .

It wasn't my doing that Rose is here. But it IS mine that he came.

And yet it was impossible – *impossible* – to abandon Rose . . .

'You want me to throw the shells for you?' the old man asked gently.

'The man is my friend.' January heard the desperation in his own voice.

Heard, too, what Père Eugenius back in New Orleans would have said: *This is your punishment for having that pagan priest back in Cuba throw them for you the first time.*

And, like his choice between Hannibal and Rose, he had no answer for that.

The old man's shell tray reminded January of Olympe's: wooden, and very old, carved with the Twin Brother Gods, whose arms circled the perimeter of the board. Papa Grillo shut his eyes and rocked back and forth as he tapped the edge of the tray with the wand, recited the prayers to Papa Legba, then started in on all the legends connected with the shells in a high, rambling voice. Some were the same that Lazaro Ximo had recited, in the dark *bohio* in the walled slave village on Hispaniola Plantation. Others January half-recognized from when Olympe would do what she called a 'full tale', though generally she just threw the beans on the board. Papa Grillo sprinkled dust on the board and went on endlessly, rocking and reciting while the evening darkened around them and the women called their children to supper. Outside the compound, birds were crying their territories in the trees.

He's doing this to keep me here until dark. January turned, irresolute, to study the old man's wrinkled face and shut eyes. *Did he send one of the children to fetch help from town?*

The Egbo?

Tullio might not be the only person working for the planters . . .

The thought of sleeping in one of these rickety little huts – and he was tired enough from walking that he knew he'd sleep, even if he didn't drink whatever was in the gourd he'd been offered – made his stomach clench. The thought of sleeping in the woods was worse.

When Olympe did the 'full tale', she'd give the querent stories connected with where the beans fell: the gods, she said, would guide the right choice. Other voodoos, he knew – and Olympe sometimes, if the question was a simple one – would just scatter the beans as Ximo had done, sometimes all at once and sometime a few at a time. At long last Papa Grillo came to the end of his invocations and began to shift his shells from hand to hand, dropping a few as he did so and studying the way they fell into the dust on the tray. Then in his shrill, droning voice he began a story of a hyena and a crocodile and of a night when the moon bled blood on to the land.

A liar, a bokor, a sorcerer, Tullio had said. *Men who go in his door don't come out again.*

The last daylight was draining from the air with visible speed. Small fires burned before each of the houses around the court, where families gathered around pots of stew. Children ran back and forth laughing between them, with outspread arms, pretending to be birds, the way January and his little friends had done in the quarters at Bellefleur, and a woman called out (as his own aunties had) to stay close, else Tonton Macoute – the evil spirit Uncle Gunnysack – would come along and snatch them right up! (Shrieks of terror.) Frogs – those guardians of the way to the Underworld, the Greeks had believed – peeped and burped and rattled in the hot dark beyond the palings.

'Well, I'll be damned.' The *hougan* widened his eyes, startled at the shells on the board. 'It say, your friend is safe.'

'What? Where? How—?'

'That it don't say.' The old man shrugged. 'Or at least it don't say to me. But there it is, clear as clear—' He paused, and his white brows puckered as he regarded January again, more closely. 'It also say, brother, that it's better you don't sleep in the forest tonight. That Tullio, he tell his friends in town of you. Don't need no *loa* to tell me that, for sure, nor you neither I bet. They know it's twenty miles to Gonaïves. They be following you. You sleep in the jungle, they come for you.'

January made no reply to this. He didn't believe Tullio had been what he said he was, but it didn't mean Grillo was to be trusted, either.

Your friend is safe so you can relax and stay here . . .

He was hungry, too. Above the smell of woodsmoke from the

courtyard came the scents of stew and chicken grilling in lemon juice.

'Don't think ill of my mistrust,' he said at last. 'And I thank you for your reading, about my friend and about my wife.'

'Don't be a fool, man,' retorted the *hougan* roughly. 'You know they watching my gate here for you when you come out.'

January shook his head. 'I take my chances,' he said. 'You can help me one more way, if you will—'

'I can help you by locking you up like the *moun sòt* you are!'

'Other than that.' January couldn't keep himself from measuring how many strides it would take him to reach the compound gate, and whether he could get over it . . .

As if he read this in his eyes, Grillo made a disgusted gesture and gathered up his shells. 'What you need, then?'

'Tell me about Dr Maudit.'

TWENTY-FIVE

'Ah—' Grillo's breath slid from his lips in a long sigh. Stillness in the flickering dark of the peristyle.

'Did he kill M'aum Amalie?'

'He kill them all.' There was a trace of surprise in the *hougan*'s voice that January hadn't known this. He shook the holy dust from the carved board, blew on it, and wrapped it up again in a tattered velvet shawl. 'M'aum Amalie and her little maidservant, those two girls from Le Cap, the two men he buy for them, at three thousand francs per man – light-skinned as white men they were, and the next thing to blond, and handsome—'

'The houseboys?' demanded January. 'For three thousand francs? For a place where his master never lived? I know what he did to the men he'd buy, and a cheap slave, an old slave, a man ill or crippled, would have served him as well.'

'The Devil asked him for different things at different times,' responded Grillo. 'Sometime he'd go to market, in Port-au-Prince or Le Cap, three days, five days, every day for two weeks sometime, looking for who the Devil would point out to him. He'd look at ten, twenty men a day, feel this man's backbone or that man's knees

. . . and he'd buy women big with child as well.' The old man's brow darkened like thunder. 'And after all that he'd buy a man with a hunchback, or a crippled leg. Then the Devil changed his mind, and he looked and looked – months he looked – only at the whitest, the fairest, the men that look like white men down to the freckles on their noses. Men that was trained up as servants, 'cause you know that's who they did train as servants. The bright ones, the *mamelukes* and *musterfines*. Like the mulattos, givin' themselves airs. Maybe the Devil, he got a taste for soft white flesh, 'stead of old black crocks like me.'

He chuckled, a horrible sound. 'Old Michie Absalon, he paid Maudit two million francs, that M'aum Amalie would deliver of a healthy boy. Maudit sold his soul to the Devil and gave him sacrifices, so be that M'aum Amalie would birth a healthy babe. And that's what she did.'

January was silent, thinking again of the girl Jacinta, alone among her husband's family at Hispaniola.

'Little good it did her.' Papa Grillo's white brows shot up, corrugating his whole forehead with wrinkles. 'She knew too much then. She seen the Devil Maudit called up. She could tell her husband what he was doing. Maybe the child was the Devil's child. But the Devil told Maudit to kill her, and Maudit did, on a night of wind and storm and hurricane that blew the roofs off the churches from Jérémie to Port-au-Prince. Then he sent the baby to Michie Absalon, and Michie Absalon, he looked after Maudit for the rest of his days.'

'Until he came back here,' said January softly. 'Who told you this?'

'Everybody know it. A man who ain't so smart – who just got a regular mind –' the old man tapped his temple with a gnarled finger – 'the Devil turns him into a werewolf, to do his evil. But a man who's smart, who got brains and education, the Devil can use him more.'

In the dark behind his eyelids January saw again the neat, hideous engravings, of organs laid bare and bones disarticulated: a brain cradled in the sawed-off goblet of a head with open eyes staring in horror. 'Do you know why he came back?'

'The Devil called him,' replied Grillo promptly. 'That's the trouble with working for the Devil, see. You owe him. In his old age, when his strength was giving out so he couldn't do so much evil any more, the Devil told Maudit to come back to Haiti. And the Egbo were waiting for him when he did.'

They came for him about two miles outside of the town.

Red Beach lay where the hills broke, and a shallow pass led into the farmlands of the valley beyond. When he left the *humfo*, January followed the track in that direction, and about a mile from the village left the path and climbed swiftly up into the woods. Terrible confusion reigned in his heart: never, ever had he thought he would simply walk away from Hannibal, yet there was no way – *none* – that he would abandon Rose. He knew what he had to do to save her, and at this point he had no idea even in which direction to walk to help the fiddler, if he could be helped. If he wandered around the countryside looking, he wouldn't last long enough to even locate him. That much he did know.

He guessed, too, that he was being followed. Whatever the mulatto planters in the south were paying for a *zombi*, the worn-out condition of the farmers' clothing, the shocking dilapidation he'd glimpsed on the edges of the town, told him that people here would do pretty much anything to feed their hunger.

Particularly if the one who suffered was only a stranger who had no business in Haiti anyway and who might very well be a spy.

Under the thick canopy of ceiba and pinón, the darkness was nearly absolute. He tried to keep the moonlight from the edge of the woods in sight, at least until he could find an outcropping of rock or a thicket of oleander that would hide him from those who knew the country, but even with eyes acclimated to the darkness it was hard to judge exactly what he was seeing. Listening behind him, he heard nothing.

In time he sat down with his back against a tree – which he hoped wasn't infested with spiders, like many he'd seen throughout the day – and drank the last of his water, thankful that he'd slept at noon. He could hear drums beating again, the sound of his childhood, like the cries of the night birds.

This was what they fought for, he thought, seeing in his mind the dark faces, the gleam of eyes in the firelight, the work-calloused hands clapping. Remembering his own childhood – drunken master, crowded cabin shared with other families, the daily possibility of losing everyone and anyone he loved at a moment's notice, the daily possibility of a beating . . . and the magic of the nights, when there'd be a dance or storytelling in the moonlight by the bayou.

The slaves who rebelled, the Africans who did the impossible, the unthinkable . . . This is why they wouldn't give up. Against all odds and with the world screaming in horror at their ingratitude to their masters, they set themselves free.

And they're free still.

Beside that, even the danger in which he stood, in which Rose stood – the hunt for past secrets, the peril of being stalked – dwindled to the status of flowers on a rock.

Just let us alone. Let us drum our drums, let us dance our dances, let us worship our gods and raise our children.

Poor, yes. Struggling, yes. Manipulated by leaders who thought only of squabbling for power amongst themselves. But the people said, 'We'll never be slaves again.'

Silence fell, sudden and shocking. January's heart seemed to freeze.

There was only one creature in the forest for whom the others fell silent.

A rustle, somewhere near. The stealthy scratching of feet treading with exquisite care in the leaf-mast underfoot.

They can't see in the dark, any more than I can . . .

His ears searched, listening for where there was silence, for those shifty, whispered cracklings. *If I run they'll hear me.*

Can they smell my flesh?

Suddenly, it seemed to him that he could smell theirs. Tobacco and dirty clothes, stale rum and body dirt. Tullio had smelled of it, on the path through the cemetery. The farmers, too, a hundred years ago that morning. After all day in the boat, another day on the road, and sleeping on the ground in between, *I must be rank enough also, to find in the dark.*

He'd hidden from enough people – starting with his childhood master and the 'pattyrollers'– to know that movement would show him up quicker than anything else. He had his pistol in his belt, but knew he'd only get one shot with it before being overpowered, and with his rifle, not even that much. So he sat where he was until the smell faded a little. (*Did it fade or am I just used to it?*) But the night noises didn't return. Gently, gently, he crawled into the forest – into the darkness.

Tullio's men? The Leopard Society? Were they really cannibals, or was that just a tale?

Will they be waiting for me tomorrow, on the empty road to Gonaïves?

Can I make it twenty miles over the mountains alone like this? And what happens when I get there?

He put his hand on what was obviously an anthill, bit his lip until he tasted blood, to keep from jerking, leaping, crying out. Backed away slowly, wondering if the next step would be on to a centipede or into the den of a tarantula the size of a dinner plate.

For the first time, he doubted his endurance. Not just, *Can I avoid the Egbo or the Tullios of this world and make it to L'Ange Rouge before Jericho's men get there with Rose?* But, *Will the land wear me down?*

Even traveling outside New Orleans, in the land where every white man was a potential captor who regarded him as free money on the hoof, at least he knew the rules. He knew that most slaves could probably be trusted: to hide him, to guide him, to give him water that wasn't drugged or advice that wasn't lies.

Here, there was no assurance at all.

With the first trickles of daylight he found himself close enough to a spring to hear it chuckling. He soaked his hand, grossly swollen with ant bites, and drank, then followed it to the edge of the trees. With a whispered prayer to the Blessed Virgin (*if she's still speaking to me after two shell-throws and a conversation with Ogoun . . .*), January moved from tree to tree, skirting wide around the village and staying just close enough to the overgrown, potholed trace of the road above the sea to guide himself. Trying to listen and watch in all directions at once, like a rabbit in the open with the dogs baying near.

Wondering what he was going to do when the forest gave way to scrubland again.

Hunger gnawed him. There were *lakou* in the hills and certainly in the valley a few miles on the other side of them, but famished as he was it might simply be too dangerous to try to buy or beg food there. The families that made up those farming compounds might help him, but their male members were almost certainly members of one or another secret society.

Keep walking, he told himself. *You can do this.*

Cloud gathered over the ocean, tumbled up against the mountains above him. The wind felt thick. Over the water he could smell storm.

Keep walking.

He focused his mind on Rose, on what Salomé Saldaña had told him of the little plantation of L'Ange Rouge.

The thought was forming in his mind of what it was that Lucien Maurir had done, there at the feet of the mountains, by the salt lakes twenty miles from Port-au-Prince. *He must have left notes. Even if he HAD made a pact with the Devil, Maurir was a scientist. Of course he'd keep notes.*

Purchasing crippled slaves, purchasing handsome slaves, *the next thing to blond . . .*

Was that just his taste? Light-skinned as white men? How light had Caliban been, who had died on the beach with him?

They have to keep her alive. And I have to find those notes – whatever it is they prove – before they reach L'Ange Rouge and put myself in a position where I can't simply be overpowered. As he'd known last night, a pistol and a rifle would be of little use to him against five men.

Not if they had Rose among them.

Twenty miles to Gonaïves, and who knew what spiritual brethren of Tullio he'd meet when he reached the little port? If he reached it. Another week of walking to get to Port-au-Prince, and he'd have to buy or beg or steal food somewhere, somehow.

Maddox and the Creeks were heading for Gonaïves. That meant they'd have to get horses and cut north through the mountains to Le Cap. *Is Jericho meeting them there?* They were three days ahead of him, and when they'd been to La Châtaigneraie they'd come south again by land rather than risk a brush with President Boyar's navy.

Dear God, don't let them be killed by the Egbo before they ever reach L'Ange Rouge . . .

One thing's certain, January reflected wearily. *Somebody needs to go back to Jeoffrey Vitrac's father-in-law and tell him that his scheme to colonize freed slaves to Haiti isn't going to work.*

Ahead of him, a small stand of boulders jutted from the forest's edge toward the road, surrounded by ceiba trees. Ground high enough to provide concealment for an hour's sleep . . .

'*Poli di umbuendo*, my beautiful one,' said a familiar voice, light and hoarse, as January came near. 'I suppose we can inquire in town where the place lies, but I'd rather we weren't taking out advertisements in the local newspapers declaring our intentions . . . That'll teach me to be discreet about the assignations of one's friends with strange women—'

'There will be many,' replied a woman, in heavily Creole French,

'who can say *there was the place*. But none will set foot there.'
And on the soft air floated the scent of cigar smoke.

January stepped around the side of the rocks, and saw, tied to a
piñon tree, a donkey. Two more steps, and he looked up to the high
surface of the boulders, to see Hannibal – his arm in a sling, and
rather like a cheerful Baron Samedei in his tattered black coat,
patched and salt-stained and bloodstained, and his high-crowned
hat – with a young woman whose red tignon was tied in the five
points of a voodoo priestess. Hannibal had just taken her hand to
kiss, and the woman turned her head and met January's eyes.

She took the cigar from her mouth and smiled.

'And here's your friend now,' she said.

TWENTY-SIX

'I knew they had to have at least touched on the beach somewhere
near where that old villain put me ashore,' Hannibal explained
as the woman – her name was Mayanet, she said – dished
congri from a gourd for January. 'I could smell the smoke of their
fire, so I stayed low and kept to the bushes when I came around
the headland between my landing place and the next beach. They'd
made a shelter, and they didn't look in much of a hurry to leave:
they were repairing something, and Maddox, the pear-shaped blond
gentleman, appeared to be seasick . . . God knows, after that voyage
I wasn't feeling entirely well myself.'

'How many were there?'

'Five. Maddox and four Indians, one of them a woman, and very
fetching she was—'

Mayanet dug him hard in the ribs with her knee as she stepped
across to hand January a bottle of what turned out to be ginger
water. She was a tall girl, Spanish and Indian mixed with African
in her features. In addition to the way her tignon was tied, the
amulets around her neck – leather, string, and iron – proclaimed
her a *mambo* despite her apparent youth. He would have put her
age in her twenties, save for the wry amusement that aged those
enormous eyes.

Like Olympe's. And like his sister, her profession made her the mistress of too many secrets for her ever to be really young. When she stretched out her hand to give him the bottle he saw her bony wrists were marked with shackle galls.

'I hid in the trees along the cliff foot for the rest of the day, well back from their camp, and occupied myself picking centipedes off my coat. They – the Indians – kept Rose tied in the shelter, but didn't ill-treat her. I had about four pistol balls in one pocket and a penknife in the other, and enough powder to startle a spider if I took it unawares, so I knew if I fired they'd simply rush me. They left a man on guard when they went to sleep, and I waited until he went off into the bushes to piss – or maybe to recite the Act Three soliloquy from *Hamlet*, I don't really know – then crept forward to untie Rose. God knows where we would have run to if I'd succeeded.'

Mayanet's dark eyes moved from Hannibal's face to January's as the fiddler spoke, and January guessed she'd spent enough time in one of the larger towns to understand French. Her clothing, too, though much faded, spoke of the towns.

'Either the guard came back early, or someone else was awake, I didn't see exactly. Somebody started shooting, anyway. I shoved Rose around behind the palm trunk and wasted my one shot on the two men who came charging at us from the direction of the fire, and I tried to finish cutting the ropes with the penknife. I got hit in the shoulder, which hurt like fire – a broken collarbone, I think – and I knew I wasn't going to do much more in the way of rope-cutting. So I dashed about three feet – so they wouldn't keep firing in Rose's direction, palm tree or no palm tree – stumbled and nearly passed out, and dragged myself into the trees. I must have fainted in earnest then, because I came to in Mayanet's hut, and the upshot was that she said she'd seen me attempt to save Rose and that she would help me, in spite of her brothers being in some sort of secret society that mistrusts gentlemen of my complexion on principle.'

'The Egbo seek to kill evil,' said Mayanet, with her sidelong smile, 'as the gods direct them. But the gods know the difference between a man who comes to this land to do evil, and a man who comes only to save a woman who is bound and a prisoner among men.'

'Are you acting for the Egbo in this?' asked January curiously.

'I act for myself, always.' She blew another cloud of cigar smoke. 'My brothers would tell me to kill you, if I ask them about it. And they tell the other Egbo of you, and of this white man –' her glance flicked to Hannibal with fond amusement – 'so it be best we be in Gonaïves by nightfall. My grandmother got a *humfo* there, she put us up the night. These Indians, this white man . . .' She made a dismissive gesture with her long fingers. 'They come seek the gold of the Crimson Angel. But it's cursed gold, blood gold. If they take it out of where it's been hid, it'll spread more evil. Best it stay where it is.'

'I don't think it's the gold they're seeking,' said January, when they made ready to take to the road again. Hannibal insisted that he could walk, and Mayanet gave January a significant look, as if they'd been friends for years.

'You want me to tell your big friend to put you on that donkey? You do as you're told, white man.'

'If people see a white man riding while two blacks walk they'll shoot me for an aristocrat.'

'Not on that donkey, they won't,' retorted January, and Hannibal – wax-pale and shaky from blood loss – laughed and mounted the sorry little beast. While January had eaten, Mayanet had woven a hat for him from fronds of the fan palms that had grown nearby; the relief from the sun was a blessing.

He went on, 'They may want the gold, yes. But I think Dr Maudit hid something at L'Ange Rouge, proof of some evil or crime that will threaten the son of Absalon de Gericault if it's found. That son – Guibert de Gericault – has sent *his* son to kill my wife – his cousin – and her brothers. He guessed they'd seek the treasure, once it was known that somebody knew its whereabouts – as the old woman Salomé Saldaña knows. He fears that in seeking it, they'll find the thing that's hidden with it, whatever that is. I don't know whether Rose convinced the Indians to go after the treasure as a way of keeping them from killing her – she's perfectly capable of it – hoping that would give me a chance to follow and rescue her, or whether the Indians decided on their own to double-cross their employer, or whether this is part of the original scheme. But I do know that unless I get to L'Ange Rouge first, and find that secret thing – that thing that was so important to Dr Maudit that he got himself killed looking for it – they'll kill Rose. And they'll kill me when they catch me, leaving our child—'

He broke off, the memory of Baby John coming back like broken metal grinding against bone. Like the clang of an iron gate, locked across a road that his heart cried to take. His son raised by Olympe and Paul, never to know his parents or what had become of them. His son – Rose's son – taking his first steps, speaking his first words . . .

'I left him in a safe place,' he said at length, seeing Mayanet's dark eyes intent on his face. As if her gaze compelled an explanation – or as if Baby-John-in-the-Future, young John January who'd grown up an orphan, asked him for an accounting of his stewardship of the life that had been in his keeping – he said, 'We had to go. We had to flee for our lives, and we left him safe with my sister. But it's not the same.'

For a moment something changed in her eyes. The confident hardness softened, as if someone else, for a brief moment, looked out from behind that gleaming strength. She whispered, 'No,' and her eyes shone with tears. 'Nothing is the same, as your own child.' She flung away her cigar, closed her hand around the donkey's sorry bridle, and walked for a time in silence.

The road between Red Beach village and the town of Gonaïves dwindled to barely a track, though January saw small boats skimming the turquoise gulf. 'Anyone wants to come and go, they do it by boat,' said Mayanet, when January remarked on this. Her brisk confidence had returned, and she dug around in her pockets for something – *another cigar?* 'The roads are in a bad state, where they go through the mountains, and if you don't run into bandits, you run into men from the Army, looking to draft men. Spanish, too, that come over from the Spanish side of the island. We won our freedom, all those years ago,' she added, shaking her head. 'There not a man on the island nor a woman neither, nor the littlest baby at breast, that wouldn't do it all over again, to be free. But since we been free, it's all been fighting . . . You know for awhile there was two Haitis on the island, Christophe as Emperor here in the north and Pétion ruling a republic in the south, after Dessalines' own men killed him?'

'Didn't anyone conquer you?' inquired Hannibal. His right hand clung tight to the donkey's bristly mane, and under the brim of his old-fashioned hat his eyebrows stood out dark against a face white with fatigue and pain. '*Divide et impera* – surely whilst you were fighting amongst yourselves it would have been child's play for the French or the British or the Spanish to come in and retake the Pearl of the Antilles?'

'Napoleon tried it,' January replied. 'He failed, and after that

France, Britain, and Spain were having their own problems – and
I sincerely doubt the American Congress was willing to annex
an island full of slaves who'd successfully murdered their
masters.'

'They cursed his men.' Mayanet's white teeth showed in the
thin line of her smile. 'The voodoos in the hills. When the French
ships drop anchor in Cap Francais, all the voodoos of the country
make a dance, wherever they are. They call on Ogou and on the
Baron Samedei, they call on the gods of this island. They call
on the gods that were the only things we bring with us from
Africa, the Guédé and the gods and the spirits that live in the
trees and the rain. They killed the wild goats and the bulls, and
drank their blood, and the gods came down and promised us the
whites would not make us slaves again. Then the Guédé sent
the bad air, the stinking cloud of their breath, and breathed on the
whites in their ships. And all of them died.' Her smile widened.
Pleased.

'It's a bad death,' said January quietly. 'Yellow fever.'

'You call on the gods for help,' reasoned Mayanet, 'you take
what they send. The death they die in their ships wasn't so bad as
being buried up to your neck in dirt near an anthill and honey poured
on your head, the way they killed my grandpa when he hit an
overseer.'

Hannibal sighed. 'And people asked me why I drank.'

Gonaïves, spread between the curve of its bay and hills sprinkled
with pine woods, was the largest town January had seen in Haiti
and bore the marks of both French prosperity and the decades of
chaos and poverty that had followed. A sprinkling of large houses
remained on its deeply rutted streets, galleried like those of New
Orleans and concealing most of their life behind high courtyard
walls. A few seemed to have been kept up after a fashion, the
French doors on their upper galleries open to the muggy afternoon
breeze, but even these had clearly not been painted in decades.
Still, as the travelers made their way down Rue Egalité, an aged,
but well-maintained, carriage passed them, drawn by two black
horses that were more or less matched: the coachman, January
observed, was far lighter than anyone he'd yet seen in Haiti, as
were the occupants, two women in gowns that informed him that
somebody was still importing both silk and the latest magazines
of fashion from Paris.

'*Les filles* Peuvrets,' commented Mayanet as the ladies in the carriage put their heads out its window to stare at Hannibal. 'Their papa brokers sugar from the whole of the Artibonite Valley. They go driving every afternoon, my grannie says, just to show everyone in town they have a carriage.'

'If anyone asks,' replied Hannibal, 'you will tell them I'm your servant, won't you?'

They weren't the only ones to stare. From the broken-down buildings, the shacks of mud-daubed wattle, the narrow alleyways that stank of piss and garbage, hosts of children emerged to gaze in astonishment at the first white person they'd ever seen, though undoubtedly, January reflected, they'd heard stories. Market women – mulattos and quadroons, mostly, and a few fairer yet, with baskets balanced firmly on tignons the size of watermelons – followed, with perfect politeness yet unabashed curiosity. Men came out of the doors of tiny shops, in the aprons of artisans. January heard the buzz of Creole so thick that it defeated even his childhood recollections, and someone called out a question to Mayanet.

'The gods send him to me,' she replied, with her sparkling grin, waving back at Hannibal. 'He mine like a parrot.'

The market women laughed.

They had almost reached the end of the town when a voice behind them called out, 'Halt, if you please!' in sing-song French. With a clatter of hooves a man in uniform caught up with them, mounted on a starved and broken-down bay horse. His uniform was elaborate, though January's eye, trained by years of marriage to a dressmaker, picked out the age of the gold braid on sleeves and epaulets: cut off and transferred from garment to garment, possibly dating back to the coat of a French officer. Like the Peuvret carriage, it was flotsam from another world, which could not be replaced.

Haiti was an island. They had won their freedom, but the price of their victory had been the loss of all those things that the world of their masters could provide: paint for houses and gold braid for uniforms, and men of education to teach their children that something existed beyond the world they knew.

The sword the official drew was reasonably new, like the ladies' dresses had been. Some trade still came in, for the little bit of sugar that still went out. 'Who is this man?' He spoke to January and Mayanet equally. 'What is his business here?'

Hannibal removed his hat, produced a visiting card, and bowed. 'Jefferson Vitrack, at your service, sir. A representative of the American Colonization Society.'

'American, eh?' The official frowned and dismounted, snatched the card from Hannibal's fingers and studied it with narrowed eyes. January found himself remembering one of his aunties back at Bellefleur Plantation when he was a child, saying, '*Put a mulatto on a horse and he thinks he's white.*'

'And what you know about those other Americans, eh?' demanded the official. 'They land outside the town here, with their guns and their money; they buy horses from Milo Maribal the smuggler, they sneak off north like spies—'

January's heart turned over in his chest, but he kept his face and body still, as he'd learned to do as a child. You never, *ever*, let anyone in authority know you knew what they were talking about until you knew which way the wind blew . . . And Hannibal, whose experience with authority had been gleaned in completely different circles, managed to look shocked at the very idea that he'd know anything about such evil-doers.

Mayanet merely sniffed. 'Maybe they sneak off so you don't put 'em in jail, eh, Linfour?'

'I assure you, Colonel,' said Hannibal earnestly, giving the man the highest rank he could, 'I was cast ashore here while on business from the Society—' He drew Jefferson Vitrack's letter of introduction from the Society from his breast pocket – *he must have gotten it, and the card, from Rose* – but Mayanet plucked it away as the official reached to take it.

'I speak for these men,' she said in her honey-dark voice. 'I and my granmère. You want their papers, you come out to the *humfo*, where I got to make dinner for my grannie now. We prove to you they're not spies.'

Linfour – *Sergeant? Major? Captain?* – looked uncomfortable at that idea, and Mayanet took that moment to turn and lead the donkey toward the clusters of trees and huts that lay beyond the buildings of the town. The officer took a step after them, hesitated, then called in commanding tones, 'You be sure to bring these men to my office tomorrow, without fail.'

Mayanet kept walking, as if she owned the entire valley.

The man did not follow. Beyond the bounds of the town, January observed that most of the people working in the fields – corn, tobacco, and rice for the most part, spread around the walled compounds of *lakou* – were African.

Hannibal sighed. '*Legum servi sumus ut liberi esse possimus* . . .'

'*Res eo magis*,' replied January, '*mutant quo manent*. But they came through here. And it sounds like they're headed for La Châtaigneraie.'

TWENTY-SEVEN

When they reached *Mambo* Danto's *humfo*, out past the cemetery, the old woman confirmed what Linfour had said. 'These *blan's*, they had it all set up with Milo Maribal, that runs sugar and rum out to sell in Trinidad. He got a little compound on the headland west of town. He buy horses, food, lot of things – the Egbo say that boat come in Sunday night.'

'And they went north?'

The tiny priestess, like a little black ant, regarded January for a moment, then glanced at the *gris-gris* around his neck. 'They went north,' she affirmed.

Two days would take them to Cap Haïtien. Then they'd have to come back south . . .

If they were lucky.

'Will the Egbo attack them?' he asked urgently, but the old woman's attention had been drawn to Mayanet, who was helping Hannibal down off their sorry donkey.

'And what's that, eh?' Exasperation edged her voice, but she went to help, and January turned to take most of Hannibal's slight weight as his friend slipped from the saddle. The old *mambo* caught Mayanet's wrist in her hand, and for a moment she studied the shackle welts, something like sadness in her eyes.

With gruff kindliness, she added, 'Every time you go out, *caye*, you come home with stray dogs!' Her Creole was barely comprehensible, like the poor who'd swarmed the streets in Gonaïves. 'Now here you got a stray white man!' She jerked her head toward one of the huts. 'You lay him down in there an' I see to him – Mano!' she called out to one of the young boys, who'd come crowding in from the fields to stare. 'You go tell your mama, kill a couple pigeons for the pot for these guests, eh?'

The hut was simple, but as clean as any building could be whose walls and roof were thatch and palm fronds. The front room contained little more than a table and an altar elaborately decorated to honor the *loa*; the rear chamber held a simple bed and what looked like a child's cradle, long disused, covered over with scraps of mosquito-bar. Hannibal whispered, 'I'm fine, I'm all right,' and crumpled on to the bed unconscious.

To *Mambo* Danto, January said, 'I can look to him, M'aum. I'm a surgeon.'

She said, 'Are you, then?' and went out, returning shortly with bundles of dried yarrow and juniper, and other cleansing herbs, and a tin of water steaming from the fire. Out in the yard, January could see Mayanet talking with others in the compound: there seemed to be six or seven families in the *lakou*, all related, who worked their plot of land in common. They treated the younger priestess as January had sometimes seen people behave toward his sister Olympe, the genuine affection in their embraces and kisses colored with awe and a touch of fear. This was someone who had the Knowing, they would say. Someone who had the Power. Even Gabriel and Zizi-Marie walked carefully around their mother.

As January gently braced the broken collarbone, the children crowded into the doorway. 'You a *hougan*?' asked one of the boys. 'A root doctor? A *bokor*?'

January glanced over his shoulder. The children were gazing at Hannibal in open fascination, wanting a look at the source of so much of the evil that they'd heard of.

'No, I'm a surgeon,' he said, speaking slowly so they could understand his unfamiliar dialect of Afro-French. 'Like the doctors in Port-au-Prince. But I went to school in Paris, over in France.'

Their eyes got saucer wide at the mention of this place.

'The *blan*' taught me medicine, the same as they learn.'

The boys – and some of them were the young men, come in from the fields with the ending of the day – crowded closer as January changed the makeshift dressings. As he worked he said, 'My friend was shot by bad men, trying to save my wife when the bad men kidnapped her.'

'Is that the bad men come in on the boat Sunday night?'

'That's them,' replied January grimly. 'You don't happen to know if they had a woman with them? A mulatto woman—'

'There was two,' said a little girl. 'One of 'em had a gun.'

'My mama say she gonna take me to Port-au-Prince, see the

doctor there,' volunteered one child. 'After we get the coffee picked, so she can pay for it. I got sore eyes.'

'Well, let me get Michie Sefton here wrapped up,' said January, carefully winding strips of the faded cloth *Mambo* Danto had given him around Hannibal's ribs and shoulders, 'and then I'll have a look at your sore eyes. Maybe we can save your mama and you a trip into Port-au-Prince.'

When he emerged from the hut it was full dark, and torches had been kindled in the little peristyle in the courtyard. Mayanet carried a gourd dish of *legrim* – the savory stew of the island – in to Hannibal, though January doubted that the fiddler was well enough to eat. More *legrim*, and dishes of yams and rice, stood on the table in the peristyle, which doubled (as such structures often did) as an outdoor meeting place or workspace, when not in use for the voodoo dances. Somewhere in the night, drums were beating, and families gathered around their cook fires in their hut doors, while children darted around like swallows.

Mambo Danto sat at the table in the peristyle and waved to January to join her. 'You come a long way, my granddaughter say, you and your friend. My grandson Ti-Do, he tell me the Egbo follow these *indios* north, but he say most of the Egbo in the east. Spanish come over the border, across the mountains and up the Cul de Sac, *Trinitarios* under Guerrero.' She shook her head. 'He a bad man, Guerrero, a whore who kill his own people for money . . . Only, nobody here got any money, so we all got to watch out. Those who follow these *indios*, all they can do now is watch.'

While January ate, he talked to *Mambo* Danto about the *lakou*, and the way life was lived in Haiti: the world cut off from the world of the whites, who saw it and everything in it as property which had been reft from them unlawfully. A republic trying to build itself with a population that was over nine-tenths illiterate, men and women who had never known any other occupation than work in the cane fields, still burdened with that legacy of ignorance.

Back in the hut, he'd heard the smaller children whisper to their elders, *'What's Paris? What's France?'*

For them, the world ended at the margin of the sea.

A population easily swayed by words, by dreams, by exhortations or by drumbeats in the night, without sophistication in sifting rival stories, without the breadth of experience that says, *Hang on a minute, is that person lying to me?*

They had won their freedom because they believed, with a belief that had never paused to ask questions. In freedom, most of them had only that uneducated, unquestioning belief, and the ingrained desperation for survival at any cost. When their leaders started fighting for power among themselves, no contender had lacked for followers.

The whites had gone, but they'd taken with them everything that might possibly give this land the hope of succeeding as a nation among nations. In the same spirit that had moved the rebelling slaves to systematically destroy every sugar mill, every grinding house, every cane field and coffee orchard so that no conqueror would be able to re-establish bondage in this once-profitable hell, the whites – those who'd survived the vengeful massacres in Cap Haïtien and Port-au-Prince – had removed education, had removed the Church, had removed anything resembling the wherewithal to purchase guns and train soldiers to defend the freedom that they'd won.

The fact that, over forty years later, these people were still free, still living as they chose to live, was literally jaw-dropping. January wondered how much longer it would be permitted to last.

Yet, seeing the faces of the boys and girls turned now and then towards him in the torchlight, he knew that most would never know a world beyond their island. The girls would have babies because that was what girls did, and most of those babies would die. The boys would work in the fields and snuff quietly out at the age of thirty or so, of pneumonia or fever or infected small injuries.

They would be what they were, while beyond the shores of Haiti the world changed around them, and others made decisions for them that would alter their lives.

After he'd eaten, January examined the boy with the sore eyes, for whom *Mambo* Danto had prescribed an eyewash of diluted honey: 'The sore come back and come back . . .'

'Use salt water,' advised January, and while he was demonstrating how to mix that – and two or three other remedies for conjunctivitis whose ingredients he guessed would be available – a young woman came diffidently up and asked, was it true he was a doctor like they had in Port-au-Prince, and might he look at her baby who wasn't able to eat properly? In the end, January looked at about twenty people in the *lakou* – sprains, toothaches, slow fevers, coughs, and a pregnancy which seemed to be doing just fine under *Mambo*

Danto's guidance, but the young mother just wanted to check with an *Otanik* Doctor, as she said – a *real* doctor.

Mambo Danto, at January's side, listened with the absorbed expression of one who is taking mental notes.

'I remember that for next time,' she said, when he'd finished gently resetting a broken hand. 'Thank you.'

'I come here starving, a stranger in a strange land,' he returned, 'and *you* thank *me*?'

Danto laughed and shook her head. 'I do what I can, but you been to school. There's some things I can't do.'

'And there's some things I can't, either. But the trouble your child saved us –' he used the term *p'titt caye*, a child of the *humfo* – 'that's worth me seeing everybody on this island.'

He sat silent for a time, trying to force back the panic that came to him every time he thought about Rose, bound north four days ago with Maddox and his Creeks . . . to meet Bryce Jericho? To be killed in the crossfire if Jericho and whatever men he'd hired overtook them? To be killed by the Egbo, or the *Trinitario* band currently moving in the green glades of the mountains?

Two days from Gonaïves to La Châtaigneraie, maybe . . . From there, four to come south again to L'Ange Rouge. Of which two were already spent, and how long would it take him and Hannibal to reach the place, with or without help from Mayanet? No way of knowing how to find them, other than to be at that place before them.

To find whatever it was that Lucien Maurir had hidden . . .

Blood and gold. Gold and blood . . .

From the shadows of the nearby hut, Hannibal's voice spoke softly – quoting Catullus, of all things – and the drift of Mayanet's cigar smoke tinged the air.

'The god is in her, isn't it?' he asked softly, and *Mambo* Danto glanced quickly sidelong at him with her dark eyes.

On the altar in the hut's front room, January had seen the images of the goddesses: the sensual and perilous Erzulie – Ezili she was called in New Orleans – who would kill a man who refused her kisses. The fishtailed La Sirene, mother of sorrow; the skeletal death-goddess Maman Brigitte. And the one who was called Marinette in New Orleans, Marinette who had a thousand forms and natures, both evil and good. Her image was often taken from old French and Spanish prints of the soul in Purgatory, the dark-haired woman shackled in the flames yet calm, knowing she will come through and see God in the end. *She is strong*, Olympe had told him, showing him the picture on her own altar back home. *One of the strongest. She knows pain, she come through the fire. She's a protector, a protector of women.*

Mambo Danto sighed. 'Since Maria was a little girl, the goddess Mayanet would come on her at the dancing. After her own little girl died, she became a *mambo*, and sometimes Mayanet stay in her for days. Now, Maria wasn't never a meek girl: she *agidi*, got a strong head on her. Maybe that's why Mayanet take to her. But when the *loa* inside her, you see the marks on her wrists, from the chains in Purgatory. When she's herself, the skin smooth as a baby's.'

January nodded. He'd seen stranger things, when as a young boy he'd slip out at night and go to the brickyard on Rue Dumaine where the voodoos danced. He'd seen, too, in France, nuns and holy men whose devotion to the Passion of Christ had induced the bleeding echoes of His wounds on their bodies, in imitation of the sufferings on Golgotha. 'Is she one of the Egbo?' he asked softly.

'They only men.' The old priestess folded wrinkled, tiny hands. 'Her brothers in the Egbo, an' it may be if you meet them on the way to this old *sucerie* you lookin' for, she can save you.'

Young men came to the door of Mayanet's hut, speaking in low, tense voices. He heard the words 'Spanish spy' and '*blan*" – white man – and when she appeared against the darkness within they gestured toward the night beyond the dim torchlight of the *humfo* yard, where drums tapped some urgent message.

Mayanet blew a line of cigar smoke and asked, 'You want maybe I should read the shells for you?' Her eyes mocked them – the eyes that had, for one moment on the road yesterday, filled with tears when he'd spoken of his child.

Now she looked every inch a goddess, cool and shimmering in her ownership of the land and men's souls. Framed against the darkness, her raised arms braced on the door frame and her dark Spanish hair curled like a gypsy's, she exuded a fey peril, like a leopard herself. January wondered if she had the reputation of a werewolf also, though there had never been a wolf in Haiti in all its history. Such was the power of the legends of the whites, even after they were gone.

'No, no,' said the young men hastily, 'we got no quarrel, M'aum, if you speak for him.'

'I do,' she said, and smiled.

And watched them as they retreated across the court, to one of the fires before some other hut.

In the darkness the drums rapped out their warning, little answering big. Spies and strangers were abroad in the land.

They must be hunted and killed, hunted and killed.

Rose would hear them, January knew, lying bound in the darkness among the men who had killed her brother.

And trusting that all would be well.

TWENTY-EIGHT

They left the *humfo* before first light, Hannibal, January, and Mayanet, with *Mambo* Danto along to take the donkey back. In Gonaïves, Mayanet found a fisherman at the harbor who agreed to take them across the Gulf to Port-au-Prince, and if anyone told Captain Linfour that his suspected spies were back in town, he didn't come down to the waterside to check.

Crossing the Gulf of Gonâve – blue sky, blue sea, blue as the veil of the Mother of God, with the mountain shadows shortening and shortening and gold light coming up into the sky – January prayed: for Rose, for Hannibal, for Baby John. *Blessed Mary Ever-Virgin, none of this mess is Rose's fault, or Hannibal's. Help me get them out of this safely.*

Beyond the low green hills to the east lay the fertile Artibonite Valley, once one of the richest sugar-producing bottomlands in the world. Mayanet, still smoking the stub of her cigar, sat in the stern, her eyes turned south-east for the first glimpse of the Haitian capital, and January had the uncomfortable feeling that however much this woman believed herself to be the chosen mount of a goddess, it wouldn't keep her – or himself and Hannibal – from being shot.

Maybe there is no way out. Maybe the whole island lay under a curse – from the 20,000 whites slaughtered by Toussaint and Christophe and the vengeful fury of the rebelling slaves; from the uncounted hundreds of thousands of slaves, worked to death, tortured to death, beaten to death in the name of profits and good order. From the thousands of mulattos in the towns that the invading French had simply massacred, and from the 24,000 French soldiers and seamen who had succumbed to yellow fever during the abortive invasion . . . The very air of the island, thick and humid, oppressed the soul.

Maybe we'll simply disappear here, the way poor Jeoffrey Vitrac set off for New Orleans with the hopes of tracking down the family treasure and never came back.

Leaving his wife to mourn him – thank God she has wealthy parents to care for her. Leaving Baby John to grow up motherless and fatherless, never knowing what became of us or why we left him to others' care.

Blessed Mary Ever-Virgin, help us. Me and Mayanet . . .

If I get out of this alive I'll be doing penance for ten years . . .

'There it is.' The goddess pointed with the stub of her cigar. 'Port-au-Prince.'

Backed by wooded hills, Port-au-Prince lay in the very gullet of the crab-claw Gulf of Gonâve, its wide streets and spread-out houses making it seem even lower than New Orleans. January recognized the flags of France and Britain, of Holland and Austria, on the jackstaffs of the few merchantmen in the northern of the city's two harbors – the source, he supposed, of the stylish silks he'd glimpsed on the mulatto bourgeoisie in Gonaïves. But only a handful of ships floated at anchor, bumboats coming and going from the wharves with water, supplies, sacks of coffee and hogsheads of sugar and indigo.

Inland, the resemblance to New Orleans was increased by the stucco of the unpainted houses, the low cottages with shed-like galleries facing the streets. It was New Orleans as he recalled it from his childhood, the half-Spanish city before the Americans had built their white wooden houses upriver of Canal Street. The ring of fortifications remained, which had vanished from New Orleans, and the forts which guarded the harbor flew the black-and-red banner of the defiant black republic.

Slave owners, take heed.

Slaves, take heed.

It CAN be done.

Before leaving the *humfo* that morning, *Mambo* Danto and Mayanet had stained Hannibal's face, hands, and neck with a dye of coffee beans and oak bark. 'My reward from Heaven,' remarked Hannibal as they came down the gangplank of the little fishing vessel, 'for all those sets of papers I've forged to let octoroons pass for white.' It would fade within days, but there were enough men in Port-au-Prince – as there were in New Orleans – of Caucasian features and African hue for him to pass unchallenged through its streets, particularly under cover of darkness. *Hell, our butler was lighter than I am!* Guibert de Gericault had written to his friend.

And, reflected January, *he probably was . . .*

And there they were, in every lamplit doorway and beneath the torch flares of the harbor, men with the dark, straight hair of Spanish or Indians or Frenchmen, with high-bridged European noses and thin European lips. Market women barely darker than a drop of ink in a quart of water: *Next thing to white,* Papa Grillo had sneered.

If their grandparents had been slaves at all – and not *librés,* as most of January's neighbors were back in New Orleans, born free of free parents like any white in the city – then those grandparents had been house slaves, maids like Ginette and her sister Reina, servants like Claudio and Fia back on Hispaniola in Cuba, like Alice Vitrac's maid Lallie in Grand Isle.

Emmanuelle and Calanthe – Ginette's mistress and her fellow-*plaçée* – had been nearly white, he thought, looking around him as they left the leaping gold light of the cressets around the harbor, passed into the blackness of Port-au-Prince's streets. And Dr Maudit had spent months, haunting the slave-markets, choosing just the right light-skinned manservants, not satisfied with just any, searching as the Devil instructed.

Searching for what?

He thought he knew.

Mayanet led them to a *humfo* in the so-called 'New City', the high ground around what had been the government complex under the French. The *hougan* there welcomed them, but January noticed how the man's glance went from Mayanet's hard, over-bright eyes to the weals on her wrists. 'They say you goin' to find the Spanish that come in from San Juan,' he said.

'They say that, hunh?'

He spread his hands. A workingman's hands, January noticed. This was no man who lived solely on what the members of the *humfo* donated. 'The Spanish killed two men by Lake Enriquillo, and then headed north into the mountains. Guerrero, they say. They say you got a Spanish with you.' He looked at Hannibal, who tried to look indignant.

He lowered his voice to a whisper, and went on, 'They say they're after a treasure . . .'

'An' what you think more likely, Azo?' Mayanet asked. 'That I go help the Spanish steal some gold? Or that I go meet them and destroy them with the thump of my fist, with the smoke of my cigar?'

Azo the *hougan* looked uncomfortable, like a priest, January reflected, confronted by a parishioner's blind willingness to stake life and property on the off-chance of a miracle.

Nevertheless, he gave them food and a bed on the floor of the *badji* – the sanctuary – amid the paraphernalia of worship: Papa Legba's crutches, Baron Samedei's hat. Clusters of necklaces hung from nails on the wall; *macoutes* full of gaudy, faded flags lay in the corners. The city *humfo* was not part of a *lakou*, but was supported by contributions from those who came to dance there on feast days and used the services of its *hougan* as healer, counselor, warlock and friend.

'I must say,' remarked Hannibal as they crept under a tattered tent of mosquito-bar overlooked by the glimmer of the moonlit altar, 'I'm going to be fearfully disappointed if we reach the de Gericault plantation and find it looted long ago.'

'The treasure there,' returned Mayanet, stretching out beside him. 'People might hear of it, but nobody touch it, all these years. It's cursed . . .' She shrugged and pulled off her tignon, shook her long, black hair down in a torrent over her shoulders. 'Your enemies all die of it. You don't need to worry.'

She lay down and was asleep in moments. On the altar, the ever-present spiders of Haiti – yellow banana-spiders, a tarantula bigger than January's spread-out hand – crept and picked among the beaded gourds, the whittled images, the plates of tobacco and half-empty rum bottles of the altar. Toads in the gutter beyond the closed jalousies kept up a basso chorus as they hunted centipedes as long as a child's arm.

'Well,' sighed the fiddler, 'I should worry a great deal less if I was assured that the curse wouldn't strike us as well.'

TWENTY-NINE

A zo drew them a map, filled a *macoute* with provisions for them, and dug into the slender coffers of the *humfo* to rent them a donkey. Hannibal protested that he was much better – he'd slept for most of the voyage across the Gulf, and under his camouflage he seemed less ashen – but January was glad of a beast to carry provisions as well as to keep 'Monsieur Vitrac' from slowing them down. Mayanet had acquired a machete back at her grandmother's *lakou*; in addition to his rifle and pistol, January borrowed an iron pry-bar from among the furnishings of the altar of Ogou, the blacksmith god.

They passed through the wooded hills that rose behind the so-called 'Government' district of Port-au-Prince, and through Pétionville, where the mulatto sugar-brokers and planters had their homes, the first new dwellings January had seen on the island. Few were awake at this early hour – in fact, one carriage-load of well-dressed ladies passed them, who appeared to be just on their way home to bed – and January mostly saw servants, noticeably darker than the mulattos he'd glimpsed on the streets of Port-au-Prince. In the hills beyond, he saw orchards of fruit trees planted to shade coffee bushes, and an occasional large house like the *casa de vivienda* back at Hispaniola Plantation, where the owner of the land dwelled in comfort while tenant-farmers sweated tending the crop.

Through breaks in the trees, he could look down from the high ground on the dark-green sea of sugar fields along the river, the island's fortune and curse. When they crossed the river, and came down out of the hills, they passed a rather ramshackle Big House and a sugar mill that still bore charring on its stone. It had been rebuilt, but to January's eye looked truncated, smaller than it had once been. The fields had been ratooned too many times, choked with weeds and maiden cane.

They walked further, into the valley called the Cul de Sac. In wet years, Mayanet told him, the rivers from the surrounding mountains would pour into the saline lakes of Azuei and Enriquillo, and they would drown the low-lying valley, merging into a single body of water. The land here was marsh and brush, thick with young palm trees and bananas, palmetto and bougainvillea. Where there were sugar fields, January saw the work gangs were smaller than those of Louisiana, laboring stoically in the heat.

'Damn planters.' Mayanet took the cigar from her mouth to spit.

'Without plantations you have no Army,' returned January reasonably. 'Then you have the French back, or the Spanish—'

She spat again. 'That for the French, and the Spanish. Why can't they leave us alone, eh? Leave us to work our fields and grow our food . . .'

'Why didn't they leave our parents and our grandparents alone to work their fields and grow their food in Guinea?' He used the word for Africa that they'd used in the quarters – that magic Africa that had probably never really existed, that world of peace and plenty to which the souls of black folk would return when they died.

If his father had ever told him how he'd come to be captured, whether in war or by raiding tribesmen from the other side of some nameless river, January could not recall. He'd been seven when last he'd seen that tall coal-black man with the tribal marks carved on his face. He couldn't even recall their final hour together, because he and his mother and his sister had been informed very suddenly in the middle of the morning that they'd been sold. His father had been out in the fields already.

When he'd come home, his family had been gone. And that was that.

And that, he supposed, was as much explanation as anyone would ever need, for the rebellion in Haiti. He concluded softly, 'Because that's not what they do.'

Late in the afternoon, when they had left all sugar fields far behind them and pushed on through the jungles above the road, January heard a man's voice down on the road below them – barely a track, now, as it threaded deeper into the lowlands of the Cul de Sac. A wordless groaning bray, like a goat, though he knew it was a man. Mayanet caught his arm as he thrust his way back downhill.

'Best you don't,' she said.

He hesitated, and the man moaned again, a bleak sound, dying. He scrambled down the sloping ground, through foliage thick with every sort of insect life in the world: centipedes, tarantulas, Haiti's myriad varieties of ants; gnats and flies without count. He saw the man at once, crawling on hands and knees along the track, reeling back and forth like a drunkard. His hands were raw and bloody and swarmed with ants and flies, his eyes and mouth were clotted around with them, like the orifices of the dead. A huge, infected machete-slash in his arm crawled likewise with insects; the smell of rotting flesh almost choked January as he ran up to the man.

When he brushed the flies from the sufferer's face, the eyes that stared at him were blank, comprehending nothing.

Mayanet's voice behind him said, 'Leave him, Ben. He knows nothing. He'll be dead by dark.'

The man made that horrible bleating noise again. January gave him a drink from his water bottle, and the water only splashed from chapped and swollen lips. His flesh was scorched with fever.

'He knows nothing,' she repeated, and January turned on his heels to look up at her, standing over him with her eyes like iron. 'He's *zombi*. His brain is gone. The *bokors* got him, poisoned him, and when he died, brought him back and dug him up and sold him to one of the planters to work.' She shrugged. 'There's nothing you can do.'

Behind her in the trees, Hannibal's face was blank with shock. Around them twilight was just beginning to slant the light through the coco palms and the hibiscus, the steady, creaking cry of a million, million insects joined by the rising peep of frogs. The man on his hands and knees before January was either white – Spanish or Portuguese – or else a mulatto of the kind that Hannibal had imper-sonated last night in town. *A stranger . . . who got no business here*, as Papa Grillo had said.

'There's no way back for him,' said Mayanet. 'He's *zombi*. He's gone. They only turned him loose out of the work gang 'cause he'd slipped with his machete, 'cause the cut went bad. There's nothing we can do.'

January said quietly, 'There is.' He knelt and gave the man water again – he managed to gulp a little of it, that time. Then he straightened up, took Mayanet's machete from her hand, and brought the blade down with the full force of his arm on the man's crawling neck. He'd cut cane, and he knew how much strength was needed to sever the tough stems; it surprised him that beheading someone wasn't harder than that. Hannibal turned away, chalky under the remains of his crude make-up, and staggered. January wiped the blade on the dead man's clothing, went to catch his friend by the arm.

'I'm all right.' Hannibal tried to pull away, his voice hoarse.

January handed the blade back to Mayanet and almost carried his friend back up into the jungle off the road, where he'd left the donkey. He had to lift him bodily to the animal's back.

'I'm all right.'

They reached L'Ange Rouge about two hours before dark. The Big House was set – as Salomé Saldaña had described it – on a rise of ground a mile up a little valley, where a spring came down out of the mountains. A mile and a quarter of thickly wooded ground lay between the mountains' footslopes and the lake itself, jungle growth mixed with the wild tangle of canes, so thick that January doubted either man or beast could have pushed through to the brackish water.

January circled the shoulder of high ground, to make sure no one was camped there, before moving cautiously in.

There wasn't much left of the house. Like the planters in Louisiana, those in Saint-Domingue had tended to regard the 'Big House' of a plantation as little more than a sleeping space and business office. The real home, the place where they brought up their children, was in town – in Paris, if they could manage it. They'd generally been built of wood, and the conflagration that had swept the island in 1791 had left little behind.

He easily found the stone piers that had supported the house, overgrown with oleander and fern. There was a well not far away, exactly where Salomé had described it from her mother's account. Its cover had long rotted, and the smell of decay in the water drifted up to him when he bent over the open pit. While Hannibal and Mayanet made a sort of camp in the ruins of the sugar mill – its stone walls still solid, built to withstand hurricanes, though the roof was gone – January scouted through the thickets of palmetto and found the stone foundations of Dr Maudit's accursed house, and of the two stone cells that had been attached to it, also as Salomé Saldaña had described.

Standing in that place, he could see her sketch of the plantation's layout, scratched in the dirt floor of that Havana *bohio* by firelight. He'd copied it into his notebook, as soon as he'd returned to his lodgings, even as, hating himself, nearly twenty years ago he'd copied the horrifying engravings in *Les Procédées de la Société des Sciences Francaise*.

The originals had been drawn here, on this spot.

And he'd used the information they'd given him, about malformations of the spine and bones, about the effects of certain drugs, about what sorts of conditions were likely to arise from cousins marrying cousins: used them to save lives, to plan surgeries, to guide those who came to him for help, to guide his own hands in cases of difficult pregnancies and births.

How could the means of salvation for so many come from this place? From that man? From those deeds?

For, by this time, he was pretty certain what it was that Lucien Maurir had done.

And he'd done it, January knew – as he moved systematically along the thick stone foundation wall that had separated Maudit's house from the cells of his subjects – in order to get access to that knowledge. In order to find human beings whom he could skin and dissect alive without fear or compunction, and a man wealthy enough, and sufficiently beholden to him, to support him in his researches.

It was knowledge for which he'd been more than happy to pay the asking price.

Be a physician, Faustus, heap up gold, Marlowe had written of another doctor who had been willing to pay that price.

And be eterniz'd for some wondrous cure . . .

Are not thy bills hung up as monuments,

Whereby whole cities have escaped the plague,

And thousand desperate maladies been cured?

As January had guessed, there was a safe built into the stone foundation of the cells. It was blocked with a stone, wedged in tight; the largest stone in the wall, and the only one that had been shaped. Probably ship's ballast originally, of the sort that was used for paving New Orleans streets. A hole had been drilled in one side of it, and that hole was aligned with a substantial crevice between two neighboring stones. With the last light fading from the tropical sky, January wedged his iron pry-bar in and pushed.

The space behind the stone was about a cubic foot.

He left Amalie de Gericault's diamonds – *getaway money? The price of a modest home in Paris?* – where they lay. There was gold there, too, as Salomé had said, and a few pearls and earrings and pins. What remained of Calanthe's jewelry, and Emmanuelle's, after Ginette had seized what she could carry. There was even a little

Dutch-gold collar-pin with a painted porcelain miniature on it, the sort of thing a servant girl would wear.

Reina's. Mammy Ginette's sister – Madame Amalie's maid.

He carried the notebooks back to the sugar house, where Mayanet had built up a little fire.

THIRTY

Amalie de Thoyomène de Caillot de Gericault
L'Ange Rouge Plantation
Saint-Domingue

July 21, 1785

To: Neron de Gericault
Chateau Vieux-St-Michel, auprès d'Angouleme
Hôtel de Caillot, Rue des Italiens, Angouleme

Brother,

I pray God this reaches you. I have given every sou I possess to my maid Reina to carry it to Port-au-Prince, and to render it into the hands of a sea-captain who will, I pray, get it to you. Please, please, I beg you, come and get me out of this nightmare.

Absalon will have written you that I have at last borne him a healthy son, christened Guibert in the Cathedral in Port-au-Prince. My recollections of his birth are confused. I have reason to believe that I was drugged when my pains began, I know not for how long. But the child they brought to me, and placed in my arms, was, I will swear it, not a newborn child. He was of a size and a countenance at least a month old, and though they tell me I was ill for many weeks, I know – by the growth of the young birds in the nest outside my window, and the kittens of the gardener's cat – that it was nothing like that long.

In my dreams I birthed a girl, a tiny mite of a thing but living, and whole.

I saw her face.

The child I see in the arms of the wet-nurse is not mine.

You know Absalon's determination – his obsession – to have an heir to the de Gericault title. I have written you before how he has employed the man Maurir, to determine some way to alter the will of God, to strengthen me through magnetism and electricity and the consumption of everything from sheep's whey to ground bones so that I can bear healthy children. I thought I was rid of the man – the tales the Negroes tell of him are frightful! But in February, when my baby quickened within me, my husband sent me here, to L'Ange Rouge, his plantation in the Western Province, where Maurir has been for nearly a year. On this plantation, my dear Reina tells me, are also the women Emmanuelle and Calanthe, Absalon's two mistresses. Both were with child when I came here, Reina says, but neither in such condition by Absalon, but by the two young footmen, Champagne and Grasset.

Neron, I very much fear that Maurir – promised the Good God only knows what reward by Absalon! – has substituted the child of one of these women for my baby, for the poor little girl I saw – I know I saw! – cry and flail in Maurir's hands when he delivered her of me. Both women are what they call in the islands mameloque – women of color whose only taint of African blood comes mixed with five generations of white. Both footmen, who seem to have no duties in the plantation house here whatsoever, are of the same extraction, like Absalon fair-haired and blue-eyed. They are like Absalon as well in height and build, and, it sometimes seems to me, like him also in cast of countenance, as if Maurir bought them solely for that purpose (one of them, Reina tells me, is widely known as a thief and a troublemaker, whom no one would take as a servant).

LATER – Brother, I know not what to do, but I am afraid! Someone – I think it is Maurir – searched my room last night; thank Heaven I carried this letter hidden on my person! But the ink and the pens were taken away, and I had to get poor faithful Reina to steal some from Mssr Gautier's office. Gautier has reassigned Reina to the kitchen, and has given me a new maid, a sly creature named Nana, one of his several slave mistresses. She sleeps in my room: there are few moments when

I am not watched. Maurir has written to Absalon that I am ill, and has told the Negroes that I am mad. Twice he has tried to drug me, and I fear to eat or drink anything that I have not myself prepared – further evidence of madness, he says piously. But he is a man who understands drugs, has experimented with them hundreds of times on the poor Negroes here. I see the creatures whose minds he has destroyed, numbly obeying his commands and knowing neither where they are nor what they do, and I wonder, is this what he plans for me?

Would Absalon care, so long as he has his healthy son of the de Gericault heritage?

I begin to fear not!

I feel trapped in a spiderweb of shadows, knowing nothing, able to believe nothing, to prove nothing! Reina tells me that both of the mameloque mistresses bore girls, one of them stout and healthy (and indistinguishable, she tells me, from a white baby), the other a poor little scrap who died within hours.

Yet I hear these women laughing with each other, see them playing with the baby – at a distance, for I am not allowed to leave the house, 'For my own good,' Maurir insists – and neither weeps, nor bears the appearance of a woman who has lost a child.

Does this mean anything? I don't know! Does it prove that I am sane and not mad? Absalon would say, 'Negroes do not feel such a loss as we would.'

If Maurir would do this – kill my baby, substitute the healthy boy that Absalon would pay almost anything to achieve – what would he not do? I don't know that, either.

I pretend that I love Guibert. I pretend that I believe what Maurir has told me happened: that I bore a boy, and was ill for some weeks, while the cook's gray kittens remained kittens and did not grow long of leg and foolishly daring of spirit . . .

Can I base all of this on some lies and some cats? I don't know!

I swear to you I am not mad! These are not the sick fancies of a woman after birthing a child! Neron, Neron, if you cannot come yourself, send a man whom you trust, a man who will not be taken in by Maurir's lies – by the lies that Absalon wants to believe, if indeed Absalon is himself not behind this terrible scheme!

Save me, I beg you! Come – or send someone who can be trusted, someone who will not believe the lies of plausible madmen! – and take me out of this place, this nightmare, this hell. Truly, you are my last and only hope.

Your sister,
Amalie

January turned the sheets over in his hands. The first one had been the flyleaf of a book – Volume Seven of Madame de Scudery's *Clélie* – and the second, a blank page of what looked like a ledger. They had at one time been creased and folded together very small, as if for concealment inside a woman's corset or shoe. Broken fragments of red sealing-wax dotted the blank side of the second.

It had clearly never been delivered.

And Neron, Comte de Caillot and holder of the title of Vicomte that should have been his cousin's, a broken man, and homeless, had come at last to shelter under Absalon's roof for the remainder of his life, never knowing his sister's fate.

Wordlessly, he passed the letter to Hannibal, turned his attention to the notebook into the back cover of which it had been tucked.

It was reddish pigskin leather, furred with mold. The edges of the pages were stained dark with it and clung stiffly together as he turned them. The first half was devoted to everything Lucien Maurir could glean about the de Gericault family, from Absalon – who had studied his family's history with a maniac's single-minded attention to every fragmentary detail – and from Amalie. Aunt Serafine back in Angoulême who miscarried eleven times and was never able to carry a child to term. Uncle Clovis who walked with two sticks. Cousin Raymond in his wheeled chair, pushed about the paths of Vieux-St-Michel by a manservant all his short days.

Who had their parents been? How many grandparents had they in common? Had their mothers miscarried before or after their births? The blocks of scribbled notes were interspersed with diagrams of a family tree which even to January's eye looked unwholesomely entangled.

In the jungle blackness all around them, the buzzing of insects mingled with the distant beating of drums.

The second half of the notebook meticulously detailed the purchase of the two footmen Champagne and Grasset, accompanied by sketches and descriptions that the scientific physiognomist Johann Lavater would have approved of for detail and specificity. The angle of the nose, the placement of the eyes, the shape of the ears and set of the cheekbones . . . along with a description in similar terms of Absalon de Gericault. The descriptions almost matched.

One of the last pages of the book contained anatomical drawings and notes, of what looked like the dissection of a newborn baby girl.

Heat went through January: rage, shock, disgust.

Of course. The man was a scientist. He wasn't going to pass up the chance to study so inbred a specimen . . .

By the look of it, the infant had been healthy and normally formed, save for her tiny size, barely five pounds.

His hands shook as he closed the notebook, turned to the next. More notes on the purchases of slaves, covering the years from 1779 up to 1791. The early years he'd buy – presumably with Absalon de Gericault's money – one or two a year, noting the physical condition and tribe. Sometimes, but not always, a name. African names: Bassy, Kigoa, Mongo. Nearly all had some defect: curved spine, bad hips, withered limbs or feet. Some were simply 'old.'

These men, these women . . . January was queasily aware that he'd probably seen their pictures, in Maurir's articles about dissected hearts and spines.

After 1782, the names became French or Spanish, and in the pinched, spidery handwriting was noted the percentage of European heritage. Five pages were devoted to the obsessive catalog of French Creole terminology:

A white and a negress produce: *A mulatto*
A white and a mulatto produce: *A quadroon*
A white and a quadroon produce: A métif [an octoroon, in New Orleans terminology]
A white and a métif produce: *A mameloque* [in New Orleans, a musterfino]
A white and a mameloque produce: A quadroonee
A white and a quadronee produce: *A sang-melée*
A white and a marabou – the outcome of a union between a full-blood African and a quadroon – *produce*: *A quadroon*

<u>But:</u>
A quadroon and a marabou produce: *A quadroon*
A quadroon and a griffe – the child of a black and a
quadroon – *produce: Another quadroon*
A black and a griffe produce: A sacatera . . .

'It always seemed to me a fearful waste of energy,' remarked
Hannibal, looking over his shoulder at the lists. 'How many white
grandparents you have . . . Does it really make a difference, when
even one black ancestor is enough to make you a slave and rob
you of your rights?' He sat back on his heels, the sheets of
Amalie's letter between his skinny fingers, the light of their tiny
fire flickering in his dark eyes. Behind him, the long, low bench
of the furnace rose like some monstrous tomb, where the heat
from the single fire had rushed to boil the five great kettles set
in a line.

'I know your mother claims to be a quadroon, and half her girl-
friends say *they're* musterfines, and they spend half their days
whispering about who's lying on the subject.'

'It matters if you're trying to convince some white protector
that your daughter is an octoroon instead of a quadroon,' said
January gently. 'Octoroons are more fashionable – God forbid he
should tell his friends he's taken on some girl who's merely a
mulatto.'

Hannibal winced.

'They give all kinds of names to each other as well,' pointed out
January. '*Chacas* and *catchoupines* and *bitacaux* . . . Would your
family have stood for it, if you or one of your cousins had announced
they were marrying an Irish girl? Africans were cheaper than
"Creole" slaves,' he added. 'Those born on Saint-Domingue were
generally healthier and were usually used as house servants, the
same as they are in Louisiana. The traders brought in Africans by
the boatload.'

'But their children couldn't pass for white.' Hannibal read for a
time past January's shoulder, then said, 'After 1785 he's buying
more. Look at all those—' The long, thin finger reached around his
arm, touched the open page. 'Fifteen in 1786, seventeen in 'eighty-
seven . . .'

'But he's gone back to Africans.'

There was another silence, in which the beating of the drums had quickened, the tireless, maddening skreek of the insects seemed very loud.

'He must have intercepted Amalie's letter.' Hannibal gestured with the pages in his hand. 'One wonders what became of Miss Reina.'

'I suspect Ginette wondered,' replied January grimly, 'when her sister didn't come back from Port-au-Prince. And I suspect that when the hurricane hit that fall, and everyone took refuge in the sugar mill, she took the opportunity to search Maudit's laboratory . . . It's what I'd have done. What Rose would have done. Whatever she found there, she fled into the jungle and spent the rest of her life in hiding.'

'Whatever it was she found in Maudit's laboratory,' January said, 'Ginette must have known she'd never be allowed to leave the plantation. You notice that nothing more is heard of Emmanuelle and Calanthe, Champagne and Grasset . . . It was too easy,' he went on softly. 'Too easy for slaves to simply disappear. They were dying like flies anyway, of overwork, or malnutrition. No one would ask. And no one on the plantation who missed them would dare breathe a word. Maurir was absolutely safe to—' He broke off as Mayanet sat up, head cocked, like a dog that smells fire.

The drums had ceased.

So had any sound of the insects.

January dumped the water pail over the fire. The smoke was like a shout in the rank darkness, but in any case, he thought, attackers would know they'd be in the sugar mill. He thrust the notebooks into one of the straw *macoutes*, led the way at a silent run through the old grinding-room – a great roofless circle – to the wide doorway that opened into what had been the shed area, where the field gangs had in times past piled the cut cane. In his heart, the place was as familiar to him as his house on Rue Esplanade: he and his little friends had played in the Bellefleur sugar mill nine months of the year – risking a beating from their mothers and worse from Michie Fourchet. His father had cut cane and carried it on his shoulder to the mill, and every man January had known as a child had done so as well.

Only three years ago, to hunt down a murderer and a machine-wrecker, he had himself worked the *roulaison* season, and the smell of sweat, the smell of blood, the smell of weeping despair and an exhaustion fathoms beyond any white man's experience seemed to whisper to him from the walls, mingling with the echoes of woodsmoke and burned sugar.

The sheds were long gone. In forty years the jungle had grown up to the mill's stone walls. January halted in the arched doorway, listening. Footfalls crunched, light and swift, in the long furnace-room where they'd left the ashes of the fire. Through the connecting arch he saw a shadow pass across the starlight of the outer doorway at the building's other end.

A moment later an amber square of lantern-light, and a man's voice said in English, 'Someone was here. The ashes are warm.'

Another man said, 'Shit.'

Then Rose's voice, and the glint of starlight on the oval lenses of her spectacles. 'If it's my husband, he won't have gone far. I didn't see any sign of Maudit's stone house, but in all this under-brush it has to be there—'

'It's there.' January's voice echoed eerily in the dark of the mill. 'And I have the notebooks – and the proof you're looking for. So let Rose go, and we'll talk.'

THIRTY-ONE

'Those proofs are useless to you!' called out the first man's voice quickly, the one who had come in to check the ashes. And Rose: 'It's all right, Benjamin. These aren't the men who killed Jeoffrey.'

Against the lantern light he saw her silhouetted as she walked to the archway that separated the milling chamber from the furnace room and stood looking into the darkness. The man who must be Seth Maddox came with her, holding her arm in a grip that looked firm but not violent, and Rose (*Thank God! Thank God! Virgin Mother of God I'll never talk to a voodoo god again . . .*) did not look like a woman who has been abused or hurt.

The shock of relief was so powerful that January felt almost dizzy, as if he'd been braced against physical pain which had been suddenly lifted.

She was well. She was unharmed.

The lantern light caught the ends of Maddox's fair, curly hair: definitely the same man January had seen on Rue Esplanade outside his house. Three other men and the woman moved up behind him, barely more than silhouettes. The Muskogee Creeks.

Hannibal and Mayanet had already stepped away from the outer doorway in the shadow of which January stood, invisible even to Rose. He could see her looking around her in the velvet blackness. Prickling with caution, he flipped a rock into the shadows of the circular milling chamber, and then, while Rose and the Indians whirled sharply in the direction of the sound, ducked out of the doorway and scrambled up the rubble that heaped the outside of the mill house wall. Trees hid the wall's broken top, and from their concealment he called down to Rose, 'Did they tell you that?'

The Indians spun again, rifles at the ready, searching for the sound of his voice. He was above their eye level now, and though he guessed they were fair trackers, he could see that the blackness and the close-crowding trees confused them. To him, they were dimly gold-lit fish in a pond below him. He could have killed any one of them with a rifle shot – another with the pistol if he were very lucky . . . and if willing to take the consequences.

'Mr January—' Maddox's tone was conciliating. 'I promise you, we're not working for Gil Jericho. We watched your house – and we, uh, induced Mrs January to come with us – because we need whatever proofs those are, that were hidden in Maudit's house . . . Notebooks, you said?'

'Notebooks and a letter.' Hannibal's light, hoarse voice came from the lightless abysses somewhere to their left. It took January a moment to figure out that the fiddler was just outside one of the windows on that side of the ruin, pressed close to the wall.

It had its effect. The Creeks swung their rifle barrels back and forth in the lantern light, trying to aim in all directions at foes they could not see.

'They prove that Gil Jericho isn't the son of Absalon de Gericault,' said January, drawing their attention again. 'That he was, in fact, switched into the family by the doctor hired to make sure that his mother bore a healthy child – the doctor who knew that *neither* parent was capable of producing healthy offspring. The child baptized Guibert de Gericault in Port-au-Prince in 1785 was, in fact, the son of an octoroon house-slave named Grasset and a free woman of color named Calanthe Delamare—'

'I knew it!' Maddox literally hopped up and down with triumph. 'Listen, Mr January. We need that proof.' He gazed all around him in the darkness. 'We need it bad. You can take half the gold – you sure as hell have earned it! But we need that notebook.'

'What they're saying is true,' Rose added. 'I haven't been harmed. Hannibal, are you all right? *Illi desperatis, non sunt inimici nostri.*'

Her captors looked at her warily, and January could see Maddox's lips move as he laboriously tried to summon enough schoolboy Latin to decipher what she'd said – *they are desperate men, but not our enemies . . .*

'I am grateful to learn that I have had my collarbone broken by a friend,' retorted Hannibal in the same language.

'This Jericho,' said the Indian woman, stepping forward, 'is in the Alabama legislature, in the land office. The family of his wife – the Bryces – are powerful in the state government. They're running him for governor next year, with the understanding that he'll turn my people from our lands, as the government of your country turned the Cherokee out, when gold was discovered on their land. Last year, gold was found on ours. The tribe's elders tried to keep it hidden, but Jericho and the Bryces got hold of it. Now they're trying to secure our land for themselves. We seek to stop him, I and my kinsmen – Three-Jacks, Blueford—'

Her gesture took in the other men. 'Also Yonah Chickenroost, who was killed when someone tried to take your wife from us.'

'That was us,' said January imperturbably. 'Her being tied up fooled us into thinking your intentions were suspect – that and the fact that you dragged her, struggling, off the beach in Santiago . . .'

'We need those proofs,' repeated the woman. 'If she escapes us here in Haiti, she can take refuge. We read about the Red Angel, came to New Orleans, only to find that Vitrack had it and was seeking the treasure. We followed him to your house—'

'How did you know about it in the first place?' asked January. 'And where do you come into this, Maddox?'

'You don't got to be a Creek, to not want to see Jericho and old Tancred Bryce running the state. How I know about the Red Angel – well, years ago my friend Clint Cranch told me—'

January recognized the name of another of the men who'd stayed at the Verrandah Hotel.

'—that a nigger woman on his place claimed her grandma worked for Jericho's father back on the Red Angel plantation, before the blacks took over Haiti. She said Jericho's mama switched a high-yella baby in, because she couldn't have a child of her own. Said that a doctor helped her do it, and that doctor later got himself killed, goin' back to the place to get the proofs of what he done. Setta here –' he nodded toward the Indian woman – 'and her kin is old friends of mine. We knew somebody in the family would go lookin' for it. And we knew if there was proof, it'd be with the treasure.'

'It is a gamble, you might say,' spoke up Setta, watching, listening all around her. 'But it is our lives – the lives of our people – on the table, and this is our only chance.'

'And you can't say we've done a speck of harm to your lady here.'

'Nor would we have harmed her brothers,' added Setta. 'We thought Jericho's son Bryce headed to New Orleans after the Red Angel as well, and when we heard of Vitrack's murder we knew he'd be after you, too. We heard he sent men to get the other brother, on Grand Isle, but when you came on to Cuba all of them came after you, and we had to do what we could, to lay hands on your lady before they did.'

'You can't think putting Jericho out of running for governor is going to keep the whites from your lands.' January had moved along the top of the wall while Maddox was speaking, groping his way as soundlessly as he could and praying he wouldn't put his hand down on a tarantula. 'You know there will be others.'

'We don't seek to ruin him,' the Creek woman said calmly. 'If Governor Bagby wins the election, well and good. If Jericho wins, we'll go to him. Those notebooks, that letter that you found – proofs that he would do literally anything to keep from his wife's family – will be the blade that we will hold over his head, the spiked bit in his mouth, the ring through his nose by which we shall lead him. But these we must have.'

January said, 'Release Mrs January.'

'Throw down those papers first,' returned one of the Creeks, whom Setta had named Blueford. *Conyngham*, January identified the name – the other would be Three-Jacks Killwoman . . . 'We didn't go through tracking down Vitrack, and following you three to Cuba, with Jericho's son and his hired men on our heels as well as on yours, only to have you sell those proofs back to Jericho and his wife's bastard of a father.'

'Or keep 'em for yourselves,' added Maddox, 'and get your own little cut of the Creek lands.'

January started to say, 'And what's to keep you from—?' when Mayanet shouted from the darkness:

'Get down!'

The next instant, below him and to his right, January saw a man appear in the outer archway of the milling-chamber, rough-clothed, dark-faced, like the mulatto Spanish of Cuba, a musket in his hands. The man shouted, '*Tira el arma!*' and instead of dropping his rifle Three-Jacks Killwoman swung around and fired it at the intruder.

In the darkness, two more shots cracked, and Maddox grabbed Rose by the arm, the Creeks retreating through the doorway into the old furnace-room. A moment later two more Spanish – Guerrero's bandits, January guessed – charged into the mill chamber from the darkness and tried to rush the door. But the Creeks had already wrestled a huge section of broken roof across the opening as a barricade, and they fired across it. One Spaniard fell; Rose called out, 'Benjamin!' and there was another spattering of shots from somewhere close.

January crouched on the top of the wall, conscious of movement, now, in the trees and underbrush all around the mill.

A man's voice yelled from the darkness, 'Send the woman out, Maddox!'

'That you, Bry?'

'I have twenty men around you,' called out Bryce Jericho. 'Now, I can just come in and shoot all of you, and that's the end of my father's problem, or you can send the Vitrack woman out and have her show us where that old man hid his treasure. Then we can see if there's any kind of thing there with it or not. If there's not, we can all go home.'

'If there's not, you can shoot the six of us and you can go home, you mean,' retorted Maddox. 'You think I don't know your daddy told you to kill all of us, to shut up that rumor about his bein' a high-yella nigger?'

January lay flat on the top of the stone wall, crawled – carefully – to the edge of the heavy tree-cover, as Bryce Jericho yelled, 'That's a goddam lie!'

Enough roof remained of the furnace room that January couldn't see in; a makeshift barricade had been put up across its farther outside door as well. The starlight dimly outlined Bryce Jericho, recognizable by his military coat, and the pale glint of his hair. He stood next to a palm tree, sheltering from any shot from within the sugar house. The man next to him, short and squat as a bull, must be the bandit-leader Guerrero – *a whore who will kill his own people for money . . .*

Because of the stony ground on which the building stood, the brush around this side of the sugar mill was short, but January could see the glint of gun barrels in the taller foliage between it and the ruins of the house. He counted eight. Muskets, probably. Cheaper to procure than rifles, and probably easier to come by on the island.

And far, far less accurate.

The Creek Blue Conyngham shouted back: 'Why your father send you, if it's a lie, eh? Why he try to kill M'am January, why he try to kill her brothers, if he didn't know it's true? You come on ahead, Jericho! You want to die 'cause your father tell you you should? So he don't lose his nice government job and maybe have to work for his living like the rest of us? You just come ahead!'

January worked his way back to the rear of the building, where the trees came up close to the rear door of the milling chamber. From there he could see movement in the thicker jungle, the flick of starlight on musket barrels. The only way in was through the milling chamber and under the gun of whoever was manning the furnace room's barricaded door.

The Spanish were watching that door, not the top of the wall. He crept to the branches of a huge ceiba tree that overhung them, slung his rifle over his shoulder and scrambled – carefully – through the foliage, with a whispered word of thanks for the stoutness of the tree's branches under his weight. He felt cautiously for the branches of the surrounding trees where they mingled with the ceiba's crown, found one that felt promising (*please, God, no centipedes . . .*) and scrambled down, feeling with his bare toes for footholds. Listening to the voices on the other side of the sugar mill . . .

Gunfire crackled. Some of the Spanish ran forward; January dropped to the ground, saw against the dim mix of lantern reflection and starlight the men who stayed put still crouched on the edge of the trees. Through the outer arch of the milling chamber he saw one Spaniard double over and fall, the other two ducking back to the shelter of the wall – the Creeks inside had rifles, not muskets. Slower to load but able to hit a chosen target.

The Spanish who'd remained in the trees were watching, too.

They'll kill Rose, he reminded himself, sliding the largest of his knives from his belt. *And that's not the first thing they'll do to her.*

It was nothing, to slip up behind one man, put a hand over his mouth – the man was nearly a foot shorter than January and half his weight – and slit his throat with a single hard jerk of his knife. Reflex spasmed the victim's hands, and the crash of the musket was like thunder, but the firing in the sugar mill covered it. He dragged the body back into the dark of the jungle, helped himself – mostly by touch – to the man's powder horn. Shucked off his shirt – the sleeves were wet with blood – and moved, silent as a shadow, to where he thought the next man would be.

The men who'd tried to rush the milling chamber door fell back; one of them ran into the trees, virtually into January's arms. He let out a yelp as January grabbed him by the throat, stabbed him up under the breastbone. A voice from a few yards further in the trees called softly, 'Paco? You all right?'

January roughened his voice into a hushed half-whisper. 'Fucking spider!'

He took the time to drag Paco's body back before circling in behind the man who'd called out to him, killing him swiftly and neatly, the blood of his own heart hammering in his ears so that he could barely think. His only thought was, *Three less on this side . . .*

He was only a few feet behind a fourth man when there was a flurry of shouting, a fury of gunfire from the other side of the mill. His chosen victim – and every other man in the trees still alive – rushed the archway; January put a rifle bullet into the back of one man, dashed back to where Paco had fallen, scooped up his musket and fired into the massed backs of the men as they crowded through. Saw a man go down, clutching his belly; reloaded – as his hands had done, automatically, unthinkingly, in the morning fog behind the cotton bales at the Battle of Chalmette – and fired again while the men were smashing through the barricade into the furnace room.

No one was shooting at them – *they must have rushed both doors . . .*

He loaded both his weapons, then ran for the rubble pile on the wall. He reached the wall's top even as he heard Bryce Jericho yell, 'Don't kill her!'

Shit . . .

He ran along the narrow stones, dropped to his knees and squirmed through the tangle of burned rafters until he could look down into the furnace room.

After the night outside, the feeble glow of two lanterns there seemed bright. Seth Maddox lay near the broken barricade that had closed the outer door of the furnace room, blood pooling under his head. One of the Creek men sprawled near him, groaning and clawing at a spurting wound in his chest. Blue Conyngham lay near the wall, his head in the lap of the woman Setta, as two of the Spaniards pulled Rose away from her side. Rose's face was bruised and blood smeared the sleeve of her dress; her brown curls tumbled over her shoulder, and her chin was powder-burned, her eyes as coldly calm as ever behind their oval spectacle lenses.

Bryce Jericho walked out from among his Spanish allies with a knife in his hand, dragged the Creek woman to her feet by her hair, and put the knifepoint against the outer corner of her left eye. He glanced over at Rose. 'You going to show us where the old man hid his treasure?'

Rose nodded. The men nudged each other and grinned – when Rose walked past them, Bryce now holding her arm with the knifepoint pressed to her side, one of them grabbed her skirt and made as if to pull it up. The others laughed and followed them outside. 'Bring the wench, Guerrero,' called Bryce over his shoulder.

So they all walked out, leaving Three-Jacks Killwoman to bleed out where he lay, and Blue Conyngham to whisper, 'Setta—' and try to crawl after them.

January slipped down from the wall, ran to where he'd left the *macoute* and pulled out the red pig-leather notebook that held the de Gericault pedigree, the notes Maurir had kept, that final, horrible dissection and Amalie's despairing letter to her brother.

The lanterns bobbed in the darkness, in the direction of the ruins of Maurir's house. Guerrero's men followed in a straggling line, joking among themselves and laughing. January heard Setta squeal and then curse. He followed, slipping from tree to tree among the fan palms and banana plants, pistol in one hand and notebook in the other, and he knew that even if he gave the notebook to this man – to that strong-built, fair-haired young man who in the lantern light did indeed have a little bit of the look of Jefferson Vitrack – it wouldn't save either himself or Rose.

Common sense told him that the only thing he could do – since any attempt to shoot Jericho, to get Rose away from them, to stop them from raping and killing her before his eyes would only end in his own death – the only thing he could do would be to flee. And to use the information in the notebooks to destroy Gil Jericho and his son Bryce.

To prove them Negroes – members of a degraded caste – before the eyes of the voters of Alabama. To get the powerful Bryce family to cast Jericho out, to force his wife to disown him, to proclaim Jericho's son Bryce a bastard. To pull down in flames everything they worked for and killed for . . .

And Rose would still be dead.

Dead horribly, in the ruins of what had begun as an accursed squabble over money and position, in a blood-soaked land.

Blood will bring you gold . . . gold will bring you blood.

And there was nothing he could do about that.

When he'd wedged the square stone back into its place in the foundation, January had thought he'd done so firmly. But by lantern light now it was plainly visible, standing out a good inch from the rest of the wall. It was a matter of only moments for them to find the iron pry-bar, lying in the weeds along the wall.

But I didn't leave it there, thought January. *I hid it . . .*

'What the hell is this?' Jericho drew out a folded paper from the treasure hole. 'Bring that lantern close, Guerrero.'

'But the treasure is there?' the bandit chief demanded, kneeling to look. 'The diamonds—'

'You'll get your damn diamonds,' snapped Jericho, and he thrust the paper at Rose. 'What the hell is this?'

'It's in Greek.' Rose took it. And, as calmly as if that had been part of the legend all along, went on, 'Lucien Maurir used Greek as a secret language, because the slaves couldn't read it.'

January's almost said, '*What?*' This was the first he'd heard of that theory, and there had certainly been no Greek document in the safe when he'd pulled out the stone a few hours before.

'Can you read it?'

'Of course.'

He dragged her close to him, held the knife up for her to see. 'And you'd better read it right, wench.'

Rose bowed her head suddenly and cringed, and caught her breath in a sob that to January – who knew her – sounded so completely manufactured that he couldn't believe Jericho wasn't aware her sudden capitulation was fake. She whispered, 'I swear to you . . . please don't hurt me, sir. I'll read it right. Bring the lantern close . . .'

Jericho grinned, brandished the knife again and took the lantern from Guerrero, and held it up above the document in Rose's hands. January held his breath.

Without Jericho's hand on her arm, Rose dropped like a stone to her knees, at the same moment that Hannibal – who had evidently been crouched on the other side of the foundation wall all along – stood up, put his pistol to Jericho's temple, and blew out his brains.

THIRTY-TWO

Every man of the Spanish force was so frozen with shock that nobody made a move except Rose. She sprang to her feet and over the wall; Setta yelled, 'RUN!'

One of the men holding Setta struck her, others fumbled for their muskets, and Hannibal – who clearly hadn't counted on the other woman being present – hesitated. Guerrero grabbed him by the dirty sling around his neck and brought up his own pistol, and January stepped out of the trees and fired. The rifle ball shattered rock splinters from the wall five feet away – the shot was almost impossible by lantern light – but the bandit-chief jerked around, and Hannibal dropped behind the shelter of the broken foundation wall as a half-dozen muskets roared. Guerrero lunged over the wall after him, and the muskets swung toward January, and with silent, whispering violence, a score of arrows sliced from the darkness and pinned the bandits through throat, temples, chests . . .

Setta dropped, as Rose had done moments before, but the men around her were no longer paying her heed. They ran—

And the trees around them seemed to produce men, silently, like sharks emerging glistening from dark water. The lantern light picked out the whites of eyes, the glint of teeth like leopards' in the darkness. The flash of ax-blades and knives.

Men passed on either side of January, naked save for the knife belts around their hips; passed him as if he were invisible. Some of the Spanish brought up muskets, and they were the ones lucky enough to be killed at once, with arrows.

The others took longer to die. Some of them – to judge by the screaming – a lot longer.

A hand took January's arm and drew him back into the trees, away from the killing ground. The smell of cigar smoke and womanliness told him it was Mayanet.

He was still shaking when he and Mayanet reached the sugar mill. Rose, Hannibal, and Setta clustered around the lantern in the milling chamber, near the stone plinth that had once held the rollers and tank. Blueford Conyngham lay next to Setta, his head on her thigh and his eyes closed, his breathing the shallow drag of a man unconscious. The Creek woman's dark glance moved constantly from his face to the five or six naked men – the local chapter of the Egbo, January guessed – who squatted around the walls, arms folded around their knees. One of them stood when Mayanet and January entered, gestured toward Hannibal.

'So this *blan'* your *p'tit-ami*, eh?'

She looked the Egbo up and down. 'What if he is, Marande, eh? What's it to you?' She fished in the pocket of her dress, took out two cigars and offered him one. 'The *blan'* out there had these.'

January ran across the room, fell to his knees beside Rose, caught her against him as if he would break all her bones. Now that the danger was over – or he sincerely hoped the danger was over, anyway – he was shaking, and he realized his arms were gummed with drying blood. 'God, you're all right,' was the only thing he could say. 'You're all right—'

'It's a good thing I didn't have any money on my chances,' she managed to say, 'because I'd have bet it all the other way.'

She looked past him sharply when Mayanet said, 'This was with them,' and produced something small that twinkled, red and gold like suspended flame, from its golden chain.

Rose stood and walked over to the other woman. 'It was my brother's,' she said.

January, following at her heels, saw that it was the Crimson Angel.

But when Mayanet held it out to her, Rose shook her head. Mayanet regarded her for a moment with speculative dark eyes, then nodded and put the pendant back in her pocket. 'You wise lady, M'aum Janvier. And you—' She turned back to Hannibal, slumped in the lantern glow like a ravaged scarecrow, chalk-white under the remains of the dye.

'You get him out of this country.' The Egbo Marande jerked his lighted cigar at the fiddler. 'You get him out fast.'

'Point me in the direction of the nearest boat,' said Hannibal, taking five or six sawing breaths to get the words out, 'and I will run the length of the island to get on it.' His good hand was pressed to his side, his left arm in its ragged sling tight against his chest, as if his shivering were from the cold.

'Silly man.' Mayanet pulled him to his feet and put her arm around his waist. 'You put that Greek letter in with the treasure, silly man?'

'Of course he did,' said Rose. 'It was one of the odes of Theocritus he copied back in Cuba, rather than steal the whole book. But at the top of the paper he'd written in big letters, *Drop down.*'

Mayanet laughed and offered Rose another of Bryce Jericho's cigars. Rose smiled and shook her head.

'So you Benjamin's wife, eh?'

'Benjamin's wife,' agreed Rose. 'And one of the last descendants of Absalon de Gericault.'

'I don't think much of your family.' Mayanet shook her hand like a man. Then she smiled, not the wide sharp smile of the voodoo-god, but of the woman Maria, who remembered loss and love and pain. 'But you got good friends.'

The Egbo were gone in the morning. In the gray of dawn, Rose cooked rice and sausage from the supplies Seth Maddox had brought down with his party from Cap Francais. The Maddox horses and mules, and those belonging to Captain Guerrero and his men, were gone. 'You think they could at least have left us a couple, eh?' groused Mayanet as she walked with January to the spring that had at one time powered the waterwheel of the sugar mill. 'But that Marande – all he think about is what the Egbo need.'

January guessed that the muskets and gunpowder the Spanish *guerrilleros* had carried were gone as well.

They stopped on the way back from the spring for January to replace the stone in the foundation wall. He couldn't imagine how Hannibal had managed to lever it free long enough to thrust within it Theocritus' 'Thirteenth Idyll', with a hasty instruction to Rose scribbled at the top. The fiddler had been very quiet through the night. January remembered how he himself had felt after the Battle of Chalmette, the shock and the sense of disorientation at having killed a man.

From her pocket now Mayanet drew the thin gold chain, on which dangled the red-winged angel of enamel and gold. When she tossed it into the safe with Absalon de Gericault's money and Amalie de Gericault's diamonds, it made a satisfied little *ting*.

'You want anything in there?' She tilted an eyebrow at him.

'Good God, no!' He straightened up, looked over his shoulder at the ground between the mill and where they stood, on the site of Dr Maudit's accursed house. Buzzards had already gathered over the bodies of Jericho and his men, grunting and hissing as they fought for the best bits. Columns of flies and every ant in Haiti swarmed, a dark glitter in the pre-dawn brightness. 'I've been taught there's no such thing as the voodoo, but I can smell a curse, and this place stinks of it. The man who spends that gold is going to be trying to wipe the stain of it off his hands for the rest of his life.'

Together they levered the stone back into place and thrust it tight. But as they walked back to the sugar mill, January was aware of Mayanet looking at him sidelong under her lashes. As if the thing within her – god or demon or simply the flame of madness – understood that he hadn't told all of the truth.

Blood and gold . . . Gold and blood.

Even though he hadn't a penny and wasn't sure how they were getting back to New Orleans, it wasn't the gold that whispered to him as they readied for the journey back to Port-au-Prince.

After breakfast, January put the bodies of Seth Maddox and Three-Jacks Killwoman into the chamber of the old furnace. There was nothing to dig with save the pry bar and their hands, so he and Setta carried rubble from around the outer wall to block up its entrances, in effect forming a sort of bench tomb of the masonry. While they did this, he asked Setta about the slave woman who first had told Maddox about Gil Jericho.

'Siney, her name is. One of the sewing women on Clint Cranch's place in Covington County.'

'Would Siney be short for Mélusina?'

'I never heard her called that.' The Creek woman frowned a little. 'Jericho tried to buy her from Cranch, and later slave-stealers tried to kidnap her. No proof who'd sent them, if anybody, but Cranch sent her to Maddox, who has a place down in Limestone County. She'd be about Rose's age. She took her daughter with her to Maddox's place. A slave's word's no good in court of law, but once we let Jericho know we've got that notebook of Maurir's, he'll have more to worry about than going after Siney. Cranch'll stand our friend and back our play.'

'Will you do one thing for me?' said January, when he handed her the red-backed notebook that contained the history of the de Gericault family's almost obsessive inbreeding and bone disease. 'Ask Cranch what he'll take to free Siney, and write to me. I owe her mother – and I owe her. Without Salomé Saldaña's help I'd never have found that notebook, nor Amalie de Gericault's letter. I expect you know,' he added as the tall, brown-skinned girl opened the back cover and touched the stained and faded sheets, 'that Jericho will deny it.'

'We expect that.' Her strong chin came up, and her glance strayed through the milling chamber door, to where Hannibal limped with tea from the breakfast fire, to where Blue Conyngham sat, weak but clear-eyed in the makeshift dressings January had put on him last night. 'But he ain't going to say, "Publish and be damned." He'll scream, "Fake," but he won't let so much as a whisper of it get out. We got him by the balls.' Her strong hand – weathering already with hard work, though he guessed she was barely twenty-five – made a satisfied fist on the notebook's cover. 'I'll see to it Cranch frees Siney.'

And indeed, a year later January received a letter from Captain Castallanos of the *Santana*, letting him know that Mélusina Saldaña and her daughter had reached Jamaica in safety and had been reunited at long last with her mother Salomé. The work of the goddess Mayanet, who protected women? The hand of the Crimson Angel, whose tiny image – sold to a smuggler to save frightened and inno-cent people from death – had started the train of events?

Or just – as Rose would have it – events tumbling at random in the shaken jar of Fate?

As it was, after speaking to Setta, January walked back to the fire and put his arms around Rose. Though the jungle that filled the narrow valley where the plantation had stood seemed deserted now of human life, it was silent, save for the constant, ghoulish clatter of the buzzards behind the mill. January saw no foxes, or field rats, no four-legged vermin of any kind, and guessed that the

Egbo had left guards to make sure the unwanted strangers got on their way. Mayanet had departed for the nearest *lakou* after the treasure had been closed up again, since it was clear that neither Hannibal nor Blue Conyngham were fit to journey on foot the eighteen miles back to Port-au-Prince.

'What do you bet me that what she brings back is one of Maddox's mules?' said Rose.

January returned her half-grin. 'Even if I had a sou in my pocket,' he returned, 'I wouldn't fling it away on such a wager.'

'They did treat me well, under the circumstances.' Rose glanced through the doorway at the stones piled in the opening of the furnace. 'They'd watched our house to find out what Jeoffrey meant to do – and they were fairly certain neither he nor his father-in-law would countenance the plan to blackmail Jericho. They were as shocked as I, when Jeoffrey was killed, and weren't entirely certain what you and I would do with the information, if we got it. Once its existence was known, they *had* to control it.'

'What was left of La Châtaigneraie?' asked January curiously, and Rose shook her head.

'Nothing. The foundation of the mill house, and of what I think has to have been a slave jail. None of it looked anything like the plan that Ginette made for me, all those years ago. I knew at once we had to come here.'

They returned to the fire, and January poured out two cups of rather molasses-flavored tea. Rose hadn't had much appetite for breakfast – the smell of the corpses behind the mill was growing stronger with the rising of the day – but January had eaten in worse places. Among the supplies the Egbo had left were two bottles of rum – a generous allotment. Though Hannibal still huddled, quietly shivering, against the old mill chamber's central plinth, January observed that the liquor hadn't been touched.

They talked for awhile, quietly, of the journey back to New Orleans: there were enough foreign ships in Port-au-Prince that it should be no trouble finding safe transportation. 'We may have to work our passage,' said January. 'Or go as far as Kingston or Santiago and have to work there for money to get farther—'

'Kingston.' Rose blew on her spectacles and polished the lenses on her torn and dirty cuff. 'I'm told the British are fairly firm about enforcing penalties on slave-traders. And nothing will induce me to touch the de Gericault gold.'

'I thought you were a skeptic, my nightingale, and didn't believe in curses.'

'I don't,' she returned. 'It's a matter of good taste.' More quietly, she added, 'I'm not going to take even a penny of money my so-called cousin murdered Jeoffrey for. Let it lie here and rot.'

Setta Goback had a simpler view of the matter, when she came over to join them. 'There's enough ill-luck in that compartment to sink this island, let alone a ship,' she said. 'Blue wanted to take some – he says we've earned it, which I think we have, as have you and Mrs January. I only hope –' she touched the folded *macoute* that contained Dr Maudit's genealogical notebook – 'that God will guard us from this one, since it's for the cause of saving our ancestors' lands. Otherwise, I'd put it on the fire.'

Her words echoed in January's mind as he packed up their few belongings, and Rose and Setta climbed to the top of the wall, to look out for Mayanet's return.

The blood will bring you gold, but the gold will bring you blood.

From his own straw gunnysack, January unwrapped the other objects that had lain so long in the stone foundation of Dr Maudit's house.

Where thy treasure is, there shall your heart be also.

But what, he wondered, constituted treasure?

January felt only a passing pang at walking away from diamonds wrought from sugar and soaked in dead men's blood. It would be pleasant to have enough money to feel secure, but he knew that hard times would pass.

Knowledge, once given to the flame, is gone.

And he was physician enough to know that however knowledge had been acquired, it was precious. A treasure that would save the lives of other men, the tears of women over the birth of children to come.

Did Lucien Maurir, he wondered, *risk his life – lose his life – to retrieve proof of Guibert de Gericault's true parentage?*

Or was he seeking this?

January's fingers, sensitive and skilled – and yes, he knew, hungry for the touch of his true trade, the skill God had given him – turned the pages of the other notebooks. Seven of them, and each filled with the records of processes, experiments, observations. All those articles he had read with such guilty avidity in the garret in Paris: they were here, in their primitive and far more complete form.

Oh, that I might see Hell, Faustus had cried, *and return again safe – how happy were I then!*

The structure of the brain. Minute observations of the workings of the muscles around the eye. Pages of notes about the beat-by-beat reactions of the heart to various types of stimulus: drugs, heat, cold, pressure. The functions of the gut, not dead and half-decomposed as he'd been forced to study that amazing labyrinth of digestive tissue, but recorded live and in action.

On every other page, January thought, *that's what I needed to know the time I took care of old M'am Passebon . . . That was EXACTLY the way poor Allys Berté's baby was tangled up in her womb . . .*

And it wasn't – he told himself it wasn't, and knew it for mostly the truth – that this knowledge, the extra skill that these notebooks would help him develop, would in time bring him white clients, clients with enough money to lift him and Rose and Baby John beyond the vagaries of bank failures and 'tight-money times'. That this would give him the edge he needed, to compete with surgeons in Philadelphia or New York.

In his heart he knew these notes were precious in themselves. That they would save lives. That the information he could learn would let HIM save lives.

One life saved for every life these cost? He wasn't sure whose voice whispered that to him. Olympe's, maybe. Maybe Mayanet's . . . maybe that of the maid Ginette, fleeing into the jungle in a hurricane because of what she had found in Maurir's house, what she had seen. Maybe Reina's, or those others whose names he'd read in Maurir's list of purchases: Bassey, Kigoa, Mongo. Having caught Reina, January guessed, Lucien Maurir wasn't a man to waste a subject. He wondered if Ginette's sister had been alive or dead when the maidservant had seen her body.

He turned the pages. He saw the mention in passing of the two mameloque footmen – *the next thing to white* – and for a moment had a vision of the son of one of them, Guibert de Gericault, Gil Jericho, pacing the floor of his big house in Mobile. Praying, waiting, wondering how long it was going to be before his own son would return . . .

How horrible, Rose had said of the men in the New Orleans morgue, when they'd gone to see Jeoffrey Vitrac's body, *to be waiting and never to know.*

He would only know when Setta Goback and Blue Conyngham appeared on his doorstep, with proofs that would render him *their* slave for life . . .

And what further blood, what further retaliation, would come of that?

Maurir had made the notes at the time of his experiments. His fingerprints remained on the corners of the pages, brown smudges of old blood.

January didn't exactly believe in curses – not even here, in the land dark and soaked with them. He didn't really think that the dead men and women whose neatly-sketched hands and bellies, spinal cords and dissected genitals, beckoned his eye from those pages, were going to reach out from the other world and poke holes in the hull of the ship that carried him home.

Could I REALLY touch Baby John's face, with hands that had turned these pages and not burned them afterwards? Could I really look at Rose, if I turned down the path that said: sometimes you have to get information wherever you can . . .?

The fact that he hadn't himself opened those bellies, sawed off the tops of those skulls, made no difference.

He looked up and saw Hannibal watching him with those quiet dark eyes, bruised with fatigue and blacker than any coffee he'd ever seen. 'Why does it bother me?' he asked softly.

'Because it should,' the fiddler replied. 'It's not that I have apprehensions about riding in a ship with those things in it . . . and it's entirely up to you. But if you'd looted Seth Maddox's pockets after the fighting was done – always supposing you'd gotten to them before the lovely Mayanet did – it would be much the same.'

January grinned without mirth. 'Don't tell me you played honestly at all those card tables in Havana, collecting passage money for us.'

'Benjamin!' Hannibal pressed a hand to his heart. 'Your suspicions cut me to the quick! We needed the money,' he went on, with a quirk of his eyebrow. '*Pecunia non olet*, as the Emperor Vespasian observed – and I'm sure Rose's esteemed great-grandfather would have claimed that he needed his birthright just as badly. The law proclaims that it is wrong to keep the profits of a crime, not out of spite toward the guilty, but because keeping the proceeds is an incentive – a permission – for others to commit crimes for the sake of the rewards. And it is perilously easy to commit crimes against the helpless. This island was built on them. And there,' he added, and struggled to his feet, 'I see by their excitement, the ladies have sighted Mayanet coming up the trail. I for one am ready to go home.'

He put on his hat and limped toward the wall where Rose and Setta stood, waving their headscarves. January turned back to Dr Maudit's notebooks.

Blood and gold, he heard the god Ogoun whisper to him in the insect-creaking darkness of the Cuban jungle. *Gold and blood.* For a moment he thought he glimpsed the Crimson Angel, holding out to him a hand filled with cleansing fire.

In the archway that led to the hot forenoon outside, Hannibal and the three women were embracing, admiring the two stout mules that had almost certainly been part of the Egbo's loot last night. Black, quadroon, Indian, and white . . .

It was time to start the journey home.

He put the notebooks on the fire, poked them up until all the pages had caught, then walked away from them, unable to watch them burn.